Praise for Jonathan Janz

"The best horror novel of the year."

—Brian Keene on *The Sorrows*

"Reminiscent of Shirley Jackson's *The Haunting of Hill House* and Peter Straub's *Ghost Story*, this should please readers who appreciate a good haunting."

—*Library Journal* on *House of Skin*

"This is a great haunted house story. It's a great haunted people story. If *House of Skin* had been stripped of its supernatural elements, it still would have been a fascinating read." (*4.5 out of 5*)

—Literal Remains on *House of Skin*

"Jonathan Janz is a skilled writer, his characters are well-crafted and believable, and *The Sorrows* is pretty damned impressive."

—Horror World

"A chilling and creepy tale of the first order... Jonathan Janz knows what frightens you."

—Ronald Malfi, author of *Floating Staircase,* on *House of Skin*

Look for these titles by
Jonathan Janz

Now Available:

The Sorrows

House of Skin

The Darkest Lullaby

Coming Soon:

Dust Devils

Savage Species

Jonathan Janz

SAMHAIN
PUBLISHING

Samhain Publishing, Ltd.
11821 Mason Montgomery Rd., 4B
Cincinnati, OH 45249
www.samhainpublishing.com

Savage Species
Copyright © 2013 by Jonathan Janz
Print ISBN: 978-1-61921-568-9
Digital ISBN: 978-1-61921-599-3

Editing by Don D'Auria
Cover by Angela Waters

First Samhain Publishing, Ltd. electronic publication: September 2013
First Samhain Publishing, Ltd. print publication: September 2013

Dedication

This book is for you, Mom. For most of my childhood you were a single mother, and I know it wasn't always easy. But you were patient and supportive of me. You gave me love, security, and just as importantly, encouragement. You encouraged me to be creative, and you encouraged me to follow my dreams. Thanks to you and the sacrifices you made, I'm now living my dreams. Thanks for everything. I love you, Mom.

Acknowledgments

My first reader is a horror fanatic and an all-around book lover named Tim. He saw *Savage Species* before anybody else and made some crucial contributions to the novel; thank you, Tim, for your invaluable help. Thank you to my incredible editor, Don D'Auria, for his expertise, his kindness, and his continued support. A huge thank you to my agent, Louise Fury. The serial novel was Louise's brainchild, and it was Louise who encouraged me to use *Savage Species* for this project. Thanks also to Dawn Martin, who went above and beyond for the book. Another thank you goes to Angie Waters, who continues to design excellent covers. I also owe a huge debt to Kevin, a police sergeant who spent several hours patiently teaching me about guns.

There are many authors who influenced this work. They range from Algernon Blackwood to H.P. Lovecraft to Richard Matheson to Stephen King to Joe R. Lansdale to Brian Keene. But no writer had as direct and profound an influence on *Savage Species* as has Richard Laymon. Were Richard alive today, I'd shake his hand and talk his ears off about how much he has taught me and how thankful and proud I am to own his books. Richard Laymon was a true original, and if there is any literary justice in the world, he'll continue to be read for the next hundred years.

Lastly, I want to thank my family. My wife continues to love and support me despite this bizarre writing obsession, and for that I'm deeply grateful. Thanks to my son, who often listens to excerpts of my books and is always encouraging and excited about what he hears. Thanks to my middle child, a beautiful girl inside and out, for making me feel special. And thanks to my youngest, the amazing daughter who made our family complete. I love you four more than words will ever explain.

"Out there, in the heart of the unreclaimed wilderness, they had surely witnessed something crudely and essentially primitive. Something that had survived somehow the advance of humanity had emerged terrifically, betraying a scale of life still monstrous and immature. He envisaged it rather as a glimpse into the prehistoric ages, when superstitions, gigantic and uncouth, still oppressed the hearts of men; when the forces of nature were still untamed, the Powers that may have haunted a primeval universe not yet withdrawn."

Algernon Blackwood
"The Wendigo"

Part One
Night Terrors

Before

It was a week before the grand opening. A week before the bloodbath.

Shane Dulin slowly climbed toward consciousness.

There was a smell like raw hamburger juice and a silence so complete he was sure someone had shoved wads of cotton in his ears. Weakly, he pawed at his ears, and though there was a stiff, crusty coating on the side of his head, there were no cotton balls to obstruct his hearing.

Shane opened his eyes, but everything remained black. A sickening dizziness grabbed hold of him. His chest tightened, his breathing grew labored and shallow. Wherever he was, it wasn't just dim, it wasn't just *dark*, it was blacker than fresh tar, blacker even than the goddamn slash marks his mom used to make on his papers even when he brought home a *C* or, on a few glorious occasions, a *B*. What kind of mother was that? he wondered. What kind of mom graded your papers *after* they'd been graded and invariably reduced the score?

He felt cold all over. Cold and weak and frightened. He realized with growing distress that his lungs wouldn't work properly.

Shane tried to suck in air to fight off the encroaching panic, but his attempt was futile. Jesus God, it felt like some huge object, an anvil or his mother, was sitting on his chest, but as the nerveless feeling in his limbs began to dissipate he realized he was lying on his stomach, and that was why his breathing was restricted. He was laid out face down on some rough, moist surface.

What the hell *was* this?

Shane made to push away from the dank rock floor, but as he did a holocaust of pain gusted through his legs. Shane howled, flopped down on his belly and pummeled the slimy rock with palsied fists, but now that the floodlight of pain was glowing nothing would diminish its merciless brilliance. Shane cursed, thrashed his head in the slime and sobbed harder than he had in his life.

The pain continued to intensify.

A long time later—or perhaps it was only a matter of minutes—Shane grew accustomed to the agony. Or rather he created other pains so his mind wasn't wholly focused on his shrieking legs. He'd bitten clear through his bottom lip, the teeth easily shredding the soft tissue until his incisors ground together like bits of gravel. He'd awakened a throbbing ache in the side of his head, which told him the crust he'd fingered earlier was dried blood. He knew this should have alarmed him—he couldn't imagine bleeding from an ear being a good thing under any circumstance—but it did help him stabilize his caroming thought processes and begin to analyze his situation.

You're on your belly, he told himself, *and though you're near water, you're not in danger of drowning.*

At least he didn't think so. Shane swallowed, made himself go on.

Your ear hurts, you've beaten the shit out of your fists and bitten through your bottom lip and on top of that there's something seriously wrong with your legs.

Shane speculated about his legs but forced himself to stop. Things were already bad enough without adding to his catalogue of miseries. A wave of dizziness steamrolled through his head, but Shane forced himself to continue assessing...

Though it's a struggle, you can breathe. You can't see, but your other senses are working.

Yes, Shane thought. He realized this was true. His hearing wasn't impaired—it was simply *that* quiet. He couldn't imagine a place this silent existing on earth, but wherever it was...

Shane sucked in startled breath. He had it.

Holy Mary Mother of God, he thought, his sluggish thoughts quickening. *You're working on the new state park, the one that's opening next weekend. You're behind schedule, and you're tired of that bitch park ranger Linda Farmer driving you and the rest of the crew like a bunch of damned mules.*

Shane made a face in the darkness. It wasn't like the goddamn park couldn't open if the walking bridge wasn't completed on time. But to hear Linda Farmer tell it, constructing a rope bridge over a half-flooded river was not only necessary for the park to be complete, it was also the easiest job in the world. As if she'd ever built anything before in her life. The woman wore so much makeup she looked like a deranged clown. If she couldn't even make herself look presentable, what the hell could she know about building bridges?

Shane shook his head, his anger elbowing away some of the pain. If Patterson, the foreman of the crew Shane was stuck working with, had any balls, he'd have told Linda Farmer to take her demands and her clown makeup and jump in the river. The image actually brought a half smile to Shane's face, agony and all.

Then the smile vanished and his eyes grew very wide.

He'd shared with Patterson his thoughts on the matter of the rope bridge, and Patterson the Prick had elected Shane to paddle across the river in that damned canoe to find a good spot where they could begin staking out the opposite side of the bridge. Like there was any good place. The river was wide enough to begin with. But with the flooding and the muck it dredged up, Shane had been forced to climb out of the boat and slog an extra fifty feet before he found relatively dry ground. He'd stopped—pant legs soaked to the thighs and his work boots weighted down by water and mud—to take a piss and to curse Tom Patterson and Linda Farmer and his mother, who'd caused him to hate school so much he barely graduated and never even applied for college. He'd been thinking about how unfair it all was, how nobody saw his potential or understood how smart he really was, when he first noticed the cave.

Patterson had told them there wouldn't be any surprises. Though the land was low-lying, the beady-eyed foreman had informed them, the Peaceful Valley Nature Preserve's terrain was fairly uniform.

Eyeing the cave entrance, Shane had chuckled. *Uniform, my ass,* he thought.

He made his way to the cave entrance and peered inside. Seeing nothing, he was about to trudge back through the muddy floodplain when something—Curiosity? A nasty urge to learn all he could about this new discovery so he could shove it in Patterson's face?—compelled him forward into the gloom. Shane remembered edging forward, stoop-shouldered, while a gleeful momentum pushed him deeper and deeper into the dark...

That was all. Had he hit his head? He must have knocked it against the low cave ceiling and lost consciousness. How else to explain the scrim of dried blood painted on the side of his face or the amnesia with which he seemed to be afflicted?

But what about his legs?

Maybe, he reasoned, he'd stumbled forward—down a sharp decline, perhaps—and skewered his legs on some jagged rocks.

Shane heaved a frustrated breath and peered into the murk. It didn't add up. None of it did.

He froze at a furtive scraping sound from somewhere behind him.

Shane licked his lips, his pulse accelerating. It sounded like a small animal. A possum, maybe? It made sense. Possums were nocturnal creatures. He'd crossed the river some time during midafternoon. That meant it could be dusk or later by now, and the animals that came out at night would be stirring.

Sure, he thought, it was a possum. And though disgusting creatures, they were not dangerous ones, unless of course they had rabies—

"Oh Jesus," Shane whispered. The wounds in his legs. Had the possums been at him?

A nightmarish image of the black-eyed, white-haired creatures feasting on the meat of his legs with their disease-infested fangs made his stomach curdle. Gasping, he scuttled forward on knees and elbows, but almost instantly the conflagration in his legs forced him to the ground again. Shane moaned, beat the ground with lacerated fists. He wanted nothing more than to escape this stinking tomb and breathe the beautiful river air again, but first he had to figure out why his legs ached so badly, why with every movement, no matter how infinitesimal, it felt as though his shins had been spitted and were roasting on an open flame.

With a sharp tug of misgiving, Shane reached down and inspected the sides of his legs. His breathing stopped.

At first, he refused to credit what his fingers told him. The messy, squishy horrors he touched could not be his upper thighs. Then, though the movement brought on a flare-up so intense Shane felt nauseated, he bent at the waist and forced his fingers to explore his hamstrings.

It was at that point that he realized where the raw meat smell was coming from.

Shane shrieked, clambered forward over the slimy rock, oblivious to the protests of his ruined legs, advancing in a wild series of tortured spasms that only served to heighten his pain and terror. His thoughts churned like turbid gray water, unconsciousness tugging at him like a drowning swimmer.

He'd crawled perhaps ten or fifteen feet when he heard the weird squelching noises echo somewhere behind him. Shane paused, immobile, for a long moment. Then, with a cry, he surged forward again, peering into the darkness for some sign of the cave entrance. If only he could see the daylight or even the starlight, he'd be able to fend off whatever vile animals had been gnawing on him. He imagined the possums chewing on his flesh. Or raccoons, those goddamned garbage eaters. The nasty beasts, they were so unclean they probably carried the goddamned bubonic plague.

The noises behind him grew louder: smacking sounds like bare feet on a wet floor, the clicking of toenails on stone. Shane shivered. If it was a possum or a raccoon, it was one hell of a big one. Shane heard a deep growl.

He crawled faster. His legs were a howling blaze, his heartbeat a jittering jackhammer. But ahead—he couldn't believe it—there was a faint cone of light. It brightened and clarified as he drew jerkily nearer, and though he doubted his savaged legs would support him, for the first time Shane attempted to gain his feet.

Anguish so huge it obliterated thought squeezed him with a bone-splintering fist and hurled him face first onto the coarse stone. He vomited long and hard on the cave floor and found himself writhing in his own regurgitated lunch. It didn't matter, though. Nothing mattered anymore, nothing but the pain. Shane abandoned himself to it. He squealed and flopped on the ground in a paroxysm of anguish. It was bright enough to see now, he realized, and unthinkingly he caught a fleeting glimpse of his lower left leg. With a deathly chill he lifted the leg again to confirm what he'd seen.

His left foot was gone. Reefed with flaps of bloody skin, only a pale, ragged stub of shinbone remained.

Unable to breathe, Shane peered down at his other foot.

It was gone too.

He threw up again, but this time there was nothing in his stomach to eject. Beneath the noise of his own retching and sobbing, Shane heard the approach of whatever horrid vermin had done this to him.

It's not fair! he thought. If only they'd given him a chance. If only his dad hadn't run out, if only his mom wasn't such a soul-crushing sow, if only his foreman didn't treat him like the rest of the illiterates on the crew. None of them appreciated Shane, which was why he'd ended up in this fucking cave. He was going to die here, he realized. He was dying already—he had to be. He'd lost so much blood it was a wonder he could still draw breath.

The footsteps sounded just behind him.

Whimpering, he pushed up on an elbow and craned his head around, expecting to see a glittering pair of black eyes staring back at him.

But the eyes weren't small. They were the size of baseballs.

And they weren't black, either.

As Shane watched in atavistic dread, the glowing green eyes loomed nearer, nearer, until the pale figure crouched over him. Though the creature was bent-backed and moving on all fours, Shane could see it was far taller than any person could be. But this wasn't a person. This was...this was...

Shane gasped as the creature scooped him into its long, emaciated arms. And though he desperately wanted to, Shane could not look away from its luminous green eyes. Cradling him like an infant, the

13

creature lowered its long, pale face. The twin odors of feces and animal sweat closed over Shane like a shroud. And before he could utter a plea for mercy, the creature's sharp, powerful jaws crunched through his face.

Chapter One

Eighteen hours before Jesse Hargrove witnessed the brutal slaughter of more than two hundred people, he was riding shotgun in Emma Cayce's beat-up white 1975 Buick Electra.

"Pretty out here," Jesse said.

"Could be worse," Emma allowed.

"What?" Colleen asked from the backseat. "Being in the forest doesn't give you the urge to sing John Denver songs?"

Emma glanced ruefully in the overhead mirror. "I'm finding it tough to concentrate on the scenery given the reception we're bound to get."

Colleen shrugged her blocky shoulders. "Isn't my fault the park director's a bitch."

Emma gave her friend another sharp glance in the mirror. Not for the first time, Jesse doubted the wisdom of calling the passenger's seat back at the newspaper. He'd thought sitting next to Emma would force her to notice him, that riding in back would've kept him off her radar like always. Yet now he wanted nothing more than to fade into invisibility. Situated as he was, he felt like a neutral country about to be obliterated by warring superpowers.

"Never met someone so stubborn," Emma muttered.

"You're taking the bitch's side?" Colleen asked.

Oh hell, he thought and hunkered closer to the door.

"I've never even spoken to the woman," Emma said.

"You don't trust my judgment?"

"You're not exactly charitable with people."

Jesse stiffened as they approached a sharp bend. Emma's eyes were fixed on Colleen's, and the Buick was barreling toward the woods ahead. The tree trunks looked as wide as the car.

He ventured to brush his fingers along Emma's bare arm, and even under these circumstances, the touch of her skin sent a wave of lightheadedness through him.

"What?" Emma snapped, and started to look at him when Colleen shouted "*Turn!*" from the backseat. Emma spotted the curve, her pretty green eyes doubling in size. Then she yanked the wheel left, the unwieldy old car groaning in protest. Their back wheels sprayed gravel while their front tires scrabbled for purchase on the loose macadam. Jesse tried not to shit himself, but it was going to be a near thing. Despite the seatbelt he was jerked sideways, the side of his face mashing against the window. He eyed the trees rocketing at him with dim terror. *I'm going to die*, he thought, *and I've never even kissed Emma.*

One moment Jesse was certain the swirly brown tree trunk would end his life; the next they were lurching forward, the Buick overcorrecting and yawing toward the other side of the lane. If another car appeared, they were toast.

"Cut the wheel, stupid!" Colleen was shouting. "Turn into the skid!"

"*Shut up!*" Emma shouted back, though she was doing exactly as Colleen said.

The back end continued sluing like a drunken pendulum. Jesse tasted hot bile in the pit of his throat. He didn't think he was going to void his bowels, but if the car didn't stop fishtailing soon he just might puke.

Emma uttered a growl and wrenched the wheel again. This time, the Buick's tires got a better grip on the lane. Just when he was sure they were safe, Emma stomped on the brakes. The seatbelt tore into his chest, the top of his curly hair actually brushing the windshield.

They skidded to a stop, the Buick sideways in the lane.

"Apologize," she said.

"What?" Colleen asked.

"Apologize for calling me stupid."

"I'm not apol—"

"*Now!*" Emma screamed.

Colleen's eyebrows lifted. "You almost killed us."

Emma tore off her seatbelt, faced Colleen on her knees, poked her index finger over the seatback. "It's your fault we're out here. I said we needed to be nice to Shannon, didn't I?"

"Shannon's a dunce."

"Who happens to be chief editor," Emma said. "I told you to be civil to her—"

"Kiss her ass, you mean."

"—but you had to shoot your mouth off like always."

"She deserved it."

"So now every time a good story comes up we get stuck doing fluff pieces."

Jesse said, "It *is* going to be one of the largest state parks in the Midwest."

Emma glared at him. Jesse shrank against the door.

"He's right," Colleen said. "A new state park is a big deal. I'd rather spend the weekend out here than listen to people barking at each other in Tibetan."

"Mongolian," Emma corrected. "And it happens to be the best story of the year."

"Do you even know why they're protesting?"

"The inhumane treatment of mine workers."

"I'm bored already."

"Of course you're bored," Emma said. "If it isn't about some asinine reality show, you're not interested."

"I get attached to the characters."

"Dumb people doing dumb things."

Colleen crossed her arms. "We going to sit here in the middle of the road, or are we gonna check in?"

"Check in," Emma muttered, resettling in her seat. "Not only are we stuck covering chipmunks and squirrels, we've gotta waste an entire weekend in a tent."

"Didn't your family ever go camping?"

Emma jerked the Buick into gear. Jesse breathed a sigh of relief as they rolled back into their own lane. Not that there were marked lanes out here. If not for the occasional hand-painted wooden sign, there'd be no indication they were in a state park at all. Over thirty square miles of forest and marshes, the Peaceful Valley Nature Preserve was proving as unspoiled as advertised. Now, if Emma would stop driving like she had a death wish, they might live to enjoy it.

"We never camped," Emma said. "Mom was usually working or out with some guy."

Jesse opened his mouth to ask Emma about her dad, but the sour expression on her face convinced him otherwise.

"We camped all the time," Colleen said. "A few times we brought the pop-up, but most of the time we used tents." She turned to Jesse. "That reminds me, where are you spending the night?"

Hopefully, Emma's sleeping bag.

"I'll rent something, I guess. I was thinking about going without a tent, actually."

Colleen cocked an eyebrow. "You bring bug spray?"

"Uh-uh."

"I'd recommend a tent."

They neared a brown shack with a large window comprising most of its front. Slowing, Emma rolled down her window and reached into her purse. Jesse lowered his window, too, and though the air outside was wet with humidity, its warmth felt good on his face.

A tall man with a thick, black mustache appeared in the window and watched them stolidly. Though it was already late in the day and the western sun was falling, the man wore Ray-Bans that only revealed a vague hint of his eyes. He reminded Jesse of a surly traffic cop.

Emma flashed her credentials. "We're with the *Shadeland Truth*," she said. "Linda Farmer should be expecting us."

"Speed limit's fifteen," the man said, leaning out the window on his forearms. Up close he appeared to be in his early fifties. His brown shirt said DNR, which stood for Department of Natural Resources. Jesse remembered one of those guys coming to his science class in junior high. The DNR officer was supposed to give them a lesson on boating safety, but instead spent most of the hour telling them horror stories about the corpses he'd fished out of the lake and the wide-reaching powers of his position. The DNR, that long-ago officer had claimed, could take away your car and your house if you went fishing without a license. They could also retrieve your body if you were decapitated by an outboard motor.

"I didn't see the speed posted," Emma explained.

"Going too fast to read the signs, I expect."

Jesse braced himself for another argument, but Colleen leaned forward and intervened. "How long have you worked for the department?"

The man lowered his shades enough to reveal the smallish eyes beneath. His eyebrows were almost as bushy as his mustache. "Nineteen years this August. What's your name, miss?"

"Colleen Matthews," she said, sticking her hand through Emma's window.

The man shook it. "Glad you came. Staying all weekend?"

"We're doing a story about the opening," Emma said. "Colleen spoke with Linda earlier."

"Oh," the man said, chuckling. "You're the ones she was talking about."

Emma shot Colleen a look.

The man nodded toward the rear of the shack. "Linda's busy at the moment, but she'll be out any time. You guys want a map?"

Emma said sure, and the officer handed her a glossy pamphlet. She tossed it on Jesse's lap without looking at it. He pocketed it, figuring it might come in handy for erection coverage later.

The man gestured toward the register. "I don't have the first clue how to use this thing, so you'll have to wait until Linda gets done."

"I got the impression our stay was paid for," Emma said.

"I wouldn't know about that," the man said and withdrew into the shack.

Emma regarded Colleen in the mirror. "Well?"

Colleen shrugged. "We didn't talk price."

Emma turned all the way around, the blue fabric of her sleeveless shirt drawing taut over her breasts. Jesse felt his mouth go dry.

"What *did* you talk about?"

"Whether or not a state park should've been built here."

Emma surveyed the woods. "Doesn't look to me like they built anything."

Colleen counted on her fingers. "Sand volleyball courts, playgrounds, dump stations..."

"What's a dump station?" Jesse asked.

"Where RVs empty their shit."

"Ah."

"I merely asked if we had to stay on one of the marked sites, and Miss Park Nazi flew off the handle. Said if we made a fire outside a designated area, we'd be fined and kicked out of the park. I said, 'What, you're worried about wildfires?' She said she wanted to maintain the integrity of the land. I said the Indians didn't play volleyball. It went downhill from there."

Jesse grinned, but extinguished it when he noticed Emma's scowl. "You don't have to pick fights with everybody," she said.

"I only fight with people who take themselves too seriously."

A figure emerged from the back door of the shack. She was short and skinny, all angles and bones. Her short, blond hair had so much hairspray on it, it resembled a helmet. And despite the official-looking, white, button-down shirt and navy blue shorts, something about her reminded him of the groupies he saw in those glam rock videos from the eighties. The woman stopped and beckoned them forward.

"Oh boy," Colleen said. "Wants to show us who's in charge."

"Would you be civil?" Emma asked. "For once?"

"She's the one with the attitude."

Emma's whole demeanor changed. Jesse thought of an anchorwoman telling off her co-host before they went on air and then smiling into the cameras. She beamed as the Buick crunched forward to where the short woman stood. "Hi, Ms. Farmer. We're from *The Shadeland Truth*."

"You Colleen?" the woman asked.

Emma's smile didn't waver. "I'm Emma Cayce, this is Jesse Hargrove, and—"

"Your friend needs a lesson in politeness."

Jesse glanced back at Colleen, who looked unabashed. He waited for her to make some wisecrack, but she settled for a quiet smirk.

Emma nodded. "Colleen can be abrasive at times."

"*Hey*," Colleen said, but Emma was going on. "We're so grateful you agreed to talk to us, Ms. Farmer."

"Good publicity," Linda Farmer said. "I trust you'll paint us in a positive light?"

Emma's face tightened almost imperceptibly. "Of course."

"You can park over there," Linda said and indicated a row of spaces. "I'll show you some of the salient features of the park, then you can interview Ron."

The mustachioed man in the brown shirt and, Jesse now saw, skin-tight brown shorts stepped out of the shack.

Ron the DNR officer said something to Linda, whose face lit up. Jesse marveled at how much mascara and lipstick she wore. Emma and Colleen exchanged a look. They'd noticed Ron's shorty shorts too.

"We'll take the Gator," Linda said.

They parked and followed Linda toward a small green vehicle that reminded Jesse of a golf cart. As they climbed in, Ron pulled away in a white pickup truck with the DNR insignia on the door.

"Is he your special friend?" Colleen asked Linda.

Linda Farmer turned in her seat and stared at Colleen, who for some reason had opted to ride next to her. "Let's get something straight, Ms. Matthews. I have a college degree, too. In forestry. Four years at WIU, same as you. I probably bring home double what you make at that pissant little newspaper, so you can just drop the patronizing attitude."

Jesse glanced at Emma, who'd swallowed her lips to hold back laughter.

Colleen met Linda Farmer's stare for a moment. She said, "I apologize if I offended you."

Linda nodded curtly and started the Gator.

As they began to roll forward, Colleen said, "Should I call you Professor?"

Chapter Two

Charly barely heard Eric pull into the drive over the screaming on the baby monitor. She'd have gotten to the nursery thirty seconds ago, when Jake began crying, but her hands were slathered in paint thinner.

Her oldest daughter had decided to decorate the foyer wall.

Charly braced herself for Eric's reaction. If she was lucky, he'd enter through the garage and not use the entryway, which had been splashed with garish swaths of purple and green, Kate's favorite colors. Using her elbow—one of the few places on her anatomy not smeared with paint or tingling with paint thinner—Charly eased open the front door curtain.

She frowned. It wasn't Eric's Escalade at all, but rather a little red sports car she'd seen before but couldn't immediately place. Then the driver cut the engine, and Charly saw the tall, longhaired brunette climb out.

Great, Charly thought. *President of the Eric Florence Fan Club.*

Easy, a voice soothed. *Most women's basketball coaches have female assistants, right? Would you rather he let you screen the candidates to make sure none of them are attractive?*

Charly grinned. *Actually...*

Stop it, the voice told her. *Meet them on the lawn and put on a good show like always. But first wash your hands. You smell like an old rag someone tossed on the garage floor.*

But...Jake, Charly thought. *The poor kid's been cranking for well over a minute now.*

He's fine. Babies are supposed to cry.

Charly's smile faded. That sounded way too much like Eric for her liking.

She peered out the window again and discovered her husband and the tall girl standing in the driveway, Eric demonstrating some sort of basketball move on her. Whatever it was, it apparently required him to nestle his crotch against her rear end.

Charly's lips thinned.

She moved resolutely up the stairs. She poked her head inside the nursery and said, "Just a minute, Jakers, Mommy's gotta wash her hands before she picks you up."

Over the light blue crib liner she saw one pink foot peek briefly at her before dropping out of sight. Jake's screaming intensified.

Charly twisted on the water. Below she could hear the side door opening, muffled voices. She scrubbed her hands, her forearms, and struggled to retrieve the new assistant's name from her memory. Mallory? Melody? Maleficent?

Melanie, the voice reminded her. *Melanie Macomber, like that Hemingway story you read in college.*

Charly shut off the water and dried her hands. Across the hall it sounded as if Jake was about to shatter the nursery windows.

"You got good lungs, kiddo," she said and hurried to the crib. Jake's blue eyes—her eyes—flitted to her, and her heart ached a little at the tear streaks on his temples, the scarlet hue of his face. Cradling him, she whispered, "Mommy's sorry, Jakers. Mommy's sorry."

He quieted down after a few moments of rocking, so she shut off the baby monitor—who needed a monitor anyway when the kid had a voice like a fire truck siren?—and lugged her six-month-old down the curved staircase. She reached the landing and heard Eric and Melanie talking in the kitchen. When she and Jake came in, Eric said, "Hey, Junior."

Hasn't noticed the purple-green horror, Charly thought. He also didn't attempt to hold his son, but that was nothing new.

"Aww," Melanie said to Eric, "he looks just like you."

The hell he does, Charly thought. *My blue eyes, my nose. Maybe he has Eric's chin, but even that's debatable.*

"He's even more adorable than you said," Melanie cooed.

Did he happen to mention his daughters? Charly nearly asked.

"Oh, Mrs. Florence, you must be so proud."

Charly suppressed a sneer. *Mrs. Florence. Thanks a lot for aging me, you little tart.*

"I am very proud, Melanie. And please call me Charly."

Eric had his iPhone out, texting someone. Probably a recruit or one of his current players. Charly couldn't reach him if her life depended on it, but his basketball players...

"Goddamned reception," Eric muttered. "I get a decent signal out here maybe once a month."

Melanie smiled at Charly. "Your new house is beautiful."

"Better than that shack we lived in before," Eric said without looking up.

"You mean my childhood home," Charly said.

For the first time, Eric seemed to notice she was in the room. His expression indicated she'd be better off in another part of the house.

"Charly's sentimental," Eric explained. "She won't get rid of anything that belonged to her parents."

Melanie's perfectly plucked eyebrows formed an inverted V. "Your folks aren't living?"

"Would you like something to drink?" Charly shifted Jake to the arm that hadn't fallen asleep and opened the fridge. "We have Coke, juice, water—"

"I'm fine, Mrs. Florence."

"Oh," Charly said, "I forgot to ask. Where's your car?"

"Had a flat," Eric said. "Thank God Melanie was still at the gym."

"Don't you have a spare?"

Eric shrugged, eyes on his phone. "One of the custodians can change it for me tomorrow."

Charly turned away so he wouldn't see her expression.

"You decide about that new zone offense?" Melanie asked.

"Don't like it," Eric said. "That skip pass is dangerous."

"Your daughters are downstairs," Charly said. "In case you wanted to interact with them."

Eric and Melanie both turned and watched her. After a long moment, Melanie picked her keys up and said, "I better get going, Flo. Thanks for the hospitality, Mrs. Florence."

Charly eyed the tall girl a moment. She couldn't tell whether the tone had been ironic or not, but Melanie Macomber was indeed a stunner. Six feet tall, dark brown hair that reached halfway down her sculpted back, cheeks speckled with just the right number of freckles. The girl's eyelashes looked like they belonged to some animated princess.

Charly put on what she hoped was a sweet smile. "Please come over for dinner sometime."

Melanie nodded noncommittally, gave Eric a smile and went out.

When the front door closed, Eric said, "Feeling threatened?"

Charly opened the fridge and lifted out the ground beef. "Speaking of feeling threatened, Sam Bledsoe called."

Eric grunted. "Bet you liked that."

Jake seized a handful of her hair, yanked. Teeth bared, she gently pried open his iron grip. "He'll be here any minute to check on the construction next door. He said you could talk to him then."

"Nice of him to fit me in."

"Please be nice, Eric."

"You're nice enough for both of us."

Footsteps sounded from below, their daughters tromping up the basement stairs. Kate appeared first, followed by Olivia. Olivia went straight to the computer desk, presumably to draw circles on her notebook, but Kate just stood at Charly's side.

"Does Dad know about the wall yet?" she whispered.

"What wall?" Eric asked.

Charly winced, drew Kate closer.

"I drew a purple walrus," Kate said.

Eric watched her from the kitchen table. "Purple walrus."

"I made his tusks green."

Eric looked at Charly for an explanation. Beyond her husband, Charly saw Olivia's four-year-old face pinch with worry.

"Most of it's already come off," Charly said. "She used acrylics, so there are only a few places where I had to use thinner."

"Wait a minute. She did what?"

"She's already apologized," Charly said. "I took away her dolls, and she'll have to load the dishwasher—"

Eric's face reddened. "What the hell's the matter with you?"

Against her leg, Charly felt Kate flinch.

"It's *fine*," Charly said. "She knows she made a mistake—"

"Then why does she keep screwing up?" Eric said, rising. "Christ, Kate, you think your teachers are gonna put up with this kind of crap?"

Charly squeezed her daughter. "You and Olivia go back downstairs, honey. We'll eat in a little while."

Kate darted away and escaped through the basement door, but Olivia moved very slowly, her large brown eyes—Eric's eyes—never leaving her father.

Eric was shaking his head and pacing about the kitchen. *You asshole*, Charly thought. *How about you try loving them, too?*

"You plan on doing that when she gets in school?" Eric said, his voice echoing through the kitchen. "Shielding her whenever she misbehaves?"

"Her teachers won't overreact the way you do."

"Then they aren't doing their job."

"It's kindergarten, Eric, not the Marines."

"Keep coddling her, see where it—"

The doorbell sounded. Eric got that look in his eyes, the one he reserved for referees who made calls against his team. "Good," he said. "About time he showed up."

"Please don't be rude to him."

"Oh no," Eric said, moving through the kitchen doorway. "We wouldn't want to hurt your boyfriend's feelings."

Charly hugged Jake, whose wails were starting to make her teeth chatter, and said, "Mommy's gotta put you down for a minute, honey." She walked him over and deposited him in the pink swing they'd used for all three kids; Eric had wanted a new one, claiming the color might turn his son into a homosexual. As she laid him down, Jake frowned as though about to scream, but when the circus animal mobile began twirling to the cheerful music, he relaxed and grinned up in delight.

"...hope you do a better job next door than you did on this place," she heard Eric saying.

"What can I help you with?" Sam said. His voice sounded pleasant enough, but when she rounded the corner and saw him, she could see the strain around his eyes. He looked like he hadn't slept in days, and his light blue work shirt was badly wrinkled. Still, she thought, it brought out the deep blue in his eyes. He was a good five inches shorter than Eric, but she liked his build. Compact. Arms hard from manual labor. *Bet he's not afraid to change a tire*, she thought.

Standing there with only a few feet between them, she was able to contrast her husband to this man more clearly than ever. Eric with his gel-shiny black hair, Sam's hair dark brown and probably finger-combed in the mirror of his pickup truck. Eric wore the red-and-white WIU women's basketball T-shirt and light gray shorts; Sam had on a button-down blue polo and the same dark blue jeans she'd always seen him in. She doubted he owned anything else.

And of course there was the age difference.

"For starters," Eric said, "the windows in the breakfast nook already have condensation on the inside."

"That's because you insisted on choosing the company."

"Your men installed them."

"The problem's not the installation. You went with the cheaper product."

"They're brand-new, for Christ's sake"

Charly said, "He did try to tell you, honey."

Eric gave her a look that made her insides do a somersault.

Then he turned back to Sam. "How about this? You fix every problem you and your crew have caused or you'll be hearing from my lawyer. Sound good?"

Charly held her breath, watched Sam wrestle with the anger that was no doubt consuming him.

Sam exhaled heavily. "I'll do my best, Mr. Florence."

"So far," Eric said, turning, "your best is pathetic."

Charly and Sam watched him go.

When the basement door closed, Sam said, "He seems like a fun guy to be married to."

"I'm so sorry, Sam."

"Part of the job, I guess."

She eyed him for a moment, let her gaze linger on his strong features. "Can I walk you to your truck?"

"I'd like that."

They moved in silence through the side door.

Sam said, "How're the kids doing?"

"Okay," she said. "Jake's a bad sleeper, so that's made for some long nights lately."

"Your girls okay?" They moved slowly toward his royal blue pickup truck.

"My oldest has been feeling her oats."

Sam grinned. "That her handiwork in the foyer?"

Charly nodded. "She's a future Rembrandt."

"I would've said Jackson Pollock."

"I don't know who that is."

"I wouldn't either if my daughter hadn't minored in art history."

"I didn't know you had kids."

"That's because we've never been alone together."

Charly's throat burned with the onset of hives. Damn them, they came on at the worst times.

"I better go," Sam said.

Charly felt a sharp pang. "I'm sorry for the way Eric spoke to you."

"He always like that?"

"I call it his coaching mode."

"I call it being a prick."

She laughed. It felt good. Sam made to get into his big dually, then paused, something shadowing his face.

"What is it?" she asked.

"Your daughter," he said. "You know, the artist."

"Yes?"

"Don't be too hard on her, Mrs. Florence."

With that, he climbed in, closed the door, and started the truck. Charly watched him drive away, a dull ache starting in her stomach.

Chapter Three

"Two hundred acres of deluxe sites," Linda Farmer said, "full electrical hookup, water, you name it. Next to that the primitive sites with fire pits and two parking spots."

"But no trees," Colleen said.

One bony hand on the wheel of the Gator, Linda regarded Colleen sourly and said, "There're plenty of trees in Peaceful Valley, Ms. Matthews."

"Where your bulldozers left them alone."

Jesse glanced at Emma to see if she was as uncomfortable as he was, but she only looked bored.

He couldn't blame her. The deluxe section of the campground appeared lifeless despite the many RVs and popup campers sprinkled around the vast, treeless oval. Jesse fingered the lens cap of the Canon anxiously. He could take pictures of these campsites, but what was the point? It wasn't like they were advertising for the AARP.

He dragged a palm across his forehead and wiped sweat on his cargo shorts. The heat was oppressive out here in the most open part of the park. How bad would it be inside a smelly old tent?

The Gator continued its smooth ride over the newly paved concrete. Marking each site was a large rock with a fluorescent yellow number on it. In the center of the deluxe section rose a large bathhouse. As Jesse watched, an elderly couple parked their bicycles against the building and hobbled to their respective bathrooms. He raised the Canon and snapped a shot of the old man scratching the seat of his trousers.

He grinned at Emma. "That what we have to look forward to?"

She gave him an inquisitive look.

"The old couple," he said, gesturing toward the bathhouse.

She went back to staring vaguely ahead.

Smooth, he thought.

"What're those poles for?" Colleen asked.

"Tetherball," Linda said stiffly.

Colleen nodded. "Just the way the Indians used to play it."

Linda opened her mouth to respond, but Emma cut in. "Have you heard anything about the construction worker?"

Linda's lips thinned, but she didn't answer.

"Shane Dulin," Emma prompted. "His mother thinks he got lost in the marshes that surround the park."

"He probably ran off with some woman," Linda muttered.

Colleen arched an eyebrow at her. "As long as he doesn't ruin the Grand Opening, right?"

Linda brought the Gator to a rapid halt. "You aren't going to do a hatchet piece on our park, are you?"

Colleen giggled. "Hatchet piece."

The anchorwoman Emma resurfaced. "Of course not, Linda. We want to celebrate the unique joys of Peaceful Valley."

"Coulda fooled me. Your friend here keeps running her mouth, I'll ask you to leave."

"You can't do that," Colleen said without annoyance. "This place is funded by the state."

"And I'm charged with protecting it," Linda said. "Are you gonna knock off the crap or not?"

"I'll behave."

Linda glared at Colleen a moment longer before sliding the Gator into gear. As they jostled over a speed bump, Emma's leg brushed Jesse's. Her smooth skin, he discovered, was sheened with sweat. Man, what he'd give to see her in a swimsuit. Or less.

Jesse shifted on the hard plastic seat. On second thought, maybe it was better he didn't see the rest of her. Lord knew he fantasized about her enough already. If he ever did see her naked, he might just have to leave his job at *The Truth* to masturbate full-time.

"The deluxe section continues over there," Linda said, pointing to their left. "That's where you'll find the showers."

"You mind if we just go to our campsite?" Colleen asked.

Linda's nodded dourly. "Maybe that's best."

"What about the Native American," Emma said, leaning forward. "What was his name?"

Linda looked away.

"Frank Red Elk," Colleen said.

"Could you tell us where to find him?" Emma asked.

Jesse had been on the verge of asking, himself. Frank Red Elk was the lone descendant of the original Algonquins who had briefly resided here. The online sources Jesse had referenced and the history books he'd found back at the campus library had cited poor living conditions and a tendency to flood as the reasons for the land's sparse population. But to Jesse it didn't make sense. Aside from the heat, he was finding the park a rather neat place. He'd certainly be coming back to take shots of the forest.

"Ms. Farmer?" Emma asked.

"I heard you," Linda said without turning. "He lives along the old canal road. Just head east."

"I thought everyone was forced to take the buyout," Colleen said.

"That's a pretty dramatic way to put it," Linda responded. "Those homeowners were paid twice what their properties were worth. More in some cases."

"But not Red Elk?" Emma asked.

Linda frowned. "You'll see some woods ahead. Beyond that the primitive sites start."

Jesse looked at Emma, but she only shrugged. Soon the sounds of loud rap music made him forget about Frank Red Elk.

Colleen said, "Is that part of the opening ceremony?"

Linda was shaking her head. "Damned liars."

"What is it?" Emma asked.

"Grad party," Linda spat. "A couple fraternities at WIU asked if they could have it here, and Ron told them yes. I said it was a bad idea and now look at them."

The Gator emerged from the thicket of evergreens. To their left sprawled dozens of cars and scores of tents. On several sites there were people dancing in the beds of pickup trucks, and in four or five places Jesse saw kids tossing beanbags into slanted wooden boxes. Cornhole, they used to call the game back when Jesse was an undergrad.

Linda floored the Gator, bypassing the milling groups of young people, and made a beeline for a campsite about thirty yards beyond the party. As they crunched to a stop, Jesse beheld three people ranged around a campfire. One was a balding man in his late fifties who wore a checkered shirt, black socks and white tennis shoes. Across the fire from him were a man and woman in their thirties. The man was tall and broad and handsome. The girl was wraith-thin, her frizzy black hair trimmed too short. It was toward the older man that Linda Farmer marched.

"You said there wouldn't be alcohol," she said.

The man's smile was serene. "I said there wouldn't be too *much* alcohol."

"Those kids might be underage."

"They're graduating seniors, Miss Farmer. Many of them are twenty-four or five. You know how long it takes kids to get through school these days."

"Can they produce ID?"

The balding man gave Linda Farmer a you-can't-be-serious look. "We're light years from the nearest town, Miss Farmer. These young people aren't hurting anybody."

"If they drink too much, they could."

"I'll make sure they don't get out of hand."

Emma was out of the Gator, her Dictaphone extended. "And who are you, sir?"

"Wait a minute," Linda said.

"Gordon Clevenger," the man said.

"And what is your association with WIU?"

Clevenger regarded his loafers. "I'm head of our history department."

Emma waved the Dictaphone toward the students. "How did you..."

"The seniors needed a faculty member to chaperone their get-together. I volunteered."

"Why did they need a chaperone?" Emma asked. "Graduation was a month ago."

"Technically, some of these students need summer school credits to graduate. And," Clevenger said, smiling a little, "in order for their fraternities to pay for the celebration, they needed official sponsorship."

"I'm not happy about this," Linda said, hands on bony hips.

"They're not bothering anyone, Miss Farmer."

"The moment they do, I'm shutting you down."

With that, she marched back to the Gator and fired it up. Emma smiled at Gordon Clevenger, who winked at her. They got back into the Gator.

"Riveting interview," Colleen said. "That one might snag you a Pulitzer."

"He was sweet," Emma said. "Who were the other two?"

"His TAs," Linda answered. "The good-looking one was Marc Greeley. The mousy girl...I forget her name. Ruth something, I think. Personally, I never understood why a college professor needed assistants. They only teach two classes a week, and they still get somebody to grade papers for them? Hell, I wish I had it that easy."

"Is this all primitive camping area?" Emma asked.

Linda nodded. "This and the next half mile. You can select whatever site you want."

"We only get one campsite?" Colleen asked.

"All your paper would pay for," Linda answered with just a trace of relish.

Awesome, Jesse thought, though he kept a neutral expression. Maybe he shouldn't rent a tent after all. If he began the night under the stars, the girls might take pity on him and invite him into their tent. At the very least he could see what Emma wore for pajamas. What if she slept in a cut-off shirt and underwear?

As if sensing his train of thought, Linda glanced back at him and said, "I'll have a couple of the boys set up a tent for you."

Jesse forced a smile. "I appreciate that, Ms. Farmer."

Chapter Four

Sam meandered along the edge of the woods. He knew he shouldn't have come back to the almost-empty subdivision tonight, but home seemed too depressing, and it was way too early to head to a bar. He knew it was a bad idea to be out here, that if Eric Florence spotted him he'd launch another tirade about the shoddy construction of his house, but something about Charly seemed to magnetize Sam. Though it was hopeless and sad and more than a little dangerous, being closer to her made him feel better.

He cast a glance along the strip of desolate lots and rued the day he signed the contract. He and the developer both agreed that the Indian Trails subdivision had a lot of potential; the land was breathtaking, it was protected on three sides by government property purchased for the state park and the neighborhood afforded homeowners the privacy of a three-acre plot.

The problem was, nobody was buying.

When the basketball coach and his wife signed on that winter, Sam was sure his investment would pay off. Since then only one more lot had sold, and no more buyers were showing interest.

Sam stopped and spat toward the valley. How much longer would his creditors wait for him? Six months? Half that?

He turned and peered down the line of woods until, in his periphery, he spotted Charly Florence's house.

With a flutter in his belly, Sam realized Charly was standing on the back deck. She had her baby boy on her hip—didn't she always?—and was bouncing him gently to get him to stop screaming. Sam could hear the little guy caterwauling as though someone had ahold of his ear and was giving it a vicious twist.

"Teething, I'll bet," he said.

Charly shifted the boy to her other hip, caressed his back, bounced him some more, her pretty knees flexing as she tried in vain to make the little guy feel better. *Where's your husband?* Sam wondered. Then, *How'd you ever end up with that jackass anyway?*

Better stop that kind of thinking, his father's voice admonished. The man had been dead six years this August, but Sam still talked to him every day.

He lingered on Charly's turned back a moment, the shimmering blond hair, the curve of her hips, the killer legs. Just the way a woman should be, he thought. Not plump, but a little meat on her bones.

He turned away with an effort. A woman like that, with her dazzling smile, her playful personality and best of all, a brain in her head...why did she have to be chained to a bastard like Eric Florence?

Sam sighed. He couldn't escape the Florences these days, it seemed. When he wasn't daydreaming about Charly, he was checking his voicemail to see what complaint her husband had lodged that day. Sam had gone to the drugstore earlier to get something for his allergies. He happened to buy a newspaper, and who should he see on the cover of the sports page? Coach Eric Florence and his Western Indiana Golden Eagles. To torture himself, Sam had read the whole article. How Florence had been promoted from lead assistant to head coach after the old one was fired, how he became the youngest coach to lead his team to the Sweet Sixteen this decade. How he'd signed a lucrative extension that spring. His highly rated recruiting class.

The article failed to mention how much of an asshole he was.

Sam slapped a mosquito on his forearm. When he lifted his hand, his palm was smeared with blood and mosquito guts.

What are you doing out here? his dad's voice asked.

Where am I supposed to be? he answered.

It's Friday night—go to the Cactus and meet a nice woman.

Pick up a barfly, you mean, and engage in a meaningless one-night stand.

Better than feeling sorry for yourself while the mosquitoes drink you like a cocktail.

You've got a point there.

Sam turned back and let his gaze wander to Charly's back porch.

She was gone.

You know, his dad told him, *some people call what you're doing stalking.*

I bought up the lots, didn't I? Don't I have a right to inspect them?

You've inspected them four nights this week. That's stalking.

"So I'll bring my binoculars next time," Sam said. He cut across the lot labeled EIGHT until his boots met gravel. From there he made the short trip back to his pickup truck. The blue exterior was coated with dust, the tires spattered with old mud. Sam took out his George Strait keychain, opened the door, reached in and fired the ignition. He'd stand out here awhile so the dually could cool off.

He almost convinced himself he wasn't just hoping for another glimpse of Charly.

Charly thought, *If Jake doesn't stop screaming soon, my eardrums are going to burst.* He'd been cranking since morning, and it was what time? She paced the floor again and checked the clock on the nursery dresser: 9:37.

It wouldn't have been so bad if she could've trusted Eric to brush the girls' teeth and read to them, but that would require his leaving the basement—his *man cave*, he called it, a phrase that sent chills of irritation down her spine. What he did down there she had no idea. He claimed he was watching game film, but every time she walked in on him he was either on the phone or visiting some fantasy football website.

He made good money, yes, but couldn't he donate just a little of his time as well? *My job is to provide for this family*, he'd declared on multiple occasions. *Your role is with the house and the kids.*

Saying kids like an afterthought.

Jake's wailing broke off a moment, and Charly held her breath, hoping the hurricane had passed.

Then he erupted again in a voice loud enough to make her eyes water.

"Please, Jakers, please," she said. "Please let Mommy have a break."

Jake thrashed in her arms, his little eyes brimming with tears.

Oh, where the hell was Eric? When she was on the phone with someone, he could hear every word; he often grilled her after she hung up just to make sure she wasn't talking to some man. But when Jake was screaming or one of the girls got hurt, Eric was as deaf as a stone.

And tonight he'd insist on sleeping in separate rooms. *The way you get in and out of bed to check on the baby drives me nuts*, he often said.

A damning voice spoke up within her: *Then why don't you confront him, Charly? Stick up for yourself instead of being steamrolled?*

What am I supposed to do? she asked weakly.

Give him an ultimatum, came the answer. *Be a man and raise your family or get the hell out.*

But he makes the money.

Of which you'll get half.

But—

No buts! He's got himself a fine situation, doesn't he? You give him free cooking, free housekeeping, free sex—

Not every time.

Most of the time. And he gets to remain a perpetual adolescent. Hanging out with his buddies. Doing God knows what on recruiting trips—

Please stop.

Staying in hotels with his female assistants—

Charly shook her head, Jake's wails escalating.

You try to run from it but you can't.

No.

The kids are young enough. He's barely a factor in the girls' lives.

Please stop.

Divorce him, Charly.

He won't let me.

You coward! You measly, mewling, spineless excuse for a woman!

Charly rushed out of the nursery, Jake braying into her shoulder.

You're ruining four lives, and all because you can't face him, can't do what needs to be done.

Charly flipped on the bathroom light, placed Jake in the little blue baby chair. His beet-red face fixed on hers a moment, incomprehension plainly stamped there. Then he let loose with an anguished, trilling cry that reminded her of a deranged chipmunk.

"Please, baby, *please* give Mommy a break."

She tore open the medicine cabinet and knocked a pair of orange prescription bottles into the sink. Neither was the one she sought. She scanned the remaining three bottles on the top shelf and spotted the one she was after, the sleeping pills her doctor had prescribed.

She threw a glance back at Jake and sucked in air. He'd twisted in his chair so that one leg was dangling over the edge, his red face mashed in the fabric.

Should've buckled him in, her conscience admonished.

"*I know*," she said, teeth clenched.

She wrestled Jake back into place, clicked the white buckles, and looked in the mirror.

The haggard face staring back at her looked like someone else's.

Grimacing, she shook out a couple pills, hesitated, then tapped out two more.

Oh that's smart, her conscience said. *Why don't you smoke some crystal meth and really screw the kid up?*

"Go to hell," she said and popped the quartet of lozenge-shaped pills into her mouth.

Maybe you'll choke, the voice said merrily. *Then your children can be raised by their devoted father!*

A horridly vivid image imposed itself in her mind: Eric playing a video game with his buddies while Kate and Olivia fed Jake bits of carry-out pizza.

Charly leaned over the toilet and let one of the sleeping pills plop into the water. Then, giving herself no opportunity to change her mind, she filled a plastic cup and downed the remaining three pills at a gulp.

Fantastic! Now you'll only be out cold for twelve hours instead of sixteen! But I'm sure good old nurturing Eric will make sure Jake gets his breakfast.

Tears stinging her eyes, Charly bent over the chair, unbuckled Jake and lifted him. He was still crying, but his demeanor seemed slightly less frantic. *Probably wore himself out,* she thought. Patting his round rear end—definitely overdue for a diaper change—she returned to the nursery, where she slumped in the nursing chair and drew up her shirt. As Jake latched onto her breast, his blue eyes rolling white in ecstasy, she caressed his sweaty head. *The pills won't be in my milk yet,* she thought, *and on the off chance they are, maybe they'll help you sleep.*

Charly stretched out a leg, hooked the footstool with her toes and dragged it closer. She propped her feet up and leaned back. Jake's warm body had mostly stopped shuddering, his drags on her nipple long and forceful. It relaxed her too. Charly closed her eyes and put Eric out of her mind. She supposed Kate and Olivia were still waiting on their bedtime stories, but the girls were sympathetic toward her plight. Though she made sure never to badmouth their father in front of them, Charly was sure they sensed the injustice. They saw who fed them, who tended to their needs. They could do without reading for one night...they could see that their teeth got brushed...they would be fine...

Charly awoke with a start. She'd been snoring. She opened and shut her mouth, a foul taste slicking her tongue.

She remembered Jake.

Gasping, she looked down and discovered him sleeping cozily in her lap.

Charly blew out a quavering breath. Good lord, she could've dropped the poor child. It was pure luck that had prevented a serious accident.

What were you saying about being such an amazing mother?

Charly peered across the room and saw by the digital clock it was 11:06. Yawning, she carried the baby over to his crib and gently laid him inside. She remembered the baby seat in the bathroom earlier, Jake nearly writhing his way out.

"My strong boy," she said, patting his hindquarters.

Charly checked to make sure the red light of the baby monitor was on, then she went out, shutting the door as quietly as she could.

Chapter Five

Jesse was sweating his balls off. The heat within the tent was equatorial, the scorched air stagnant and rank.

Worse, he hadn't brought anything to cover his arms and legs, so even if he did decide to escape from this stinking sarcophagus Linda passed off as a tent, he'd be eaten alive by the mosquitoes. Could a person catch malaria in Indiana?

Jesse breathed through his mouth, but the odor still made his eyes water.

The smell of these tents always reminds me of the forest, Linda Farmer had said.

Sure, Jesse thought. *A forest filled with decomposing bodies and dog shit.*

Whoever had set the tent up possessed quite a sense of humor too. Outside, the ground looked uniform enough, but the area under Jesse's tent resembled the surface of the moon. Divots and mounds near the door, the ground near the window a horror show of rocks and shards of what felt like broken glass. And that didn't even take into account the heat. If he didn't get outside soon he'd combust.

Jesse struggled to take in air, willed his bladder to stop complaining. He'd already gone outside to piss three times. Emma thought little enough of him as it was; if he kept making trips outside she might add incontinence to the reasons why she'd never sleep with him.

Footsteps sounded outside his tent. Jesse sat up, listening.

Emma? Unable to sleep and wanting company?

Not likely.

Colleen, then? What would she be doing at—he checked his watch—a quarter of midnight?

Probably the same thing you've been doing. Better not disturb her or you'll get one heck of an eyeful.

Jesse pictured Colleen's manly body squatting in the weeds and shivered.

"Hey," a voice outside whispered. "You awake?"

The voice was male. Jesse crawled to the window and strained to see who it was, but the figure stood just out of his vision.

"*Hey*," the man said again, more urgently this time. "You up?"

Slowly, the familiarity of the voice coalesced into a mental picture.

Marc Greeley, the professor's handsome assistant.

Sniffing around Emma's tent.

No!

Jesse clambered to the door, but the tent zipper caught. As he struggled with it, he heard Emma's voice, drowsy with sleep, respond, "What's up?"

Was she annoyed? Or was there the merest come-hither lilt in her tone?

He wrenched the zipper loose and raised it another few inches before it stuck again.

"That you, Jesse?" Emma's voice called.

He wiggled the zipper, but it was stuck fast. Damn it! He'd always been terrible with zippers. From earliest childhood, give him a coat to zip up, and he'd have that sucker broken in five minutes. He remembered a time he'd pissed himself in elementary school, six inches from the urinal and unable to open his fly.

"Come on out," Emma said.

She sounded sincere enough. Unsurprisingly, Greeley didn't encourage him to join them. Jesse grinned. *Don't want me honing in on your new prospect, do you? Well, I've got news for you, buddy. She's not the one-night type. And I'm not gonna let her go without a fight.*

Emboldened by Emma's invitation, he endeavored to slide an arm through the gap at the bottom of the tent door. It looked about a foot-and-a-half tall, but when he sought to push through, his body caught fast, only the top of his head and one arm poking out. Jesse's grin shrank. He drew his arm in and made to push his head through the gap. He could only imagine how ridiculous he must look. Like a crowning newborn, replete with the world's curliest head of infant hair. This time he got his face all the way out, but his shoulders lodged in the opening. His chin upthrust, he smiled at them in the guttering firelight. Emma looked amused, but Marc Greeley watched him with unconcealed disdain. Jesse pushed forward, the fabric of the tent stretching.

"Need some help?" Greeley asked.

"I've...got it," Jesse grunted.

Drawing his arms as close to his body as he could, he gave one last push with both feet and tore loose from the tent.

Jesse flopped out and lay gasping in the dirt.

"That was impressive," Marc Greeley said.

Suck it, Jesse thought. He got to his feet and dusted himself off.

"You okay?" Emma asked. She was eyeing him with a mixture of sympathy and mirth. He permitted himself a quick glance at her body. She was still wearing the clothes she'd had on earlier. No cut-off shirt or low-cut panties. *One mystery solved*, he thought.

"Splendid," he answered. "So...what's going on?"

Greeley regarded Emma. "I was having trouble sleeping. You know, all that noise..." He smiled, his white teeth gleaming. "...and I wondered if you wanted to walk a little."

Emma regarded him neutrally.

"I'm up for a walk," Jesse said.

Greeley arched an eyebrow at him.

"Might as well," Emma said. "I'm awake now."

They started toward the paved road, but Emma stopped. "What about Colleen?"

Greeley gave her the dazzling smile. "She looks like she can take care of herself."

"What's that supposed to mean?"

Greeley started. "Oh, I only meant...well, she has a steely demeanor, doesn't she? She's not the type to get pushed around."

Jesse studied Emma's face to see if Greeley had wormed his way out. She looked skeptical, but her anger seemed to abate. They continued across the road toward the sound of bubbling water and started down a dirt path.

Emma asked, "How long have you been a TA?"

"Technically," Greeley said, "I'm an associate professor."

"What's the difference?" Jesse asked.

"The difference is that I'll be a full professor in a year. Two at the most. Clev will be retiring about that time, so it should be an interesting phase for the history department." Greeley glanced at Emma—to see if she was impressed, Jesse was sure—but she appeared lost in thought.

The tree-lined path led to a river Jesse estimated to be about sixty feet across. Around them the winding drone of the cicadas filled the forest.

Standing on the shore, Greeley went on, "Of course, history is only one of my interests. My real love is disasterology."

Emma glanced at him. "You made that up."

"Not at all," Greeley said. "There are professors of natural disasters at many major universities, and though my chosen field is Native American History, I take the study of disasters and their effects on various peoples just as seriously as do those with the title."

For the first time, Jesse spotted the glowing red eye of the Dictaphone poised at Emma's side. If Greeley had noticed it, he wasn't letting on. Jesse paused, looking around. Beyond Emma and Greeley, the moonlight reflected on the moving water and tossed brilliant white spangles into the air. Jesse's gaze moved over the river's surface, along the trees that had been inundated by the high water. From downriver some enormous bird came winging in Jesse's direction. He glanced down the bank at Emma and Greeley, but they were lost in conversation, oblivious of the huge shape winging their way. Jesse squinted into the darkness, amazed at the bird's size. Its wings looked ten feet across. Maybe even fifteen. Just when Jesse began to worry it would swoop down and snatch one of them into the night sky, it rushed over them, veered west and headed upstream.

Jesse watched after it, uneasy. The damn thing looked prehistoric. Chilled, Jesse hurried down the bank after Emma and Greeley.

"Kind of an odd pairing, don't you think?" he heard Emma remark. "Native American History and disasters?"

Greeley permitted himself a grin, as if relishing some secret. He said, "Ordinarily I'd agree with you, Miss Cayce, but in this instance I find the two share a rather fascinating...convergence."

"And what is that?"

He favored her with a speculative look. Bending over and picking up a smooth stone, he said, "Much is made of the systematic extermination of the Native American peoples. Westward expansion, Manifest Destiny, the Trail of Tears." Greeley paused and glanced down at Emma's Dictaphone. "Can that thing pick up what I'm saying?"

"It can."

He nodded. "Good. Now, popular thinking places blame on the white man. Europeans raping the virgin forest, killing indiscriminately, destroying the idyllic existence of the natives."

"You disagree?"

"Not at all, Miss Cayce. To the contrary, our nation's treatment of Native Americans is far more reprehensible than even the most graphic accounts have depicted."

"So you're categorizing the genocide as a natural disaster."

"Oh, it was a disaster all right, but hardly a natural one. No, utterly preventable, which makes it all the more tragic."

"Then I'm afraid I don't see the connection."

"Have you ever asked yourself," Greeley asked, rubbing the wet sand from the stone until it gleamed in the starshine, "whether or not it was *all* really attributable to the white man?"

"Of course. Are you denying it?"

Greeley shook his head and skipped the stone along the surface of the water. It deflected three times before sinking with a muted plop. "No, Miss Cayce. Let's take the Algonquin tribe that migrated here and tried to make its home on this land as an example. Because the abhorrent treatment of the Algonquins was so endemic to that period of time, everyone assumes that the people who inhabited this valley were subjected to the same treatment."

"Weren't they?"

Greeley became animated. Raising an index finger, he said, "There isn't one account of an Algonquin being mistreated in Peaceful Valley. Further, there isn't a single recorded battle between settlers and the Algonquin people within a fifty-mile radius."

Emma shrugged. "That was a different time, very little technology. Word traveled slowly."

Greeley smiled and nodded as if he'd expected that. "Yet in every other 'forced resettlement', there were numerous eyewitnesses and second-hand accounts of skirmishes, scalpings, wholesale violence. So why," he asked, eyebrows lifting, "is there such a paucity of evidence with regard to what happened here?"

"You think there was a natural disaster, a flood or something?" Emma asked.

"There was indeed a flood, but why wasn't the land resettled after that?"

Jesse waved a hand over the river. "Because it's surrounded by marshland. The state had to build up the road in half a dozen places to make sure people could get in and out."

"Ah," Greeley said, "but people are here now, aren't they?"

Emma frowned impatiently. "What are you saying, Mr. Greeley?"

"I'm saying that something other than the white man killed the natives. I'm saying that whatever it was—and I'm not talking about *marshland*, Mr. Hargrove—slaughtered the whites who ventured into this valley, as well."

Emma leaned forward. "And that was...?"

The speculative look returned to Greeley's face, and with it a shrewd gleam that Jesse didn't like. "Let's save that for later, Miss Cayce. You'll be staying through the weekend, won't you?"

She clicked off the recorder. "We leave first thing Sunday."

They moved back toward the road, Greeley producing and holding aloft a glowing iPhone. "I know we're in the lowlands, but this is ridiculous."

Emma regarded him sourly. "What a shame."

Greeley went on as though she hadn't spoken. "Another sign that they rushed this place."

Jesse glanced at him. "What do you mean?"

"The road into the park has already started to dimple, a sure sign it'll crumble into the marshes within the next few years. There's no first aid station and only one bathhouse. And to top it all off, they didn't even bother to put up a cell phone tower to make sure people could stay connected to the outside world."

Jesse shrugged. "I'm sure there's a landline in the check-in booth."

"Doesn't help me a bit," Greeley muttered. He shook the phone again as if it would respond to physical abuse. "Damn thing. Come *on.*"

Emma said, "Guess you'll have to interact with us."

Greeley looked at her dubiously. "Don't tell me you've got a prejudice against modern technology."

"Maybe I think people should spend more time with each other and less time gazing blankly into machines."

They reached the road, and as they did Jesse spotted several figures forming in the darkness. He heard laughing voices, perceived the glint of bottles reflecting the starlight.

"That Greeley?" one of the figures asked. There were seven or eight of them, and as the group neared, Jesse realized a few of them were wearing skimpy bikinis.

"Hey, Marcus," one young man said, his handsome face grinning over a beer bottle. Jesse took in the guy's spiky blond hair, his washboard stomach, and felt his insecurity flare. "What's going on? You leave Cavanaugh back at the campsite?"

"Done swimming already?" Greeley asked.

"Gotta be fresh for breakfast club," another guy said. This one had shaggy black hair and a goatee.

"What's breakfast club?" Emma asked.

"Everybody wears costumes and gets drunk," Jesse explained. "They had it at WIU when I was there."

A small smile. "You ever go?"

"Once," Jesse said. "Most of the time I slept in on Saturdays."

One of the girls asked Greeley, "You're coming, aren't you?"

Greeley shook his head matter-of-factly, as if big-breasted coeds flirted with him every day. "I doubt it."

"We'll be at the playground," the goateed guy said.

Another guy stepped forward from the darkness. This one was strong as hell, his crew cut giving him the look of a soldier or a professional fighter.

"What about you?" he asked Emma. He took a swig of beer, grinned.

"We might," she said, "after we do an interview."

The muscular guy stepped closer. "You can interview me." An aroma of beer attended him, and he wobbled as he spoke.

"We better get going," Greeley said, reaching for Emma's arm.

"What, she yours or something?" the guy asked.

Jesse's flesh tingled. An atmosphere of violence had arisen around them, and he suddenly longed for the quiet of his stinky tent.

But Emma surprised them all by taking Jesse's arm. "I'm with him," she said.

Greeley stared at them in stunned silence. Jesse tried to remove his amazed look, but didn't succeed. Emma's warm body pressed against him. The grip of her fingers sent delicious ripples of heat up his arm.

And with the rest looking on, Jesse and Emma headed toward the campsite.

Chapter Six

Charly rose through the fog as if on a slow-moving conveyor. She listened for Jake's screaming, and sure enough, there it was: shrill, heartbreaking, endlessly grating. She opened her eyes and turned her head on the off chance Eric had come to bed, but of course he hadn't. There were nights lately he'd never come to bed at all, instead crashing on the basement sectional. While she walked the carpet between the master suite and the nursery until she finally gave up and took Jake into bed with her.

And when Eric did sleep in the same room, he invariably crammed fluorescent orange plugs in his ears to muffle Jake's cries. She asked him once if he felt guilty that she did all the work with Jake.

Eric just looked at her blankly and said, "Why would I feel guilty?"

Charly glanced at the clock, saw it was past two in the morning. Groaning with frustration, she swung her legs over the edge of the bed and ambled slowly to the communicating door. She was about to open it and repeat the nightly exercise in futility when something made her stop. She pictured Eric as he'd been earlier that afternoon at the kitchen table: skin healthy and brown from golfing with his friends, his soft hands and his long limbs at ease. None of the strain she noticed around her own eyes, none of the baby mileage. And his belly wasn't a shriveled white sack of loose skin either. If her older sister was to be trusted, Charly's full breasts—the one feature she felt had been improved by child-rearing—would eventually droop like windsocks on a breezeless day.

Charly let her hand fall from the doorknob, her lips a white line.

By God, let him take a turn.

Coming fully awake for the first time since swallowing the pills, Charly experienced a galvanizing jolt of elation. She felt almost giddy imagining the look of stupefaction on his face when she demanded that he—gasp!—actually parent his son.

It had been a relief, she thought as she reached the foyer and headed for the basement door, to learn they were having a boy. Charly suspected Eric would have, like some medieval king, continued inseminating her until she produced a male heir.

At the top of the basement stairs she stopped and listened. It looked dark down there, but that didn't mean anything. His man cave was tucked safely within the recesses of the basement, presumably so he wouldn't be troubled by domestic matters.

Moving into the darkness, Charly rehearsed what she would say. Rip open the door and greet him in a booming voice: *It's your turn, honey! Remember the child we had in January? Well, he's been screaming for over nine hours now, and I had this crazy idea that you might try to comfort him. I don't want to cut into your technology use or your recruitment of alluring assistant coaches—oh yes, honey, I noticed—but it's time to get your ass upstairs and pretend to be a father.*

Charly squinted into the murk, thinking she'd see a narrow sliver of illumination under Eric's office door, but the darkness of the basement was impenetrable. She grasped the knob, took a deep breath, and pushed the door open.

Empty.

The only illumination from within was provided by the blinking lights of the modem and the wireless Internet device. Even Eric's laptop was closed.

Charly frowned. Then where was he?

Disquieted but—and this made her furious at herself—a little relieved, she left the basement and returned to the main floor. A quick pass around the family room, the kitchen, told her Eric wasn't here either.

From above, she heard a floorboard creak.

Charly's skin misted with goosebumps. It wasn't so much the creaking that unnerved her, but the lack of her son's wailing. She'd become so used to it over the past six months that its cessation was startling.

The floor groaned again.

Charly tiptoed into the foyer and gazed up at the ceiling, as if the answers might be written there. Kate often got thirsty in the middle of the night, and for that reason Charly usually made sure to place a glass of water on her nightstand. Of course, Charly hadn't been there to furnish her daughter with water tonight, so perhaps Kate had stolen across the hall to slake her own thirst.

Charly mounted the stairs and began the slow climb. It was also possible, she reminded herself, that Olivia had gotten scared—she'd been suffering lately from what the parenting books called night terrors—and had perhaps climbed into her mother's bed only to find it empty. The idea made Charly's chest ache with guilt.

She ascended the steps faster, sure now that Olivia would be standing bewilderedly in the middle of the master suite. *Where were you, Mommy?*

Almost to her bedroom door, Charly heard another sound and stopped, her heart suddenly galloping, because it came not from the girls' room, or even from her own, but rather from the nursery. She stepped closer to the nursery door and felt a muggy breeze whisper over her bare toes.

Someone had opened the window.

Had her husband been in Jake's room the whole time?

As preposterous as the notion seemed, it was the only explanation. Jake's screaming had ceased entirely, and the window had, indisputably, been opened. In fact, Charly thought, nose wrinkling, there was a fulsome odor seeping through the nursery door, a scent that reminded her of dead leaves and wormy soil.

A caul of dread lowering over her, Charly reached out, opened the door.

Across the room, no more than twelve feet away, she discerned the figure stooped over the crib, her husband soothing little Jake with weird clittering sounds. She'd never heard Eric make those sounds, and she'd never noticed how pale he appeared in the moonlight. God, almost luminescent. And when she padded quietly into the room the stench swam over her like an opening coffin. Her gorge rose, and the hot breeze brought instant perspiration to the base of her neck.

But that didn't explain the undeniable sense of wrongness that made every cell of her body vibrate with terror, nor did it answer the question of why her husband was naked, why his back was far too long and steepled with protruding vertebrae, why when he stood erect his head reached nearly to the nine-foot ceiling.

As the figure turned, its lank, sparse hairs trailing over its bony shoulders like black wire, Charly clapped a hand over her mouth.

A creature with huge and leering green eyes was clutching her baby. She took a step toward little Jake, whose body didn't move at all.

The creature's mouth twisted in a hideous grin, the eyes widening in lunatic hunger. A viscous drop of slaver strung from the curved, elongated teeth and pooled on her sleeping son's forehead.

Before Charly could lunge forward and reclaim her child, the creature took two long strides and lifted itself onto the open windowsill.

"*Jake!*" was all Charly could say as she rushed forward.

The creature cradled her baby to its muscular white chest and leapt through the window.

Chapter Seven

They drove to Frank Red Elk's house at around 7:30 the next morning. A few of the college kids had migrated over to the playground, but thus far breakfast club seemed pretty subdued. *Give it a few hours,* Jesse thought. *If the rain holds off, the place will be good and loud by midmorning.*

"How bad is the storm supposed to be?" Emma was asking Colleen.

One wrist resting on the steering wheel, Colleen said, "About as bad as it's been in a decade."

"Why didn't you say anything?"

"The story is due Sunday night," Colleen answered. "I don't feel like hunting for another job, do you?"

They rumbled past the little path Jesse, Emma and Greeley had taken down to the riverbank last night, and as they continued on, the forest on either side of the Buick grew wilder and wilder. Jesse thought of Greeley's cryptic talk about the Algonquins and the whites, wondered what the hell the man had been getting at.

The Buick jounced over the potted road. The pavement had ended, and the surface on which they now traveled made Colleen's speed more than a little frightening. He reached out, grabbed hold of the seat to steady himself. The car dipped in a deep crater, the muddy water spraying the windshield.

"Is someone chasing us?" Emma asked. "Slow the heck down."

"Quit being a wimp," Colleen said. "This car's a dinosaur anyway."

"The engine was rebuilt last year."

"So there's nothing to worry about."

The Buick juddered again.

"Never met a person so bullheaded," Emma grumbled.

"You couldn't live without me," Colleen said as they splashed through another pothole.

Jesse buckled up.

Colleen guided the big white car smoothly around a curve. When the road straightened out again, Jesse discovered a long section of it had been inundated by rain.

Jesse said, "We're turning around, right?"

Colleen said into the overhead mirror, "I thought men were hell raisers. Didn't you ever do donuts in an icy parking lot?"

"You can't drown in icy parking lots."

The Buick hurtled toward the swamped stretch of road. Jesse estimated it was underwater for at least fifty yards.

"Seriously," Emma said, "you're stopping before we get to that."

Colleen accelerated.

Emma seemed to sink in her seat. "Dammit, Colleen."

The Buick slammed into the lake of water, but rather than going completely under or stalling, the white car plowed forward, tank-like, the water reaching halfway up the tires.

Jesse realized he'd lifted his rump off the seat, as if that would keep him from drowning. Though they'd slowed down appreciably, they still made steady progress. Beneath the roar of the motor, Jesse distinguished the rush of water, the wet thuds of the tires as they bounced over the rugged lane.

Emma was shaking her head. "You're such an idiot."

Colleen remained silent, her eyes fixed on the road. Soon they reached dry land. Easing the Buick to a stop, Colleen turned and peered back at the flooded section. "Good thing we came early. By noon, this whole place'll be cut off."

They drove a couple minutes.

The Buick climbed a gradual rise, had started to follow the lane left, when Emma shouted, "*Wait.*"

Colleen depressed the brakes.

"Back there," Emma said, pointing. "Didn't you see it?"

Jesse and Colleen shared a puzzled glance.

"The turnoff," Emma explained. "There were tire tracks leading into the forest."

Colleen threw the Buick into reverse. After they'd backtracked a hundred feet or so, Emma said, "There."

Jesse followed the faint tire tracks into the woods, and there, just visible from where they sat idling, he glimpsed what looked like an abandoned house. One story tall, its clapboard siding weathered a dingy gray, the structure was little more than a shack.

"That can't be it," Colleen said.

But Emma pointed. "Look."

Jesse followed her pointing finger and spotted a red truck bed.

"Someone's there," Emma said.

Colleen hesitated.

"Oh, come on," Emma said. "You'll hotrod through a lake, but you won't drive down a wooded lane? I thought you were braver than that."

Though he didn't want to say anything, Jesse was inclined to side with Colleen. The dwelling reminded him of every horror movie he'd ever seen involving young people meeting untimely dooms. Well-adjusted members of society didn't reside in such places. Guys with names like Leatherface and Jason Voorhees did. Jesse half-expected to see a masked killer come charging out of the front door, a machete in one hand and a severed head in the other.

Emma opened her door.

"Where are you going?" Colleen asked.

"To interview Frank Red Elk," she said and slammed the door behind her.

As she strode up the lane, her sandals keeping to the grassy strip between the two wheel ruts, Jesse lingered on her sculpted calves, the roundness of her rear end in the jean shorts. He turned and discovered Colleen watching him.

"You need to disguise it better."

Jesse tried to smile. "Disguise what?"

"Your undying devotion to Emma."

He opened his mouth to argue, but Colleen was going on. "I don't blame you. If I were a guy, I'd be in love with her too. Just try not to follow her around with that puppy dog stare so much. It makes you look unintelligent."

Charly hovered above her body, watching events unfold like a passive spectator. The setting and plotline reminded her of a crappy made-for-TV movie, something that might play on the Lifetime network. But the surreal events, the absurdity of it would've been better handled by someone like Stanley Kubrick:

Shot fades from black to an interior view of a newer, affluent home. Protagonist, a blond woman in her late thirties, sits on a white leather couch while people bustle about. The woman was probably once pretty, but now appears careworn, her hastily thrown-together attire—blue jeans and a white tank top she fished out of the laundry— make her look like what she is: a harried, shaken mother whose worst nightmare has just come true.

An overweight but kindly police officer enters. Unlike the others, he maintains a respectful silence. Unlike the feds in short-sleeved polo shirts and khaki slacks, the kindly cop doesn't try to ingratiate himself with artificial smiles and platitudes. It's the difference, the housewife thinks, between doing things by a script and doing things by feel. And, she supposes, the fact that the feds have done this before inures them to the situation. By contrast, the cop doesn't appear at all desensitized.

When the handsome but soulless feds finish talking to her, rather than lunging forward to take their place, the cop hangs back a bit longer, studying the pictures on the mantel, seemingly in no real hurry.

The housewife can bear the silence no longer.

"Have you heard anything yet?" she asks him.

He speaks without turning. "Nothing."

"Shouldn't you be out there?"

"There are plenty of people looking."

The housewife finally snaps. "You don't have the slightest idea what you're doing, do you?"

He turns to her, no anger in his face. "Yes, ma'am. I just think they're going about it wrong."

The housewife stands, goes into the kitchen to get herself a beer.

She hears him come in behind her. "Want one?" she asks.

"Better not," he says.

Twisting off the bottle cap, she takes a swig and turns to look at him: the loose jowls, the mournful eyes, the mouth that always seems about to smile sadly. He's holding his hat before him in a way that's somehow endearing, like a polite little boy apologizing for breaking a neighbor's window.

"You think I'm crazy too," she says.

The merest ghost of a smile. "What makes you think they believe you're crazy?"

"They talk to me like I've escaped from the group home. Ever since I told them what happened."

"It *is* pretty hard to swallow."

"The hysterical housewife, deranged with grief—"

"I didn't say that."

She looks away, guzzles some beer. She burps loudly and wipes her mouth, wondering how her daughters are doing with Chris's folks. She needs, just about more than anything else, the comforting noise of her daughters fighting over the Trikester that Kate had outgrown and that went to Olivia, except Kate didn't like seeing Olivia on the pink tricycle she used to ride. Then Olivia's high-pitched screaming would pierce the day, and Charly would storm outside to officiate and mete out punishment. It drove her nuts, keeping those two from killing each other, but right now it was exactly what she needed.

That and her baby boy.

The sobs grab hold of her like the hands of some cunning strangler. She drops the bottle in the sink and bends double, the storm of tears racking her weary body. She feels the cop's soft hand on her shoulder, but where the hell is Eric? Every time the feds question her he's in another room, and she still hasn't gotten an answer about where he was last night when Jake was kidnapped.

The cop's arm encircles her shoulders, draws her against his kneeling body. Her equilibrium fails and she sinks toward him, and then they're sitting together like that on the kitchen floor when Eric walks in. His face is already red with anger; she doesn't even kid herself it's because he's been crying. She wonders if on some level he's worried about their son. Or maybe his selfishness doesn't even allow the occasional slip into normal human behavior.

"What's going on?" Eric demands.

Charly returns his stare, wondering, *Does he actually think I'm having a romantic moment with this chubby sheriff?*

Next to her the cop says, "I thought she needed some help, Mr. Florence."

"What's wrong?" she asks Eric.

"The cocksucker's here."

She frowns. "What?"

"What do you mean, what? *Bledsoe.* That cocksucker Bledsoe just pulled up."

Though she knows Sam can't do a thing to help get Jake back, for the first time since the creature stole him from his crib, Charly feels a surge of hope.

Eric starts to go out.

"What are you going to say to him?" she calls after him.

Red-faced, he rounds on her, "I'm going to tell him to get his ass off my property."

"He didn't do anything wrong," she says, rising.

"And you can shut your goddamned mouth."

The cop, who has risen with her, suddenly seems to grow in stature. "Don't speak to her like that," the cop says.

Eric utters a breathless little laugh, as if Kate or Olivia had just deigned to challenge his authority. "Listen, fatass," Eric starts. "It's none—"

"You want to explain to your wife why you and that girl were in the car last night?" the sheriff says.

Charly feels her mouth drop open. She stares at the cop, who blushes.

"I'm sorry, ma'am. That was a terrible thing to say, especially right now. It's not my place—"

"Now you start in," Eric says. "Just like those FBI guys. Look, do any of you have any idea what it takes to run a basketball program? She's an *assistant,* for chrissakes, she was diagramming plays—"

"At two in the morning?" Charly asks.

"Parked at the end of a gravel road?" the cop puts in.

"We were in the *front seat,*" Eric says and levels a finger at the cop, "and you need to keep your mouth shut. What's your name?"

"Why weren't you here?" Charly asks.

But the doorbell rings and Eric says, "Your boyfriend's waiting."

"Tell me the truth," she says, voice stronger than it's ever been with Eric.

He flaps a dismissive hand at them and goes out.

Charly glances up at the sheriff.

He shakes his head, "I'm sorry for blurting that out. I don't know what came over me."

"What's your name?"

"Larry Robertson," he says. "Call me Larry."

She leans up and kisses him on the cheek. When she pulls away his blush is so deep his skin is the color of Merlot.

She gives him the best smile she can muster. "Thank you, Larry."

This close, Jesse could see the peeling white paint, the sagging eaves that hung like gaudy earrings off a once-pretty actress's aging lobes. Whatever money Red Elk had gotten from the state hadn't been used on home repairs, that much was certain. Jesse brought the Canon up, snapped a couple shots of the house. From this range, he could get all of it in the frame and some of the woods too. The place was so deeply embedded out here in the forest, it seemed a part of it, as though the leprous white house had grown as naturally as a maple or an oak.

"What a dump," Colleen said.

"Hey," Jesse said under his breath. "Take it easy."

Colleen stopped on a crumbling concrete archipelago that once might have been a sidewalk. "What?"

"Keep your voice down," Jesse said.

"We in church all of a sudden?"

Jesse rolled his eyes. "Don't you think you should show a little more respect?"

"For what?"

"This house is probably all he has."

"Then he should buy a new one."

Emma had gone up to the screened door, was peering inside.

"He's almost a full-blooded Algonquin," Jesse explained. "His family's lived here for generations."

"In this?" Colleen asked, thumbing toward the house. "You claiming this used to be a wigwam or something?"

A shape moved behind a filmy window. Jesse shook his head, moved past Colleen. "Never mind."

"You're too sensitive."

"Or I happen to think the Native American has been treated badly for centuries."

Colleen groaned. "Not that crap again. Look, have you oppressed anybody?"

Jesse's mouth worked a moment. "Not directly, no, but my forefathers—"

"What forefathers?"

Emma looked up. Someone was at the door.

"I had an uncle moved here from Germany back in the seventies," Colleen said. "Does that mean he should spend the rest of his life apologizing for Hitler?"

Jesse mouthed the word *shush*. The large silhouette stood unmovingly behind the screen door. Emma was staring up at the figure with unusual reticence.

Colleen went on, "I'm sorry this guy's great-great-great grandparents got forced out by a bunch of people who happened to have the same skin color as me, but that doesn't mean I have to walk around with a guilt complex the rest of my life."

Emma cleared her throat. "Are you Mr. Red Elk?"

The figure didn't respond. Jesse was gripped with the strange feeling that the man was watching him particularly, waiting on him to rebut Colleen's argument.

"We're from the paper," Emma explained. "*The Shadeland Truth?*"

"Shannon Whirry," the figure said in a deep, resonant voice.

Emma glanced back at them, disconcerted. She turned to the man standing in the screen door. "My name's Emma Cayce," she said. "This is Jesse—"

"You've got her tits," the voice said.

Emma drew back. "Excuse me?"

"Shannon Whirry was one of the biggest soft-porn stars of the nineties. She had these perfectly formed breasts. Milky skin, a little beauty mark on the side of her face..."

"Mr. Red Elk," Emma said, "we've come to talk to you about the new park. We wanted to get some insight into the history of this land and how you feel about—"

"My favorite one of Shannon's films was *Mirror Images II*. There's a great girl-on-girl scene where this hardcore porn star sticks her tongue in Shannon's ear and rubs her titties from behind."

Jesse was just able to manage an offended expression when Emma turned to him.

Colleen, however, wasn't hiding her amusement. "I remind you of anybody?"

The door opened a bit and Jesse beheld the tight white underwear, the gnomish belly hanging over the waistband. Red Elk's skin was dark, his frame large and intimidating. Jesse put him at about six-three, two hundred and forty pounds.

"A soft-porn star?" Red Elk said, scrunching his nose a little. "Nah, you don't have the body for it. You do kind of favor a young Rosie O'Donnell, though."

Colleen's grin evaporated. "Thanks a lot."

"You asked."

Emma shook her head. "Mr. Red Elk...are you available for an interview?"

He appeared to size them up. Then he gave a little shrug. "You can come in if you want." He receded into the house. As he went, Jesse saw the tighty-whities shifting with the man's buttocks.

Emma held the door open for them.

"Real charmer," Colleen said as she stepped inside.

Chapter Eight

"You won't even know I'm here," Sam said as he moved around the side of the house. Eric was stalking him, less than three feet away. Charly and Sheriff Robertson jogged after them.

"You're a really stupid guy, you know that?" Eric spat.

"If the sliding door is sticking on you," Sam said, "I need to fix it."

"My son was *kidnapped* last night," Eric said, the tendons of his neck jumping.

"Which is why I'm staying out of your hair," Sam said. "Of all the issues you raised, this is the quickest fix."

"Are you fucking deaf?"

Charly had seen her husband in a rage before—heck, on the sidelines it was never a matter of if he'd blow up at the refs, but when; Eric had a reputation as one of the fieriest young coaches in the nation, a label in which he seemed to revel—but she'd never seen him strike anyone.

That's why she was so startled when he punched Sam in the back of the head.

Sam stumbled, the toolbox he carried clanking loudly, but he didn't go down. She was sure he'd whirl on Eric and beat his face in—in fact, she yearned for it—but rather than retaliating, Sam kept moving as if he'd never been struck.

"Stop it, Mr. Florence," Larry Robertson called. He was badly winded already, his voice strained.

"Stupid *fucker*," Eric growled. Charly reached out to hold her husband back, but before she could he planted both palms in the middle of Sam's back and shoved. Sam fell forward in a heap, the red toolbox tumbling in the grass beside him, its hasp coming undone.

Sam pushed up onto his hands and knees and said, "Listen, Mr. Florence—"

But before he got any more out, Eric slashed down at him with a balled fist and cracked him in the side of the face.

Robertson finally reached the pair. "That's *enough*, Mr. Florence."

Eric spun away from Robertson and cocked an arm back for another blow. But before he could level it at Sam, Robertson threw a shoulder into him.

Charly watched in satisfaction as her husband went down in an awkward heap.

"What the hell?" Eric shouted at Robertson.

He looked stricken, like a little boy who's just received a smack on the butt for smarting off. She hoped Robertson would leap onto Eric's prone form and deliver a sound trouncing, but the sheriff merely went over and helped Sam to his feet.

"You okay?" Robertson asked.

Sam nodded, but Charly saw the trickle of blood running from the corner of his mouth.

"I own this property," Eric said and pointed at Sam. "He's a trespasser, and I can damn well deal with him how I please."

Robertson eyed Eric coldly. "For one thing, you're not the only one who lives here. The missus has rights too." He looked at Charly. "You want Mr. Bledsoe to leave?"

"No," she said.

Eric made a scoffing sound. "Big surprise."

"Secondly, just because someone is on your land, that doesn't give you the right to assault him. Which means I just witnessed an unprovoked attack. Do you want to press charges, Mr. Bledsoe?"

Sam palmed blood off his lip. Then, glancing at Charly, he said, "No, I don't."

"You gotta be kidding," Eric said. "Press charges? This asshole does a shitty job on our house—"

"I also suspect," Robertson said, his voice rising over Eric's, "that Mr. Bledsoe here could whip your skinny behind if he so desired. That he hasn't done so yet shows me how sensitive he is to your situation." Robertson stood over Eric. "Now you can either control your mouth, or I can take you in for striking this man."

Eric stared hatefully up at Robertson.

"Good," the sheriff said. "Now, let's forget this happened and focus on getting your boy back."

He offered Eric a hand, but rather than accepting the help, Eric pushed to his feet and made for the house.

Robertson stared after Eric sourly before saying to Sam, "You sure you're okay?"

"I'm fine," Sam said and bent to retrieve his toolbox.

Robertson looked at Charly, and she realized how the confrontation had taxed him. His short black hair was matted with sweat, and he was still breathing heavily. *If he doesn't get in shape soon*, Charly thought, *he'll have a heart attack by his sixtieth birthday.*

"I better check in," Robertson said. He nodded at Charly. "If you think of anything I can do to help, please call me."

She said she would. Robertson ambled to his cruiser, and she was left with Sam.

"I'm sorry Eric hit you," she said.

"I didn't come here to fix your back door."

Charly returned his stare for a long moment. Then she said, "Eric was out with his assistant coach last night."

"I assume this assistant isn't a man."

"She's very pretty."

"Can't be as pretty as you."

Charly felt a little sick to her stomach. She fought an insane urge to throw her arms around Sam and squeeze. Sex could come later, she thought—a lot of sex—but right now she needed comfort. Sheriff Robertson had gone a long way toward helping her feel as if she weren't completely alone, but Sam filled that need in a much more fundamental way.

Charly exhaled pent-up air. "So why did you come?"

"Can you walk with me a little?"

She frowned, glanced back at the house. "It's sweet of you, really. But I need to stay here. Maybe I'll go pick up my girls and bring them back—"

"I'm not asking you on a date."

She tried not to look hurt.

"I want to find your baby," he said.

"It's sweet of you, but I don't think—"

"I spent some time today walking around the woods. The description of your kidnapper gave me the idea."

"And?"

He hesitated.

"Wait a minute," she said. "How did you know what the kidnapper looked like?"

Sam gave her an apologetic look. "I've known Larry Robertson for years. He shared a couple details…"

She steeled herself for more condescension. "So you think I'm crazy too."

"Not a bit," he said. "Your story's the only one that makes sense."

She watched him closely to see if he was putting her on.

"Think about it," he said. "They didn't find any sign of forced entry. The dogs couldn't pick up the scent outside. They're focusing all their attention on the tire tracks—"

"It doesn't matter," she said. "A creature like that doesn't exist."

"You said it sprang out of your window."

"So?"

"You didn't say 'jumped,' you said 'sprang'."

"What's—"

"When you ran to the window, you didn't see the creature below, right?"

Try as she might, she couldn't fight off the flood of images:

The monster's horrid grin as it cradled her baby.

The long, walking-stick legs striding toward the window.

The monster climbing onto the sill.

But the worst had been the appalling cleverness in the creature's eyes. The sadistic way it appeared to luxuriate in her terror...

"Charly?" Sam asked.

"I thought I saw it rise into the air."

"Maybe it did."

She grunted. "It was the middle of the night, I was half out of my mind..."

"I found a place in the woods where the undergrowth was pushed flat."

She stopped and studied Sam's earnest face.

He said, "There were branches snapped in half, saplings that looked as though something very powerful had come through."

Charly shook her head. "But the thing I saw was skinny. Really, really tall, but skinny."

"It leaped into the air," Sam said. "That's why the dogs couldn't find its scent. Or maybe because it wasn't human."

Charly pushed palsied fingers through her hair. "Look, I really need to call Eric's mom to check on the girls."

"Check on them," Sam said. "Then come down the hill with me."

She swallowed. "You think that thing took my Jake down there?"

"I think it's likely."

"Sam..."

"Call your mother-in-law," he said, "and meet me back here in ten minutes."

Red Elk's living room reminded Jesse of some police procedural show, the scenes in which the detectives scoured the home of a suspected murderer and found signs of mental imbalance and disrepair. There were fast-food sacks crumpled on a scarred coffee table and a ratty green couch that looked like something you'd find by the side of the road. The reclining chair bled yellow foam in several places, and the coarse fabric wasn't recognizable as any color in particular. Empty beer cans littered the floor, and on the arm of the recliner, Jesse spotted an open *Penthouse* magazine. He forced himself not to look.

He knew he should get permission before shooting in here, but this was too good to pass up. Jesse snapped a picture of the couch and another of the recliner before he heard footsteps coming.

Red Elk, now wearing a tight pair of blue jeans but still without a shirt or socks, was carrying the remains of a six-pack by the plastic string.

"Hope you like Red Rocket," he said, putting his own can of Old Milwaukee down on the coffee table. Red Elk tore off a can for Emma and lobbed it to her, repeated the process for Colleen and finally tossed Jesse one. The beer can was sweaty, as though it had been sitting out. When Jesse cracked it open and sipped, this suspicion was validated. *Nothing like cheap, lukewarm beer at eight in the morning*, he thought.

Colleen opened her can, took a healthy swig. Emma held hers against the belly of her shirt. Jesse took another drink and allowed himself a long look at Emma. When she moved the beer can away from her body, using it to gesture at a painting on the wall—"Is that one of your forefathers?"—Jesse noticed the way her shirt clung to her stomach. He felt the skin at his temples go tight and something in his chest throb.

Red Elk took a moment before answering her. When Jesse looked up, he understood the reason for the delay.

Red Elk was watching him watch Emma. The big man wore a crooked grin.

Turning to Emma, Red Elk said, "I usually call kin my relatives, but yes, I guess you'd say they're my forefathers."

Jesse said, "You mind if I take a picture of the painting?"

"You've already taken some," Red Elk said. "Why ask permission now?"

The man plopped down in the recliner, his shoulder-length black hair catching some of the blue light shining in from the next room. Jesse peered inside the kitchen and saw a rectangular device dangling in the middle of the room.

"God*damn*, I tied one on last night," Red Elk said, leaning against the headrest and closing his eyes.

"Excuse me," Jesse said, "but is that a...bug light?"

Red Elk nodded. "I took off the guard so the big ones could make it to the sizzlers."

Jesse lowered his gaze and felt a moment's queasiness at the dusty ring of dead bugs in the middle of the kitchen floor.

"The best are the moths," Red Elk said. "You know, those big mothers with eyes on their wings? They flap toward it like kamikazes and take ten minutes to fry."

"Is that sanitary?" Emma asked.

Red Elk opened his eyes, which were very bloodshot. "I don't eat 'em, miss."

"Don't clean 'em up, either," Colleen added.

Red Elk turned to Colleen, a little grin on his face. "You're kind of a spitfire, aren't you?"

"A plus-sized spitfire, apparently."

"Now, don't be sore, I was only teasing you."

After Emma cleared some Burger King sacks off the couch, they sat down.

"Mr. Red Elk," Emma began and clicked on the Dictaphone, "let's start with your full name and date of birth."

"Turn that damn thing off."

Emma looked at him with raised eyebrows.

"I don't like talkin' to a little red light. Makes me feel like you're about to shoot me or something." He turned to Jesse. "You ever seen *The Terminator?*"

Jesse nodded. "The part where Schwarzenegger goes to the night club to kill Linda Hamilton—"

Red Elk sipped his beer, nodding and smiling. "And he puts the laser dot on her forehead..."

"Could we focus a little?" Emma interrupted.

Jesse and Red Elk glanced at her, then exchanged a look.

Red Elk said to her, "The tits are Shannon Whirry's but your face reminds me more of Mia Zottoli back when she had longer hair."

Emma sighed. "Is she another porn star?"

"Soft porn," Jesse said.

"That's right," Red Elk agreed. "It's a big difference, miss."

"You must really like soft porn," Colleen said.

"Hell, yes," Red Elk agreed, leaning forward. "It's got all the passion that's missing in a hardcore flick, but you still get to see the goods."

Emma cleared her throat. "So how did you find out about the plans to make this a state park, Mr. Red—"

"Not to mention," he continued, "you don't have all the gross stuff you got in real porn. Yeah, it's nice when you do it yourself with a good woman, but who the hell wants to watch some big-dick guy with a shaved nutsack spurt his seed all over some skank's face?"

"*Mister Red Elk*," Emma said.

Jesse stared at the floor and tried to stifle his grin.

"Yeah, darlin'?"

"Could we talk about things my paper can actually print?"

Red Elk tilted his head appraisingly. "I take that back about Mia Zottoli. You're a lot prettier than her."

"For God's sakes."

"I heard they gave you a lot of money so you wouldn't sue," Colleen said.

Red Elk turned to her, not the slightest bit abashed. "Depends on what you call a lot of money."

"Two hundred grand?"

"Somewhere in that range, sure."

"What'll you do with it?"

"I imagine I'll keep doing what I've always done, 'cept I'll do Vegas two, three times a year."

"Mr. Red Elk," Emma said, "do you feel your people were mistreated?"

The big man chuckled. "Mistreated? Miss, that's like sayin' this guy here," he said and nodded at Jesse, "thinks you're mildly attractive."

Jesse stared wide-eyed at him. Colleen snickered. He dared not look at Emma to see her reaction.

"You think she doesn't know?" Red Elk said to him. "She ain't stupid, buddy. Every time you think she's not lookin', don't you think she feels those big doe eyes of yours crawlin' up and down her body?"

Emma said, "Was anyone in your family slain, Mr. Red Elk?"

He stopped, the merry twinkle in his eyes vanishing. "Could be, miss. But not the way you think."

"No murder raids, resettlements, anything like that?"

"Some," he said.

"Disease?"

"Sure, but only if you count diabetes and colon cancer."

Emma gave him a confused grin. "I'm not sure where—"

"Do you know how many arrowheads they found when they excavated for the park?"

Emma shook her head.

"A handful," he said, "and those were ancient, probably from the Potawatomis or the migrating Iroquois."

"So?" Colleen said.

"You go to any cornfield in Indiana, and a trained eye will find several arrowheads in no time at all. They're all over the place despite the fact that the last arrows were fired in this area over a hundred—" He broke off and bent over.

Emma sat forward. "What is it, Mr. Red Elk?"

He made a miserable face, clutched his swollen belly. "Ah, man...you'd think I'd learn by now. Whiskey always gives me the shits."

"We can come back later," Emma said, but he was up and out of his chair.

"Gotta drop the kids off at the pool," he said, jogging toward a door. He slammed it shut, and almost instantly they heard a ripping sound followed by a prolonged splash.

Colleen made a disgusted face. Emma said, "Maybe we should wait outside."

She rose and stepped over to the door. "Mr. Red Elk, we'll come back later if—"

A groan and another messy, splashing sound.

"We'll come back," she said.

Chapter Nine

Jesse was sure Frank Red Elk was the weirdest thing he'd see all day, but when he and the girls came through the pine trees and beheld the large, circular playground, he knew this sight was in contention. They'd heard the music from nearly a mile away and smelled the beer the moment they climbed out of the car. But this...

Jesse regarded Emma, who was laughing softly.

A hundred or so young men and women covered the playground equipment and the areas between in a bulging mass of skin. Granted, it was hot—probably eighty degrees already with humidity that made you feel greasy all over—but the bikinis the girls wore would've been risqué for the French Riviera. A few boys wore costumes: togas made of old sheets, heads swaddled in unconvincing turbans. One guy had fashioned an oversized diaper out of a pink blanket. The rest appeared dressed for the beach.

Jesse realized Colleen was no longer with them. He looked around and spotted her next to a row of five beer kegs lined up under a pavilion in the playground's center. An overweight young man, his tanned, hairless belly spilling over a tiny red Speedo, filled a plastic cup of beer and handed it to her. She drank, wiped off the foam mustache and beckoned them over.

The music originated from a red pickup truck stationed at the southern edge of the circular playground. Someone, thank God, had replaced the rap music with Van Halen's "Runnin' with the Devil".

To their right a group of guys were spotting scantily clad girls as they breezed across the playground on a zipline. Immediately opposite the zipline, several people played on the swings and took turns looping down a curly slide. Jesse saw as they neared that a large group had gathered to watch people doing keg stands. At the moment a big-breasted girl, her light blue bikini barely preventing her boobs from suffocating her, was standing on her head sucking down beer. The onlookers chanted for her to drink. Just when Jesse was sure she'd bust out of her top, the girl brought her legs down, swayed a moment, then dashed for the pine grove that surrounded the playground.

"Lightweight!" one guy yelled.

As they pulled up next to Colleen, another drinker took the last one's place. Jesse recognized the spiked blond hair, the washboard stomach from the night before.

Austin favored Emma with a broad grin, and with an athleticism

Jesse couldn't help but admire, Austin leaned down, his spikes embedding in the sand, and popped up in a headstand. Another guy, the one with the black goatee, fed the tube into Austin's mouth. The crowd started chanting, "Go! Go! Go! Go!" the young man's throat working furiously to ingest the flow of beer.

"Fifteen seconds," the goateed guy shouted, and everyone cheered. Austin remained upside down several moments longer before spluttering out beer and scissoring his legs to the ground.

He gave Emma another grin and exchanged high fives and fist bumps with the adoring crowd.

Jesse watched him sullenly. Wasn't it enough the guy was great-looking? Did he have to drink like a champion and move like a professional athlete too? He wondered idly if Austin was the kid's first or last name, but he was too annoyed to ask.

"Here you go," a voice from behind them said.

They all three turned and saw the muscle-bound guy holding out a pair of plastic cups. Emma and Jesse both took one.

"Come swing with me?" Musclehead asked Emma.

"Maybe in a little while," Emma said.

He nodded and ambled toward a pair of guys tossing a football back and forth.

Emma asked Colleen, "How's the beer?"

"Tastes like bear piss," Colleen said.

"Suits me," Emma said and drank.

Jesse hesitated. He normally enjoyed beer, had drunk plenty of it in college, but his stomach gurgled at the prospect of getting a buzz at—he checked his watch—ten thirty in the morning.

Colleen was watching him, the challenge plain on her face.

He drank.

She was right. It tasted like bear piss.

"I see you found the party," a jovial voice called.

They turned and watched Gordon Clevenger, Marc Greeley and the one named Ruth approach.

Clevenger patted Jesse on the shoulder. "Has the lovely park ranger been by?"

"Not yet," Colleen said. "She's still hair spraying her bangs."

Greeley was looking around uneasily. "You don't think the older campers will complain about the noise?"

Clevenger shrugged. "There's enough of a buffer zone between here and the RVs for the senior citizens to enjoy their canasta."

A pretty girl wearing a tiara and a snug black bikini appeared and handed the professor a beer. "Ah," he said, "thank you, Your Highness."

Her smile flared brighter, and she turned it on Greeley a moment before rejoining another girl on a teeter-totter.

"Drink," Emma said.

Jesse turned to her and felt a little queasy at the way she was watching him. Her brown eyes remained locked on his, but her expression was inscrutable.

He drank. She did too. As the beer entered his stomach, some of his nervousness began to dissipate. He drank again. Emma did too.

"Want me to sign your toga?" they heard Colleen ask.

A mountainous guy—he had to be a lineman on the football team—had appeared beside Colleen. His eyes were recessed, his brow protuberant. He looked like an overgrown and not particularly intelligent child. Jesse noticed the black Sharpie in his hand, the signatures all over the white sheet he wore. The sheet wasn't nearly large enough for him, but when coupled with his prodigious size, the guy reminded Jesse of an evil gladiator in some sword-and-sandals epic. Or a villain from the Old Testament.

Goliath handed Colleen the Sharpie. She accepted it, grasped him by the waist and drew him closer. She grabbed the white fabric over his crotch, lifted it, and signed her name. Goliath grinned widely, exposing two missing front teeth.

"You wanna drink with us?" he asked Colleen.

"Why not," she answered, and she was gone.

Jesse turned to Emma and felt his stomach lurch. Greeley had led her toward the merry-go-round.

You son of a bitch, Jesse thought. He knotted his fists, took a step toward Greeley.

"Maybe you should drink a little first," a voice at his shoulder suggested. He turned and saw Clevenger smiling sympathetically.

"There are plenty of girls here," Jesse said through clenched teeth. "Why does your assistant have to hit on Emma?"

"Because she's the prettiest, I suspect. And she even has a brain."

"He doesn't deserve her."

Clevenger nodded. "You're probably right."

Emma laughed at something Greeley said. The tall man had begun to spin her slowly on the merry-go-round.

Clevenger folded his hands behind his back. "If Greeley tries to take advantage of her, you have my permission to beat him to a pulp. Until then, how about that beer?"

"Make it two," Jesse said and followed him to the keg.

He was drunk by noon.

It snuck up on him, the way it always did now that he was no longer a college student. Somewhere between his third and fifth cup of beer, he'd begun to feel a pleasant tingle at the base of his neck. He'd joined Professor Clevenger, who turned out to be a horror movie buff, in a spirited debate about which was the best *Evil Dead* movie. But when he excused himself to refill his cup, he had to freeze, his arms held aloft, while the entire playground canted like a storm-tossed ship. For one terrible moment he was certain he would vomit all over the sand, and wouldn't that be a great way to impress Emma? He closed his eyes to stop the world from tilting, and in the distance heard the rumble of thunder. Then, a soothing breeze began to waft over him, the storm front moving in. He opened his eyes to see that the sun had been obscured by an ominous wall of clouds, and though the sky at that moment was overcast, the farther east he gazed the darker the clouds grew.

Jesse felt a flutter of apprehension. He turned and beheld Ruth, Clevenger's mousy TA, surveying him from the shadows of the spruce trees. A flicker of anger passed through him, but after a moment he realized it was because he associated this woman with Greeley, the jackass who'd stolen Emma. He forced himself to relax, to not hold Ruth's association with Greeley against her. Jesse smiled. When she realized he'd noticed her, Ruth straightened, and a hint of color rushed into her pasty face.

"You must be Professor Clevenger's assistant," Jesse said, going over.

"Ruth Cavanaugh," she said. With a half-hearted smile, she added, "Sorry about the staring thing. I'm feeling kind of out of it today."

Jesse felt large standing next to the girl. He guessed she'd have a hard time breaking a hundred pounds. "Don't you feel well?"

"It's the oddest thing."

She hugged herself, massaging the shoulders of her green shirt. Like her long black skirt, it was made from some thick material, which meant the girl should have been roasting in this heat. But Ruth shivered, hugged herself tighter.

"Hey," Jesse said, putting a hand on the back of her shoulder. "You okay?"

At his touch she peered up at him with an odd, penetrating look that, had they not just met, Jesse would have taken for lust.

Then the reticence bled back into her face. She looked away, said, "I've felt strange since last night. I went hiking in the bluffs..." She shook her head, laughed mirthlessly. "Stupid thing to do, I know. Going off by myself like that. But the caves...there were such interesting sounds in there. Such...*emotions.*"

Jesse watched her uneasily. "What sort of sounds?"

"It must have been a bat. Or a bunch of them. One minute I was standing before an immense tunnel. I shined my flashlight down its length, but it seemed to go on and on. Then I became aware of a sound. Then there were many sounds. The next thing I knew the cave was full of strange shapes—huge, monstrous shapes—and then I was lying on my back, this terrible stinging all over my chest."

Jesse hesitated. A brief image of the night before tickled uneasily at his memory. The black shape swooping over him by the river...the slow beat of vast wings...

"Did something attack you?" he asked.

"I don't think so," Emma said. "But I've had the most peculiar sensations and...*thoughts* since then. My dreams last night were full of...I haven't had dreams like that since I was little." Her eyes flitted upward. "It was like being a superhero."

Jesse waited for the rest of it, but Ruth had fallen silent.

"Is there anything I can do for you?" he asked.

Her eyes, for the briefest of moments, held a glaze of mockery. Then it was gone. "I'm fine, Jesse. I just need to rest."

She moved away from him, and watching her go, Jesse realized something that disquieted him. He hadn't told her his name.

So? She heard it from Clevenger. Or Greeley.

Jesse supposed that made sense, but the unease persisted. He pushed it aside and faced the playground.

Now, he thought, *where to find Emma?*

He glanced about, locating the rest of the usual suspects: Goliath pushing Colleen on a swing; Austin and Goatee doing body shots with a quartet of hotties; Clevenger regaling a group of students with some story; Tiara Girl, Light Blue Bikini, and another girl lying on a beige blanket, their brown bodies a curvy tableau of sweaty flesh; Ruth Cavanaugh sitting sadly on a large rock.

No sign of Emma or Greeley.

He was both surprised and embarrassed at the tightness in his chest. *What the hell?* an incredulous voice demanded. *You gonna cry because your dream girl decided to have a quickie with a handsome stranger?*

She's not having sex with him.

Deal with it, the voice taunted, *and quit being such a baby. If you looked like Greeley, she'd have sex with you instead. So why don't you stop with the self-pity and hook up with someone too? Preferably some girl who's more your speed.*

But try as he might, he couldn't ward off the sense of betrayal. What had been a cheerful buzz was now a sour weariness.

Dammit, Emma, Jesse thought. *Why'd you have to do it this weekend?*

He knew she dated. How could a girl that perfect stay at home all the time? But as long as he wasn't aware of her social life, he could maintain the fantasy that she was waiting for him. But to meet a guy right in front of Jesse's face and go off with him...

He needed to urinate.

Jesse meandered past the kegs and through a game of cornhole. Though the beanbag fluttered by Jesse's face, missing him by only an inch or two, no one commented on his passing. He heard thunder again, louder this time, and continued on.

His sneakers stepped from the mulch to the wide concrete sidewalk encircling the playground. He moved slowly around the perimeter until he spotted a break in the pine trees. Sidling through the gap, he moved fifty feet or so up a gentle rise and stopped, his back to the playground. If he turned, he could take in the view of the partying, of all that female flesh.

Buck up, he told himself. *The day is young, and the drunker the girls get, the better your chances.*

Jesse unbuttoned his cargo shorts, got hold of himself, and began to urinate. Before him the tall grasses and weeds went on a little ways before the forest thickened again. The woods back there looked very deep, very dark. He shifted a little, his urine shooting out in a steady stream. Had he peed since he started drinking earlier? He strove to remember, and as he did he became aware of something to his right, a paleness that made him turn and stare at an object about twenty yards away.

Jesse's urine flow stopped. He tried to breathe but found he couldn't. He couldn't even blink.

The creature was at least nine feet tall.

The skin was stark white. Its limbs were impossibly long, the arms hanging nearly to the ground. And though everything about the creature was thin—emaciated, even—its body radiated power. The tight, corded muscles swarmed down the arms and legs like pale ivy. The pectoral muscles were striated, defined, and they gave the impression of being stretched over the skinny frame and bundled tight by the pallid flesh.

The creature was gazing avidly at the playground. Jesse watched in numb dread as a long stream of spittle dangled from its bloodless lips. Its breathing was slow, the creature's entire frame rising and falling with each respiration.

Hungry, he thought. *It's positively ravenous.*

Though Jesse still couldn't move, he was able to peer beyond the creature. What he saw made his lips quiver.

Four more of them, staring down at the playground.

Jesse swiveled his head slowly to the left and discovered four more creatures taking in the view. *They're going to attack*, he thought. *They're about to descend, and no one down there has the first clue.*

Run! a voice in his head shouted. *Get your skinny ass out of here!*

Do that and you're dead, another voice declared. *They don't see you right now. For whatever reason, they don't see you.*

What, you think you're Casper the Friendly Ghost? Of course *they see you. They're just waiting for the right moment to begin the carnage, and you're gonna be the first appetizer.*

Jesse was thinking this when one of the creatures broke forward. As it did, another followed suit. A pair of them straightened and bellowed a high-pitched, blaring scream that made his balls shrivel. The creature directly to Jesse's right—the first one he'd spotted—was watching him now, a grin of predatory delight stretching its face.

I'm going to die, Jesse thought.

With a supreme effort, he tore his eyes off the creature staring at him and saw the other beasts closing on the playground. They moved in weird, loping strides, their arms propelling them as much as their legs.

Bad Company had begun to sing "Feel Like Makin' Love".

At the creatures' first cries, several of the young people on the playground had turned and stared up the rise confusedly. One or two of them turned to run. The others simply stared openmouthed at the approaching beasts.

Jesse turned back to the creature nearest him. The eyes were huge, green, iridescent, the irises as large as hockey pucks. Its white face stretched in a fearsome grin, the teeth—holy *shit*—were of normal width but were as long and sharp as ice picks.

It grinned at him a moment longer. Then, with astonishing quickness, it crouched and sprang, its tall, wraith-like body knifing through the air and disappearing into the pine grove.

Twenty-foot jump, Jesse had time to think.

Then the screams began.

Chapter Ten

As near as Jesse could tell, the first person to die was a guy who wore baggy green shorts that revealed a good deal of his plaid boxers. The guy had an average build, which meant he was a bit stronger than Jesse.

He never had a chance.

The creature that had grinned so hideously at Jesse before hurdling the pine tree landed only a few feet away from the young man. Unlike some of his cohorts, Baggy Shorts hadn't noticed the swarm of creatures approaching, so he must've been doubly shocked when he turned to find the nine-foot monster towering over him. He opened his mouth to say something—it was impossible to guess what; Jesse wasn't a lip-reader—when the creature plunged his freakishly long fingers into the boy's chest and pried open his ribcage. The creature buried its face in the boy's torso, blood and hunks of lung dribbling down its neck and muscled shoulders.

A warbling scream diverted Jesse's attention. He glimpsed a blur near the merry-go-round, a buxom girl in a pink bikini sprinting that way as though if only she could get on, the spin of the ride would save her. A pale creature rode her down before she reached it, the razored nails pistoning at her bare back like a cat clawing a carpeted pole. Ribbons of flesh flew up like bloody streamers, the girl's wild thrashing adding to the twisted gaiety of the moment.

There was a flurry of commotion atop the curly slide. The enclosure at the top of the slide had clear plastic bubbled windows, and within those windows, Jesse could see elbows and fists flashing. Then the plastic window was splashed with a syrupy gout of blood, the whole enclosure rocking from the carnage within.

Beside the curly slide was an open, straight slide; some poor kid had sought sanctuary up there, too. The boy—he seemed too young to be in college, a little brother maybe?—was pushing away from a creature whose feet were still climbing the stairs. The boy's back was to the slide, and if only he could break away from the advancing monster, he could slide on his back all the way to the mulch. But the creature, Jesse now realized, had hold of the crotch of the boy's blue shorts. It wasn't digging or tearing yet, but that was because it was climbing into position, ensuring the boy wouldn't get away.

Do something! some distant voice in Jesse's head called. *He's only a kid.*

Can't, Jesse thought dimly. *Wouldn't matter if I intervened. He's already dead.*

As if the creature had heard him, it positioned itself on its knees at the top of the slide and lifted the boy by the crotch. Gibbering in terror, his spindly arms flailing, the boy rose higher, his body upright as it floated toward the open jaws. The boy's body tilted forward slightly, as if the creature intended to kiss him. With a sickening crunch, the creature bit down on the boy's larynx. Freshets of arterial spray drenched the chewing creature. Its stringy black hair dripped with blood. Before Jesse could look away, it reached the back of the boy's neck and the teeth snapped the spine with an audible click.

Jesse gasped as a siren-like wail erupted just on the other side of the pine trees he was gazing over.

"*AGHHHH!*" the voice screamed as it drew closer.

Don't lead it over here, Jesse thought and felt a blush of guilt.

A girl burst through the pines and scrambled up the hill toward him. He took a step toward her, more out of instinct than a genuine desire to help. She was a plain girl who wore a yellow cut-off shirt and jean shorts. She was streaming blood from an ankle and limping badly. She'd gotten a few steps up the weedy hill before her ankle gave, pitching her forward onto her belly. She stared up at Jesse with huge eyes and yelled, "*Help me!*"

Jesse was taking another step toward her when a white figure exploded through the pines and landed at the bottom of the hill. She heard it but did not turn, instead emitting another siren howl. The creature pounced on her legs, then set to digging through the seat of her jean shorts, a frenzied red soup dousing its steam-shovel hands. Jesse whimpered, shoved a wrist to his mouth and strode unsteadily along the hill until the screaming carnage was behind him.

Twenty feet ahead a figure broke through the pines, followed by another. Young men both, neither of them familiar.

"Alex!" the trailing boy yelled, but the other boy—Alex, presumably—kept hoofing it toward the rise. *He just might make it,* Jesse marveled. The boy didn't seem athletic. He had a straw-colored shock of hair and a bony, freckled torso. Yet he moved with an alacrity Jesse only wished he could match.

"*Please, Alex,*" the other boy begged. Alex's friend was already winded. His pudgy gut rippled with each lumbering step, and to make matters worse, Jesse realized, the larger boy was drunk.

"Alex, I need your he—"

The boy never finished because a creature shot out of the screen of pine boughs and landed on the hill in front of Alex. Alex stared at the creature hulking over him, and just when Jesse was sure there'd be another bloodbath, the creature favored Alex with a malevolent grin, extended one knobby finger, and slashed a diagonal swath across Alex's forehead. A crimson rill flooded the boy's face as he crumpled. But rather than setting upon the boy, ripping him to pieces the way the others had done to their victims, the creature stood erect and glared down at Alex's friend.

"Oh jeez," the pudgy boy was whimpering. "Oh jeez no."

The creature took two long strides, and just when Jesse thought the pudgy boy might escape into the pines again, a long, sinuous arm swept out and snatched the boy from the ground. The creature gripped the boy by one plump calf. Despite his girth the boy rose rapidly through the air, the creature handling him as effortlessly as one would an overstuffed rag doll. The pudgy boy yowled in terror as the creature swung him upside down toward its opening mouth, the teeth crooked and mottled with brown. In one brutal motion the creature bit into the boy's beefy thigh and wrenched its head to remove the meat. Then the teeth snapped again, splintering the boy's femur, and his body, sans leg, tumbled headfirst to the earth.

The boy wailed in an inhuman voice, a fountain of blood jetting from his femoral artery. The creature held the severed leg by the knee and began gnawing at the twitching, hairy calf.

"Oh shit," Jesse muttered, half in horror, half in nausea. He turned and made for the pines separating him and the playground. If the jutting branches poked his eyes out, at least he'd be spared the sight of this bloodbath. The soft needles brushed his skin as he waded forward under a pine tree, then a thin branch came zinging toward his face and thwacked him on the bridge of the nose. He doubled over, his eyes instantly full of water. He swayed on his feet, remembering he himself had drunk quite a bit of beer, and a new sound grabbed his attention. Jesse opened and shut his eyes to shake off his disorientation, and as he regained focus he caught a glimpse of something waxen moving on the other side of the tree trunk. Despite the fear roiling in his guts, Jesse staggered forward, taking care to dodge the thick branches. It was very dark under the sheltering pine needles, but when he came around the corner of the thick trunk, he saw what was happening all too well.

Oh no, he thought. His scrotum tightened in terror and revulsion.

It was Tiara Girl, her black bikini top still on but her bottoms nowhere to be seen. She was on her back, her throat opened in a bloody, meaty smile. The creature that licked at the wide slit, its tongue dragging the length of the gash in forceful scoops, was also raping the dead girl, its skinny, muscled ass flexing in rhythm to the Bad Company song. Jesse could see how long its phallus was, more like the forearm of a tall man. It was grunting, moaning, defiling the poor girl's limp body as it slurped at her death wound. Her eyes were fixed open in a permanent stare, and Jesse noted with helpless sorrow that the sparkling tiara had somehow remained fixed in her black hair.

Before he knew what he was doing, Jesse reached up and snapped off a branch.

The creature didn't look up.

Jesse lifted a sneaker over a low bough and crept closer.

What are you doing? a voice in his head screamed.

I have no idea, he thought, but he kept moving anyway. He stepped over a branch, and finding it was higher than he'd thought, he ended up straddling it and having to wiggle his hips a little to distribute his weight to the other side.

When he lowered to the ground and turned to the raping monster, his stomach plummeted.

The creature was grinning at him.

Jesse froze where he stood, unable to go through with it. What the hell did he think he was going to do, anyway? He stared dumbly down at the branch in his hand. It was two feet long, not very thick. More like a baton than a bludgeoning weapon.

I'm dead, he thought. *Dead in just a moment.*

The creature stood, its jutting phallus glistening with blood. The thought of the monster tearing up the girl's insides was what finally did it, brought the toast and banana and coffee and beer geysering up into the back of his throat. The creature reached for the stick in Jesse's hands, but Jesse wrenched it away, then jabbed. Somehow, the sharp, broken end of the branch pierced the creature in the abdomen. It snarled, ripped the branch out of Jesse's hands, and before it could open his ribcage or rape his dead body, Jesse wheeled and plunged through the pine branches. He heard it roar, then came a chorus of snapping branches and throaty growls. The growls drew nearer, but Jesse refused to turn now. It would land on him and pin him and eat him but by God he wouldn't look into its wicked green eyes as it did. Jesse spied the leaden sky stippling the wall of branches, knew he was about to emerge onto the playground, and once out there he'd be dead within seconds, the thing leaping on him and tearing him apart.

Something hooked Jesse's ankle and sent him sprawling headfirst into the blanket of dead pine needles. He flopped onto his back, realizing he'd simply tripped over a root, and watched the monster leap onto a branch directly above him. For a moment, it sat perched over him, its snarling face lusting for his blood. Jesse screamed. The thing plummeted down at him. He rolled over to evade it. The white salamander body thumped down where he'd just been. Jesse clambered forward and discovered how close to the open air he was. Something slapped the heel of his sneaker, the creature groping for him. Jesse shot out a hand, bellowed for help. His elbow broke through, his head.

The creature caught him and hauled him backward.

Jesse stared up as its leering face loomed closer.

Don't kill me! he wanted to scream, but the sight of the mad, iridescent eyes stole his voice. The teeth, he noted with clinical fascination, were inward curving, like those of some species of sharks. That way, he remembered from watching *Shark Week*, the predators would be able to hook their prey, batten onto them so that even if their victims were able to disengage their bleeding bodies, the damage would be so great they'd be easy to finish off.

The hooked, scythe-like teeth drew closer. Jesse felt a droplet of rain on his hand, realizing with sick irony that he'd almost made it outside the sepulchral darkness of the pine tree, that part of him *had* made it outside the shadows. If only he could've gotten to the daylight...if only he could've—

You'd have died anyway, and you know it. Just pray it doesn't rape you the way it did Tiara Girl.

Jesse whimpered, his chest heaving, as the creature reached for him. He realized with amazement that it was clutching a branch with its bottom feet and dangling bat-like over him.

The taloned hands reached the mat of pine needles next to his shoulders, and the sighing jaws swam nearer. He closed his eyes and waited for the end.

Something clutched Jesse's wrist. Then he was yanked out from under the creature, his head smacked by fluffy pine branches.

He opened his eyes and stared up at his savior.

Colleen.

"*Look out!*" she screamed.

The creature emerged from the pine tree, its eyes slitted with rage. Colleen backpedaled, and Jesse, still on his ass, dug with his heels and palms to scuttle away. He bumped something, gasped and turned to see a pale figure towering over him. He was sure for a moment it was one of the beasts, but then he saw the toga, the beefy arms.

Goliath.

The gigantic man wielded a wooden baseball bat—Goliath was apparently a purist of the game—and was fending off a snarling beast.

Colleen bumped into Goliath's broad back; he shot a glance back at her and saw the creature who'd nearly killed Jesse approaching.

"Smash it," Colleen said.

Goliath gave her an exasperated look and raised the bat. The creature closest to the huge man was snarling and snapping at him. The creature closest to Jesse was still watching the trio of potential victims with a confident, calculating look that was somehow worse than the other creature's feral one.

Goliath swung, and the snarling creature ducked with a quickness Jesse wouldn't have thought possible. Then, cobra-like, it darted forward and hopped back, and Goliath was holding his chest in dismay. Jesse caught a brief glimpse before Goliath's enormous paw covered it up, and he was able to see the ragged clump the creature had chomped out, half of Goliath's pectoral muscle gone, the nipple replaced by a flowing scarlet bed of hamburger.

Goliath raised the bat, but the pain in his chest arrested the motion midway.

The creature didn't hesitate.

Leaping forward, it fastened its feet in Goliath's sheet-covered hips and with its fingernails began shredding the sides of the huge man's face. The ears were gone in an instant, the temples flayed. Goliath's high-pitched screaming was terrible, and almost as bad was the drizzle of blood that sprayed over Jesse and Colleen.

The mixed odors of raw meat and feces made Jesse ill. He felt himself mentally retreat, his body suddenly a nerveless husk. His knees buckled.

The creature from the pines crouched over him.

Chapter Eleven

Jesse kicked it in the face. Its head barely moved, but its slitted eyes darkened in outrage.

It lunged for Jesse's face. He whipped his head to the side, felt the whoosh of the creature's mouth as it missed him by inches. He flung his arms up to ward it off, then they were both crushed by flailing bodies.

In the melee he took an elbow from Colleen, who'd been knocked down by Goliath and the creature feasting on him. The huge man was a goner, but somehow he was still struggling for life. Something limp smacked Jesse's face and he realized with revulsion that it was the beast's pendulous breasts, apparently the first female creature he'd encountered. As he scrabbled away from the mass of twisting bodies, he discovered it also had more hair. The filthy black strings pendulummed as the female beast shredded Goliath's chin. He was swatting the creature in the head, but it seemed unaffected by the club-like blows.

Jesse pushed to his feet, took a few jogging steps before glancing back and seeing Colleen fighting for her life in the pile. Goliath and the female creature had somehow interposed themselves between Colleen and the creature who'd attacked Jesse, but the cadaverous monster was extricating itself, would be free in moments. Colleen, however, was hopelessly pinned under Goliath's hemorrhaging body.

Go back! She saved your life, asshole!

Jesse moaned, knowing the voice was right. Acid boiling in his throat, he drew closer, bent and grasped the bat. Its handle was slick with sweat, the barrel speckled with black ichor, but it nevertheless felt good in his hands. The rapist creature burst loose from the pile, pounced on Colleen. Before she could get her hands up, the creature pinioned her wrists to the ground and slid its long wormy tongue up her throat. Jesse saw tears squeezing from the sides of Colleen's eyes, and without further hesitation he brought down the bat like he was splitting a cord of wood. The barrel thunked solidly against the back of the creature's skull.

It slumped on top of Colleen, but Jesse could see immediately it hadn't lost consciousness. Far from it, the creature was cupping its dripping pate with one taloned hand and pounding its other fist in anger on the playground mulch.

"Again," Colleen croaked.

Jesse gave her a baffled look, and she pushed up on the writhing creature as hard as she could. Teeth bared from the strain, she growled, "Hit the bastard again!"

Jesse did. This time he crushed the side of its face. The creature yowled in agony, and Jesse brought the bat down again, the Louisville Slugger cracking the forearm covering its face.

He swung again, thinking, *Not so tough now, you gutless rapist*, but Colleen seized his arm, yanked him backward. Stumbling after her, Jesse saw why Colleen had dragged him away.

The female creature had paused, Goliath's now limp body messy with gore, and was watching its fallen comrade intently.

"Run!" Colleen yelled.

Jesse followed. He couldn't believe how fast Colleen ran. They shot by the seesaw, headed for the concrete sidewalk that led out of the playground. Jesse glanced to his left and was immediately sorry he had.

Three of the creatures had swarmed over the jungle gym, reminding Jesse very much of lizards sunning themselves on a rock. Yet it wasn't even noon, and the sky had grown dark. A couple more droplets of rain pattered on his arms, and the western thunder rumbled. Bad Company had ceased its ballad, and in its place Jesse heard the first few notes of AC/DC's "You Shook Me All Night Long".

The kids trapped inside the jungle gym didn't seem to notice the song change.

There was a short, red-haired boy and three girls in bikinis, one of whom Jesse now remembered as Light Blue Bikini Girl. Under any other circumstances, he was certain the red-haired boy would've thanked his stars to be trapped with three gorgeous girls in skimpy swimwear, but this wasn't being snowed in at a cozy mountain cabin or being marooned on a tropical island.

This was being trapped in a cage by monsters.

The creatures, Jesse realized with sick understanding, were taunting their prey. One creature would curl his freakish tongue out at Light Blue Bikini with lascivious menace and actually chortle whenever she'd recoil. Another creature—this one was shorter and broader than the others, its skin a dingier shade of white—was dangling its arms through the gaps in the jungle gym, making halfhearted grabs at the girls as they evaded it.

Before they made it past the jungle gym, Jesse witnessed one more atrocity.

One of the creatures had sneaked behind Light Blue Bikini. Quicker than Jesse could believe, it snagged her by the calf and dragged her screaming through a gap in the bottom bars. She clawed the mulch to return to the safety of the barred dome; her braying screams were the loudest Jesse had yet heard.

Her shrieks must've agitated the creature because it gave her body a rough shake. Her blond hair jostled as her head smacked the ground, but she only screamed louder. Lips drawn back in a snarl, the creature grasped her by the ankles, pivoted, and swung her entire body through the air in a whipping arc. Her face and shoulders smashed the ground, the sound of her snapping neck cutting off her screams.

The last thing Jesse saw as he tore his eyes away were the two other creatures dropping inside the jungle gym and setting upon the other victims in a flurry of claws and teeth.

They neared the sidewalk, the shrill screams of Angus Young only partially masking the death wails erupting all around them. The number of creatures seemed to have grown. A frenzied scan of the playground revealed at least a dozen of the beasts, every last one smacking and chewing on the body of a victim. Jesse was also sure the number of college students had diminished, and not just because they'd been eaten. There appeared to be about half the number of people there'd been only minutes earlier, and very few of those present were still alive.

Still, somewhere in his muddled thoughts, he understood there might be hope for them. If so many had escaped from the playground, he and Colleen might too. The creatures were too concerned with devouring their victims to worry about the ones who were getting away.

He was thinking this when a creature stepped onto the sidewalk in front of them.

Ten feet tall at least, the creature was also more muscular than the others, its green eyes larger. *A fine specimen*, some voice within Jesse's mind commented, a remnant perhaps of all the crappy sci-fi movies he watched at three in the morning.

It extended its arms as if barring their way. Or perhaps it was about to embrace them both. A surge of panic so bright it nearly blotted out all other thought flooded through him, but an object resting against Jesse's leg seemed to nudge him back to reality.

The bat.

Jesse raised it, called out, "Get down!" to Colleen. The creature's hungry grin widened in amusement, and Jesse realized how feeble his weapon was. The creature leaned closer as if offering its face up for batting practice, but before Jesse could swing, a noise erupted to their right.

The creature turned, and at the last moment Jesse realized what the sound had been.

A blatting horn.

The black pickup truck steamrolled through the high weeds and smashed into the creature, which flipped sideways onto the windshield before tumbling over the roof and flopping into the bed. The truck skidded sideways just as it reached the pines, and for a moment Jesse was sure it would tip. But the wheels jounced down, the creature in the back bouncing up and landing limply, dead or unconscious.

He and Colleen shared an amazed look.

Then the door opened and they discovered who'd saved them.

Musclehead.

Jesse had forgotten all about the night before, when he and Emma—

Jesus Christ, he thought. *Emma!*

He'd completely forgotten about her, and on the heels of that thought he remembered Greeley, the two of them disappearing at the same time.

Maybe they got away, he thought and was immediately ashamed to find he only wanted one of the two safe.

Musclehead gestured toward the open door. "Get the hell in!"

Colleen grabbed Jesse's wrist and dashed with him to the black truck. Colleen lunged inside first, and Jesse followed. As he did he caught a glimpse of something black at Musclehead's side.

A handgun.

Jesse knew nothing of firearms, but the gun in Musclehead's hand filled him with a sudden flash of hope. So did the dark crew cut, the square jaw, and the bodybuilder's muscles. The guy looked more like a Marine than ever as he slammed shut the door and jerked the truck into reverse. They halted, Musclehead's strong hand reaching up to shift the truck into drive, and an alabaster shape plummeted down from the pines and crashed down on the hood.

Snarling, the creature drew back a fist and punched through the windshield like paper, its talons whickering through the air an inch from Jesse's face. As calmly as if he were a cop positioning a radar detector, Musclehead leaned out the window, the black gun gripped in his left hand, and squeezed off four deafening shots. The first missed, but the next two made the creature twist sideways, a spray of black blood misting the webbed windshield. The fourth shot knocked the creature off the hood. As if he did this sort of thing every day, Musclehead drove over the creature with a dull crunch, and in a moment they emerged from the sidewalk and into the parking lot outside the playground.

Jesse's windpipe constricted. He realized why the creatures had let so many people escape the playground.

Jesse stared gape-mouthed.

The entire campground was acrawl with the beasts.

On the main road alone Jesse counted twenty or thirty. In the sprawling, primitive camping area he beheld twice that number. The creatures were all running people down, feasting on them, or scouring the darkening day for more victims.

When the black pickup bounced onto the main road, half a dozen sets of huge, green eyes fixed on them. Rain pattered the windshield.

"Can you see?" Colleen asked.

"Good enough," Musclehead responded. Staring at the square jaw, one corner of the man's mouth rising with the tiniest glimmer of mirth, Jesse realized the man was enjoying this. Had probably daydreamed about it all his life. Of course, Jesse had too, but deep down he'd always known if there were an outbreak of vampirism or a zombie plague, he'd turn into a quivering jellyfish. Thinking of Tiara Girl, he supposed that assumption had already proved true.

Not fair, a part of him protested. *I did go back and try to help her.*

Not soon enough, his conscience declared, *not nearly soon enough.*

Musclehead turned to Jesse. "You know how to shoot?"

"With that?" Jesse asked.

Musclehead smiled. "This one's mine. There's a shotgun under the seat."

Colleen got on the floor, said, "My dad taught me guns." She came up with the shotgun. "Shells?"

"There's a live one chambered and five more inside. There's more in the glove compartment."

Jesse longed for a better weapon. He'd positioned the bat between his legs with the handle sticking up, and now it made him feel like a child on the way to little league practice.

The rain was falling steadily. Through the passenger's window, just beyond Colleen's grim face, he watched a creature rip a man's head off.

Jesse shut his eyes and leaned against the seat.

"Where're we going?" Colleen asked as the pickup accelerated.

"Where you think?" Musclehead asked. "The fuck outta here, of course."

Mercifully, they passed the last of the primitive sites and the wholesale murder occurring there, and into the stand of forest separating the two main camping areas. Jesse caught a glimpse of a pale figure hunkered over something obscured by the underbrush, but the bobbing of the creature's head told him all he needed to know.

Musclehead asked, "What the hell are they?"

Colleen only stared.

Jesse said, "It's like they've been waiting for this."

Musclehead glared at him but said nothing. Then the truck emerged from the canopy of forest. Colleen gasped.

The RV area was overrun by creatures.

Chapter Twelve

In a movement Jesse suspected was wholly involuntary, Musclehead eased off the accelerator and let the pickup drift down the lane. There'd been fifteen or twenty RVs and other assorted camping vehicles when they'd come in; now there were double that.

And nearly all of them had been overturned.

Jesse had no idea how many creatures there were in the deluxe section, but his mental estimate was somewhere between seventy-five and a hundred. Like gaunt, fairy-tale trolls, the figures marauded over the campground, ripping and maiming as they went. Jesse beheld an old woman, her neatly permed white hair swinging wildly from side to side, being devoured by a creature with its face buried in her midsection. Moving away from the same campsite, another creature dragged a white-haired man through the grass. At first Jesse thought the creature was grasping the man's belt, but then he realized the object was too long for that, that it was a string of the man's intestines the creature was clutching.

Get us out of here, he thought. *Just get us out of here.* But to his horror, the pickup was still decelerating.

"What're you doing?" Colleen asked.

Musclehead was staring at something ahead and to their right. "Gonzales," he whispered.

Squinting through the cracked windshield and the metronomic sweep of the wipers, Jesse discerned a man swinging a crowbar at an advancing creature. The man backpedaled, his mouth twisted in a deranged grin. As the truck crunched to a halt, Musclehead said, "Wait here."

"What are you—" Colleen began.

"That's my friend," Musclehead said and climbed out.

Jesse wished Musclehead had shut the door. He and Colleen watched as the creature slapped the crowbar away from Gonzales and then whacked him in the side of the head with an open hand. The blow sent Gonzales flying, his puny-looking body crashing against an iron fire pit. As the man rolled over—not dead, but not exactly flourishing either—Jesse noticed the black facial hair and recognized Goatee from the night before. *Poor son of a bitch*, Jesse reflected. *Guy came out here for a little fun and is going to be eaten alive by a white-skinned monster instead.*

Before the creature could rend Goatee's flesh, however, a gunshot cracked, then another. The creature stood rigid and actually glanced down to assess itself, the runny black liquid leaking out of its chest and belly.

Its face came up to stare at Musclehead. Seeing the monster's wide green eyes, its lips stretched wide, Jesse couldn't breathe. He'd never seen such unbridled viciousness in a face.

Musclehead shot it between the eyes.

Jesse was stunned to see it tumble backward.

Without pausing to make sure it was dead, Musclehead hoisted his friend in a fireman's carry. Then, Gonzales's shaggy black head jiggling pitifully, Musclehead hustled him over to the truck. With a gentleness that would have moved Jesse under other circumstances, the big man placed Gonzales in the driver's seat and eased his head against the seatback.

"These two are gonna take care of you," Musclehead said. "They owe me."

Gonzales, Jesse noted, was conscious, but definitely in a fog. He lolled his head in Jesse and Colleen's direction and offered them a wan smile. Colleen started to say something, but before she could get it out, they felt the truck rock slightly.

The storm was kicking up now, but the wind had to be stronger than he thought to buffet the full-sized pickup that way. He glanced a question at Colleen, but she held her arms out, as if awaiting the next tremor.

"Hey," Gonzales said, his grin brilliant within the glossy black nest of beard, "I remember you from last ni—"

He never finished because the window behind them shattered and a pair of white hands clamped over his head.

Colleen shrieked, and Jesse practically climbed on top of her to get away from the grasping creature. Gonzales yowled in terror and flung out an arm toward Jesse, but the only thing Jesse could think about was the monster in the back of the pickup. Somewhere below his conscious mind, a sardonic voice said, *Guess you'll never make fun of the characters in a horror movie again, huh? That's worse than not checking the back seat.*

Gonzales was being towed backward through the window. His hairy legs kicked madly, his arms slapping Jesse, the roof, anything they could reach. But the creature drew him slowly, almost methodically, through the jagged aperture. Beside him Colleen puked on the dashboard, and now he saw why. Gonzales's skin was being peeled from his body as he was dragged through the hole. Shards of glass plowed vermilion grooves through his chest, his arms. The flesh over his ribcage seemed to unzip as if he were molting. Jesse turned away and regarded Colleen, whose upper lip was creamed with vomit. Her face twisted in horror again, and again she puked, this time down the front of her shirt. Against his will Jesse turned to see why and thought, *I'm losing my mind.*

The creature had succeeded in dragging Gonzales all the way out. Now it stood in the truck bed with a long-toed foot fixed on the man's upside-down crotch. It was tugging on the skin of the man's legs as though trying to free him from a pesky pair of tight pants. Only this was the man's skin, and the creature was ripping off gobbets of it as it yanked, chewing the pink stuff like a lion at a fresh kill.

"Oh man," Jesse muttered. "What're we gonna tell Musclehead?"

"Tell who?" Colleen asked, but at that moment the man returned.

"Can't find Austin," he was saying, not yet noticing the soaking red stain where a minute before his friend had sat. "Maybe he got out before the…" Musclehead trailed off, his eyes widening in disbelief.

His eyes shifted from Jesse to Colleen. "Where did…"

Jesse pointed sheepishly through the window. Musclehead's mouth fell open in an expression that would have been comical at any other time. His mouth twitched, the brawny man actually on the verge of tears. He moved around the side of the truck, raised his gun, and aimed it at the feeding creature's face. Jesse remembered the shotgun, had a sudden urge to wrest it from Colleen's hands and atone for letting Gonzales get skinned. The champing creature appeared totally immersed in his dining, so Musclehead edged closer, the gun jittering in a palsied rage.

"Look at me, you—"

One moment the creature was feasting; the next it was leaping into the air, its agility incomprehensible. Musclehead was too amazed to track it as it described a graceful flip high over him. It landed behind him, and as he turned to blast it the creature surprised Jesse again. Rather than decapitating Musclehead, as Jesse was sure it would do, the creature flicked the gun out of his hands. The gesture was rapid and neat, but the wounds it made were not. Three of Musclehead's fingers had been torn off, the stumps pumping fresh blood into the air. Instead of lunging at the muscular man and rending him to pieces, the creature scraped a grubby index fingernail through the flesh of Musclehead's brow. Blood swam over his face in a sheet. Musclehead sank to his knees, his gaping mouth barking out hoarse sobs.

The creature regarded Jesse, on its face a look of obscene merriment.

"*Drive,*" Colleen shouted.

She was climbing onto her knees and taking a bead with the shotgun, the barrel inches from Jesse's head. He lunged toward the dash just before the cab filled with the earsplitting roar of the blast.

"*Get your ass over there,*" she demanded, shoving Jesse toward the wheel. He moved numbly to the driver's seat, saw Musclehead had left the engine running and slipped the gearshift into drive. He cast a nervous glance out the open driver's window to see if the creature was about to leap through, but it was on its knees, its back to the truck.

"I nailed it in the eye," Colleen said.

Jesse glanced in the rearview mirror meaning to see the creature's blasted face, but he caught a glimpse of Musclehead instead, the man lying on his side, still holding his bleeding hand.

"Should we go back?" Jesse asked.

"For what?" Colleen asked, fumbling with the glove compartment.

"Musclehead," Jesse explained, "the guy who saved us."

"Leave him or all three of us'll die." She located the box of shells, slid one more inside.

From their right came a bounding figure. The creature jumped off one foot, swooped toward them. Colleen pushed into Jesse just as the creature hammered the passenger's door, its fists crashing through the window. The glass hailed over them. Jesse jerked the wheel, and the creature almost lost its grip. The pickup bounced over campsites, crushed a grill on an iron pole, veered away from an overturned pop-up camper, then made it back to the main road. The creature's skinny legs scrabbled for purchase on the dented door, then swung up, perching on the windowsill. Then its entire, nine-foot frame was squatting in the open window, its incredible gauntness and flexibility allowing it to snake its head into the cab and leer at them. Its long phallus swung between its legs, reminding Jesse of the creature he now thought of as the Big Nasty, the one who'd raped Tiara Girl.

The creature groped for the shotgun. Colleen kicked its reaching hand out of the way and leveled the weapon at its crotch. Its eyes widened a moment before she pulled the trigger, the blast evaporating the creature's abdomen in a haze of black gore. The creature bellowed in agony and fell backward into the road.

They'd driven about thirty yards when Jesse noticed the object lying on the passenger's seat. *Oh crap,* he thought.

Colleen followed his gaze to the severed penis. A foot long, it looked like an enlarged breakfast sausage someone had left out of the fridge.

"Could you..." he said and nodded at the penis.

"I'm not touching that."

"Use the gun," he said, "you know, to nudge it—"

"*Look out!*" she screamed.

Jesse turned and saw the professor standing in the middle of the road, his palms thrown out to stop them.

We're going to run him over, Jesse thought.

The same dread knowledge was imprinted on Professor Clevenger's owlish face. He flung his forearms over his head as if that would save him. Jesse ripped the wheel left and felt the back end slue. He was sure it would swing around and crash into the man like a wrecking ball, but the impact never came. As they spun in the road, Jesse glimpsed the professor standing where he'd been, his arms still thrown over his face in that warding-off gesture. The truck shuddered to a stop.

"*Get in*," Colleen shouted across Jesse.

The professor slowly lowered his arms and pivoted toward them, his expression both joyful and unbelieving.

"You think we can make it out?" Colleen asked as the professor hustled toward them.

"If we can—" Jesse started, but broke off when he spotted something about fifty yards away.

In the middle of the deluxe section, surrounded by a dozen pale figures, several RVs had been overturned. A couple were still upright, though the figures were working on them too. It was next to the largest RV, however, that they saw what prevented them from answering when the professor climbed in the passenger door next to Colleen and said, "Thank God for you two. I can't tell you how much..."

The rest of his words were lost in the rush of foreboding that had gripped Jesse.

"We have to go over there," he said, dry-mouthed.

Colleen nodded, but she looked very frightened.

Jesse put the pickup in drive and cut across the main road. Weaving in and out of campsites, they approached the giant white RV with green and blue stripes decorating its flanks.

And the big white Buick parked outside it.

Part Two
The Children

Chapter One

"Why aren't we heading for the exit?" Clevenger asked.

"Our friend is there," Colleen said. "We're not leaving without her."

Jesse nodded, but he was already having his doubts. For one thing, they were heading toward the epicenter of madness, the proliferation of creatures worse here than it had been at the playground. Secondly, the logistics of their rescue mission were virtually impossible. What was he to do? Crash into the RV and hope that, rather than killing everyone inside, the truck would rip a wide enough swath for everyone to climb through? And say that did work, what then? What if the mountainous RV had become the last bastion for two dozen survivors? Was he to fit them all into the bed of the pickup?

And who was to say Emma was in the RV at all? She might've died in the first wave of attacks, and someone else could've commandeered the Buick. Maybe Greeley had hung her out to dry and, finding his road to safety blocked, ended up at the motor home. That would be a hell of an irony, wouldn't it? Jesse would risk his life only to learn that his reward was a supercilious handshake and the knowledge Greeley had slept with Emma before she died.

Enough, his mind shouted. *Quit playing the spurned suitor and focus on what you're doing.*

That was good advice, he knew. Because Emma could indeed be in there after all. Jesse'd never believed in psychic powers, but he had a vague premonition now that Emma *was* inside the RV, and if she was, she sure as hell needed his help.

He imagined ripping open the door of the camper and finding Emma huddled inside. *Thought maybe you could use a hand*, Jesse would say with a lopsided grin. Then Emma would throw herself into his arms—

"*Jesse!*" Colleen shouted.

He plummeted back to reality in time to see a pale figure rear back and hurl something at them. Only when it was halfway to the truck did Jesse identify it, and by that time it was too late.

The old man crashed through their windshield and sprawled out, convulsing, across their laps.

"Oh my holy God!" Clevenger screamed and pawed at the man's shattered body. The old man's bald pate had been sheared most of the way off, the flap of scalp smacking Jesse's bare knees as they bounced toward the RV.

The creature who'd lobbed the senior citizen at them was hunched in an aggressive stance about twenty feet in front of the motor home and was waving them forward in a come-and-get-it taunt.

"Run him over," Colleen said, her voice reasonably sedate for having a convulsing octogenarian in her lap. She buckled her safety belt. Jesse did too.

They were closing on the RV.

This close to the big camper, Jesse discovered there were creatures on each side rocking it back and forth. Blue letters said SEABREEZE, and behind the wheel Jesse spied a terrified woman of perhaps sixty watching the truck approach.

Just when he thought the creature who'd heaved the man through their windshield would leap into the air or dive out of the way, the pickup scuttled up a slight incline. At the speed they were traveling, the dirt mound acted as a ramp. The truck leapt into the air, and the creature realized its error too late. As it sprung, the pickup crashed into its lower legs, sending its upper body hammering down where the windshield had been. Its head crunched sickeningly on the dash before its limp body jounced up and over the roof of the truck. One of the creatures trying to overturn the RV whirled and saw them bearing down on it. It too attempted to move but Jesse understood how badly he'd misjudged the distance.

He tried to stop but it was much too late.

The pickup rammed the motor home, the pale creature crushed between the vehicles.

Professor Clevenger slammed into the dash with a bone-jarring *whump*. The RV rocked away from the impact, teetered on its side a moment, then toppled. From inside the RV, Jesse heard shrieks of pain and terror. A creature appeared from nowhere and, berserker style, plunged through the motor home's windshield. More screams from inside. Then came a volley of staccato blasts, someone firing a gun within.

The rain was gushing now. Jesse shielded his eyes. Peering through the gaping hole where the truck's windshield had been, he watched a creature leap onto the overturned RV's side. Surely unaware there was a creature there, someone from within the camper threw open the side door and attempted to climb out. Whoever it was let out a yelp of surprise and tried to close the door, but the creature was too quick. It reached down and fished the person out, a short woman Jesse now recognized as Linda Farmer, the camp ranger. Movement to his right drew his gaze and he saw Colleen drawing a bead on the creature, who was lifting Linda into the air, her legs flailing madly. The scimitar teeth leaned toward her exposed neck, but just before the creature ripped out her throat, the side door of the motor home swung open and Ron the DNR officer emerged. He leveled a black gun and squeezed off a fusillade of shots. The creature dropped Linda, took a couple wobbly steps at Ron, then crumpled.

Ron clambered along the top of the overturned camper to retrieve Linda's weeping but intact body, but before he reached her, a creature pounced on him. Rolling onto his back, Ron thrust the gun up to shoot the creature, but it backhanded the pistol, the black object skittering uselessly along the white metal before disappearing over the edge. The creature raised its taloned hand to kill Ron, but before it could, a crack of thunder sounded and a gaping hole opened under the creature's armpit.

Beside the truck, Colleen pumped the shotgun and advanced on the creature. Rather than clutching its side or bellowing in agony, the creature turned and let loose with a combination bark and hiss that made Jesse's flesh crawl.

Then the creature leapt at Colleen.

She dropped but had the presence of mind to squeeze the trigger. The buckshot struck the creature in the kneecap in a spray of liquid and tendons. The airborne creature, seemingly unmindful of its wounds, flashed a clawed hand at Colleen and yanked out some of her hair. The creature landed, turned and crawled toward her, its ruined leg trailing behind it. It was only a few feet away but Colleen, grasping her bleeding scalp, didn't notice. The creature's fangs glistened in the torrential rain.

Then Jesse realized he was moving. In his periphery he saw the professor look up, startled, from his place on the floor of the truck.

The creature reached Colleen before Jesse, but it was taking its time, either unaware of Jesse's approach or unafraid of his intervention. The shotgun had tumbled into the puddled grass, a few feet away from where the creature was grasping Colleen by the front of her shirt and hauling her toward it. Jesse bent and retrieved the shotgun. He pointed it at the creature and squeezed the trigger, but nothing happened. The creature's long, serpent-like tongue uncurled and slicked a line across Colleen's shut lips. She was grimacing, shoving ineffectually against the creature's ivory chest.

Her terrified eyes focused on Jesse, whose finger was locked on the trigger that wouldn't pull. Staring at Colleen, he had a sudden memory of her shooting this creature in the armpit and advancing on it.

A voice in his head shouted, *Pump it, you moron!*

Jesse pumped the shotgun, heard the wet click. The creature slid a slimy hand down the front of Colleen's pants. Jesse squeezed the trigger.

The explosion was deafening.

Colleen shrieked and held her ears. At the same moment the top of the creature's head seemed to disappear, a chunky black fountain of brains and skull fragments showering the besotted earth. Colleen was holding her ears and lying on her side, but her eyes were on Jesse's. Impossibly, he realized she was smiling.

Jesse rushed to her and got his arms around her. Rather than slapping him like he'd thought she would, she crowded into him, and for the first time that day he didn't feel like a complete coward.

Something seized his shoulder. Jesse gasped and dropped Colleen. He'd raised the shotgun to protect himself from a new creature, but it was Ron the DNR officer shouting something unintelligible at him. Jesse glanced down at Colleen, whom he'd let drop into the mud. *Some savior I am.*

"The other girl," Ron said, "the one you came with."

Jesse felt a surge of hope. "Emma?"

Ron nodded impatiently, hooked a thumb at the RV on its side, which was jerking spasmodically amidst a demon's chorus of wails. A terrific battle was taking place inside.

"She's not..." Jesse began.

Ron nodded emphatically. "She's in there."

The needling rain had cooled the day, but as Jesse stared at the tremoring RV he grew absolutely frigid.

"How many?" a voice at his side asked.

Jesse turned to see the professor standing beside them. The older man was holding his chest, his wispy hair plastered to his forehead. He looked like he was in bad shape. But there was a resolve there too, a grimness around the eyes that gave Jesse hope.

Ron said, "How many what? People or those white bastards?"

"Either," the professor said. "Both."

"Ten or eleven people, at least three monsters."

Jesse experienced a horrible afterimage of Tiara Girl's dead body being defiled by the creature under the pines. Only it wasn't Tiara Girl's face.

It was Emma's.

He made for the gaping front window of the RV.

"Hold on," Ron shouted. He jogged over, picked up his pistol. Thrusting it into Clevenger's hands, he said, "You take this, stand guard over Linda." Ron nodded at the blonde woman who lay in small heap a few feet away.

Clevenger let the gun dangle from his hand, as if the touch of it made him ill. "Where will you be?"

Ron fetched the shotgun from the grass, checked its chambers and handed it to Colleen. "Saving as many as we can," he said.

Jesse and Colleen followed Ron to the RV window. Jesse cast about for some sort of weapon, but all he could see were rocks, shards of broken glass. Finally, he spotted a slender steel rod, about two feet long. It looked like it had come off of the motor home, but he couldn't be sure. It wasn't much, but it was better than going in empty-handed.

"You got four shells left in the Remington," Ron told Colleen. "Be smart about how you use 'em."

Jesse was wondering what Ron's plan was when the man stopped in front of the missing windshield, bent and produced a black pistol from an ankle holster. The man's mustached upper lip rose as if he were about to shout something intimidating, some cool piece of movie dialogue perhaps—"*Yippee-kay-a, motherfucker*"—when the man's face seemed to drain of color, the black gun drooping to his side. Jesse and Colleen pulled up alongside him, and Jesse saw why he'd reacted the way he had.

The interior of the RV was a bloodbath.

There weren't three creatures in there, but five. And there hadn't been ten or eleven victims, at least not by Jesse's estimation.

Of course, it was difficult to tell.

There were at least twelve headless bodies piled up at the bottom of the overturned motor home. Some of these looked like refugees from the playground massacre; the rest were elderly, the black socks and leisure wear giving them away. Two of the creatures were in the process of slaughtering more victims, both elderly women. Jesse saw with benumbed horror that there was a small child's headless body in the pile too.

"Oh my God," Colleen said, and for the first time since he'd known her, she looked and sounded absolutely powerless.

One creature was painted with blood, its iridescent green eyes the only things that weren't crimson. It was on its knees, immersed in hammering the bathroom door beneath it, clawing at the plastic to get to whatever poor soul was hiding on the other side.

Another of the creatures who was feasting on an old man ceased burrowing into the guy's belly and opened its bloodstained maw in their direction.

"Dammit," Ron said. "Dammit all to hell."

One of the creatures was in the rear of the RV, barely visible beyond all the carnage, but its current occupation was clear enough. The victim appeared somewhere between seventy and eighty—it was tough to see from this angle. The mattress had fallen off the frame and was lying diagonally in the rear of the RV, and it was atop this canted mattress that the creature was raping the old woman.

Colleen said, "Are any of them…"

Jesse glanced at her, his mind a jumble of disordered thoughts. Then he remembered.

Emma.

He made himself reexamine the pile of corpses in an attempt to identify Emma. But how, without their heads… Jesus, this was insane.

"Here it comes," Ron was saying. Jesse whipped his head around and saw the DNR officer backpedaling. Ron was staring up at something, and when Jesse turned again he beheld the creature stalking toward him, the thing so damned tall it had to crouch despite the fact that the shell of the RV was so huge.

It's crouching because it's treading on corpses.

Jesse shot a glance at its spindly legs and realized this was true. Each time the creature took a stride, the headless bodies shifted like broken dolls in the bottom of some kid's closet. Then it was looming over Jesse, Colleen shouting for him to run.

Jesse reared back with the metal rod and swung. The bar smacked the creature in the side of the face and lashed its skin open. The messy wound immediately rose in a livid weal, and the creature glowered at Jesse in ravenous fury.

Then something cracked behind him, the creature's gaunt frame jerking as Ron shot it twice, three times. It listed to the right, then fell.

It was at that moment that the red-painted creature pried open the bathroom door.

Jesse heard a high-pitched wail.

Oh God. *Emma.*

He surged toward the shattered windshield, unmindful of the creatures feasting just inside.

Ahead, the creature lowered inside the bathroom, and Emma's screams grew frantic.

Jesse reached the creature, peered down over its shoulder and saw Emma lying in the shower stall kicking at the beast. It was standing in the stall too, chortling at her, its bloody talons flashing out now and then at her flailing tennis shoes. A weird vertigo swam over him as he struggled to process the bizarre angles of the overturned motor home.

Jesse fought it off, gritted his teeth. Emma was weeping freely, the creature actually squatting over her now, daring her to inflict damage. Toying with her, the sadistic bastard.

"Hey," Jesse yelled. The creature's crimson back froze. Emma shot a glance at him and through her panic and her tears he saw recognition and what might have been hope.

Wish there was a reason for it, he thought.

The creature spun on him, snarling. Before Jesse could react, it exploded out of the stall, slammed him into a hard surface. It seized him by the seat of his shorts and flung him toward the rear of the RV. Jesse hit the back wall hard. Dazed, he turned and saw the creature stalking toward him like some freakish jaguar. Jesse pushed away from the blood-covered creature, but that meant nearing the tilted mattress, where the unholy copulation was still taking place. As he scuttled toward the mattress, something slid beneath his knee. Jesse glanced down and realized he was sitting on a sliding closet door. He endeavored to pry the door open, but his weight prevented it from moving. God, with the motor home on its side, his physics were all off.

The crimson creature snared his ankle, reeled him in. Jesse grabbed the closet door and scraped it open. Something thudded against Jesse's grasping hand. He shot a look back but the other creature was still on the mattress, still making violent love to the old woman's corpse.

Jesse looked up and beheld the crimson creature's dripping fangs.

His fingers happened on an object by his hip.

A yellow pencil.

Jesse pumped it into the side of the creature's face and actually watched the lead tip puncture the thing's cheek. It yowled in surprise and pain. It clutched the pencil with one hand, and with its free hand it backhanded Jesse a terrible blow that sent him somersaulting backward, his feet rising and his head going gray. He thought for a second he was tumbling into unconsciousness, but he realized too late he was literally tumbling through the open sliding closet door.

He struck the back of the closet with a muffled thud. Something gasped and slapped at him, and he thought, *Oh hell, not another one.* Then he opened his eyes and felt the wooziness and terror burn away.

Marc Greeley.

Hiding in the closet.

"Whatever happened to women and children first?" Jesse asked.

But Greeley wasn't listening, didn't even seem to be aware Jesse was human instead of monster. Greeley gibbered and sobbed and hurled piles of clothes at him.

"Greeley," Jesse said.

Greeley whipped him with the cuff of a sports coat.

"*Greeley*," he repeated, but the man only burrowed deeper into his fortress of senior citizen casual wear.

Jesse dug through the layers of clothing until he beheld the man's frightened face. Grabbing him by the chin, Jesse shouted, "You've gotta help me!"

The anesthesia of terror finally seemed to dissipate. Greeley blinked at him in a look that wasn't quite recognition. Greeley opened his mouth to respond, but as he did his eyes flashed to something over Jesse's shoulder.

Jesse knew without turning what it was.

The blood and saliva pattered down into Jesse's hair.

He whirled on the creature, aimed a haymaker at it, but it jerked its head back and Jesse's fist crashed into the side of the closet door.

Broken, he thought. It hurt like hell, but the pain was the least of his worries.

The monster was lowering into the closet with them.

Chapter Two

The sound that issued from Greeley's mouth was scarcely discernible as human. The maniacal squall crescendoed louder and higher, a rictus of ultimate terror inscribed on Greeley's once-handsome face. Methodically, almost delicately, the creature stepped inside the closet with them. Greeley clambered away until he was bunched in the roof of the closet, his quaking limbs gathering as many items of clothing as he could to cover himself. The creature's satanic face leered with delight. Then, clearly unconcerned with Greeley, it turned its attention to Jesse.

The crimson beast seized him by the chest of his T-shirt and hoisted him aloft.

Jesse rose out of the closet, borne higher and higher, mesmerized by the hideousness of the creature's face. The scimitar teeth opened, and above them he watched the huge green eyes glaze in anticipatory delight. Jesse felt doom spread over him, his entire body going slack. He had no weapon, no hope against this beast. He rose higher, higher, the creature's mouth opening farther than he would have thought possible.

Thunder exploded to Jesse's left. He and the creature turned that way and saw Colleen holding the smoking shotgun. Movement from the back of the motor home drew all their attention.

Only then did Jesse realize that the monster raping the dead woman on the bed was the Big Nasty.

The creature holding Jessie growled at Colleen, but Jesse scarcely heard it. His only thought was of the Big Nasty, which had jolted at the gunshot and was now climbing off the old woman. The raping creature hadn't detected Jesse yet, but when it did...

Panicked, Jesse grasped the crimson beast by the arms. Surprised, the creature turned to face Jesse just as he whipped forward and headbutted the creature as hard as he could. It was an insane ploy, but it worked, at least for the moment. Its nose shattered; the creature uttered a clipped scream, released him and stumbled away. Jesse landed on Greeley, who let loose with a wet-sounding fart.

Emma climbed out of the bathroom. She had a terrific bruise on her cheek that had already begun to purple. The look she gave him would have, under any other circumstance, sent him into a giddy euphoria. But her gratitude and respect for his suicidal rescue mission was extinguished in the flood of menace filling the front of the RV.

The feasting creatures had risen.

They were stalking toward Colleen.

Colleen was nodding her face upward in quick, secretive jerks as she backed away from the approaching creatures. He frowned at her, until he heard Emma whisper, "Lift me."

The side window was open above them. If they hurried...

A guttural growl sounded from the back of the RV.

The Big Nasty was coming.

He bent, grasped Emma by the waist. Whimpering, she climbed up his body and got a shoe on his left shoulder.

The Big Nasty was ten feet away. Beside it, Jesse saw the crimson creature rising, a look of depthless rage twisting its face.

Emma had reached the aperture, had her elbows on both sides of the shattered window. She glanced down at Jesse. "How will you get out?"

"Go," he commanded.

With a pained look, she obeyed, slipping easily through the opening and peering down at him on hands and knees.

The Big Nasty's growl had morphed into a continuous drone that sounded half-canine, half-insect. Jesse wanted to follow Emma, but he knew he'd never make it. The long, cadaverous beast would snatch him out of the air. Jesse had a nightmare image of the Big Nasty raising its face to rip out Jesse's genitalia in one giant chomp. Even if he were able to evade the creature, he didn't know if he was athletic enough to jump that high or strong enough to draw himself through the window if he did make the jump.

The shotgun exploded. The Big Nasty's eyes shifted to the front of the RV.

Colleen had lured the creatures outside.

Impulsively, Jesse bolted to the left corner of the shattered windshield, heard the Big Nasty's livid cry of surprise. Jesse dove through the opening, and as he did his shoe clipped one of the beasts in the calf. Out of the corner of his eyes, Jesse saw the creature give a little jolt, but he didn't wait to see if it was going to pursue him. Emma was sliding down the rain-swept roof of the RV. Jesse met her as she hit the ground. She threw a terrified glance beyond him, and he knew one or more of the creatures had followed, would pounce on them if they hesitated. Clenching Emma's hand, he compelled her around the corner of the overturned Seabreeze and pelted toward the Buick, which had its lights on, a figure sitting in the driver's seat. He thought at first it was Colleen, but that was impossible. She'd been just as far away from the Buick as he had been.

But who—

The Buick rolled toward them and through the rainspattered window he discerned Clevenger, his eyes huge with fright. Jesse's first thought was that the man was abandoning them, saving his own skinny ass. Then the window lowered and he shouted, "Back seat!"

At the same moment, Jesse glimpsed Colleen scampering toward the Buick, four of the beasts right behind her. He got the back door open, practically shoved Emma inside. He made to climb in as well when he looked up again and saw that Colleen wasn't going to make it.

"Gun!" he shouted.

Colleen threw him a frenzied glance, then lobbed the shotgun toward him in an awkward chest pass. One creature reached out, snagged the tail of Colleen's shirt. She faltered, her face a mask of horror. Jesse caught the shotgun, shifted it, fired, and was amazed to see the creature bearing down on Colleen jerk back in pain and consternation.

He'd gotten it in the mouth.

It went down, long fingers slapping over its mangled face. The others, however, ignored their fallen comrade, and kept up the pursuit of Colleen, who still looked like she'd never make it to the Buick.

Jesse drew a bead on the creature nearest her.

Within the car beside him, Emma screamed. He whirled out of instinct to see the Big Nasty charging at him, a look of triumph on its demon's face.

Jesse aimed at its gaping mouth and fired.

Its face snapped back and the rear of its head exploded.

It landed on Jesse and slammed him into the car. They crumpled together beside the Buick, the unearthly stink of the creature invading his nostrils like a pestilence. God, like dirty diapers and flyblown meat. Jesse gagged, a dry heave rolling through him, but Clevenger was shouting something, Emma clenching the waistband of his shorts and hauling him inside. A blur of bodies scudded past, Colleen pursued by the beasts, one of whom had barred her way to the Buick.

Jesse thumped down beside Emma. She shouted something at Clevenger, who'd begun to reverse the Buick.

"...can't leave her," Emma shouted.

Clevenger had his arm around the passenger's headrest, was staring fiercely out the back window. "Not...leaving...anyone."

They angled toward where Colleen was sprinting, the pursuing creatures toying with her now, enjoying her helplessness. Clevenger swung the car sideways, the Buick skidding to a halt. He lunged across the seat and threw open the passenger's door.

Colleen was nearly to it, but a pale creature was almost upon her.

Clevenger brought up the gun Ron had given him, fired. The beast doubled over, wailing, but another creature surged past it. It reached for Colleen, too, but Clevenger unloaded on it, squeezing Ron's gun until it clicked empty.

But there was one beast left, and they were out of ammo.

Jesse's bowels froze as a horn blasted from their right.

He glanced that way in time to see a red pickup truck, the one that was still blaring classic rock, bounce over a campsite and barrel into the creature chasing Colleen. The creature's thin body crunched against the windshield. The pickup slammed its brakes, sending the limp, skinny body tumbling into the grass. Then, as the creature raised its head in a daze, the pickup lurched forward and ran it down, one front tire crunching over its bony shoulders. Jesse had time to identify the driver of the red truck: Austin, the blond-haired beer guzzler.

Wheezing, Colleen plopped down in the passenger's seat and rammed home the door.

To their amazement, the other creatures set off after the pickup, which circled toward the overturned motor home.

Jesse watched a figure emerge from the top of the RV, wave its arms madly at the red pickup. It was Greeley, of course. The coward.

Jesse eyed Emma to see if she'd seen the tall man on the RV, but she had a hand on Colleen's shoulder, was asking if she was okay. Colleen nodded weakly.

Ahead of them, the red pickup slowed enough to allow Greeley to leap into the bed. But two dozen creatures were converging on the truck.

"Get us the hell out of this campground," Colleen moaned.

Clevenger shook his head. "Have you seen the road?"

Jesse did and felt his stomach clench.

The creatures were pouring out of the forest, the way out of the RV park a squirming mass of white limbs and bared teeth.

Colleen saw the creatures coming, said, "Please get us moving."

Knuckles pale on the wheel, Clevenger nodded to the east. "What's beyond there?"

Jesse said, "That's where we camped, remember? The playground—"

"*I know that.* What I'm asking is what's on the other side of that? Roads, trees, what?"

"There's nothing," Colleen said. "Just forest and marshes. Now can we—"

"Frank Red Elk lives back there," Emma said.

Clevenger opened his mouth, perhaps to ask who the hell Frank Red Elk was, when something hammered Jesse's window. They all shrieked, and Jesse practically climbed into Emma's lap. He shut his eyes, certain it was the Big Nasty somehow returned from the dead to take its vengeance on him. The snarling lips, the eyes as round as full moons, the—

"Got room for two more?" a man's voice asked.

Jesse opened his eyes to see Ron the DNR officer grinning through Clevenger's window.

"Get in," Clevenger said.

Ron nodded and hastened back to the grass. Jesse rolled down his window to see what the man was doing. God, he wished they'd get moving again. Fifty or sixty yards beyond them the red truck was outpacing the pursuing creatures. *Soon, they'll get tired of chasing Austin and realize we're still here. Fresh meat. Sitting—*

Jesse visored his eyes from the deluge and discovered one of the creatures had indeed given up on the pickup and was heading their way. It looked fierce.

Have you seen one yet that looked friendly? a voice in his head demanded.

"Hurry!" Clevenger shouted out the window. Jesse turned to see what Ron had gone back for.

Linda Farmer.

Tenderly, he lifted her from the sodden grass. If he'd seen the beast approaching yet, he was being awfully nonchalant about it.

Emma screamed. Ron whirled and gasped. Panicked, the DNR officer bolted for the Buick.

"The window," Clevenger called.

Ron nodded as he ran. The creature strode after the fleeing pair, Linda's unconscious body flopping in Ron's grasp.

The creature bore down on them. Ron reached the Buick, swung Linda headfirst toward the open window. Jesse had time to be grateful that the windows weren't childproof, were the kind that rolled all the way down, when Ron's gaze shifted behind him. The half turn was just enough to throw off his aim.

Linda's head rammed the closed door.

"Oh shit," Emma said, a hand to her mouth.

Ron turned with a look of comic surprise as Linda Farmer's unmoving body thumped down on the concrete. Ron made a move as if to pick her up and try it again when his eyes shuttered wide and he was lifted into the air. He drew his pistol and fired twice at the creature, which dropped him from a height of ten feet. Ron plummeted to the grass and landed badly, one arm trapped beneath his broad frame. Jesse heard a sick crunch and winced.

Clevenger was out of the Buick at once. At first Jesse thought the professor would wade into battle with the creature, but the balding man was lifting Linda Farmer, shouting at Jesse to open the back door.

Should have done that anyway, moron. Ron might still be alive.

He is *still alive*, Jesse tried to argue, but at that moment, the creature clamped its bony hands over Ron's head and lifted him high into the air.

Clevenger rushed across his vision carrying Linda Farmer, but despite the obstruction and the torrential downpour, Jesse still witnessed far too much.

Ron's face scrunched in exertion as he strove with his unbroken arm to pry the creature's hands off his face. His expression descended into agony as the creature's shoulders began to tremble. Jesse realized the thing was smashing Ron's head between its hands. Ron's legs began to kick.

"We've got to..." Jesse muttered feebly, but he knew it was too late.

Ron emitted a high-pitched howl. His face seemed to elongate. Runnels of blood spilled over his bottom eyelids. More blood dribbled over the creature's flexing knuckles. Ron's nostrils let loose as well, and the drumming of his legs diminished. Then, as if it were sampling from a waiter's tray, the creature drew Ron closer and bit off the man's face.

It turned to the Buick.

Clevenger pushed Linda Farmer's body into the front of the car, where Colleen drew her the rest of the way in. He shoved the Buick into drive just as the blood-spattered creature darted at them.

Please go, Jesse thought, but he was too numb to speak. So much death, so much horror...and they couldn't even try for the exit. He shot a look at Emma and saw the tears rimming her eyes. She probably felt just as he did, that there was no hope for them.

"Is she alive?" Clevenger asked, glancing at Linda Farmer.

Colleen nodded. "Brain-damaged, but alive. Of course, she was slightly brain-damaged already."

Ahead and to their left, the red pickup bounced over campsites, a legion of creatures in pursuit.

Clevenger hunched over the wheel, struggling to make out the road through the freshets of rain sweeping the windshield. Emma's wiper blades were worn out, but Jesse doubted even brand new ones would've done much good today.

"Can't you go faster?" Emma asked.

Clevenger glanced at her. "Not safely."

From their right a creature came crashing through the forest, its face maniacal with hunger.

"*Floor it*," Colleen shouted.

Clevenger stomped on the accelerator and the big car jumped. The beast lifted its arms as if to swing them down King Kong-style and flatten the roof. Jesse watched the muscles rolling under its taut skin and wondered again how a creature so emaciated could generate so much power. He thought of the one who'd murdered Light Blue Bikini, the way it had swung her body through the air and dashed it on the ground...

The creature thrashed its gnarled fists down. Colleen and Emma screamed and leaned away. Just when he thought the knobby fists would punch through the roof of the Buick, the big car gave a lurch and scuttled by.

"Good driving," Jesse said.

Clevenger didn't respond, kept guiding the Buick toward the approaching gap in the trees, the stand of woods that separated the two main camping areas. *We're going back by the playground*, Jesse thought. *I can't believe we're actually going back to that slaughterhouse.*

As long as you're putting distance between yourselves and the Big Nasty.

The Big Nasty is dead, he reminded himself. *I don't think it's walking away from that hole in its head.*

Don't be too sure. How many of their corpses have you actually seen?

"Impossible," Jesse muttered aloud. Emma glanced at him, and he opened his mouth to explain. Then he realized how stupid it would sound.

Still...he turned in his seat to peer behind them. The rainfall cast a leaden blanket over the entire RV section, but here and there he could still make out a few landmarks. The overturned Seabreeze where they'd almost died. The bathhouse beyond that. He'd shotgunned the Big Nasty to the left of those things, beside the winding road unspooling behind them. It was there he focused his gaze.

The rain was so unrelenting that the day had gone a bleak, gunmetal hue. Nevertheless, something in the general area where he'd shot the Big Nasty drew his attention. Jesse scrunched up his eyes to see better. It was crazy, but he'd sworn...

A new species of dread awoke deep inside him. Despite the staccato machine-gunning of the rain on the roof, despite the roars of the creatures and the wails of the dying...despite all of it he still heard the thump of his own heartbeat, felt a febrile pulse in the pit of his throat.

He wanted to believe the shape he discerned was his imagination. He wanted desperately to persuade himself it was a mirage, a trick of the precipitation, the white contours just the natural dance of the storm.

"What is that?" Emma asked beside him.

She'd joined him on her knees staring out the back window, her face slack with disbelief. Jesse suspected his face looked much the same way.

The figure strode on legs as tall as extension ladders, the gaunt body towering above the other creatures, towering above the few RVs still upright, towering ten feet above the bathhouse.

Jessie thought, *I'm not seeing this.*

So you and Emma are witnessing the same illusion?

Jesse swallowed and squinted into the rain. The figure kept coming, but rather than pursuing its current course, it stopped, lowered its great head. Then, looking like an albino salamander, it descended onto all fours to examine something. The Buick was almost to the woods now, the great creature at least a football field behind them, but Jesse could still see the freakishly long fingers reach out. Then something on the ground stirred. Before Jesse could see what it was, the woods swallowed them up.

Chapter Three

"Something smells," Clevenger said.

"It's our forest ranger," Colleen answered. "She's fertilized herself."

Jesse peeled his eyes off the back window and beheld the limp body lying facedown across the professor and Colleen, the woman's head turned sideways on Colleen's right thigh. Linda Farmer's makeup had bled in clownish streaks, giving her the appearance of an over-the-hill prostitute after a really bad cry. There was indeed a chocolate-colored stain in the middle of her tight brown shorts.

"Mind if I open a window?" Colleen asked.

Emma said, "For God's sakes, I think you can live with that after all we've seen."

Colleen made a face. "You're not sitting here at Ground Zero. It's like I've got the world's largest toddler in my lap."

Clevenger shook his head in irritation. "Help me watch for them. They might come out of the forest at any moment."

Colleen pinched her nostrils. "Peaceful Valley, my ass."

Jesse glanced at Emma, who looked as if she might cry. He put a hand on her leg for comfort. She didn't pull away, but she didn't seem comforted either. She looked like she wanted all of this to be a bad dream from which she'd soon awaken.

Jesse could relate.

Clevenger sucked in air, and following his gaze, Jesse saw why. Ahead and to the left a figure wandered along the edge of the road.

"One of them?" Emma asked.

"I don't think so," Clevenger said as they neared.

Jesse peered over the professor's shoulder and wished again that Emma's wipers worked better. Within the canopy of forest, the downpour wasn't as severe, but it still impaired his vision. To make matters worse, the inside of the windshield had begun to fog.

There was something familiar about the figure; the way it moved reminded him of horror movies. An awkward shamble more indigenous to an old-school zombie than a real person.

"I know that girl," Clevenger said.

The figure turned, and Jesse recognized her too.

Ruth Cavanaugh.

She resembled a refugee of some war-torn village. Her shabby clothes hung in dirty tatters, her hair matted and wet.

They crunched to a stop beside her, and Jesse beheld the ugly red slash slanting across her face. The inch-deep trough began at her hairline, plowed through her eye, which was a gaping red ruin, continued through the bridge of her nose, and cleaved through both lips.

Emma uttered a doleful moan. Clevenger covered his mouth. Even Colleen seemed to feel bad for the small woman.

Ruth stared at them without recognition. Jesse half-expected her to pitch forward into the puddled lane. Clevenger seemed to awaken from a trance.

"My God," he said and threw open his door. With a gallantry Jesse admired, the professor cast an arm about the girl's shoulders and ushered her around to Jesse's door. Jesse opened it and scooted over to give her room.

Ruth didn't seem aware of him, didn't even seem aware of her surroundings. Clevenger put the Buick back in gear. *Thank God*, Jesse thought; idling beside the lane he'd felt vulnerable and exposed.

At that moment a large shape thundered past them. Emma cried out, and Clevenger jerked the wheel toward the shoulder. Then Jesse discerned the red tailgate, remembered Austin and his pickup. A figure was huddled in the truck bed.

Greeley.

Jesse thought of how the coward had concealed himself in the closet while Emma and the others were being attacked. He didn't expect the man to save everyone, but burying himself in a pile of clothes?

As if she'd shared his thought, Emma put a hand over Jesse's, locked fingers.

He looked at her in wonder. She held his gaze a moment before turning to look out the back window.

Her eyes widened in horror.

"*Look ou—*" she started to scream.

But the sound of the creature landing on the trunk drowned out her voice.

"Shoot it!" Emma screamed.

"No more shells," Colleen answered.

Jesse sat up on his knees just as the creature mashed its Caliban face against the back window.

"Swerve or something," Colleen commanded.

Clevenger gave her an impotent look. Beyond the creature that was now clambering forward onto the Buick's roof, Jesse could see other figures bearing down on them. A few moved like ghostly marathoners, but the majority were loping toward them like mutant cheetahs.

Daggers lanced the shell of metal above them.

Then a large section of the roof was torn away, the creature casting it aside like the lid of a tin can.

Clevenger stood on the brakes. The creature rocketed over the hood. Jesse, Emma and Ruth were slammed into the seatback. The Buick shuddered violently.

They skidded to a stop. His nose a blood-slicked ache, Jesse peered over the hood and saw the creature somersaulting forward. He turned to see if Emma was okay, but she was staring out the spider-webbed back window.

The creatures were thirty yards away.

The Buick jumped forward. Clevenger overcorrected and sent their back end plowing along the grassy shoulder. The beast that had torn off the roof was gaining its feet, preparing to leap on them again.

"Run the sonofabitch over!" Colleen yelled.

Emma's eyes flew wide. "No!"

But Clevenger was clenching the wheel grimly, teeth bared in concentration. "Would you both...just...shut your—"

Before he could finish, the Buick's back end pendulumed into the lane and crashed into the creature's stilt-like legs. The dull crunches of splintering bones sent a charge of black excitement through Jesse, and when he whirled he saw the monster's knees had hyper-extended, the creature folding in on itself. Then it was trampled by the shifting mass of pursuers.

The Buick emerged from the forest and sped through the primitive campground. Outside the canopy of trees, the brutal rain drenched the mostly roofless interior immediately. Jesse spied his foul-smelling tent sitting intact, utterly oblivious to the horrors swirling around it. There were a few creatures scattered here and there, and most of them, Jesse noted with nausea, were dragging dead bodies away from the playground. How many victims had the beasts claimed? Two hundred? Twice that number?

"They've made it," Clevenger said, shouting to be heard above the rain.

Jesse frowned and stared ahead just in time to see Austin's red truck disappear into the forest.

"If we can get to the trees..." Clevenger said.

Colleen gave him a sardonic look. "Yeah?"

Clevenger glanced at her. "You said that man Red Elk lives in those woods?"

"A couple miles in," Emma said.

"Who cares where he lives?" Colleen asked. "It's not like he's going to save us. The guy's a porn-addicted alcoholic."

Clevenger shook his head. "He may have some secret route out of here, something they won't know about."

They, Jesse reflected. It made him ill trying to figure out how *they* thought. Did they consider anything beyond the satisfaction of their bloodlust?

The car reached the forest and bounced over a series of potholes.

"Might wanna slow down," Colleen said. "We're not gonna have time to fix a flat if one of them blows."

Clevenger looked ill, but he did as he was told. The Buick was motoring along at just over thirty miles per hour. An awful thought occurred to Jesse, and he glanced at the gas gauge in dread.

Three-quarters full. Thank God.

The bend was approaching, the one where they'd almost wrecked that morning. But the professor was proving a more conservative driver than Colleen had been.

A kamikaze pilot would be more conservative than Colleen.

Clevenger slowed a little as they neared the turn, and despite half the lane being underwater from the downfall, they glided smoothly around the bend.

When they started down the straightaway, Colleen said, "That's not gonna be good."

Jesse's legs turned to ice. Not only was the road flooded far deeper than it had been yesterday, but the red pickup had crashed in the pool, was lying in on its side with smoke wafting up out of its engine.

They slowed as the water overtook the lane. Clevenger guided the Buick forward through the deepening pool. Emma gasped and said, "*Look.*"

From around the side of the overturned pickup, two figures emerged, the taller one leaning on the smaller one for support.

Despite himself, Jesse felt his spirits leap.

Austin and Greeley.

His spiked hair was drenched brown, but Austin appeared perfectly healthy. Greeley's arm was slung over the other man's shoulders, and though Greeley was limping, he too seemed intact.

Clevenger halted the Buick and got out. Jesse threw a nervous glance behind him, but the lane was deserted as far as he could see. He made to climb out, but paused when he noticed Ruth Cavanaugh's small frame bunched on the floor. Like him and Emma, she'd been thrown into the seatback earlier, but unlike them she hadn't bothered rising. She sat there staring with her one remaining eye at nothing in particular. Jesse sidled around her and opened the door.

He joined Clevenger in front of the Buick.

Austin was laughing. Nodding up at Greeley, he said, "Lucky son of a bitch. He hit that water and skipped like a stone."

Jesse got hold of Greeley's arm. Clevenger took the other, and together they guided him toward the Buick.

"What made you crash?" Colleen asked over the top of the windshield where the roof had been torn off.

"That thing over there," Austin said and gestured toward the forest.

Laboring to heft Greeley into the backseat, Jesse spied the long, white body lying motionless on the narrow strip of raised shoulder. The bare buttocks and legs stuck out, but its upper body was hidden by the woods.

"You shoulda seen it," Austin said, shaking his head. "Thing rose out of the water like a goddamned sea monster. I screamed like a little girl." He grinned, and Jesse found himself grateful the boy had survived.

Now Greeley...

Stop it, he told himself.

"Need to get moving," Clevenger said.

Austin's mirth vanished, replaced by a steeliness Jesse was glad to have on their side. Austin nodded and eyed the lane behind them. "Those sons of bitches don't quit, do they? Probably coming right now."

Jesse said, "You think we'll make it through the water?"

"We made it yesterday," Colleen said.

"It wasn't as deep then." He scanned the wide, brown pool of standing water. Like an ancient tarn, it seemed to stretch on forever.

"What choice do we have?" Emma asked, climbing into the front seat next to Colleen. "They're coming."

"We could try that," Austin said and pointed toward the edge of the lane, which rose at a forty-five degree angle. The strip of grass was perhaps wide enough for the Buick, but they'd have to take a chance on not tipping over. Examining the shoulder, Jesse was reminded of the times he'd seen men tackle steep hills on riding mowers, their whole bodies leaning to the uphill side to prevent them from toppling. Except those were lawn tractors, and this was a Buick built like a Sherman tank. Yes, he thought, warming to Austin's notion. The chances they'd flip the car were minimal.

What if you get stuck in the mud?

Jesse felt the skin at his temples draw taut.

What if the suspension gives out? What if the monsters leap out of the forest?

Good points all, he thought, but he couldn't shake Austin's description of the creature rising out of the water.

Like a goddamned sea monster.

"Let's take the shoulder," Jesse said.

Sitting half in, half out of the driver's seat, Clevenger eyed him dourly. Then, a barely perceptible nod. The professor shut his door, and Austin jogged around the car.

Jesse climbed in. Ruth Cavanaugh still sat hunched on the floor behind Clevenger's seat, reminding Jesse of a carry-on bag taking away foot room on a cramped flight.

He hiked his feet onto the seat and yanked the door shut, wondering why the biggest coward in their party got the best seat in the house. *Look at him,* Jesse thought. *Sprawled across half the backseat.* Greeley's feet were actually crowding Jesse's right hip. Impulsively, he reached down and shoved them away. Greeley looked stricken.

Turning in his seat, Clevenger swept them with his keen blue eyes. "You're sure we want to do this?"

"Take the shoulder," Colleen said.

Clevenger seemed to deflate. He reached for the gearshift, paused. "Is everybody inside?"

Austin had his hand on the top of the open back door, a distant look of horror on his tanned face.

Jesse shot a look into the forest, saw the creatures bearing down on them.

Greeley grabbed Clevenger's shoulder, shook it. "He's in," Greeley shouted. "Now drive!"

Clevenger nodded, and the Buick began to roll. The back door ripped free of Austin's grasp, and the boy whirled in shock.

"Wait!" Emma shouted. "He's still outside!"

Clevenger threw a confused glance back at them, but Greeley lunged forward, blocking his view. He seized Clevenger's face and twisted it toward the forest to their left, where one beast had already begun to descend the short hill to the shoulder. "Would you *look,* for chrissakes, they're *coming.*"

Clevenger uttered a surprised groan and accelerated the Buick. Austin began running to catch up, his legs quickly blurring. Next to Jesse, Greeley thumped back in his seat—plenty of room now, with Emma and Colleen both in the front—and reached for the open door.

Jesse clasped Greeley's forearm, jerked his chin at Austin. "We have to wait for him."

Despite the Buick's growing speed, Austin was gaining. With a dive, he got hold of the top of the swinging door, but the Buick bounced and tripped him up. Austin hung on, but the door was swaying now, the boy's legs scissoring over the rugged terrain, his face drawn in terror.

"*Help him*," Emma shouted.

Jesse scrambled over Greeley's unmoving body to offer a hand to Austin, who looked like he wouldn't hang on for much longer. At that moment, Austin uttered a hoarse cry.

The creature from the pool had followed them.

Its stiletto-thin legs kicking up sprays of water as it ran, it closed the distance between it and the Buick in mere seconds. Its intention was clear. The creature groped for Austin's trailing legs.

Jesse thrust out a hand. "*Here*," he said.

Austin threw a desperate look up at Jesse, reached out. Their fingers brushed together.

Then Greeley lashed out with a boot and kicked Austin between the eyes.

Austin dropped away, and in the surreal moments that followed, Jesse watched out the back window as the boy tumbled end over end at the edge of the lane, landed on his back, and before he could even bring up his hands for protection, the beast fell on him, its whirring talons rending his flesh.

"You bastard!" Colleen screamed.

"Should throw you to those fiends too," Clevenger growled.

"It's his own fault," Greeley whined. "He should've gotten in."

The professor's gasp made them all turn.

A creature had stepped onto the shoulder ahead.

Clevenger made a weird gurgling sound, but he didn't swerve. He seemed locked in place, a frail mannequin someone had stuck behind the wheel as a joke. They were almost upon the creature, which was tensing as if to leap forward and meet them halfway. Without a roof, Jesse thought, they'd be easy pickings.

Colleen jerked the wheel and they plowed into the water, the Buick's front end disappearing under the murk and crashing into the bottom of the flooded lane. *That's it*, Jesse thought as they bounced. *We had a good run, we lasted longer than the others, but there's no way the car—*

Clevenger yanked the wheel to the left, and they sloshed forward in a lazy curve. The Buick spluttered, coughed, but kept chugging.

The creature, Jesse realized, had leaped at them, but finding them gone had sprung up and was loping along the shoulder after them. The water was too high; the beast was gaining rapidly. And more creatures were teeming down the lane behind them, their cadaverous frames barely slowed by the high water. To their left, six or seven creatures bounded out of the forest. Jesse threw a frightened glance at the speedometer, saw they were struggling to achieve twenty miles an hour.

Ahead, a pallid shape emerged from the water like a surfacing submarine.

Chapter Four

The creature started toward them.

"Up there," Emma said and pointed to the shoulder to their right. It was narrower and steeper than the left shoulder, which was why they'd avoided it, but Clevenger obeyed and brought the Buick jouncing out of the pool.

"*Ohhh shiiiit*," Greeley moaned as they tilted sickly. The Buick rumbled over roots, large rocks. Objects scraped the undercarriage with frightful shrieks. Jesse's side of the car was downhill, his window actually slicing through the shallows, roaring with the surf and pinging each time the metal supports skimmed the water.

Greeley slid down into him. Jesse thrust an elbow into his ribs. Greeley cried out but was apparently too terrified to retaliate. The uphill side of the Buick snapped off an outcropping branch, crunched over a sapling. Jesse's window shattered as the Buick dipped, and for one vertiginous moment he was sure the car would overturn, the damn thing bouncing along at nearly a sixty-degree angle.

"*Oh no*," Clevenger cried. Through the maelstrom of noise and rain, Jesse saw the Buick race toward a squat stump. They hit it, him and Greeley flying forward and smashing the seatback, the jarring impact sending the big car sailing through the air. Jesse experienced a moment of soul-sucking weightlessness. Then the Buick crashed to the sodden earth, the driver's side half in the shallows.

A creature pounced on the trunk.

The beast scrambled over the dented white metal to devour him, but the car rocked down, its back end whipsawing to the right. The creature on the trunk almost tumbled off. Its talons, however, saved it. The creature pierced the distressed metal lid, puncturing it as easily as tacks through paper.

"Jesse," Emma said.

He turned and glimpsed the creature advancing over the trunk again.

"Where's the crowbar?" he shouted.

"Hold on," Colleen called.

The creature swiped at his head. Jesse ducked and heard the claws furrow the damp cushion of the seatback. Foam flew around him. He scanned the back seat desperately to find a weapon.

Nothing.

The creature growled, its face looming closer. Jesse covered his head and did his best to burrow into the seat. He waited for the claws to slit his flesh, for the fanged maw to guzzle his lifeblood.

But nothing happened.

Emma and Colleen screamed. Jesse opened his eyes.

The creature was bridged over him, its feet on the trunk, its long fingers gripping the front headrests.

Jesse was afforded a view of the monster's elongated phallus. It told the whole story.

The creature wanted the girls.

It reached down for Colleen or Emma; Jesse wasn't in a position to see which one. Clevenger was doing his best, was swerving the Buick back and forth within the narrow strip of real estate he'd been dealt, but the beast barely trembled atop its perch. They were gaining speed, which might help them outpace the other creatures, but what of this one, the one whose mouth was opening in salacious need? A long stream of slaver dripped from its bottom lip and was swept by the wind into Jesse's face. Arming the fluid off, he glanced over at Greeley, who looked green with horror. No help there.

Ruth, he noted, was semi-conscious, but appeared no more aware of her surroundings than a badly concussed athlete. The creature's hand darted forward, and the girls' screams spun higher. It lifted something off the seat.

Emma.

Oh Christ, he thought. *No!*

Its fingers were cinched in her hair. She gibbered and kicked, but it continued raising her higher. She'd clamped her hands over its pale fingers to keep her hair from ripping out at the roots. Colleen grabbed hold of one of Emma's legs, but the Buick hit a pothole and she lost her grip.

Its prize dangling from one powerful hand, the creature straightened and brought Emma closer. Its green eyes crawled over her writhing body, and Jesse was sickened to see its phallus distend farther, the pinkish skin shiny and taut.

Jesse took a breath, cast about one last time for a weapon. The beast was pivoting, no doubt ready to leap into the forest and have its way with Emma.

Frantic, Jesse lowered his gaze to the floor.

There, by Greeley's shoes, gleaming dully in the dreary day, he found a piece of the ruined roof, a sheared sickle of steel that just might—

Emma bellowed, and the creature prepared to jump.

Jesse lunged for the sickle, squeezed it, its jagged edge biting into the fleshy pads of his fingers.

Jesse stood in the back seat, grasped the creature's erect penis, and began sawing with the steel shard.

The effect was immediate.

It dropped Emma onto Colleen and clutched at its wounded phallus, which was hemorrhaging black liquid. Jesse disengaged the sickle, lowered it, then pistoned it up with all his strength. It imbedded between the creature's legs.

The howl that issued from the beast's mouth was unlike any sound he'd ever heard. Klaxon-loud, its demonic outrage echoed through the trees, drew every eye—human and beast—in the forest.

Triumph caroming through Jesse's chest, he jerked the steel piece downward. The creature's scrotum ruptured and emptied black fluid all over the back seat. The testicles, white and round as baseballs, plopped out of its body and onto the Buick's upholstery. Out of the corner of his eye, Jesse saw one testicle roll toward Greeley's hand. Screeching, Greeley recoiled and bicycled his legs.

The creature howled again, and though the terror in Jesse's mind escalated, a very clear image prevented him from backing down:

Tiara Girl, her dying body being defiled by the Big Nasty.

This creature was not the same one Jesse'd battled in the pine grove, but there was no doubt in his mind it would've done to Emma precisely what the Big Nasty had done to Tiara Girl. Or worse.

Despite the agony no doubt rippling through its gaunt body, the creature lowered its face to Jesse, its jaws hissing in menace.

Jesse lashed out again, this time with a quick sideswipe, and exulted as the serrated steel cleaved the sides of the creature's mouth. Its eyes widening in furious disbelief, it pawed at the fluid bubbling from its lips. It swayed on its walking-stick legs. Then the creature tipped backward, too stunned to catch itself before it hit the trunk and tumbled off.

Jesse turned and saw that Colleen was staring at him in admiration. "That was some hardcore shit, Jesse," she said

"*Hang on,*" Clevenger shouted. He guided the Buick into the pool, which was only a few inches deep now. Showers shot up in dirty brown fans on both sides of the car, but the ground was more level than before. Jesse glanced behind them and saw they were distancing themselves from the creatures, the big white car surging ahead.

"How far ahead is Red Elk's place?" Clevenger asked Colleen.

"Not far," she said. "A mile or so."

The professor nodded. "Let's hope he knows a way out of this circle of hell."

Jesse put a hand over his heart to steady its trip-hammer thud. Leaning forward, he saw Emma's chest heaving in relief and terror. Colleen had her arm around Emma's trembling back. Linda Farmer was supine on the floor, her short body using up every inch of foot room on the passenger's side. The park ranger was alive, but who knew for how long. Greeley had recovered, was watching Clevenger drive them away from the monsters. Ruth Cavanaugh was catatonic. She stared at nothing in particular and didn't bother righting herself when they jostled over a bump in the lane.

Jesse glanced at his hands, which were covered in the black liquid that had spilled out of the creature's abdomen. He started wiping them on the seat, then gave up when he realized how pointless it was.

The dull heat of fading adrenaline spreading through his body, Jesse watched the Buick near the edge of the pool, pass onto drier land, then continue down the lane toward Frank Red Elk's house.

Chapter Five

Sam stood at the edge of the forest and glanced at his watch.

12:46.

The rain had let loose almost an hour ago. Charly was more than a little late. He felt like a chump out here without an umbrella, but he suspected if he knocked on the door, her asshole husband would answer.

He checked his watch again, knew something had come up.

Sam blew out disgusted breath. What the hell was he doing out here?

And to make matters worse, look who was rolling down the lane. Larry Robertson, his police cruiser traded for a Chevy pickup like Sam's, only Robertson's was black and Sam's was blue. Robertson's was also a year newer and likely didn't carry a four-hundred-dollar-a-month payment.

Sam broke off watching the black pickup when another vehicle emerged from the thicket of woods that separated Indian Trails from the longer section of winding road. Small, red, sporty—that wasn't the ride of a federal agent. Though the car was a good way off, he could discern the shape of the driver, the long hair, the curve of the neck.

Sam watched the slowing vehicles and toyed with the idea of heading out in the open. It would be tough coming up with a plausible story, but it would be a hell of a lot better than cowering behind this tree in the storm. The rain wasn't cold, but he was growing uncomfortable just the same. He longed for nothing more than a dry change of clothes and a warm drink. Hot chocolate, maybe. Of course, he didn't have any stuff to make hot chocolate, hadn't needed any since Karen divorced him and got the kids.

A cloud seemed to rush over him. He cleared his throat and told himself it was the weather making his eyes bleary.

The sheriff stopped his truck, got out and waited for the sports car to pull into the drive too. When the red car disappeared from Sam's view, the house obscuring it, Robertson went over, probably to talk to the driver.

Now's your chance, he thought. *The moment those two go inside, you can hightail it out of here, get in your truck and head back to your five acres of loneliness. Maybe there'll be a good skin flick on Showtime tonight. You can pretend one of the blondes is Charly. It'll be seriously entertaining. Maybe even use your left hand so it'll feel like someone else is doing it.*

But something prevented him from breaking cover. If the driver of the sports car wasn't a relative of Charly's—and the glimpse he'd gotten of her as she pulled in made him seriously doubt there was any relation—who was she?

One of Eric Florence's basketball players?

Two car doors thumping, muffled voices. Robertson and the girl talking. Another door closing, softer this time. The pair entering the house.

Sam stood beside the tree and gazed at the back deck. If someone came to the sliding glass doors, Sam would be easy to spot. If it was Charly, that was one thing. If it was the husband, well, he'd probably have to fight the man. Sam had let the guy pound on him the first time, but his charitable urges had just about run dry. Anyway, he got the feeling Charly wouldn't mind if he gave her husband the ass-kicking he deserved.

The sliding door opened and a blue figure stepped out. Whoever it was, the whole body was draped in royal blue fabric, like someone had cut armholes out of a tarp. Sam was reminded of the way his kids used to put on his clothes and flap around the house.

The figure approached. Within the sagging shadows of the hood, he made out a pair of perfect pink lips, a heart-shaped chin.

Charly.

The blue poncho dragged the ground and sheathed her arms all the way to her fingertips. Her face peeked out of the drooping blue hood like a pink wildflower. She was irresistible.

Charly stopped and gestured down the length of her body. "Like my outfit?"

"Did that thing used to be a tent?"

"My dad's," she said. "He wore it fishing sometimes, but whenever it rained he made me wear it."

"The blue brings out your eyes."

"He brought it to Cubs games," she went on. "The first time I was on TV, I was eight years old at Wrigley Field. The cameras got me singing 'Take Me Out to the Ballgame', only you couldn't see anything but my mouth."

Sam grinned. "Shame."

Charly shrugged, nodded toward the woods. "We still going in there?"

"Down the tree line a ways," Sam said.

Charly glanced back at the house, her face clouding.

Sam said, "You don't have to come with me."

She shook her head. "Sheriff Robertson's in there with Eric and one of his assistants. They're trying to figure out if there's anybody Eric might have pissed off enough to...to do this."

"Seems like a stretch."

"I feel bad for Larry. He can't believe my story, but he doesn't want to admit I'm crazy to my face." She started to tear up, then drew in trembling breath and put on a strained smile. "So I left the house to give him a chance to interview Eric alone." Her smile grew more natural. "At least it gave me an excuse to come out here, right?"

Sam nodded. Her cheeks were rounder at the tops than he'd thought. She was painfully cute. He wanted to kiss one of those cheeks, right up under her eye. Taste the skin there and let his lips linger.

"We'd better get going," she said.

They'd taken a few steps when he stopped and asked her, "Robertson need to talk to you too?"

"Not likely. It's easier on both of us if I'm out of the house."

Sam couldn't imagine Charly's presence being hard on anyone, but he nodded and commenced walking.

They halted at the sound of car doors shutting. They turned and watched the red sports car reverse its way out of the drive. Two figures were inside. The assistant coach and Eric Florence.

Charly said in a voice that held no inflection at all, "Were you ever married, Sam?"

Watching the red car, he said, "We better get going."

"Think Larry's going to figure out where we went?" she asked.

"I expect he will."

"Is that good or bad?"

Sam thought about it. "Depends on what we find."

They continued along the tree line.

"Wait," Eric said as they pulled away.

"What's wrong?" Mel asked.

"Stop the car," he demanded and was annoyed when she took too long to bring the little sports car to a halt. How long it did take to depress a brake pedal anyway? Jesus, he hated riding with women drivers.

"Flo, you're worrying—"

"*Just a second,*" he spat. Mel had a lot on the ball, but in many of ways she was just like Charly. Always needing a dissertation from him to explain his feelings. Forever begging him to expand on his thoughts. Couldn't they just *sit* sometimes?

"Back up," he told her.

She watched him a moment—Jesus!—before slipping the car into gear and promptly backing into the vacant lot.

"Not *that* way," he said. "Straight back the lane, so I can see better."

"How come?"

"Oh for chrissake." He climbed out of the car and jogged back down the lane a ways to see if what he'd glimpsed earlier was real. The rain dampened his hair immediately. Eric was about to write what he'd seen off to imagination when he caught sight of Charly, wearing her father's slicker—he hated that thing; it still smelled like the dead man's cologne, and if that wasn't twisted, he didn't know what was—drifting along the wood's edge like she was in some kind of trance.

Then he noticed the man strolling beside her. Eric's mouth formed a venomous smile.

Sam Bledsoe.

The wife-stealing son of a bitch.

"Aren't we leaving?" Mel asked.

"Looks like plans have changed."

"Flo?" she said, her tone fretful. "What's wrong?"

He grinned at her savagely. "Not a goddamned thing. Drive me back to the house, Mel. We're going for a hike."

Chapter Six

They didn't see any more creatures on the road to Red Elk's, but Jesse had already been ambushed by them too many times to relax. They could be anywhere. In the woods, lurking in the shadows. Their lithe bodies were perfectly suited for concealment.

Unless they're three stories tall.

Jesse thought of the god-like creature striding through the rain and brushed away the image.

Greeley sat forward, the man's voice cutting through the white noise of the rain. "What's so special about this Red Elk again?"

Clevenger said, "He's lived here his entire life. If anyone would know of an escape route, he would."

"The man's a drunk," Greeley said. "Emma said he had pornography right out in the open."

"I don't care about his personal habits. We need a way out."

"Let's head for the bluffs then," Greeley said, his voice plaintive. This close to the man, Jesse was overwhelmed by the aroma of fear-sweat, a combination of fried food and cat urine.

Clevenger glanced at Greeley in the overhead mirror, which was somehow intact despite the roof being ripped off. "You're talking about trying to cross a flooded river."

"Why not?"

"How will we get them across?" Clevenger didn't identify Linda Farmer and Ruth Cavanaugh by name, but he didn't need to.

"They can take care of themselves."

Colleen looked at Greeley coldly.

"What?" he asked. "We're supposed to tote them around until those things catch us? You have any idea how much time that'll add?"

"Those things are everywhere," Emma said. "Crossing the river won't accomplish anything."

"I don't feel good," Ruth Cavanaugh said.

They all turned to look at her. Even though Jesse had placed her right next to him in the backseat, he'd forgotten she was there. Her frizzy black hair, matted down by the rain, formed a kind of helmet around her face. That was a blessing, Jesse thought, because it partially obscured his view of the slash mark, the one that split her face in a clotted, red diagonal. Against his will he recalled how her eye had looked, the scooped-out top and the puffy bottom half that reminded him of curdled milk.

Emma peered at her over the seat. "We're almost to the house, Ruth."

Ruth went on as though Emma hadn't spoken. "My knees feel like they're splitting apart. My head hurts too. I think I need to lie down."

"There it is," Colleen said, pointing.

"Help me watch for them," Clevenger said.

The Buick slowed. Jesse noted with misgiving the rattle of the engine, the way the whole car seemed to vibrate. It was a marvel they'd made it all the way here, but he doubted the Buick would go much farther.

They curved around the derelict house. Red Elk's truck was there along with another vehicle, an old teal Jeep. Clevenger drove right up into the front yard and halted beside the porch. From within came the throb of bass from Red Elk's stereo. They got out, leaving Linda and Ruth in the car. Climbing the porch, Jesse identified the song: Motley Crue's "Girls, Girls, Girls".

Greeley jogged past them and hammered on the screen door.

The music continued to blare.

Jesse glanced around him, probed the rain-swept forest for leering white faces.

So far, nothing.

Emma was gripping her arms, bobbing on her heels. The skin of her throat was stamped with goose bumps, her white shirt clinging to her torso. Her breasts had contracted to tight mounds. Her nipples jutted within her bra.

"Come on, come *on*," Greeley muttered. He cupped his hands around his eyes and peered through the screen door. Jerking away, he said, "Jesus."

Jesse took an involuntary step backward, sure Red Elk had been murdered.

Then Colleen shouldered past Greeley, rolled her eyes, and said, "Oh, for God's sakes." She tried the knob and found it open. She went in, and Jesse followed. Motley Crue assaulted them, the bass deep and growling. Jesse froze when he saw the naked pair on the couch. A black-haired woman was bent over, her rear end upthrust and tremoring each time Frank Red Elk slammed into her. Red Elk's paunch jiggled, his hairless buttocks flexing. The woman was older but nicely built, and she was the one who looked up first.

"Frank," she said.

Red Elk continued thrusting, his face pinched in concentration.

"*Frank*," she said, louder this time.

Red Elk uttered a prolonged groan, his muscles clenching and his head thrown back.

Jesse glanced back at Emma, who had her head down and was massaging her forehead in disgust. Greeley's mouth hung open. Clevenger had turned to watch out the front door for the creatures.

"*Frank!*" the woman he was having sex with shouted. She was scowling, apparently not because she was the star of an impromptu public sex show, but because she couldn't make herself heard over the music.

Red Elk slumped, patted the woman on the side of the rump, and stumbled back, a contented smile on his face. "Man, Debbie, I love it when you drop by."

The woman, Debbie evidently, strode toward them without a hint of self-consciousness and stopped at the stereo. The music cut off.

"Aw, come on, Debbie," Red Elk said, looking hurt. "The best part's when Vince Neil and Tommy Lee talk at the end." He turned, noticing the five new people standing in his living room.

His face expressionless, Red Elk said, "Bet you didn't think I was circumcised."

Colleen said, "Put that thing away, Frank. We've got bigger problems to worry about."

Red Elk blinked at them a moment. Then, gazing from face to face, a bleak comprehension seemed to dawn. "They came for you?"

"Scores of them," Clevenger said. "They attacked us on the playground."

Red Elk's face tightened but he nodded as if he weren't terribly surprised by this. "How many killed?"

Debbie passed Red Elk on the way to the bedroom. Her rear end wasn't small, but it was firm. Jesse put her at a well preserved fifty.

"Hundreds," Greeley said, his voice high with tension. "We need to go before they find us here."

Red Elk smiled a little. "Where you gonna go?"

"Anywhere. The park is vast, there must be some way—"

"Uh-uh," Red Elk said. "The only road's the one you came in on."

"Then give me your phone," Greeley said and began casting about, knocking things off shelves and tipping a half-empty beer can with an errant elbow. "That is, if you can afford one in this hellhole."

"This hellhole," Red Elk said, "happens to be mine. And I don't have a landline."

"Big surprise," Greeley said. He kicked an empty pizza box in disgust.

"Touch another one of my things and I'll rip your arms off."

Greeley wheeled on Red Elk. While Greeley was built well, Frank

Red Elk was thicker, a good deal of the weight hard muscle. Last night Jesse had been intimidated by Greeley's combination of good looks and erudition, but now the man seemed to shrink in Red Elk's presence.

The two stared at each other a long moment. In the kitchen the bug light crackled, the walls in there strobing as some large insect fried to death.

Red Elk had still made no move to cover himself. His softening member shone dully in the semi-dark living room. There was something oddly natural about the way Red Elk looked, despite the ratty furnishings and grungy lighting. This silent, burly specimen was what Jesse had been expecting earlier. His hairless chest seemed a mile wide, the nipples there tiny and hard, as though the confrontation with Greeley was as stimulating as the sex with Debbie had been.

Greeley looked away. He licked his lips, scowled. "For God's sakes, put some clothes on."

Debbie reentered wearing a white wife-beater tank top and the shortest denim shorts Jesse had ever seen.

Red Elk asked, "How'd you escape the Children?"

Greeley licked his lips again, a bemused grin flickering on his wet mouth. "What are you...what do you mean, *Children*?"

"Your tall friends."

Children of what? Jesse wondered.

Emma stepped closer. "What do you know about them?"

"I know we don't have much time," Red Elk said.

"Isn't there a trail or something?" Greeley asked. "Some old route no one knows about?"

Red Elk retrieved a balled-up pair of jeans from behind the recliner and began wiggling them on. "Sure, there're other ways out, when we're not in the middle of the worst monsoon season in recorded history. A normal year, it'd be a hassle getting out, but you could do it as long as you didn't mind wading through a couple miles of marshes and a few pockets of quicksand. Try it now, you better have on scuba gear."

Greeley moved toward the door. "I say we take our chances."

"You'll be dead before you get to your car."

Greeley's chin trembled. "You don't know that."

"They're here already," Red Elk said and slipped on a black T-shirt. It said *HORROR DRIVE-IN*. Beneath that, a blood-spattered pair of 3-D glasses.

"They couldn't have gotten here this quickly," Greeley said.

"*Listen*," Red Elk whispered.

They did.

Jesse shot a look at Emma, who was leaned forward, her whole self intent on hearing what Red Elk had alerted them to—the creatures in the forest.

The Children.

Emma's breath caught, and her eyes widened. She stared at Jesse in fright, and then he heard it too, the huffing of hundreds of voracious creatures, the squelching of their tensile feet on the sodden forest floor. Jesse felt an ominous heat in his bowels. Greeley backed away from the door, moving like a man wired to explode should anyone make a sudden movement. Colleen, who'd behaved so fearlessly, now seemed on the verge of tears. Clevenger's mettle also appeared to be flagging. Red Elk's dark face was merely expectant. For his part, Jesse only longed for a good hiding place. And a toilet.

The silence drew out. Jesse bit his bottom lip. The cacophony of the storm, the orgy of blood and terror at the playground, even the grueling death ride to Red Elk's...all of it, as awful as it had been, was preferable to this preternatural silence.

They all jumped as something crashed against the front door.

Greeley jumped back, and Emma uttered a shrill yelp. Jesse squirted urine into his boxer briefs.

Red Elk swallowed, seemed to hesitate a moment. Then, exchanging a glance with Jesse, he shambled over to the door. Jesse felt whatever gossamer hopes he had snap like over-tightened guitar strings. If Red Elk had a gun, he certainly would have grabbed it before confronting whatever lay outside the door, wouldn't he?

Red Elk seemed to bounce on his heels a moment, his fingers twitching at his sides. Then he reached forward and twisted opened the knob.

The door swung open.

Ruth Cavanaugh peered up at them from the gloom.

Red Elk only stared at her, his expression bewildered. Then Clevenger shouldered past him. "My *God*, Ruthie, get in here." The balding man clutched her hands and drew her inside. Ruth moved with him, but she showed no particular desire to be out of the rain or away from the creatures.

Emma rushed over and put an arm around the drenched, pitiful-looking woman. "Did you see them?" Emma asked. "Did they come for you?"

Ruth's expression remained hollow, her pasty complexion and mutilated eye making her look more than ever like she'd risen from the dead.

Colleen squared up to Ruth Cavanaugh, seized her by the shoulders. "Are those monsters outside or not?"

Ruth gestured behind her. "*Car...*"

"It's totaled," Colleen said impatiently. "Forget the car."

Ruth frowned, shook her head. "The car..."

Emma said, "What—"

But an earsplitting wail cut her off.

They all moved to the front windows.

From the direction of the Buick, the scream persisted, devolved into choked sobs. A small white object fluttered within the wrecked carcass of the car. Then a pair of terrified eyes peered over the rim of the passenger's side door.

Linda Farmer had awakened.

"We've got to get her," Emma said.

Greeley laughed. "Apparently you haven't seen how those things operate."

"Which is why we've got to help her," Emma said, spitting her words into Greeley's mordant face. "Have you forgotten the RV? How Jesse and Colleen saved us from those monsters? What if they'd let us die?"

Her desperate gaze flitted from person to person and eventually landed on Jesse. She entreated him with her big brown eyes, and for one terrible moment he was sure she'd come out and ask him to volunteer for the rescue mission.

From behind them came a weary sigh. "I suppose I better go."

They turned and looked at Clevenger, who was already moving forward.

But Red Elk said, "You're not going anywhere." The larger man barred Clevenger's progress.

Clevenger's eyes were flinty. "You're just going to let her die?"

"She's dead already."

"How do you—" Clevenger started to say, but movement from the forest choked off his words. From where they stood, they could see at least fifteen or twenty feet of the woods surrounding the Buick.

The trees seemed alive.

The creatures' pale, wiry limbs resembled shifting, denuded boughs. Their bony torsos seemed to squirm forward, irresistibly attracted to the car. Within the Buick, Linda's whole face was now visible behind the beaded glass, her gaze darting about her, trying to make sense of what she was seeing.

"Ron?" she called. "Is that you?"

I hate to tell you this, a voice in Jessie's head spoke up, *but what's left of old Ron is digesting inside one of those creatures' bellies.*

The shapes swarmed through the twisted old elms, their sinews pulsing with each step.

"*Ron?*" she said, all her smugness and authority gone.

"Why didn't we bring her in?" Emma demanded.

Clevenger's voice was tight, regretful. "I thought we'd be driving out of here."

"Let's go," Greeley whispered, his voice husky with fear.

Emma fixed him with a fierce stare. "I'm telling you—"

"He's right," Red Elk said. "Now's our best chance. While they're distracted."

Greeley didn't need to be asked twice. He nearly knocked Jesse over as he followed Red Elk toward the kitchen. Clevenger guided Ruth across the room. Colleen came too. Reluctantly, Jesse peeled his eyes off the grisly scene in the yard, but stopped when he saw that Emma hadn't left the window.

"Emma," he said, gently grasping her arm, "there's no time—"

"It's so *horrible*," she said, her voice thick.

They were surrounding the car, their huge, peridot eyes sly and gleeful. *They're savoring it*, he thought sickly. *They're reveling in her terror.*

And Linda Farmer was terror-stricken. One moment she was standing up in the roofless car, her squat frame jutting pitifully over the jagged back window; the next she was crumpling on the seat, knees bent in supplication, her hands pressed to her cheeks as she gibbered for mercy.

A creature stepped nimbly onto the Buick's hood. Another peeled away the starred windshield as easily as a moist Band-Aid. Linda began to say something when one dropped from a tree behind her and smashed the glass of the back window.

Linda whirled, squealing, and backed against the dash. A creature lunged forward, snapped at her head, and she spun again, dancing in place, bellowing in horror at the beast that had just bitten off half her scalp.

Jesse tried to swallow, but there was no saliva left, only a dull, painful click. He took Emma by the shoulders, said, "Don't watch any more."

This time she allowed herself to be led from the window. But as they moved through the living room toward the kitchen, Jesse glanced back one more time.

Through the dark screen door, he watched the creature on the Buick's hood drag Linda out of the car, rip through the back of her shirt, and sink its teeth into the meaty place on her side. Linda's stubby white legs began to kick. The creature who'd dropped out of the tree caught her foot, writhed its lips sinfully, and crunched through her Achilles tendon.

Chapter Seven

Charly feels curiously weightless as she steps onto the huge stump. Sam's hand is on her lower back, steadying her, and the thrill it elicits is not a sexual one, but rather an astonished gratitude at being taken care of. Eric has rarely been chivalrous with her, and when he has it's been for show. Sam's fingers against the ridiculous blue poncho are firm, kind. She thinks to herself, *So this is what it's like.*

She follows his pointing index finger and says yes, she sees what he's talking about, the grass and weeds down there pushed flat. She is about to ask if the driving wind or the rain could have done that to the grass, but then she spots the broken stalks of young trees, the deep imprints of what can only be cloven feet.

"Yes," she says, "I see it."

Sam looks up at her. "But your monster couldn't have made that trail."

She frowns, wanting this to lead her to Jake, but not wanting to muddy the waters with false hope. She shakes her head no.

Sam nods like he expected that. Then he takes her hand to help her down. He doesn't have the long, graceful fingers that Eric has. Sam's hands, she sees, are crisscrossed with old lacerations. Worker's hands.

"You sure you wanna do this?" he asks her.

She nods, not wanting to admit it is as much to escape the house and its haunted, suffocating atmosphere as it is to accompany him on this ill-advised investigation. *Sheriff Robertson is in my house right now,* she marvels. *Eric and that sex kitten coach as well. I must be insane to leave. What if the girls call and want to talk to me? What if the federal agents return with a lead? What if I screw up an opportunity to get Jake back?*

Sam is watching her. "You okay?"

She tries a smile. "I was just thinking…"

His face is open, sincere. "Don't tell me anything you don't want to."

She sucks in a shuddering breath. "You really think this might lead to something?"

"I can't give any guarantees."

She exhales pent-up air. "Guess we might as well try," she says.

He watches her a moment longer, then nods.

He begins making his halting way down the steep hillside. Trying not to trip over the voluminous poncho, Charly follows.

Eric threw open the front door. "Robertson!" he yelled.

He didn't hear what he wanted to—the fat slob scrambling to his feet from the living room, where he'd probably been dozing on the couch and dreaming of glazed donuts. Eric listened but he heard nothing.

"What's going on, Flo?" Mel asked as she came through the door behind him. He turned, put a finger to his lips. Christ, he swore he was always having to tell someone to be quiet. At home it was the girls, yammering about the Disney princesses or a yodeling mermaid or some other bullshit. At the gym it was even worse, his team playing grabass with each other, making jokes when they were supposed to be listening. Even his assistants were like that. Too many times lately he'd caught them whispering to each other when he was addressing the team. It was one of the worst parts about having an all-female staff. Yeah, they were better to look at, and he'd bedded all but one of them. But now they thought they could push the boundaries, chatter while he was talking because they were above the law.

Too comfortable, that was the problem. His assistant coaches had become far too comfortable, and when people got comfortable, they got permissive.

Take Charly. At first he'd ignored the subtle way her manner would change every time Sam Bledsoe stopped by to discuss the plans for the house. Eric had been in the midst of his best season at the time, and the truth was he wasn't home much. Still, he made sure he was there when Sam came calling.

Eric's eyes narrowed.

Sam.

Who called their contractor by his first name?

Okay, he thought, *maybe a lot of people, but they sure as hell don't say it the way Charly did.*

"Sam called. He said he'd stop by at four o'clock."

"Sam's on the phone, honey. He has a question about the basement."

"I like the windows Sam recommended."

Eric ground his teeth.

He knew what Charly was really saying. Strip away the words and focus on her mouth as she said the word *Sam.* Watch how the hives bloomed on her chest like a mating call. What she really meant was that she wanted to have sex with Sam Bledsoe.

"Sam called to ask about the kitchen lighting."

"Sam stopped by today, honey. He stuck it in my ass."

"Why are we being so quiet?" Mel asked.

He glared at her. "Because the sheriff's in the house, remember?" He shook his head. Man, he hated explaining himself.

"Why's he still here?"

He forced himself to smile at Melanie, the one coach he hadn't boned. *Be nice to her*, he reminded himself. *Snap at her too many times, she'll keep holding out on you.* Thinking of the way she'd dry-humped him last night in her shoebox of a car, Eric's throat went tight. Man, he couldn't wait to work it inside her, feel her squirm.

He made his expression soften. "He said he wanted me and Charly to have a break, let someone else wait by the phone."

"Sorry about that," Robertson said from the hallway. The guy was fat, but Eric had to hand it to him—he could sneak as quietly as an Indian.

"Where were you?" Eric asked.

Robertson smiled sheepishly. "I had to make a pit stop. Hope you don't mind my using the facilities."

Eric thought of the man's sweaty, hairy ass draped over one of their toilets and decided he minded very much that Robertson had taken a shit here without asking.

Let it go, he told himself. *Remember Charly and her boyfriend.*

"Have you asked Bledsoe where he was last night?"

Robertson cocked an eyebrow. "Why would I do that?"

"He was the last person to leave our house yesterday."

"That doesn't—"

"And he's taking my wife into the forest as we speak."

That stopped him. "Forest?"

Eric exulted in the man's puzzled expression. "Yeah, the forest. You know, the one that surrounds the whole subdivision?"

"Why would they…"

"I don't know," Eric said, "but I thought we might follow them to see. What if Bledsoe knows something about my son?"

Something rippled across Robertson's doughy face, something Eric didn't like. Derision, maybe? Taking exception to him calling Jake his son?

Eric felt the familiar heat growing at the base of his neck. If this hick cop wanted to start in questioning his parenting skills, he'd teach the fat fuck a lesson, regardless of his badge.

"Sam's a shrewd fella," Robertson said, more to himself than Eric. "Maybe we oughtta follow them, just in case they turn something up we missed."

"You ask me, you guys have missed everything so far."

"It's a good thing nobody asked you then."

With that, the man pushed by him and out the front door. Mel shot Eric a questioning look, but he was too pissed to talk to her. He followed the sheriff around the side of the house and heard Melanie hustling to keep up.

Good, he thought. *Move that sweet ass of yours and keep your mouth shut. It'll make my day a hell of a lot more bearable.*

They found the cave at around one-fifteen that afternoon. Sam had been staring at Charly's profile—the delicate line of nose, the kind of full lips women get injections to procure, the cheekbones he yearned to kiss—when she gasped and said something he didn't catch.

"Sorry, what?" he asked.

"Over there," she said.

He turned and saw it. Beyond a short sloping grade, on the other side of what appeared to be a shallow tributary, a cave yawned like a diseased mouth. Dead wildgrass overhung the rim of the cave forbiddingly. He estimated the entrance to be about six feet high, just tall enough to walk into comfortably. Within, the passage might dwindle dramatically, and if that happened, he sure as hell didn't look forward to navigating any tight spaces. He'd never considered himself terribly claustrophobic, but when he could avoid being closed in, he did.

"You think it took Jake there?" she asked.

He glanced at her, saw the naked hope in her eyes. "I don't know," he said carefully, "but the tracks lead in that direction."

Her forehead wrinkled.

"See the way the verge there is matted down?" he said, pointing at the hill that led to the cave. "If that was flat ground, you'd say it was a place where the deer slept. It isn't the flooding either, because everywhere else on this hillside the grass is leaning, not embedded in the mud." He nodded. "Only in that one spot there's kind of a track, like someone skidded a good part of the way."

"How do you know so much about that?"

"What?"

"I don't know..." She gestured toward the hill. "Tracking things, stuff like that."

Sam eyed the cave. "My dad was big into hunting. He'd take me with him sometimes. I never got into it as much as he did, but I guess I liked going because I got to be with him."

She studied his face a moment. "How many kids do you have, Sam?"

He glanced up at the leaden sky. "A son and a daughter."

"You and your boy ever go hunting?"

He bit the inside of his cheek, pretended to study a leaning old maple tree that looked about a year or two away from toppling. "Once or twice," he said. "Course, he's grown up now."

"Why only once or twice?"

He tried to smile, gave up on it. "It wasn't really his thing."

"Hunting or being with his dad?"

Sam looked at her in wonder. He couldn't recall a woman scrutinizing him this closely before, especially one so damned perceptive.

"We never had much of a relationship," he said.

In a soft voice, she asked, "When did you and your wife divorce?"

He let out a harsh laugh, almost a bark, and smiled down at his feet. "You get right to it, don't you?"

"I'm afraid Eric's going to follow us," she said. "I don't want to waste my chance to talk to you."

"You can talk to me whenever you want."

"We both know that's not true."

Her blue eyes were a shade lighter than the poncho, but tiny flecks dancing in her irises were just about the same royal blue.

He asked, "What makes you think your husband's following us?"

"He's a jerk, but he's not stupid."

"He must be stupid to take you for granted."

Her eyes locked on his for a long moment, and Sam held his breath. *Kiss her*, he told himself, and waited for his father's voice to talk him out of it.

But Dad was silent.

Sam urged his feet to move forward, his arms to reach for her, but under the weight of her stare, his limbs wouldn't cooperate. Like being in high school again—hell, junior high. Terrified of kissing a girl because she was too pretty. The dumbest reason of all.

Charly lowered her eyes, then turned toward the cave.

Sam silently cursed himself.

She nodded at the sooty maw, the arch of veined limestone within. "We going in there?"

"The tracks lead that way."

They headed down into a shallow swale, the sticks and leaves that eddied there reminding him of that old Mickey Mouse cartoon he used to watch with his kids, the one where Mickey made a broom carry water for him.

Charly asked, "Is this safe?"

"I didn't even know the cave existed. Maybe no one does."

"Won't it be too dark?"

"I always carry a Maglite in case I need to get in someone's crawlspace."

She grinned. "Is that code for something?"

Sam blushed.

The runoff from the creek trickled past their shins, but it didn't get any deeper. They stepped onto dry land and moved toward the cave. Sam reached out, put a hand between Charly's shoulder blades. The first time he'd done it, she hadn't slapped him, so now he touched her any chance he got.

She's married, remember?

Sam grinned. *Thanks for the reminder, Dad. I thought you'd abandoned me.*

You need to abandon trying to get in her pants.

At the rim of the cave, he stopped and plucked the flashlight from his soggy jeans.

"*Bledsoe Construction*," she read.

He held up the Maglite. "Impressive, huh?"

"You paid to have that done?"

"Kind of pointless," he agreed. "They gave me a couple free ones when they stenciled my truck."

He clicked on the Maglite and ventured into the darkness. He swept the interior of the cave and saw it went back a good ways.

They'd moved a few steps in when she said, "Earlier."

"Yeah?"

"Did you like what you saw?"

"What do you mean?"

"When you were staring at me outside the cave."

A sweltering heat ignited at his hairline, around his collar. "Hey, look...I'm sorry I—"

"Do I look angry?" she asked.

"Not really."

"So stop apologizing."

"All right."

She got moving again, and he shined the Maglite at the ground ahead of her. The air in here was fetid, no rainfall to start a breeze. Sam smelled wet rock and something that reminded him unpleasantly of semen. This wasn't a pretty place to be taking a lady, he thought, especially one he wanted to impress.

You're not trying to impress her, remember? You're trying to find her son.

He examined the sandy cave floor and made out the faintest intimation of a footprint. The print was abnormally slender and stretched, the toes as long as Sam's fingers.

The Maglite's amber glow happened on something else. Sam froze.

"What?" she whispered.

He hunkered down beside her and studied the impression. He thought at first it was a rut carved into the gritty floor by a steady stream of water. But when he used a sharp stone to rake a perpendicular line through the rut, he discovered it was freshly made. He stood and held the Maglite aloft so its glow would encompass a larger area. The line joined with another, this one running nearly parallel with the first. Sam counted three more. Other than a slow drip of water from somewhere ahead and the muted roar of the storm behind them, the cave was silent.

"Sam?" she said, gazing at the cave floor.

"Yeah," he answered, his voice nearly a croak.

"Does that look like a giant handprint to you?"

"Yes," he said. "That's what it looks like."

She reached up, took his hand in hers and pointed the Maglite a few feet deeper into the shadows. More lines.

Another handprint.

"Your kidnapper could've made that?" he asked.

She shook her head. "It was tall, but it wasn't that tall."

"But the shape..."

"The same," she said in a small voice.

"You okay to go on?"

He heard her swallow, sensed her nodding.

"You stay behind me," he said.

Wordlessly, he moved forward. He felt a finger hook one of his belt loops. Her touch sent spires of warmth pirouetting through him.

Sam waded deeper into the dark. The cave floor began to slant downward.

"Stay close," he said. Her poncho rasped against him.

Sam reminded himself not to enjoy it too much.

Chapter Eight

Red Elk's face was ghastly under the bug light. He was saying something to Greeley, who was shaking his head and looking like he was about to cry.

Red Elk turned to Clevenger. "You get this mouthy prick down there. I don't have time for this shit."

Clevenger's bald forehead was dotted with perspiration, the sparse black hairs plastered to his head here and there in exhausted curlicues. Red Elk crossed the kitchen, and momentarily, Jesse thought the man was heading out the back door. But Red Elk veered left and said something to Debbie.

"What're we doing?" Emma asked. Her face was still fish-white from witnessing Linda Farmer's death.

Clevenger shook his head, following Red Elk. "It doesn't matter. We have to trust him."

Greeley's voice rose to a petulant whine. "I'm not entombing myself in some half-assed bomb shelter...crawlspace, whatever he calls it."

"It's not a bomb shelter," Debbie said from around the corner. "It's a tunnel, and it's our only way out."

"What kind of tunnel?" Colleen asked.

Jesse followed Red Elk and saw, in the back hallway, a section of the floor had been removed and propped against the wall. Debbie was standing in the opening, her breasts even with the floor, which indicated to Jesse that they were indeed entering a crawlspace.

"Get in here," Debbie said.

Without comment, Colleen followed her, then Clevenger. Emma got an arm around Ruth's back and descended into the hole.

"So we just hide under the house?" Greeley said in that same plaintive voice. "That's the plan?"

Jesse moved past him and climbed in. Lowering to his knees, he saw that Red Elk had slid aside a square board in the far corner of the crawlspace and was swinging his legs into the opening. Muttering, Greeley got on his hands and knees behind Jesse.

Clambering forward, Jesse noticed several white tanks positioned around the dark crawlspace gleaming at him like dying moons.

They'd made it halfway to the trapdoor when Colleen, ahead of them, asked, "You guys put the floor back?"

Jesse turned in the gloom and eyed Greeley.

"No one told me I was supposed to," Greeley said.

Compressing his lips, Jesse scuttled hurriedly over to the opening and stood in the light of the back hallway. Moving in a near panic, he got hold of the section of floor, leaned it down, and fitted it into place from beneath. When he turned to locate the trapdoor, he discovered with dim terror that the crawlspace had emptied.

Crawling fast enough to kick up a cloud of dust, Jesse scrambled over to the trapdoor, began the downward climb on an iron ladder that had been bolted to the wall, and stopped when he realized he hadn't replaced the trapdoor.

He'd let the wooden door close halfway when someone hissed, "*Careful with it!*"

Jesse froze, looked up and noticed something he hadn't previously. A slender plastic tube hung through the opening and continued all the way to the ground.

"I'll rig it," Red Elk said. "Just get your butt down here."

Jesse did as he was told. He took in the dimensions of the tunnel. Eight feet wide and at least ten feet high, it meandered thirty feet or so before turning. It didn't look manmade.

At the top of the ladder, Red Elk reached through the gap, and Jesse heard scraping sounds. Then the big man took the tube and inserted it into a tiny notch carved into one side of the trapdoor. The tube, Jesse saw, ran along the floor several yards to where Debbie held the end of it pinched between her thumb and forefinger.

Red Elk climbed down and said to all of them, "We don't have time for talk, but here's the situation: If they find out we're down here, we'll put a lighter to that propane tube and the whole house will blow sky high."

There was a brief, incredulous silence. Then Greeley said, "What?"

Red Elk ignored him, moved to the opposite wall, which was overlaid with a sheet of plywood. Lifting the plywood section away and casting it aside, Red Elk revealed a pair of wooden shelves, on which lay a couple guns, a green backpack and a faded red gym bag.

"Which one of you can shoot?" he asked, picking up a gun with each hand. One was an old-fashioned silver revolver. The other was a big, black pistol that looked to Jesse like it could blow a hole in an elephant.

"I'm a daddy's girl," Colleen said, stepping toward him. "He used to take me to the range."

"You ever fire one of these?" Red Elk asked. He held out the revolver.

"Dad had a Colt just like that one," Colleen said, nodding to the big, black gun. "Why not let me use it?"

Red Elk tilted his head and grinned. "The .45's mine, honeypie.

You get the Smith & Wesson."

Colleen took the revolver, looking pleased.

Greeley went over, started unzipping the red gym bag.

"What'd I tell you about touching my stuff?" Red Elk said.

Red Elk's stony gaze was enough to make Greeley put his hands up in a gesture of truce.

"So what's in there?" Greeley asked.

"Twinkies," Red Elk said. He got up, went over to the enclave. "Bottles of water, granola bars, flashlights. A cleaver." Red Elk brought out an old bread bag that clinked metallically. "Batteries," he explained. He reached a big hand inside the gym bag and came out with something red and cylindrical.

"Is that what I think it is?" Jesse asked.

"It's old," Red Elk said, "but if it still works, I'm told a stick of dynamite can turn a ton of rock to dust."

"Now what on earth would we use that for?" Greeley asked. "Lighting that down here would bring the whole cave down."

"What's in that one?" Emma asked, nodding at the green backpack.

Red Elk set the dynamite down, reached into the backpack. "A mining helmet. A couple more flashlights. Rounds for the Ruger, bullets for Grandpa's revolver."

Colleen examined the revolver. "This belonged to your grandpa? The thing's an antique."

"You don't want it, I'll take it," Debbie said.

"You know how to use it?" Colleen asked, eyebrows raised.

"Frank can teach me," Debbie answered. She extended a hand.

"I'll keep it," Colleen said, stuffing the revolver down the front of her jeans. "It might blow up and take my face off, but I'd rather die that way than let someone like you kill me by accident."

Debbie's expression didn't change. "Who says it'd be an accident?"

Red Elk said, "Glad to see you two've hit it off."

Charly had never bought into the notions of ESP, second sight, those kinds of things. But she didn't entirely discount them either. For one, there was her unerring sense of direction. Even Eric, from whom compliments seldom came, had grudgingly conceded she was uncannily able to find her way through unfamiliar cities, choose the correct road even when their GPS told them to go another way, or navigate the largest airports without pausing to look at signs.

Then there was the incident with the toad.

One finger still hooked firmly in Sam's belt loop, she stared sightlessly at his back and recollected the time Kate, a little over a year ago, brought a toad into the kitchen and asked if she and Olivia could keep it. Charly wasn't averse to toads and bugs—not the way many women were—but she wasn't fond of the way the bumpy brown creature leered at her with those ancient, distended eyeballs.

She'd instructed Kate to carry the toad back outside and release it in the yard. Kate had promised to do so, but ten minutes later her husband had come home from practice and announced that the girls were playing with a toad in the driveway. Charly was immersed in making dinner and asked if Eric could call the girls in—with special emphasis on making sure they washed their hands. Eric had arched an eyebrow at her—any request on her part, no matter how reasonable, received this galled reaction—and told her, sure, don't worry about it. The dangerous serenity in his voice, she supposed later, had been her first tip-off, but that didn't explain what happened next, not by a long shot.

The girls, hungry and emotional about leaving their toad behind, had eventually come in to eat. Eric followed a short while later.

She awoke that night at a little past one and stared at the ceiling.

What, she wondered, had Eric done with Kate's toad?

She had a powerful urge to wake Eric up, but he'd been complaining about her restlessness quite a bit already. The fact that being pregnant with Jake was the reason she was uncomfortable—and why she also had to pee a lot—didn't matter to him. If it affected his sleep, it wasn't acceptable.

So she stole out of bed and crept downstairs. She had no idea where she was heading, but there was a youthful deliciousness in sneaking out of the house, which was what she found herself doing despite wearing nothing but a saggy black tank top and a pair of pink underwear.

She bypassed the driveway where Eric said the girls had been playing. She ignored the yard and the field across the road—the two places she herself would have dumped the toad had she been charged to do so.

Instead, Charly ambled around the side of the house, relishing the crisp night air and the somehow exciting possibility that one of their neighbors might see her out here wearing next to nothing. Her skin prickling with goose bumps, she stopped next to an old window well that shielded the cracked windowpanes and also prevented water from rushing into their cobwebby old basement. Charly knelt before the corrugated metal curvature and braced her hands on its rounded lip. Kneeling forward, she peered into the pooled shadows and at first discovered nothing but a spill of dead leaves and a few scurrying daddy longlegs. She leaned lower.

There, right up next to the cracked and dust-whitened glass, something was moving.

Without thinking about it—had she been thinking clearly, she might not have done it at all—Charly swung her legs over the edge of the well and lowered herself down. The drop was about four feet, but the desiccated leaves from a nearby oak cushioned her bare feet enough to make her descent painless. Yet when she bent down—the top of her mostly bare ass bumping the cool metal ridges all the way— she was suffused with an alarming ooze of dread. On hands and knees, she lowered her face to what she could now see was Kate's toad, or at least what was left of it. One side of its face seemed to cave in with each respiration, and a dark apostrophe of blood bubbled from the corner of its mouth. Forgetting all the conditioning of adulthood, Charly viewed the dying animal through her daughter's eyes, scooted her fingers under it as gently as she could, and brought it close to her face. As she and the toad regarded each other, a wetness started between her fingers, and she thought, *It's pissed on me. I forgot they always do that.* When she switched the toad to her other hand she saw the loop of guts dangling from its anus, a sinister horde of tiny black ants already teeming over the yellow-looking entrails. With a gasp Charly dropped the toad and immediately felt guilty for adding to its misery. Then she cast about feebly for a rock or something with which to end its suffering. But that too was denied her, the floor of the dank well comprised of hard-packed dirt. Charly swallowed and snatched up a handful of leaves. She scattered them over the toad and, moaning with sadness and an equal measure of revulsion, stepped on it. It squelched under her bare foot with a sound that reminded her of an old woman farting. When she lifted her foot, she discovered a good part of her heel was wet. *Its blood is on your feet,* she thought and had an insane urge to laugh.

She climbed out of the window well and sat panting. Again, she felt something draw her gaze, and she followed an urge that wasn't mere deduction but wasn't quite psychic power either and found, at shoulder level on the white brick façade, the dark splotch of blood where Eric had smashed the poor toad.

She pictured her husband reassuring their daughters that he'd make certain their little toad was safe. God, Kate had even named it, she now remembered. Elton John, because "Rocket Man" was one of Kate's favorite songs. Her husband probably even talked to Elton John on the way to the window well, *You're a good little toad, aren't you, Elton boy, you're a nice little piece of shit. You want me to be your errand boy, Charly? Well here's your fucking errand.* And winding up like Nolan Ryan, Charly's father's favorite player, even if he didn't play for the Cubs, Eric hurled poor Elton John toward the white brick wall like he was pitching a fastball in the World Series. Never mind that their daughters loved the toad, if only for a few hours. Never mind that the animal didn't die on impact, had to suffer the indignity of having its guts eaten by ants. Never mind—

"You hear that?" Sam asked.

Charly blinked and stared up at him in the meager light of the cave.

She listened, comfortable now with Sam even though their faces were very close. She didn't hear anything but the dim roar of the storm outside. She told him so.

"I thought I heard voices," he said, and after a brief look of deliberation, he proceeded deeper into the cave.

Charly shook her head. Now why, she wondered, had she thought of Elton John?

Because you're sleep deprived and because you're walking in near darkness.

No, she thought, *that's not all of it. I remembered the toad because I was looking for it, and I found it with some kind of sixth sense.*

Nonsense.

And that wasn't the first time either, she argued on, hope leaping within her. *If I can use that ability, harness it somehow, it could lead us to Jake.*

If you wanted to find your son, sweetheart, you wouldn't be underground.

Yes, but—

—so don't give me this "Sam led us in here" crap—

He did, he—

—wants to get laid, and you know it. He's been making eyes at you since the first time you met—

So? Maybe I like him making eyes at me—

Yeah, and maybe you're a cheap whore.

Charly sucked in a startled breath.

"What's wrong?" Sam asked, stopping to look back at her.

"Nothing."

But it was something; it was indeed. Because she now realized to whom that voice belonged. That cutting, wheedling voice she'd been hearing far too much of lately, mostly when she thought about what an asshole she'd married, and was it really impossible for her to take the kids and start a new life?

Oh yes, the voice belonging to her mother-in-law whispered, *of course you'd like to start a new life. Get yourself a fat alimony settlement, make sure you don't have to get a real job, and live the rest of your life touching men's dicks and sponging off my boy.*

Charly crinkled her brow, deeply thankful Sam couldn't see her right now, couldn't watch her face twisting as she fought and lost a battle with her own mind. She knew that's what it was, of course, for Eric's mother didn't really talk that way. Frieda Florence—God, the first time Charly had heard the woman's name, she thought Eric had been joking, came perilously close to exploding into laughter—never said things outright, never condemned Charly in any direct way. It was how she operated: insinuating, suggesting, inflicting damage without ever lacing up the gloves.

Now Frieda Florence's voice assaulted her, manumitted from the mores that suppressed total honesty, free to wreak whatever havoc she could on Charly's weary psyche.

Down here huddled close to another man, Frieda clucked, *while your husband is back at the house faithfully awaiting word on Jake. Why don't you two kiss? That would be lovely. Have yourselves a nice little makeout session while Eric tries to hold your family together.*

You don't know me, she thought, her eyes filling. *Every single thought I've had since last night has been about Jake. My heart is breaking with the comfort I can't provide him, and my breasts are about to burst with the milk I can't give him. He can't survive on his own, can't go much longer without feeding. My God, I only started him on solid foods a couple weeks ago, how will he survive—*

Sam said, "You ever do this before?"

As if rising from a great depth, Charly said, "Have I been alone with a man who wasn't my husband in the dark before?"

"I was thinking of spelunking."

"No way," she said. "The idea of it always made me queasy."

"Me too. When I started working for a commercial construction company—this was in the summer between my sophomore and junior year at WIU—"

"You went to Western?"

She could hear the smile in his voice. "Sure."

"What year did you graduate?"

"Uh-uh," he said. "You'll threaten to put me in the nursing home."

She was silent a moment before she said, "I didn't know you went to college."

"Hard to believe, isn't it? Blue-collar guy like me?"

"That's part of it," she admitted. "But it's more that you remind me of my dad."

"Yeah?"

"Your personality, at least. He was a lot taller than you."

"Ah."

She took a breath. "He was handsome like you."

A voice behind them muttered, "Isn't that sweet."

Charly cried out, her hand darting away from Sam's belt loop.

Eric rushed toward them.

Flashlight beams fluttered wildly around the corridor, the sounds of a scuffle. Sam brought his own beam around to illuminate the others. Charly distinguished Melanie Macomber with a hand to her chest and her mouth in a frightened O. Beside her, Robertson and Eric were wrestling, the sheriff endeavoring to put Eric in a headlock. But Eric was too quick and angry for him.

"Don't do it," Sam said as Eric began to break free.

"*Stupid cocksucker,*" Eric said.

Charly wondered which man Eric was referring to. Maybe both.

"Mr. Florence, I'm telling you—" Sam started, but Eric ripped free of the sheriff's grasp and came spinning toward them, one fist already cocked high. Charly sidestepped him as he hurtled toward Sam. She watched Eric's balled fist arc wildly through the air, the haymaker missing and bringing him right on top of Sam, who'd bunched in a tight crouch and immediately pistoned a fist up into Eric's gut. Eric doubled over with an astounded *oof*, and Sam popped out from beneath him. Quicker than Eric could retaliate or even stand erect, Sam jackhammered the side of his head with two lightning jabs.

Melanie cried out, and Robertson hurried toward the pair to break things up, but not before Sam hauled Eric up by the shirt front, reared back and walloped him with a roundhouse right that sent Eric crashing against the cave wall.

All three flashlights had been dropped, and it was in this surreal and spectral light that Charly watched Sam and Larry Robertson yelling at one another, their fingers stabbing the air, their underjaws awash in the faint light.

The men were still shouting when Charly heard something that cut through the commotion like a white-hot blade.

She threw her hands out, bent her head to hear, but the others wouldn't shut up. She said, "Stop yelling," and when that didn't work, she screamed, "*Shut your mouths, everybody! Please!*"

Sam and Sheriff Robertson immediately broke off quarreling and stared at her. Melanie was wide-eyed and a little afraid. Eric, too, was listening.

The sound came again, and this time Charly's heart jitterbugged in her chest.

It was Jake. From somewhere deep in the cave, her baby was crying.

Chapter Nine

"That's him," Eric said. "That's Junior."

Gee, you think? Sam wanted to say but didn't. *You sure it isn't some other kidnapped baby down here wailing for help?*

The cries were coming from the darkness ahead. Charly had started that way, her hands actually cupping her swollen breasts in a gesture of which Sam was sure she was entirely unconscious.

He and Robertson came up alongside Charly, who'd been wandering blindly into the cave. The baby's cry was a strong one, which he supposed was a good sign. But it was putting Charly through hell, hearing her baby screaming that way.

"Whoa!" Robertson shouted, and Sam halted automatically. Flicking his light down, he discovered he'd been damned lucky. He tottered another moment on the brink of a nasty fall—the drop was sheer and at least twenty feet down—then he regained his balance and put out a hand to make sure Charly was okay. She was, he now saw, but only because Robertson had grabbed hold of her and saved her from breaking her pretty neck too. Sam put a hand on her shoulder, asked her if she was all right.

"Don't touch her," Florence said behind him. The man interposed himself, put his back to Sam, and said to Charly, "It'd be nice if you at least acted like you were married."

His words scarcely seemed to register with Charly, who stared down into the pit.

"How do we..." she began, a tortured frown on her face.

"We don't," Robertson said with finality. "We go back and call for help. They'll have your boy out within..."

But he stopped, his eyes going very wide.

Another voice had sounded from the pit, this one harsh and feral and somehow *knowing.* Maybe Sam thought that because of how Charly had described the monster that stole her baby.

But Sam didn't think so. Something about the voice below reminded him of a playground bully who'd once plagued him, the kid an enormous fifth grader, Sam only in second grade. A kid named Mitch. God, what a perfect name for him. Wide-shouldered and sullen-faced, his thick, brown hair cut straight across his forehead almost at the hairline, Mitch had been held back twice by that time, which made him what? Thirteen? Fourteen by then? And Sam would've been seven or eight.

Mitch would wait by a funnel-shaped monstrosity with four colorful tubes sticking out of it in different directions. The game was like basketball and Russian roulette combined because you never knew which tube the ball would tumble out of. It became a game of precognition. Mitch loved that weird hoop more than anything, and he'd station himself there until the kids came. And because it was just about the only attraction on that pissant little dustbowl the school passed off as a playground, the kids always came. If the ball came out of the tube where Mitch was stationed, everything was hunky-dory. He'd snatch the ball out of the air, hold it aloft to torture the younglings awhile, then lob it toward the conical opening at the top. He'd usually miss because, even at his advanced age and height, he was as coordinated as a drunken grizzly bear. But whenever the tar-spattered red kickball they used squirted out of another tube, which was three-quarters of the time, he'd wade through the massed children like some crazed Gulliver and thrash the kid brazen enough to snag the rebound.

That was usually Sam.

And Sam would run around with the ball because he was faster, and everyone would laugh like hell at Mitch as he flailed his arms and puffed like an asthmatic, and sometimes Mitch would catch him and give him a good pummeling. Other times, most of the time, Sam would tire the big bastard out, return to the hoop, and make a shot. On these occasions Mitch would eject someone bodily from one of the swings and slouch there until his wind returned.

The sound coming from the pit now reminded Sam very much of Mitch, the oversized dumb bastard who nevertheless understood one thing very well: cruelty.

Listening to the voice—the laughter, it was unmistakably laughter—the old righteous indignation rose up in Sam, made his fists clench and his jaw tighten.

Robertson was gazing at Charly. "Could that be the thing you said took your boy?"

Sam had thought Robertson was like the rest, that he considered Charly an ignorant, hysterical woman for telling them the story she'd told. Now he understood the sheriff's mind was a good deal more open than most minds would be, and though he'd already liked Larry Robertson, had known him a good part of his life, the sheriff went up several notches in Sam's estimation.

He said to Robertson, "I don't suppose you've got a spare gun?"

"Hunting rifle's in the truck, but you're not going near that."

"You have anything else?"

Robertson bent down, lifted a pant leg and came up with a big buck knife with a white grip. "The handle's made from the antlers of a twelve-point buck I got a couple years ago."

Charly's breath was coming in shuddering gasps, but she was able to ask Eric, "Can I borrow your flashlight?"

Eric drew back as though she'd just asked him to put out one of his eyes with a Phillips screwdriver. "You don't need a flashlight," he said. "We're going back, remember?"

"What do you need to see?" Robertson asked in a considerably kinder tone.

She scrunched up her face in frustration, shook her head. "Oh, for Christ's sakes—"

"Here," Sam said, offering her the Maglite.

She offered him a peculiar, sidelong glance, fleeting but full of a meaning Sam was apparently too dense to grasp, and said, "No, you and Larry keep yours."

"You're calling the Feds, right?" Eric said to Robertson.

The sheriff opened his mouth to answer, but before he could, Charly darted a hand toward her husband and snatched the flashlight from him.

"*Hey*," Florence said, "what the hell—"

But the thought never completed because Charly leaped forward, her poncho billowing up like a wind-torn umbrella, and disappeared into the pit.

"*Wait!*" Robertson shouted.

Sam made a clumsy grab for her, but his fingers missed the poncho altogether. He waited, heart in throat, for the crunch of breaking bones.

"Look!" Melanie shouted. Her hands closed over Sam's right hand and aimed his flashlight at Charly's body, which was sliding down a place below them they hadn't spotted, a declivity that led downward in a hurry but wasn't a straight drop. The flashlight spotlighted Charly just in time to see her twist her body with the spiraling grade before disappearing.

"What're we gonna do now?" Melanie asked.

Eric glanced at the sheriff. "We go back to the house, right? We know where the baby is—"

Sam noted the indecision on Robertson's face, said, "That thing might be dangerous, Larry. We don't want to leave her alone with it."

Florence's mouth widened in incredulity. "What *thing*? Don't tell me you believe that horseshit about some shirtless troll taking Junior."

"You hear that voice?" Sam asked.

"I don't know what I heard," Florence said. "And you sure as hell don't know either."

Robertson had gotten down on the ground, was dipping his head over the lip of the hole. "Mrs. Florence!" he called. "Let me see where you're at!"

"She's gone," Sam said.

Robertson peered up at him, redfaced.

"After her boy," Sam explained. "She means to get him back."

"She'll get herself killed," Robertson said.

"Which is why we've got to follow her."

Melanie withdrew a step. "We're not going down there?"

Robertson fluttered an impatient hand, said, "I need to think this—"

But Sam jumped before he could finish.

In the moments before his feet left the relative safety of the cave floor, the only thought in Sam's mind was making sure Charly was all right. But the moment his body started its downward trajectory, half a dozen less noble thoughts vied for supremacy:

Are you fucking nuts?

His feet dipping into the void, Sam forgetting all about the flashlight in his right hand...

Going to die!

...his toes stretching out, yearning for something, any surface to pad his fall...

Thinking with your heart again, this is what you get.

...knuckles rapping some sandpapery surface, the grit removing the flesh as easily as old cellophane...

Could've planned this better—would another three or four seconds have cost you that much?

...drawing his feet up, which was the worst thing he could do because the moment the toes of his work boots smacked rock, his kneecaps shot toward his face and cracked his nose so hard the tears practically spurted out of his eyes...

What you deserve

...windmilling his arms...

You look like a cartoon coyote

...tipping backward...

You idiot

...somersaulting sideways...

Here it comes, oh shit

...canting off the slide...

OH SHIT!
…into darkness…
SHIT SHIT SHIT SHIT
…and then the impact.

He lay there a moment wondering how far he'd fallen and how busted up he was. His nose was a bellowing bullhorn of pain, his mouth a gritty stew of blood, sand and mucus. Though he could barely breathe, he could already smell the dank odor of this place and an acrid tinge of something else as well, something he didn't care to think about. Not yet, at least. Whatever he scented was fulsome, sinister…and where the heck was Charly?

Coughing, he forced himself onto his elbows to look around. He couldn't see anything. Sam groaned, bringing the Maglite close to his body. He tapped it on his leg, joggled it, fingered the glass cover to see if it had shattered. When nothing presented itself as the cause of the malfunction, he clicked the rubber button on a whim and sighed with relief as its small but very bright shaft of light spilled across his lap. He swept the beam around his new surroundings and counted six separate holes wide enough for a man—or in this case, a poncho-wearing goddess—to squeeze through.

Above, Robertson and that prick Florence were hollering for him to say something so they'd know he was okay. Robertson sounded genuinely concerned, but Florence's heart wasn't in it. Maybe he hoped both Sam and Charly had broken their necks so he could set up shop with that tasty assistant of his.

Sam whisked the flashlight from hole to hole, but there was no sign of passage in any of them. Not to mention that fool's chorus above him pleading with him to say something.

"I'm fine," he growled up to them. "Now shut up a second so I can collect my thoughts."

Feeling like a hung-over octogenarian, Sam climbed to his feet and immediately bonked his head on an overhang.

"*Dang,*" he muttered, rubbing the back of his head.

"Your thoughts collected yet?" Robertson called down.

"Just about."

He straightened again, making sure not to brain himself this time. The largest openings were across the way. Charly might have—

Check the sand! his dad's voice thundered.

He flashed the Maglite on the foul-smelling sand and spotted them right away—Charly's shoe prints. They were as large as a man's, something that made him smile. He'd be sure to kid her about it when he found her.

He followed them a few paces, where they veered crossways to the far left recesses of the cavern. He shined his light at the moist and glittering wall.

"If you can make it down here," Sam called, "take a hard left. The tunnel will be marked with an X. Look for it in the sand."

"Wait a second," Robertson called, but Sam had already bent low to shine the beam down the narrow chute.

Knowing he'd psyche himself out if he delayed any longer, Sam crawled forward and down toward the sound of rushing water.

Red Elk was eyeing Emma, who crouched to the man's right.

"Anything wrong?" she asked.

"Monique Parent," Red Elk said.

"Excuse me?"

"*Play Time, Dark Secrets, The Key to Sex...*"

"Not that again," Emma said.

"...*Midnight Confessions.* Cute little blonde. At least she's usually a blonde." Red Elk made a little humming sound, his gaze wistful. "Kind that just drives you crazy. She's never been in a hardcore film, which means there's something left to the imagination." Red Elk glanced up at Jesse, nodded. "Most actresses, they're just acting, and it shows. Now Monique...you know she's acting, but she's good at acting turned-on. She's classy, but she's ornery too, which makes it more fun. Was in a movie called *Desire: An Erotic Fantasyplay*, but damned if I can find it. It's one of the holy grails of soft core. I'd give my left nut for a VHS copy."

Emma said, "Could we ease up on the porn stuff awhile, Mr. Red Elk?"

"Soft porn, miss."

"Okay, but we're kind of in the middle of something here—"

"Reason I mention it is you fooled me earlier."

Emma arched an eyebrow. "What are you talking about?"

"That bra you wore this morning, it was a miracle of innovation. Either you stuffed it so full of tissue it was fit to burst, or you've gotten on to some new kind of brassiere. Those tits of yours looked three sizes too big for your body. I'm usually great at visualizing a woman naked, but you fooled the hell out of me. I mean, Monique Parent and Shannon Whirry? The difference between those two sets of tits is like the difference between a grenade and an atom bomb."

Emma stared at him with distaste. Jesse knew he should stick up for her, but he had no idea what to say. After Red Elk had decided to blow up his house, Jesse was truthfully a little bit frightened of the man. Also—and he wasn't at all proud of this—he'd noticed how large

145

Emma's breasts looked earlier too. He'd attributed it to water retention or some other mystical feminine condition.

"She wears it to get better answers," Debbie said.

Emma shook her head. "Can we *please* stop talking about my breasts?"

"If you didn't want people to notice," Debbie said, a hint of a grin touching the corners of her lips, "you wouldn't wear a push-up."

"You weren't even here this morning."

"I didn't need to be, sugar."

Colleen shrugged one shoulder. "It's not that big a deal, you know. No pun intended."

"I'm curious too," Greeley said.

Emma's mouth worked as she looked from face to face. She turned again to Jesse, but the only aid he could muster was an apologetic wince.

Emma heaved a sigh. "Okay, fine. I wore a push-up bra earlier."

"I *knew* it," Red Elk said, slapping a knee. "I knew I wasn't that far off my game."

"You suck, you know it?" Colleen said to Emma. "It's not enough to be gorgeous and built like Miss October, you've gotta stack the deck even further."

Emma scrunched her forehead. "Colleen—"

"Don't 'Colleen' me. I've got to work my ass off just to keep a job, and all you've gotta do is flash that cleavage and stick out your butt—"

"You'd do the same if you could," Debbie said.

Colleen seemed on the verge of a rebuttal when they heard a rattling sound from above.

"That's the front door," Red Elk said.

Chapter Ten

Eric listened in astonishment as the sounds from below faded. That weasel Bledsoe had actually forsaken them to follow Charly. There was disrespecting a man to his face, and then there was doing what Sam Bledsoe was doing to him: shitting on a plate, thrusting it into a man's lap, giving him a knife and fork, and laughing at him while he ate it.

If he'd been mad at the guy before, there weren't words for how he felt now. Not in his darkest dreams had he imagined he'd be humiliated this badly. Not when his first team got taken out behind the woodshed on ESPN to the tune of a hundred and six to fifty-two. Not when he'd been demoted in junior college to a benchwarmer. Not even during that awful morning during his freshman year in high school, when the senior boys gave him a wedgie so severe the seam of his jockey shorts sliced the skin around his bunghole so badly it made him bleed through his white gym shorts.

This was worse than all those times because humiliation was supposed to be a part of a man's youth, wasn't it? Wasn't that why a boy grew up, to end the embarrassment and enjoy being on top for a change? Yet here he was, forty years old and finding himself on the verge of being cuckolded by an unsuccessful construction worker.

His jaw still ached where Bledsoe had decked him. Eric ran his fingers over his chin and touched the split bottom lip, the nose that felt as though someone had taken a sledgehammer to it. Christ, he was lucky they were down here in the dark; if Mel got a good look at his mangled face she might never spread her legs for him.

A slow pulse of lust mingled with his fury. He'd fucking kill that Bledsoe, and he'd laugh doing it. Robertson was saying something to him, but it didn't matter; all Eric's attention had migrated south, where his cock was stretching his shorts tight. Sure, he got erections every day, but this...this was something new and exciting. He figured it was that depraved combination of sex and death that killers got off on, those blank, staring murderers he and Charly sometimes watched on that *Cold Case Files* show. He enjoyed the hell out of that show, every part but the end, when the killer got his comeuppance. He supposed it had to end like that; otherwise there'd be no show. People wouldn't go in for a series based on unsolved murders that stayed unsolved. But for his money the best part was the beginning, where the victim was described and you saw all those pictures of the person as a child, then as a teenager. Those were the best, the teenager pictures. He'd always experienced a slight sexual thrill when they showed some future murder victim in her cheerleading outfit or leotard. Knowing what was coming made him feel...what? Powerful, he supposed. Omniscient. *I know what's in store for you, Little Lady. You think the world is your oyster, but it's actually a nasty, ugly place. At least for you.*

And then the best part, the description of how the victim went missing and how the body was found. They nearly always showed you pictures of the corpses. None of those faggoty reenactments you got on so many shows these days. It wasn't scary or remotely interesting to watch some actress pretend to be afraid. What the hell—if he wanted that, he'd watch a horror movie, though those were bullshit too. You could do anything with makeup and special effects.

No, you got to see the real thing on that show, mm-mmm...a pale, naked body lying dead in the woods, the dirt and leaves that smudged the skin giving the corpse the appearance of some discarded doll. But these weren't dolls, uh-uh, they were real, and where Eric's mind went at that moment, other than between the legs of the victim to see how much the network dared to show, was back to the moment of the crime. There was always a rape first. Otherwise, why do it? There'd be a rape, then a strangulation. Sometimes there were signs of captivity, and man, that really sent his heart racing.

Someone was shaking him by the arm, and with an effort he tore himself out of the fantasy.

"...you think?" Mel finished.

"Do I think what?" he said as though in a fog.

"The lady wants to know if we can go back," Robertson said.

Mel's expression was pained, childish. "It's spooky down here, Flo. We can get help if we go up now."

Eric said, "We're going after them."

The blood drained from her face. She glanced imploringly at the sheriff, and Eric felt another wash of anger at her disobedience. This bullshit was going to end. Pronto.

"Tell you the truth," Robertson said, "I'm of a mind to follow them too."

"But—"

"I get your point, Miss Macomber, and there's some logic in it. We go back now, we can call in the cavalry, do this thing by the numbers."

"Then let's go."

"Problem is, by that time we might have three missing persons to search for. There've been rumors of caves in this area since before I was born, but I never credited them until today. The old codgers claim it's a veritable ant farm under this land. Tunnels leading to tunnels, caverns branching off in a hundred directions. A man wanting to disappear after he committed a crime would find it ideal."

Mel's face pinched. "What if we get lost too?"

"We'll leave a trail," Robertson said.

"Of what?" Mel asked.

How about your clothes? Eric thought.

"Whatever we have on us," Robertson said, and reached into his pocket. He fished out a white box.

"Cigarettes?" Mel asked.

"I quit officially three years ago, but I keep them around for special occasions."

Eric grinned. "Your wife know you still smoke, Sheriff?"

"Unlike others I know, this is the only thing I keep from her," Robertson said.

Eric flushed. He glanced at Mel to see if the accusation had registered with her, but thank God for small favors, she was casting fretful looks into the pit. Eric felt his good spirits return. Maybe this could work in his favor. She got scared enough, she'd look to him for solace. Perhaps the two of them could accidentally split off from the sheriff for a few minutes, just long enough for her to break down entirely. Once that happened, Eric knew from experience, the deal was as good as sealed.

No, he told himself. *Don't drift away on that cloud yet. Focus on Charly, who's getting farther and farther away while you stand here. You think Mel's the only one who'll need comfort? Charly's gonna break down too—she's a woman, isn't she?—and when that happens who'll be there to console her?*

His fists bunched into tight knots. He imagined what would happen if he stumbled upon Charly and Bledsoe screwing. He did, it wouldn't matter if *ten* cops were with him, he'd slaughter them both. They'd find Charly twenty years later, her pale legs smudged by dirt...

"Better get to it," Robertson said.

"I'll go first," Eric said.

Robertson nodded. "I'll let you."

Mel hopped in place, a pitiful, keening sound emanating from her throat.

Eric slid a comforting arm around her lower back, his fingers stroking the top of her perfect ass. "I'll be with you the whole way," he said. "It would mean a lot to me if you'd help me find Junior."

Mel sniffed, nodded. Eric massaged her lower back, the top of her butt.

Robertson was watching Eric's rubbing hand. His eyes rose to meet Eric's.

So what? Eric wanted to say. *You gonna do something about it?*
Eric moved to the edge of the pit and jumped.

In the gravid silence of the tunnel, Emma said to Jesse, "They're the only two I had that were clean."

He looked at her questioningly.

"Bras," she explained.

Jesse opened his mouth but could think of absolutely no response.

"I have four all together," she went on. "A sports bra, the push-up and two regular ones. One was dirty, and anyway, it's starting to fall apart. The wires are showing through in places. So I left it at home."

Jesse frowned, did his best to be scientific about it, to not picture Emma in just a bra. "How many bras do most girls have?"

"I have no idea. More than four, I'd imagine. Colleen has about twenty strung all over the bathroom like Christmas decorations."

"So..."

"Why do I only have four?"

She looked away, a rueful smile darkening her face. She tongued the inside of her cheek a moment, uttered a mirthless little laugh, and said, "Quite a thing to talk about, huh? Maybe you should share what kind of underwear you have on. You know, to put us on equal footing."

"Boxer briefs," he said.

She regarded him, eyebrows raised, some of her good humor returning.

He nodded. "I used to wear tightie whities because that's what my mom bought for me, but it wasn't until college that I realized they were incredibly uncomfortable."

"Is that so?"

"Like being in prison."

"I see."

"Boxers were worse, for the opposite reason. About a year ago I finally bought a pair of these from JC Penney—" He lifted his shirt and pulled out the plum-colored waistband of his boxer briefs. "It was like the heavens opened."

She chuckled.

"I'll never go back," he said. "It's the perfect marriage of security and freedom."

"You do all your underwear shopping at JC Penney's?"

"Some," he said. "I went to Abercrombie and Fitch a couple times, but I was surrounded by teenagers."

"So?"

"So I felt out of place. Isn't that sad? Not even thirty yet and already feeling like a dirty old man."

"Maybe you are."

"Old or dirty?"

"I don't know," she said. "Maybe both."

He laughed softly.

She said, "I'm dirt poor."

He looked up at her, waiting for the punch line.

She returned his stare, her pretty face both vulnerable and defiant.

"What do you mean you're dirt poor?"

"How many ways are there to take that?"

"I don't... How much do you make at the paper?"

She crossed her arms. "How much do you?"

He told her.

"About the same," she said. "When you subtract my college loans from that, there isn't much left."

"Your bio says you were on scholarship at Brown."

"Partial scholarship. Which means I'll be paying off the other half for the next sixty years." She suddenly brightened. "You read my bio?"

He colored. "I was bored one day, I just happened—"

"'Jesse Hargrove is a graduate of Western Indiana University and a native of Shadeland. He enjoys movies of all kinds—especially horror— and when he's not photographing for the *Truth*, he can be found at the local theater taking in the latest zombie release'."

He could only stare at her.

"Was that right?" she asked.

He shook his head slowly. "Verbatim."

"Well," she said and looked away.

After a time he said, "Tell me more about your bras."

"Oh that," she said and inhaled deeply. "The only three I brought camping were the two you've seen—"

"I haven't really seen either."

She punched him on the arm. "You know what I mean."

"Right, the two you've worn and the sports bra."

"Uh-huh."

"Why didn't you wear the sports bra?"

She eyed him, a frisky gleam there that made him a trifle light-headed.

"The sports bra mashes my boobs flat, and they don't need any mashing to begin with."

"I think they're nice," he heard himself saying.

Her mouth fell open, an amazed smile on her lips. "*Jesse!*"

Holy crap, he thought, what *was* he saying? "I...uh, I only meant—"
"

"Thanks," she said.

He swallowed. "You're welcome."

"Anyway, the sports bra doesn't do me any favors, and the regular one fits better."

"What about the…"

"The push-up bra?"

He nodded.

"It makes my breasts look bigger."

"That's true."

"Why do you like boxer briefs?"

"Same reason."

She laughed at that, leaned closer. The summery smell of her flesh drowsed over him. Man, it felt good to relax, if only for a moment. The warm feel of her arm against his soothed him, made him wonder for a moment if those horrors outside might leave them alone, might be content with the carnage they'd already wrought.

When their laughter dissipated, they sat quietly a minute, listening to the others whispering down by the trap door. So far, nothing seemed to have changed, and that was just fine with Jesse.

He looked over at Emma. "Why did you tell me all that?"

She shrugged. "I wanted you to understand, but I'm sure as hell not telling the others. Especially Chief Horn Dog."

"What about the cell phone thing with Greeley?"

"What about it?"

"Do you really hate technology?" he asked.

"I don't like how it takes people out of the moment."

"So you don't have an iPhone?"

"I can't afford one."

"What if you had the money?"

"I'd buy more bras."

They both laughed. Emma clapped a hand over her mouth, pressing against him.

"You two might want to keep it down," Red Elk called.

"What's happened?" Emma asked.

"Nothing much," Red Elk answered. "Just that we can hear them scratching around up there."

Jesse crowded up close to Red Elk, who stood staring up at the trapdoor.

"Have they found that section of floor yet?" Jesse asked.

Red Elk gave him a deadpan look. "They'd be down here if they'd found it."

"You covered the trapdoor with dirt?"

"Well as I could. Kinda tough to cover a door you've just closed."

"I guess so," Jesse admitted.

The silence drew out. A few feet behind them, he could make out the others in the gloom. Emma's eyes were large and watchful, Colleen's grim and narrowed. Greeley was bouncing on his heels and making little humming noises. Clevenger, Ruth Cavanaugh and Debbie stood immobile, like cardboard cutouts Red Elk had stored down here.

Jesse strained to hear the creatures above them, but save for an occasional muffled scrape, the crawlspace remained quiet.

Jesse eyed the dusty plastic tube depending from the notched corner of the trapdoor. The flatulent reek of propane was growing stronger despite Red Elk's thumb, which plugged the bottom of the tube. The lighter Red Elk grasped in the other hand was an old-fashioned one, the silver kind with a flip-top and a wheel. Its polished surface gleamed in the muted glow of the mining helmet Jesse wore.

"You sure this is safe?" Jesse asked.

Red Elk looked exasperated. "How the fuck should I know? You ever blow up a house?"

"No," Jesse said.

"Me either."

Emma looked around. "Should we...I don't know, take cover somewhere?"

"Not a bad idea," Red Elk said.

Clevenger took Colleen by the elbow and guided her and Emma down the corridor a ways.

"Get ready," Red Elk whispered.

Debbie stepped backward until she stood with the group. Greeley had retreated several feet behind the rest.

"Are they coming?" Jesse whispered.

"I can't hear them," Red Elk said. "But that doesn't mean they're not."

Jesse and Red Elk remained motionless, the only sound in their part of the tunnel the husky susurrus of their breathing. Above, the crawlspace had grown preternaturally quiet. Distantly, Jesse detected a faint tapping sound and realized it was the rain on Red Elk's roof.

A voice behind them blurted, "Oh, for God's sakes, what's happening up there?"

Greeley was marching past him toward Red Elk.

From Greeley's angle, Jesse realized with mounting anxiety, he couldn't see Red Elk raising the lighter to the plastic tube, didn't see the large, chipped thumbnail settle on the silver wheel.

A flurry of noises erupted above them. The click and scrabble of

153

talons and toenails converged on the trapdoor. Without hesitation Red Elk flicked the lighter, but nothing happened.

Oh God, Jesse thought and moved away from Red Elk.

"What are you—" Greeley began. "I thought you had it remotely charged or something."

Red Elk didn't respond, was too immersed in flicking the wheel. But the damned lighter wouldn't light.

Scratching sounds above Red Elk.

"Get out of there," Clevenger hissed.

Something creaked. Jesse's heart thundered as the trapdoor swung open and a creature's virulent face poked through the aperture.

The lighter flared into life.

The creature groped for it.

Red Elk let his thumb off the propane tube. Greeley threw up an arm. The creature pawed at Red Elk's face.

Red Elk touched the flame to the tube.

There was a high-pitched zipping sound. A blue puff of flame seemed to engulf Greeley and Red Elk. Jesse saw the creature's hideous face twist in surprise. The tube became an incandescent spire of heat.

Then the zipping sound was drowned out by a low *whump* that shook the entire tunnel.

Greeley screamed. The others began to run. Before Jesse followed them, he glimpsed Red Elk and Greeley stumbling away from the trapdoor. The creature tumbled screaming into the tunnel, its haunches and legs aflame. Greeley fell and Clevenger doubled back to help him. Blue fire spat out of the trapdoor, pooling on the writhing creature and starting a dozen bonfires on its sizzling flesh.

Another *whump* shook the tunnel, this one far stronger than anything that had come before.

The propane tanks.

Part Three
Dark Zone

Chapter One

...two, three, four...
Exhale.
One, two, three, four...
Exhale.

Charly repeated the mantra as the slimy walls closed in on her. She'd never been good in tight spaces, and the panic urge was threatening to overtake her now. The sound of rushing water filled the tunnel, and to Charly it sounded like death, like suffocation, like premature burial in a tight coffin—

No!

She squeezed her lids together. She had to think of Jake, had to think of her aching breasts, swollen with nourishing milk. Her baby needed her. Would die without her. She had to breathe...*breeeeathe...*

One, two, three, four...
Exhale.
One, two, three—

She clapped a hand to her mouth when Jake's cry sounded from ahead. My God, she was getting closer! Charly scrambled forward on elbows and knees despite the diminishing space, the cave swallowing her like some insatiable serpent. The tunnel had mostly tended downhill, with occasional meanderings right and left, and now the grade was steepening. The swooshing rustle of her poncho was magnified by the narrowness of the space, and she strained to hear over it, to detect the horrible, blessed sound of Jake's wails. The water roared below, and coupled with her stupid poncho, it drowned out Jake. Charly tugged the poncho over her head and crawled over it.

She stopped and strained to hear her boy.

Nothing.

She started forward again, the tunnel so close now on all sides that she feared she'd hit a slick spot and slide right into a wedge. Then she really would suffer a premature burial, and what kind of a blasphemous irony would that be, dying a tortured death shoved tight in a stinking cave tunnel while her baby wailed helplessly nearby?

Stop it! she ordered herself. *That's doing you no good at all.*

But the fear would not abate. She heard the cry again, but the other sound, the thunder of rushing water, reduced it to a background noise, ambient and barely audible. With a jolt of self-condemnation she realized she'd been so busy listening, she'd hardly been looking. Now she stopped and aimed the flashlight down the tunnel.

She sucked in breath.

The tunnel ended just ahead.

Clicking off the flashlight, Charly wriggled forward and listened for Jake. She knew she should be concocting some brilliant rescue plot, but there simply wasn't time. She had to go forward, had to get to her baby before something happened to him. She was almost there, she could hear the water roaring below. The tunnel squeezed around her, and Charly surged ahead now with straining jerks and lunges. Droplets of water spattered her face, a cool, drowsy mist filming her cheeks, and she wiggled forward, forward, nearly to the terminus now, forward—

Her fingers grasped the outer edge of the tunnel. She scooted toward it, her head poking through, her hips working their way against the wet tunnel rock. Her shoulders popped through the opening, her ribcage. She planted her toes and shoved, and then she was tumbling downward, vomited out of the tunnel toward—

She landed on the top of her head, her neck instantly numb.

Her consciousness dimmed, the flashlight pinned under her. Not that it mattered anyway. She hadn't the strength to open her eyes, much less move her arms. The sound of the surf waned, and in the last moments of waking Charly strained to hear her boy's voice.

She did.

Then another sound tore through it, scattering it like chaff.

A deep, feral laughter.

Sam moved through the tunnel, thinking, *You don't know for sure she went this way.*

But the footprints led here.

What if they weren't her footprints?

Who else's would they be? The goddamn hobbits of the Shire?

His Maglite picked out something ahead. Something blue.

He exhaled relieved breath and muscled his way forward, his broad shoulders now a serious hindrance to his progress. *Those shoulders nearly killed your mother*, his dad had been fond of saying.

156

Yeah, he thought as the grainy walls bit and snagged at the fabric of his shirt, *now they can finish the job with me.*

A couple more feet...

Sam halted, reached forward and ran his fingers over the smooth, blue poncho, perhaps to verify its existence. Charly couldn't be far ahead.

Purposefully now, Sam wormed forward. A tightening in the tunnel impeded him a moment, a ringed ridge that made him angle his shoulders diagonally, strain ahead with bared teeth...

There. His lower body slipped through easily, but he saw ahead that worse was still to come. He shifted his shoulders again, leading with his left arm and keeping his right arm tucked at his side like some kind of subterranean Superman.

The flashlight was in his lead hand. He took a moment to pause, arrow the light at the tunnel ahead.

"Oh hell yes," he muttered.

The opening was less than ten feet away.

Still squeezing forward in that awkward, shoulder-wrenching manner, he made it to the end, felt the cool tang of the water spray slicking his upper lip. He licked the moisture off, closed his eyes at the way it soothed his dry throat. The water down there sounded wild but it also tasted chilly and pure, and he elbowed toward the opening excitedly now, not only to catch up to Charly but to plunge his face into the spring and drink deeply.

Sam got his head through. One shoulder. The other. Before he went farther, he gripped the slick rim of the tunnel and pointed the Maglite downward.

Just in time to see the creature seize Charly's prone body by the hair.

Chapter Two

"*No!*" Sam shouted. Without thinking, he splayed his arms, grasped both sides of the opening, and heaved forward. He saw it all in the moment before he fell twelve feet to the ground.

The cavern, about twenty feet high and about twice that wide. The river bisecting it, which he suspected was ordinarily narrow and placid, because of the storms now having breached its banks a swirling maelstrom.

And just what the hell *was* that creature? He'd gotten a glimpse of the hideous thing when the Maglite strafed it, and what he'd seen had jived with Charly's account down to the last detail.

He plummeted from the tube and was able to tuck his head enough so that when his shoulders and back struck the rock floor, his body went immediately into a kind of roll. It wasn't perfect, and he'd be sore for days—if he lived that long, of course—but he thought he'd escaped major injury.

Sam completed his roll and found himself five feet from Charly and the beast. The emaciated white creature had dragged Charly to the edge of the river, just before a bend where the turbid water spumed and frothed.

The creature bent. Sam imagined it diving into the water, its subdued quarry trailing after it like a kind of streamer, disappearing into the whitewater and lowering until it reached some hidden lair, a spot where it could dine on Charly at its leisure.

Sam dropped the Maglite and dove for Charly's ankles. Grasping them, he dug his heels into the slippery rock as well as he could and hauled Charly back toward the wall. The creature uttered a raspy cry of dismay. In the faint glow cast by the downed Maglite, he saw a monstrous, almost-hairless head whirl and snarl at him. Rather than playing tug-of-war for her, the creature lashed out at him, clouted the side of his head. Sam didn't mean to let go of Charly, but he must have because he collapsed against the wall. It gave the base of his skull an awful knock. The creature pivoted as if it were finished with him and again prepared to enter the river. Sam pushed to his feet, the cavern listing deliriously, and extended his arms toward the pair on the bank.

Sam launched himself at the creature, but it was too late.

The creature rose into the air, Charly's body rising with it. Sam struck the ground, but he could not take his eyes off the two bodies, which rose and rose, halfway across the river now, descending, the white feet landing deftly on the other side, Charly's body thudding dully beside the creature.

"*Let her go!*" Sam shouted.

Though the stygian darkness engulfing most of the cavern precluded a clear view, Sam thought he made out an arched opening a few feet beyond the creature. It dragged Charly in that direction.

If it gets her in there, she's gone. You know that, right?

Sam shoved to his knees, glanced impotently about for something to hurl at the receding white figure. He could dive into the water, but the current would propel him right past Charly.

You're running out of time.

I know that!

Then do *something.*

Sam scrabbled forward to the river where his fingers closed on a good-sized rock. He couldn't hurt the son of a bitch, but maybe he could piss it off enough to draw it into a fight. After that, who knew what he'd do, but there wasn't time to think beyond the next step. He cocked his arm, sighting the base of the creature's skull.

White light swam over the creature. It spun and let loose with a spine-tingling growl.

Sam whirled, thinking he'd somehow toed the Maglite into just the right position; then the cavern was aglare with the strobe of gunfire, the concussions impossibly loud in the enclosed space. Clapping his hands over his ears, Sam peered up and saw Larry Robertson leaning clumsily out of the tunnel and firing his Sig Sauer at the creature. The sheriff seemed to defy gravity; one hand held the pistol, the other aimed the flashlight. *There's no way he'll hit it*, was Sam's first thought, but it evaporated when a howl of pain escaped the snarling lips, the creature dropping Charly and striding toward the river. Sam thought, *Yes. Get angry. Get back over here so we can give Charly a chance.*

A bullet opened the creature's right shoulder, the blood spluttering up in a black fountain. Another shot punched a hole in the thing's throat. Evidently convinced it stood no chance against the Sig Sauer—which had to be nearly empty—it spun with a frustrated growl and reached down for Charly's hair again.

A shot exploded, and all but one of the creature's fingers disappeared.

Squalling, the thing clutched the jetting stump of its hand and gaped at it with bared teeth. Then its eyes shifted to Robertson and narrowed to hateful slits.

Sam turned and peered up at the sheriff. Behind the pointed flashlight beam, Robertson's face had gone slack with terror, the expression of a man who realizes he's just pushed a superior fighter too far and is about to suffer the consequences.

"Fuck a duck," Robertson said.

"Fall," Sam said.

"Huh?" Robertson stared down at him like he was crazy.

"That thing's going to—"

But he never finished because he saw in Robertson's dumbstruck expression it was coming.

Robertson glanced behind him, and Sam realized how the sheriff had been able to hang in the opening that way. Eric Florence had ahold of his legs. "Push me out," Robertson said.

A muffled response.

Sam whirled in time to see the creature crouch down for its leap back across the water.

Robertson saw it too. "*Now*, goddammit! Push me *out!*"

Then the sheriff's plump body squeezed forward like a turd from an asshole, his eyes never leaving the creature. Sam heard but did not see it spring. Robertson's hips cleared the opening, his thighs. He fell, and Sam cursed himself for not relieving the man of his flashlight and gun, which were both skittering through the air too. Sam hustled toward Robertson's falling body to catch him. The gun and flashlight smacked the scummy floor with wet, cracking noises. Robertson landed nose-first, his lower body swinging down in an ungraceful swoop. The sheriff hardly made a sound, which Sam took as a very bad sign. The flashlight flickered but stayed on.

Ten feet away from Robertson, Sam suffered an endless moment of indecision. Fetch one of the flashlights so he could see his adversary better? Make a grab for the gun? He knew the general area of where it fell, but beyond that it was guesswork.

Sam went for the gun.

Something behind him whistled through the air. Sam hit the ground on his knees and swept his fingers over the gritty wet floor to locate the gun.

The creature landed.

An unwholesome glow backlighted the creature as it straightened and stalked toward Robertson. For the moment, it had decided to ignore Sam.

Keep ignoring me, he thought. *Ignore me long enough to let me find this goddamn gun.*

Robertson lay immobile—was he paralyzed or simply stunned from the fall?—and didn't look up as the creature towered over him, reached down with a clawed hand.

Sam turned back to the ground and thrust his hands every which way. *Where was the gun?* If he could retrieve it, and if there were bullets left—

"Where did Charly go?" a voice from above asked.

Sam shot a glance up and saw Eric Florence gaping down at them, an expression of comical disbelief stretching his eyes. Unhesitatingly, the creature reached up and seized Florence by the front of the shirt. Bellowing, Florence tumbled forward. Rather than slamming him on the ground and breaking his back, the creature actually prevented Florence from landing, holding him aloft the entire way. Sam knew he should be searching for the gun, but there was something spellbinding about the scene before him, the creature drawing Florence slowly closer, the coach's legs dangling several feet off the ground. The creature sneered at Florence, their noses only inches apart. Florence batted at its face, flailed his limbs, but it drew him closer, closer.

Unconsciously, Sam's hands had commenced their search, tapping the floor in nerveless circles.

Sam froze. His fingers had touched steel.

The creature brought its face closer to Eric Florence's, and for one wild moment, Sam was sure it would kiss him.

Then its mangled hand came up and the one remaining finger dug a trench down the side of Florence's face, the skin of his cheek gathering in a pinkish, bloody curl. Florence howled and drummed his feet against the creature.

A quick, meaty sound arrested the creature's movements. It shot a glance down.

Though it was dark, Sam could see very well the antler-handled buck knife embedded in the creature's ankle. Robertson had shoved it in to the hilt, the tip of the blade tenting the skin on the other side of the creature's ankle but not quite puncturing it.

The beast dropped Eric Florence, who landed in an ungainly heap a couple feet from where Larry Robertson lay. Either Robertson was paralyzed from the waist down or injured so badly he couldn't do anything but stab that pallid ankle and wait for the thing's retribution.

Sam brought up the pistol. Fired.

The creature's left nipple became a messy divot, the torso snapping sideways. It came right back toward Larry Robertson, who was awaiting his end with quiet dignity. The creature hunkered down over the sheriff's body.

Sam squeezed the trigger again, but this time there was a click that made his balls shrink.

Methodically, almost lovingly, the creature hooked an index finger into the meat of Robertson's left shoulder and tore a steady line down his back, opening fabric and flesh, the ripping sound turning Sam's stomach and making his gorge rise into his mouth.

Sam took a step forward, but he knew it was already too late. Robertson's eyes were darting behind him in terror, his arms thrashing around trying to disengage the creature sitting on him. Like a diner savoring a particularly well-prepared cut of steak, the creature set to work, this time spreading the torn fabric of Robertson's blue shirt and exposing the glistening incision it had made.

Sam took another step toward them. "Don't—" he started to say, but the rest of it cut off in a choking gasp. With that same hideously thoughtful expression on its face, the creature sank a hand into the gash, just inside Robertson's shoulder blade, and seemed to probe the body within for some hidden treasure. The sheriff bucked with convulsions, weird, gurgling rattles issuing from his lips, which were now spewing gouts of blood.

Sam closed the distance to the creature—who was now fishing something maroon out of Robertson's gore-streaked back—bent and grasped the buck knife. The creature froze, shot a withering look back at Sam.

Sam yanked on the knife. It came free of the creature's ankle with a slurping sound that would have made him gag if he weren't so damned scared.

Sam rose, the buck knife dripping at his side.

The creature rose too, and as it did its wormy arm pulled free of Robertson's back with a protracted sucking sound. Sam glanced at the creature's freakish hand and saw why. It clutched Robertson's heart.

It grinned, brought the heart to its fanged maw, and began to chew.

A voice above them said, "Um, what the hell is that thing doing?"

The creature glanced up in surprise, but Sam didn't need to see Melanie Macomber up there, gaping at the gruesome scene like she had a box seat at an underground Grand Guignol.

Sam rushed toward the beast, pumped the knife into its belly.

The body doubled onto him, the hand that clutched Robertson's heart smashing into his shoulder. The other arm, the one missing fingers, cracked Sam a glancing blow on the side of the head.

Sam knew this was it. If he failed to drop the creature now, they were all as dead as Larry Robertson. He muscled the buck knife deeper, twisted, jerked across his body as hard as he could. The creature squalled, its belly opening in a noxious black flood. Sam got both hands on the slick handle, ripped down. Now the flap of the creature's skin yawned very wide, something that felt like the thing's intestines spilling over Sam's wrists and forearms. It reminded him disgustingly of the time he'd helped deliver a newborn lamb, the afterbirth feeling very much like this. Hot and slimy and broadcasting a coppery stench.

Talons pawed at his neck, and before the thing could rip his head off, Sam wrenched out the knife, raised it and hammered at the creature's chest. The talons dropped away from his neck, batted at the knife. The quivering fingers closed over the blade, so Sam jerked it away, watched in grim satisfaction as another walking-stick finger was severed cleanly at the knuckle. In a frenzy now, he hacked at the creature's abdomen, and when it doubled over again, he set to shanking it in the side like an inmate gone berserk. Five times, ten, the black substance pouring from everywhere. Dimly, he heard someone screaming, assumed it was Eric Florence, then realized it was himself. The creature was leaning now, its struggles lessening.

Sam moved with it, glad of the newfound access to its throat, and shook the buck knife loose. The creature snapped at Sam's face, but it was a half-hearted lunge, like it already knew what the outcome of this struggle would be. Grimly, he raised the knife and slashed the creature just below the chin. It opened its lips as if to wail, but the only sound that escaped was a deep gurgling. The slit ranged from one side of its underjaw to the other, and to help it along, Sam reached up with his free hand, grasped the pulsing flap of skin, and yanked down. The slit became a clownish black grin, the thing's lifeblood spurting like a rancid waterfall. Sam was drenched with the ichorous fluid, but he hardly noticed. He released the flap of skin, grasped the knife with palsied hands and slammed it into the side of the creature's head. Whatever sentience had still been present in the dying creature winked out, the spidery body flopping on the floor and convulsing in a messy whir of limbs. Sam stepped over and kicked the thrashing head for good measure. When the convulsions slackened, he stepped on the hateful face, got as good a hold on the antler handle as he could, and reared back. The knife made a sound like a zipper being jerked rapidly up. He straightened and wiped the blade clean on the leg of his jeans.

Then he remembered the others.

Eric Florence hadn't moved, was now watching Sam with a species of something that might have been betrayal.

Melanie was watching Sam too. Her freckled cheeks were absolutely motionless in the tunnel exit. She still looked cute if a little simple that way, but he knew he had to snap her out of her fugue if they were gonna get Charly.

"Can you turn around enough to slide down feet first?" he asked her.

She frowned at him. He assumed she didn't hear him—the rush of the river behind him was loud enough to produce a good-sized headache, and Sam was developing a whopper of one himself—but then he realized it wasn't a lack of hearing him that had induced her expression, but rather an unformed suspicion. She was scared of him now, even if she didn't realize it herself. He imagined what a figure he must cut down here in the scarce light filtering from the flashlight beams. Bedraggled beyond description, probably bleeding himself, the creature's obsidian fluid befouling him and making him look like some medieval convict swabbed in pitch.

"Melanie," he said, "I need you to listen to me."

"Uh-uh," she answered. "I'm not listening to anything you say. I'll only come if Eric tells me too. Otherwise, I'm going back up."

Sam kept his voice level. "You won't make it."

She nodded at the corpse of the creature. "That thing is dead."

"You see a baby?" he asked as patiently as he could. "This...thing isn't the one that's got the child."

She began to shake her head.

"Which means," Sam went on, "that there's at least one more of these creatures running around down here. My guess is that there's a whole *lot* of them running around down here. You really want to be alone when you run into one of them?"

Sam avoided referencing Larry Robertson, but when Melanie's eyes flitted to the sheriff's facedown corpse, he realized he didn't need to. He was thankful she didn't have a flashlight of her own because he certainly had no desire to see the sheriff's exposed spine and half-eaten entrails again. Not in this lifetime.

When Melanie still hesitated, Sam glanced at Eric Florence. "You tell her."

"Tell her what?"

"To get her ass down here before one of those things bites it off."

Heat flared in Florence's eyes. "What if I don't want to?"

Jesus, Sam thought. After all the crap that had just gone down, here was the big bad basketball coach still trying to prove whose dick was bigger.

Sam heaved a sigh. "You two do what you want." He made his way to the water's edge.

"Where're you going?" Florence demanded.

Without looking back, Sam said, "We've got to cross. Charly's over there."

Chapter Three

Greeley didn't come unhinged until his roasted forearm began to ooze. He moved along in an awkward shamble. Because of Greeley and Ruth, whom they practically had to drag through the tunnel, they were making poor time.

"*Awww, man,*" Greeley whimpered, tilting his head to examine the juicy wound. "This is a serious burn. I need medical attention."

"Keep moving," Colleen said.

Jesse paused and waited for Greeley to continue on. The man had refused to be last in their procession, so Jesse got the dubious honor.

Greeley thrust his jaw at Red Elk. "Before we go any farther I want to know why we're putting such blind faith in this moron."

Debbie's voice was mild. "This moron saved your life."

Greeley held up his blistered forearm. "You call this saved? Blowing up the damn house? Endangering our lives?"

"The Children endangered you a lot more," Red Elk said without turning.

"I'd gotten along just fine without your help, hadn't I?"

Emma whirled, her eyes narrowed in contempt. "You're a fool, you know that? The only reason you're alive is because everyone else acted with more integrity than you. Jesse here, Colleen, Clevenger…"

Jesse's cheeks burned with pride, but he kept a neutral expression. Let the others rip the man a new asshole. Jesse was more than content to watch it unfold. He only wished he had some popcorn.

"But they ran away too," Greeley protested.

"Of course they did," Emma said, "but not until after they got us out of that RV. Or don't you recall cowering inside the closet?"

"I'm a naturalist," Greeley complained, "not some ridiculous Indiana Jones—"

"Naturalist," Red Elk said, chuckling. "That's what a guy calls himself when he wants women to think he's earthy."

"You don't know anything about me."

"There's nothing to know," Red Elk said. "You're about as interesting as one of those rocks over there."

Emma moved closer to Greeley. "Why don't you tell the others about Austin?"

Greeley made to move past. "Let's drop it."

Emma turned to Debbie and Red Elk, who were in the lead but had paused to watch the fireworks. "There was a frat guy named

Austin. We met him last night. I thought he was cute, but I figured he was immature. This jerk," she said, hooking a thumb at Greeley, "seemed like the more interesting of the two."

"Can we please move on?" Greeley asked. "They might be right on our heels."

"And you," she said, whirling and slapping Greeley on the chest, "are the one I kissed today." She slapped him again, on the shoulder this time, and he backed away. "I should have my—" Another slap. "—head examined."

Debbie gave her a wan smile. "We've all had sex with losers, honey. Don't sweat it."

"All I did was kiss him, but even that was a mistake."

Jesse repressed an urge to cartwheel around down the passageway.

Red Elk turned to Greeley. "Sounds like you blew your chance, buddy. Crying shame. I lost out on a piece of ass that nice, it'd haunt me the rest of my life."

Clevenger gestured impatiently with the flashlight, its flicker darting along the ceiling in evanescent stripes. "Can we please move? We need to put distance between us and them."

A calculating look had come into Greeley's eyes. He said to Emma, "You're so good at character assassination, why don't you ask yourself why Frank here didn't do something to prevent this horror from taking place."

Debbie said, "Like anyone would've believed him."

"We'll never know, will we? After all, your preparations were limited to saving your own hide."

"Saved your hide too," Colleen said.

"Fess up, Frank," Greeley said. "Why stockpile the weapons, all these provisions, and wire your house to explode when there was no threat?"

A change was coming over Red Elk's face. "I never said that."

"Exactly," Greeley said, striding toward him. "You never said *anything*. And because you kept mum, hundreds of people are dead, some of us are badly injured and our whole party is stranded down here."

"I told you, we just follow this tunnel—"

"I know you told us that, but so far all we've seen to corroborate your theory is a lightless dungeon. What happens if you're wrong?"

"You're a real dick," Jesse said.

Greeley spun on him. "Don't you want to know? This...*individual* constructs a bomb shelter, seals off one tunnel, and claims to have opened another—"

"It's not a claim," Red Elk said. "I've walked it."

Greeley's voice rose. "Then you *knew* about them." He stormed toward Red Elk, who didn't flinch. "If you were so sure about those things, why didn't you warn anybody?"

"I wasn't sure," Red Elk said.

The two men, nose-to-nose, stared at one another in the near darkness, Greeley's handsome face gone ugly with panic and rage, Red Elk's ageless features tinged with what might have been bitterness.

Greeley flourished his wounded arm toward the others. "Then tell us why you guarded your secret from everyone else." He glanced at Emma. "You were at his house earlier today, correct? Wouldn't it have been nice for Frank to say, 'Hey, you might want to be careful out there. There's a slight possibility of monsters eviscerating everyone in the campground'."

Clevenger was studying Red Elk closely. "Why didn't you warn anyone?"

Red Elk returned the professor's gaze. "I'll tell you everything I know, but only if we keep moving. It'll all be pointless if we die down here."

"Sounds good to me," Jesse said and cast a glance behind him.

"Agreed," Clevenger said.

As the train of survivors reformed itself in the narrow tunnel, Frank Red Elk began to talk.

After Sam, Florence, and Melanie finally got across the water, a frightened voice cried out, "Is that thing still here?"

Sam whipped the Maglite around and was shocked to see Charly sitting bolt upright on the moist floor.

Florence shouted something, but Sam paid him no mind, was too immersed in sprinting toward Charly. God, he was glad to see her eyes open again, even if they were wide with terror.

"Sam?" she whispered, getting to her knees. "Is that you, Sam?"

He flicked the beam to the side when he realized he'd been blinding her. Then he was kneeling next to her and supporting her with both arms.

Charly's forehead pinched. "Is it still—"

"It's dead, Charly. It can't hurt you now."

She studied his face, the fearful doubt lingering. "Are you sure?"

"I'll take over from here." Florence bent and made to get between them.

"Get your hands off me," Charly hissed.

Florence's chin jutted, his eyes dangerously serene. "I'll put my hands where I want to, Charly. You're my wife, remember?"

Charly glared at him defiantly.

"Now," he said, insinuating himself between Sam and Charly. "I'm going to take care of you because I took a vow to do that."

And then Charly did something that made Sam damn near faint.

That same stubborn gleam smoldering in her blue eyes, she shoved her husband's reaching hands away, leaned toward Sam, grasped his face with both hands, and planted a lingering kiss on his mouth.

Though it only lasted a few seconds, while their mouths were pressed together Charly had time to taste the salt on Sam's lips from all the sweating he'd done. She imagined her lips tasted much the same way and hoped her breath didn't stink.

Reluctantly, she drew away.

When she opened her eyes again, she saw that Sam was watching her with naked longing. She knew she should feel bad for what she'd just done, but she understood already that the mistake would have been to not kiss him, to not make clear how real her feelings were. She hoped desperately he understood it had not been a lark or some juvenile ploy she'd used to make Eric jealous. She tried to communicate all this with her eyes, to put to use whatever telepathy existed between them. She saw something flicker in Sam's face. Understanding? Hopefulness? Whatever it was, it edified her, made her feel they weren't fooling themselves down here. They'd find Jake, they'd save him and when they got back to the surface, things would be different. She'd take that dreary cast out of Sam's handsome face and replace it with the liveliness she sometimes glimpsed when he looked at her.

When she turned to Eric, her first thought was, *He's going to kill me.* The words flashed in her mind without any fanfare or melodrama. She'd never seen such raw hatred before, and it was all directed at her. Eric's face was a floating white moon in the cave shadows, his glittering eyes soulless and glassy, the eyes of a discarded stuffed animal. His breath came in slow and audible tides, something primal and portentous about the sound. He was about to come unhinged, she realized, if he wasn't there already. Charly could feel Melanie watching them with apprehension.

Want him? Charly thought without turning. *Take the jerk.*

Eric lunged at Sam.

At first Charly was sure he would try to throttle Sam until his eyes popped out, but rather than going for his throat, Eric grabbed for something at Sam's side.

The buck knife.

Charly scooted involuntarily away, then felt craven for doing so. Sam and Eric grappled for the knife, but Sam, she realized with endless relief, had things under control.

Sam cuffed Eric in the back of the head. Eric tumbled forward and landed on his elbows. He went for the knife again, but this time, Sam shifted the antler handle so it jutted out a good inch from the heel of his hand and popped Eric on the crown. This time Eric went down hard, a white-knuckled hand squeezing the bump that had almost certainly begun to rise.

"Now, I didn't want to do that," Sam said evenly enough. His smile held the slightest bit of warning. "You got your licks in on the lawn, and I returned the favor a little while ago. So why don't we call it a draw and simmer down, all right?"

Melanie was squatting next to Eric, a hand between his hitching shoulder blades. Eric slid a wrist over his mouth, examined it, then spat on the ground beside him. He got to his feet a little drunkenly and regarded Sam with glittering eyes.

"Your boy's still down here somewhere," Sam said. "We ready to move on?"

"You think you're smart," Eric said.

"I don't think anything."

"You kiss my wife in front of me, think I'm gonna let it go?"

"I kissed him," Charly said.

"Shut up," Eric muttered.

"All right," Sam said. "You don't like me, and you're madder'n a hornet that Charly kissed another man. It's your right to feel that way. But this isn't about you—it's about your child. Now let's go get him."

"He's right," Charly said.

Eric favored her with a look so black it sent chills rippling down her spine. Turning, Eric eyed the buck knife.

"Careful," Sam said, the warning smile returning.

Uneasily, they advanced into the corridor.

Chapter Four

"There are many legends about this land," Red Elk said. He nodded at Greeley. "Professor Nutless here could no doubt recite a few of them himself."

Greeley's smug grin faded.

"Most of them," Red Elk went on, "are too far-fetched to be taken seriously."

Clevenger said, "My concept of far-fetched has altered dramatically in the past couple hours."

"Mine too," Red Elk agreed. "I'd like to say I believed what I heard about the Children, that when my father told me the tale one night before bed, I swallowed it hook, line and sinker. But I didn't."

"But the propane," Greeley said, "the flashlights—"

"Dad's idea," Red Elk said. "He was more imaginative than I am. He was a real dreamer. Course, he dreamed the cigarettes wouldn't give him lung cancer, but there he was on life support at the ripe old age of fifty-one."

Red Elk shook his head. "I didn't believe in the Children any more than I believed in Santa Claus, but Dad did, and I felt like if I sold the house, it'd be like him dying a second time. So, I refreshed the food stores every now and then, checked the guns to make sure they still fired—"

"You checked them recently?" Colleen asked.

"How recent's recent?" Red Elk said. He shook his head. "I can't provide any guarantees."

"You spoke of legends," Clevenger prompted.

"The Children were one, of course. They were tied up with the Wendigo—"

"Wendigo?" Jesse asked.

"A common myth amongst North American tribes," Greeley said, his tone suddenly pedantic. Very much how he sounded in front of his students, Jesse assumed. "The gist of the legend holds that the creature—fire-footed and winged in Canada; a furry biped in the American Northwest—can transform a human being into a cannibal with a single touch. Pioneers convicted of cannibalism were said to have been gripped by the Wendigo Psychosis."

"What he says is true enough," Red Elk murmured. "To me it always sounded like a way of justifying what needed no justification. I mean, if you were gonna starve, wouldn't you eat your buddy?"

Jesse made a mental note to give Red Elk a wide berth if the provisions ran out.

"At any rate, what always sounded like hokum to me was the notion of a giant beast that could make normal people into monsters just by touching them."

Emma turned to Jesse, her brown eyes huge with dread. He thought of the monolithic figure they had seen striding through the rain. He tried to reassure her with a smile, but she only wandered on, her eyes fixed in that doomed, starey look.

"Did your grandpa dig this tunnel?" Colleen asked.

Red Elk chuckled. "You kiddin'? The cave was here already. He just connected it to the crawlspace."

"How did he know the caves were here?"

Red Elk slowed, his breathing heavy in the broadening cavern. It was now possible to walk in pairs, which they'd formed unthinkingly: Jesse beside Emma, ahead of them Greeley and Ruth, then Colleen and Debbie. Red Elk and Clevenger were in the lead. The green knapsack hung low on the professor's thin shoulders even after Red Elk had removed the Ruger ammunition and pocketed it. Jesse adjusted the red gym bag slung over his own shoulders and wished Red Elk had relieved him of the dynamite. It would be just Jesse's luck to survive the massacre at the campground only to be blown up down here because of an errant spark.

Red Elk nodded bleakly at Colleen. "If I do have a regret, it's not believing what my dad said about the caves. Or the creatures that dwelt inside them. I guess my grandpa scoffed at the notion too until he saw his own dad—my great-grandfather—murdered by one of those sons of bitches."

Red Elk was silent a minute, the chuff of their breathing and the sandy rasping of their shoes the only sounds in the tunnel. Jesse was grateful for the mining helmet, but he didn't care for the way the light beaming out of it bobbed and twisted on the scaly walls. Didn't care for it at all.

"You gonna tell us the story," Colleen asked, "or do we have to imagine it for ourselves?"

Red Elk eyed Colleen in the near-darkness. "You got a mouth on you, don't you?"

Colleen beamed at him.

"I like it," Red Elk said. Debbie gave Colleen a cool look. If Red Elk noticed that, he didn't say. "My grandpa worked on a farm above the bluffs. The farmland stretches from there all the way to the new Indian Trails Subdivision, but that's neither here nor there. What does matter is that he and his dad were working the field one day when they came to a good-sized rock.

"If it wasn't a boulder, it was in the same league." Red Elk shook his head. "Had no business trying to move the damned thing—the farmer my relatives worked for should've done the job himself or at least provided enough men to make the work bearable—but that didn't deter my great-grandpa. He told my grandfather, who was just a kid at the time, 'They don't pay us to just till the good ground.' So they chained the big rock and looped the other end of the chain over the furrow. The ox they were using strained and snorted and had gotten the big rock halfway up when my great-grandpa decided he'd help matters along by getting down in the depression the rock had made to tip it over."

Red Elk hocked, spat on the wall. "Well, my great-grandaddy never considered that rock might've been placed there on purpose."

"Like a cap?" Emma asked.

Red Elk nodded. "Bottled up what was under there. And what was under there was a big hole. My grandpa said his dad was there one instant and was gone the next, and the ox, maybe hearing something it didn't like, or maybe even *scenting* something, went wild and began bucking against the yoke. The next thing my grandpa knew, the chain slipped off the furrow. The ox took off, and the big rock thumped down, trapping his daddy inside the hole."

"Buried," Jesse said.

"Buried is right. My grandpa was young, probably only nine or ten, but he was savvy. He stood there gaping a few seconds before realizing that without the ox he didn't have a hope in hell of getting his daddy out of that hole. So he bolted after the dumb animal, which wasn't moving too fast anyway, old and encumbered as it was by that heavy plow, and before too long he caught up to it and led it back.

"Somehow he got the chains under the rock again. While he was doing this, he was shouting at the ground to see if he could hear his daddy under there. When he calmed down enough to listen, he found he could hear my great-grandpa, but the voice was muffled and difficult to make out.

"'You okay, Papa?' was what he kept callin'.

"'Move this goddamned rock!' was what his daddy kept replyin'."

Red Elk slowed, his flashlight doing slow sweeps over the floor. "Then my grandpa heard the other sounds."

A crawling dread began to ooze its way down Jesse's back, making him step closer to Emma, who didn't seem to notice.

"The noises sounded like nothing my grandpa'd ever heard before. But they scared him. His dad's voice changed too, a new kind of fright creeping into it. He was shouting for my grandpa to hurry, dammit, *hurry*, and my grandpa got up and began shoving the ox from behind to get it moving. When that didn't work, he started in beating on the old animal, punching its dusty hide and kicking its shanks to spur it into action. Well, that must've worked because the beast started grinding forward, and the rock began tilting up. My great-grandfather's hands shot out of that hole right away, and his voice, unleashed from that hellish cage, was womanish with fright. My grandpa wanted to give off pushing the animal, but he figured if he did that, the rock would smash down again and cut his daddy in half. So he kept at it, beating that old ox like a rug to get it to move.

"The rock had tilted just enough for my great-grandpa to wriggle his head and shoulders up onto the ground. He was howling with terror and what sounded to my grandpa like physical pain. My grandpa gave the animal one final kick and lurched over to where his dad was struggling his way out of the hole, and the odd thing was that the rock was more than high enough for my great-grandpa to slide through. In fact, the side of the rock had risen to an almost perpendicular angle with the ground. But despite this, my great-grandpa was still hanging on to the lip of the hole for dear life. And he was screaming louder than ever."

Red Elk sighed. "That gave my grandpa the idea that the sinkhole was much wider than he'd thought and that his daddy's feet were dangling over thin air. He grasped handfuls of his daddy's shirt and reared back as hard as he could, but that didn't help. His daddy was actually sliding back down toward the darkness."

"'Use your legs', my grandpa remembered saying.

"'*I can't feel my legs,*' was his daddy's response.

"My grandpa couldn't understand this, so he reached down to get a better hold on his daddy, but when his face got low enough, he saw something that changed his life. My life too, I guess you could say."

"One of them," Emma said.

Red Elk nodded. "One of the Children. Its green eyes blazed at my grandpa from the shadows of that hole. Its face was smeared with blood. It had hold of my great-grandpa's legs. It was chewing on one of his ankles.

"The ox must've been worn out, what with having lifted that huge rock twice and all the chasing and beating it'd been through. The weight of the rock dragged it back, the door to the hole closing and my grandpa about to be crushed under it. Grandpa was bent on not leaving his daddy though, so he held on as long as he could. Held on until the white monster in the hole dragged his father screaming into the darkness. Grandpa was just able to roll out of the way before the rock crashed down on him.

"No one believed his story, of course, and who could blame them? Little Indian boy talks about a monster eating his daddy? They hardly even investigated it.

"But my grandpa did. He explored the tunnels for years but never found his daddy. Never found the monster, either. Eventually, he decided to build the house we just blew up. Where one of the tunnels ended. That way he could stay close to the mystery and maybe get some revenge."

Chapter Five

After climbing up and down half a dozen steep slides, Sam suggested they rest for a little while in the small bowl of rock they now found themselves in. He posited the suggestion as a respite for all of them, but Charly heard the hoarseness in his voice, knew he was badly winded. Funnily enough, she found herself attracted to him for this minor deceit. Love was like that in the beginning, she knew. Everything filtered through a screen of endearment. Oh, she was sure he had his faults. Probably wore the same underwear on consecutive days and left his beer cans sitting on the table. He had something of the caveman about him and would need a little feminine civilizing. Yet the imperfections weren't glaring ones, like the ones Eric had.

Treating her like dirt, for example.

She watched Sam now in the glow of the small fire he'd made with Robertson's lighter and a few desiccated strips of driftwood he'd pocketed before they left the river below. The smoldering driftwood produced more smoke than anything, but strangely enough, she sort of enjoyed the greenish flare of ghostly light it put off, like they were witches around a cauldron. Staring into it, she was almost able to suppress the doomed anxiety that throbbed within her every time she thought of her baby.

Why are you sitting here? part of her demanded.

Because I'm exhausted. We all are.

No excuse.

We'll move soon, she thought. *The moment Sam catches his breath...*

She cast a glance that way and felt her anxiety fade. As Sam worked his house key over a milky chunk of quartz, grinding down the teeth until the metal was honed to a gleaming shard, she studied the overgrown hair on the back of his neck, wiry black curls with a few white strands salted in. His ears, too, were a trifle fuzzy. But far from turning her off, she banked these details away for later use. She could kid him about his ear hair, maybe suggest French braiding it. He'd laugh softly and ask her if she wanted to give him a pedicure too, and she'd say yeah, we can do it in the bedroom.

Then they'd go.

Sam understood when to laugh and when to be serious. Eric was serious all the time, especially when it came to Charly. Whenever Eric made a joke with her it was cutting. Thinking about it now, she couldn't remember the last time she'd kidded with him.

Melanie was watching Charly with sullen intensity.

Sam went on whetting the edge of the key. "Something on your mind, Miss Macomber?"

Eyes never leaving Charly, Melanie said, "You're disgusting."

Charly gazed back at her. "That's a little hypocritical, don't you think?"

"Nasty is what I'd call it," Sam said.

"Mel's right," Eric said. "I've pampered her too much. Doesn't have to work, doesn't have an ounce of stress." He chuckled darkly. "Unless you call spending my money stressful."

Charly fought off a surge of indignation. "I buy the kids' clothes, I shop for groceries..."

"You get your hair done for a hundred dollars—"

"Thirty-five plus tip."

"—and then you wear it in a ponytail anyways."

Sam said, "My wife paid fifty, and that was fifteen years ago."

Eric shot him a look. "No one gives a shit about your wife, Bledsoe."

"Speak for yourself," Charly said.

"You're so ungrateful," Melanie said, a bitter twist to her lips. "Flo provides you with a home, a beautiful family, all the things you need, and how do you repay him? By kissing another man. I've never seen..." Her lips became a white line, her pretty face pinching into something decidedly unattractive. "...*anything* like you. You treat Flo like some—"

"Do you have to call him that?" Charly asked.

"Excuse me?"

"Every time I hear 'Flo this' or 'Flo that' the hackles on the back of my neck stand up."

Melanie stared at her as though she'd lost her mind. "Everybody calls him Flo."

"I don't. Whenever I hear 'Flo' I think of that old TV show, what was it—"

"*Alice*," Sam said without looking up.

"*Alice*," Charly agreed. "You were too young for it, Melanie...actually, it was before my time too. I only watched it because my parents did. There was this big-haired waitress named Flo—"

"'Kiss my gritz'," Sam put in.

Charly laughed. "That's right, she'd get mad at her boss, Mel Sharpels, and end up telling him off."

Sam was laughing too. "'Stow it!'"

Charly leaned forward with her laughter. God, it felt good.

Eric had been watching the exchange sourly. "Aren't you two cute."

Charly turned, regarded him in the green light of the fire, which had already begun to gutter. "I forgot you were there, honey."

Eric's grin was ghastly. "Don't 'honey' me, you goddamned tramp."

Charly didn't flinch. "I wondered when you'd get to that."

"I'm sure you did," he agreed. "You know what kind of a slut you are."

Sam spoke mildly. "I'd bag that kind of talk if I were you."

"You don't have enough money to be me."

"Can't argue with that."

"Suck at building houses," Eric went on. "Can't make your payments on time. No wonder your kids want nothing to do with you."

"You son of a bitch," Charly said.

"Hit a nerve, did I?"

"You shouldn't talk about—"

"It's all right," Sam said.

"Sure it's all right," Eric agreed. "It's common knowledge what a deadbeat this guy is, isn't that right, Sammy?"

Sam smiled softly. "My dad used to call me that."

Eric went on, "I ran into someone at the lumber yard. I wanted to buy a swing set for the girls because I think it's important for a dad to be a part of his kids' lives."

Charly opened her mouth to say something, but the look on Sam's face stopped her. He was watching Eric with a kind of fierce vulnerability that was painful to behold.

Eric continued, "I spoke to this guy who worked there, and he told me how far in the hole Sammy here is with the lumber yard. This guy said that Sam used to drink himself senseless most nights and carry on with the girl who ran his office. Back when he could afford an office, anyway."

"These are lean times," Sam agreed.

"But back then things weren't so lean, were they, Sammy Boy? Both in the construction business and in the screwing department. Too bad your wife dropped in on you at the office one day when you had your receptionist bent over a desk."

"*Eric*," Charly said between clenched teeth.

"It's okay," Sam said. Looking Eric in the eye, he said, "I made the biggest mistake a man can make. Excepting murder and rape and that kind of stuff."

"You don't have to—" Charly began.

"We were married ten years when I cheated on my wife."

Charly's breathing slowed as she listened.

"I never had sex with anyone at the office, but I did cheat. Two different women, the first of them a one-time thing, the second went on a couple months."

"One of them your receptionist?" Eric asked.

"I wouldn't call her a receptionist," Sam said, "but yes, I did make the mistake of getting involved with an employee." He smiled crookedly. "Course, you wouldn't know anything about that, would you?"

Eric's smile evaporated.

"Then what happened?" Charly asked.

"Barbara found out from a friend, though it doesn't really matter how she found out. She confronted me and I confessed. She told the kids right away, and they stopped talking to me."

Charly heard the subtle break in his voice, asked, "How old were they?"

"Jenny was eleven, Daniel eight."

"Hurtful thing to do to your kids," Eric said.

"It was. I begged Barbara to forgive me, lived out of my truck a couple weeks. Eventually, she let me sleep at the house again, but the atmosphere there had soured. I was like a pet that nobody wanted around anymore. At some point, Barbara told me she'd give me another chance."

"What happened then?" Eric asked. "You go on a bender and bang some hooker?"

"When we'd begun to reconcile, she stayed out all night and showed up the next morning telling me she'd gotten her revenge."

"Screwed somebody else, huh?" Eric said, grinning. "Just like you."

"Just like me," Sam agreed. "The kids...I'd already lost them. So Barbara took them and moved to town. I was allowed to see them every other weekend, but after a while, we let that lapse. I wanted to stay in touch with the kids, but Barbara wanted a clean break, and I guess the kids did too. They no more wanted to be with me than they wanted to have earlier curfews." Sam smiled grimly. "Which they had at my place and was one of the many reasons they dreaded staying with me."

"You were trying to set a good example," Charly said.

"By atoning for the bad one I'd set when they were younger, sure. I guess it was too much, too late. Last time they stayed with me, Jenny was fourteen and Daniel was eleven. He told me he hated me. Jenny didn't state it in such explicit terms, but she didn't have to. I could see it every time she looked at me."

They were all quiet a moment.

Leaning back on his palms, Eric said, "Boo-hoo."

"Shut your mouth," Charly said.

Eric grinned at her. "Don't think I'm not storing all this away, sweetheart. You're gonna get what you've got coming pretty soon."

Sam's voice was no longer serene: "Lay a hand on her, and I'll rip off that little pecker of yours and clean your ears with it."

Charly favored her husband with an appraising look.

He turned to her. "What's on your mind?"

"An epiphany," she said. "I just now realized why you coach women's basketball instead of men's."

Eric grinned at the ceiling. "This oughtta be good."

"You can't intimidate men," she said. "You can't intimidate every woman either—that's why the first assistant you had quit—what was her name...Terri something..."

"I let Tanya Bogans go because she was a stupid dyke who didn't know shit about basketball."

"She was good enough for the previous coach."

"Maybe that's why they always had a losing record."

"Or maybe she refused to put up with your outmoded, patriarchal attitude."

"Outmoded what?"

"Giving all your assistants menial tasks, making them pick up your lunch."

"That's what assistants do, they assist."

"Then why do you have managers? You're telling me it takes someone like Melanie here to get an order right at a fast-food restaurant?"

"What the hell's your point?"

"My point is you enjoy it," Charly said. "You enjoy telling women what to do. Your tone is always dictatorial."

"Big word."

"It's how you treat your players, your assistants. And it's how you treat me and the girls."

"My players love me," Eric said. "So do Kate and Olivia."

"I'm surprised you know their names."

"Fuck you."

"They hardly know you. But maybe that's a good thing."

Eric shook his head, his expression marveling. "You're some piece of work, you know that, Char?"

Melanie had been watching all of this with an aura of growing asperity. Now, as they all turned to her, she inhaled deeply and with the attitude of one coming to a momentous decision, she stood, strode the three paces over to where Eric sat reclining on his hands, and put her mouth on his. As her hand settled on his chest and then began to massage, their kissing became more feverish, almost like a pair of animals rutting in the dirt. His fingers played over her chestnut hair, her bare shoulders. Charly watched in dim revulsion as one of his hands descended to her jutting rear end and massaged her. She moaned.

After what seemed like minutes, she broke the kiss, directed a triumphant glare at Charly and returned to where she'd been sitting.

"Well," Sam said, "aren't we just one happy family?"

Charly stared morosely at the fire, which had died to embers. She could no longer stomach the sight of her husband. Without thinking much about it, she scooted closer to Sam, who held the key nearer the guttering firelight and examined it.

Evidently satisfied, he got up and handed it to Melanie, who accepted it dourly.

"You use that if another of those things gets too close to you." He turned to Charly. "You've got my pocket knife. It's not a long blade, but it's sturdy. One of them comes for you, don't show it any mercy. Go for the balls."

Eric said, "I notice you kept the buck knife for yourself."

"I'm in the lead," Sam said evenly. "Something attacks us head on, it's got to get through me first."

"Who goes last?" Charly asked.

Sam nodded at Eric. "He does."

Eric laughed breathlessly. "Yeah? And what am I supposed to use to defend myself?"

"Try your breath," Sam said. "I can smell it from here."

Chapter Six

"How far is it to the end?" Greeley asked.

"Three miles," Red Elk answered.

"But it's just one tunnel, right?" Colleen said. "I mean, it's not like we're going to get lost in some subterranean labyrinth."

"Dad made it one tunnel," Red Elk agreed. "We'll have to climb quite a bit and worm our way through some tight places, but the tunnel should take us all the way there. There used to be several places where the passage forked or joined with others, but much of what he did in his spare time—other than get drunk in town—was to make sure those spots were sealed off."

Clevenger shot Red Elk a look. "Sealed off?"

Red Elk nodded. "Right up here, if I'm not mistaken, is the first fork in the road. Least it used to be. Dad stacked it so full of big rocks, it'd take those creatures a good while to open it up. That is, if they even know of its existence."

"You knew of it though," Greeley remarked. "I'm still amazed you never warned anybody."

"Knowing the stories is a far cry from believing them," Red Elk said distractedly. He'd trained his flashlight on the wall to their right, was painting the damp brown surface with slow swaths of honey-colored light. "I can just see myself talking to those jerkoffs from the state conservation board. 'Sure, I'll take your money, fellas, but before you build your state park, I think you should know that all those legends about the Wendigo, the Night Flyers—"

"Night Flyers?" Emma asked.

But Red Elk had stopped. "Well, hell's bells," he said in a soft voice.

All the yellow beams converged on a point about ten feet ahead of them, where the wall on their right disappeared.

And a huge hole began.

Greeley stared at Red Elk. "You said he blocked it off. Your dad blocked it off."

"He did," Red Elk said in the same soft voice.

Greeley nodded at the opening. "Then what the hell is that?"

"They must've unblocked it."

A gravid pause as they took it all in. "Oh Jesus," Greeley said.

"That means they could be anywhere, they could be—"

"Shut up," Colleen said.

"—ahead of us, behind us...if they know about this tunnel they could be laying in wait for us anywhere. Maybe they're leading us into a trap, letting us get this far—"

"*Shut your stupid mouth, Marc!*" Clevenger hissed. His head was tilted slightly, the man listening to something that Jesse now heard. Something that might have been the clicking of toenails on stone, the steam-shovel breathing of a predator barreling toward its prey. Sound down here was tricky, but to Jessie it seemed to be coming from all directions.

"Oh shit," Greeley whimpered, "oh shit."

Clevenger said to Red Elk, "Back to the house?"

Red Elk cocked an eyebrow. "What house?"

"We don't know that they followed us."

"They did."

Clevenger motioned down the long stone corridor ahead. "But if we go that way...you said it was three miles...we'll be so strung out..."

"And the opening," Colleen said. "For once, Greeley's right. They could be anywhere, just waiting for us."

"Going back to where we started is certain death," Red Elk said in a firm voice. "Ahead and here—" Nodding at the hole, "—could be either one."

"Pretty crappy choices," Colleen said.

"Frank's right," Debbie said.

Colleen said, "'Stand by Your Man', huh?"

Debbie ignored that. "That explosion took out a mess of them, sure. But how many did you say were chasing you?"

"Well over a hundred," Jesse said.

"You think all of them died in the blast?"

Clevenger said, "Of course it didn't kill all of them. But there would be wreckage to dig through, rocks to move..."

"Take them all of ten minutes," Red Elk said.

Clevenger expelled weary breath. Red Elk's flashlight slanted through the dust motes they'd kicked up, frontlighting the professor from below. It made skeletal hollows of his eyes, his mouth a ghastly cache of wrinkles. Before, he'd seemed so virile, a warrior poet. Now he looked like a haggard old man.

"Okay," Clevenger said. "We go on, but we should put one of the armed people in the rear just in case."

"Makes sense," Red Elk agreed.

The clattering intensified, and now there was no mistaking the growl and chuff of the creatures.

"Come on," Red Elk said and surged forward. Clevenger came next, followed by Debbie, Emma, Ruth and Greeley. Colleen dropped back next to Jesse. When they made it to the hole he shone his light inside. It was hard to tell because he refused to stop moving as he passed, but to him it appeared as though the tunnel in there quickly narrowed.

"Jesse," Colleen said from directly behind him.

He glanced at her but she had raised the revolver, gripping it with both hands, reminding him of a cop on a firing range. Only Colleen wasn't wearing earmuffs, and she sure as heck wouldn't be shooting at paper.

The guttural woof and staccato clatter doubled in volume, trebled. The creatures were coming from behind after all.

And he and Colleen were the only two back here to face them.

Jesse unshouldered the knapsack and reached inside for the cleaver. He opened his mouth to alert the others, but then he closed it, agonized with indecision. Should they give up the only thing they had going for them—a modicum of surprise—or should they attempt to martial all their forces to meet the creatures en masse?

How many? he wondered, straining to sort out the echoes floating toward them. Three? Ten?

Doesn't matter, a cynical voice declared. *One is enough. Or don't you remember the playground?*

His whole body shaking, Jesse kneeled beside Colleen and raised the cleaver.

"Won't do much good with that," she muttered.

"Wanna trade?" he asked.

Colleen shook her head. "You'd probably shoot me."

"Guys?" a voice called. Clevenger.

Jesse turned to shout a reply, but Colleen stilled him with a warning look.

Something clicked just ahead of them. Colleen swung her gun up and aimed.

Jesse thought he'd prepared himself sufficiently for an attack, but the sight of the creature loping toward them like some freakish white panther made every fiber of his being thrum with terror.

The creature halved the distance between them.

Jesse's muscles locked. He became aware of a high-pitched humming sound, and it wasn't until the creature tensed to leap that Jesse realized it was coming from his own throat.

Time slowed. The creature's mad, emerald eyes fixed on Colleen. She squeezed the trigger. Its head jerked as the pallid, wraithlike body left the ground. Colleen continued firing, tracking it as it rocketed higher, arcing toward them. In the strobing magnesium silverlight, Jesse saw bloody ponds open in its throat, its chest. Two more slugs punched through the papery flesh of its belly. Then it was plummeting toward them, a cascade of fat, ebony droplets spilling out of its body.

Jesse and Colleen leaped apart. The creature tumbled between them, somersaulted, then without a pause it dove for Colleen. Shrieking, she jumped backward and squeezed the trigger. Its head flicked back, but it kept coming, snarling and seizing her by the leg. It bared its scimitar teeth and dragged Colleen closer.

Colleen gave off firing and lunged away. She managed to get separation between her body and the creature's snapping teeth, but its pursuit was relentless. It hauled her back.

Jesse raised the cleaver.

The creature's white arm, like a bundle of thin cables, scraped along the gritty cave floor, compelling Colleen backward by her right ankle.

Jesse swallowed, measured the distance.

He swung the cleaver as hard as he could.

The blade sliced neatly through the beast's arm, just below the elbow.

The howl that exploded out of its mouth was nearly as startling as its attack had been. It bellowed at the ceiling, its whole body quaking in agony. The sinister features distended, the huge, jade eyes bulging. Jesse noted with revulsion the exposed cheekbone, the membranous flaps of an earlobe that had been torn in half by one of Colleen's slugs. It lowered its gaze to the jetting stump of its arm.

Then it turned to Jesse.

Its breathing slowed, the quaking lips curling up in anticipatory delight. Jesse was paralyzed. To his right, he heard the frenetic clatter of nails on stone and the industrial chuff of breathing—unmistakable harbingers of another attack. Grinning, the beast stepped toward him.

Gunshots erupted behind Jesse.

The creatures had ambushed the others.

Chapter Seven

Jesse couldn't swing the cleaver again, couldn't do anything. The creature seemed to whisper into his brain, hypnotizing him into submission. Its satanic eyes engulfed him, drowned him in their bloody depths.

Colleen placed the barrel of the revolver against its forehead.

Its face twitched in surprise.

She pulled the trigger.

A starburst of liquid exploded from the other side of its head, and for one terrible moment Jesse was certain the creature would keep coming. Its face loomed nearer, the discolored teeth somehow brilliant in the uneven glow of the mining helmet. It kept coming, the eyes sightless now, the noxious body tumbling onto Jesse. Gasping, he scrambled away.

More gunshots from behind. Screaming voices. A slew of capering shadows danced on the walls.

Greeley was the first to appear. Emma came next, dragging Ruth Cavanaugh along like a recalcitrant child. Debbie followed, Clevenger trundling after her and looking older than ever. Last came Red Elk, a fierce grin on his face.

"Didn't like that, did they?" he said.

"Won't stop them," Debbie said, and for the first time she seemed afraid.

Jesse could relate. The first close-up encounter with the creatures tended to do that to a person.

"What are we gonna do?" Greeley said in his newfound falsetto.

"We need to decide," Clevenger said. "Press forward or go back to the house."

"The lady or the tiger," Emma said.

"That's easy," Red Elk said. "I'd rather have the lady any day."

"Wait a minute," Clevenger broke in. "If we—"

"*Listen*," Colleen said.

Furtive sounds from ahead, slithery and dry.

As one, they began to back away.

More sounds, a whole chorus of rasping noises.

"Sounds like a lot of them," Jesse said.

They'd drawn even again with the gaping hole in the side of the corridor. They all stopped, and Clevenger shone his light inside. Wide at the beginning, it rapidly drew down to a narrow breadth. Jesse thought of a coffin, of being entombed forever.

"Oh hell no," Debbie said. "I ain't going in that *OHHHHH FUUUU—*" Her words devolved into an incoherent gibbering. They raised their flashlights in time to see the white taloned fingers clutching Debbie by the hair, hauling her toward the ceiling.

"*Dammit,*" Clevenger gasped. The creatures swarmed toward them from both sides. Red Elk dropped the gun to grab Debbie, who was half swallowed by the hole in the ceiling. Colleen whirled and blasted a creature in the face, its teeth shattering in a smoky black spray. Another pounced on Emma. Jesse brought the cleaver down without thinking and buried it in the middle of its steepled back. The heavy blade crunched through cartilage and vertebrae, the creature pawing at its back to disengage the cleaver. Jesse yanked the cleaver free with a pulpy rip and slammed it down again on the creature's skull. It slumped on Emma, its spidery body convulsing in a seizure.

He reached down, pried up one shoulder to help Emma get loose, and then his blood froze at the sound of someone in supreme terror.

Jesse whipped his head around and saw Clevenger being dragged to the ground by two creatures.

One of them had the professor by the head. Another prepared to snack on the white flesh of a thigh. Clevenger's intelligent face was slack with terror.

Debbie had all but disappeared, Red Elk still clinging doggedly to one sandaled foot and actually being lifted off the ground as she rose into the ceiling hole.

Behind them, Colleen was popping off rounds and shrieking for them to get inside, get inside. Whatever the hell that meant. *Inside the creatures' bellies?* he wondered.

"Come on," Emma said. He stared dumbly at her a moment, then let himself be pulled sideways. Then he understood.

The hole.

Greeley had already reached the spot where the corridor narrowed and was worming his way on stomach and elbows through the gritty, brown passage.

Of course, Jesse thought. *When faced with certain death, he's suddenly full of the pioneer spirit.*

Asshole.

Jesse flapped the flashlight at Clevenger. Illuminated, the pair of creatures glowered at Jesse, snarling, like they were annoyed their meal had been delayed.

Jesse took two unthinking strides and brought the cleaver down on the closest creature's forehead. It bellowed, its scream an earsplitting siren, and batted at the embedded cleaver. The other monster tensed to spring at Jesse. Whimpering, Jesse reared back on the handle to disengage the blade, but this time it was no use.

The creature sprang.

One moment Jesse was on his feet, struggling to extract the cleaver; the next he landed roughly on his side, the snarling creature taking him down. He thrust an arm between the creature's snapping jaws and his throat, but he knew he couldn't hold it off. The beast's fangs clipped Jesse's forearm, drawing blood. There was a flurry of movement behind him, then the creature's hideous face swung up, stared at something with sudden trepidation.

Jesse glanced that way in time to see Emma retrieve Red Elk's gun from the ground, whirl and aim it at the creature. The beast tossed a hand up as if to catch the bullet, but it blasted a hole through its palm and transformed one of the creature's eyes into a green and black soup.

Shrieking, it flopped off Jesse and convulsed on the cave floor.

Emma hauled the professor to his feet. Clevenger looked dazed but intact. Clutching him by the arm, Emma started forward toward the hole. Jesse paused to locate the others. Colleen had seen them, was hurrying in their direction. She'd left two white bodies in her wake.

Colleen seized Ruth, shoved her toward Jesse. "You go first—we'll put Zombie Girl between us."

Jesse threw a glance at Red Elk just as a shower of blood started to drizzle over his upturned face.

"*Debbieeee!*" he bellowed, but almost as if the unseen creature who'd gotten her had twisted a spigot higher, the blood began to splatter over Red Elk in steaming freshets.

"*You take Ruth,*" Colleen shouted at Jessie.

Colleen spun toward Red Elk, grasped him by the arm. "She's gone, dammit, now get moving before they get you too!"

Jesse climbed into the tunnel and dragged Ruth after him. The slimy feel of the tunnel rock seemed to shatter the veneer of shock that had encased the small woman. She looked up at Jesse and nodded. *Thank God*, he thought.

A volley of gunshots pounded the cave walls behind him, and he threw a glance back beyond Ruth's frizzy head to see if he could spot Colleen or Frank. For an awful moment, he was sure they'd been overcome by the creatures. Then Red Elk's blood-slicked face appeared and he started down the tunnel after them. Colleen climbed in last, revolver poised and ready to shoot any creature that tried to follow her.

She's an animal, Jesse thought. *Thank God she's on our side.*

Red Elk came to his senses, his will to live—or perhaps his loathing of the creatures—surmounting his grief over Debbie.

"Who's got my Ruger?"

Jesse peered over Ruth's white shoulder. "Here," he said and handed it to Ruth, who examined it a moment like it was an artifact from some long-ago culture. Then she passed it on to Red Elk.

They crawled forward for several minutes. The passage dwindled. Astoundingly, the creatures hadn't followed them in. Or if they had, they were doing a good job of keeping it secret.

A muffled voice sounded ahead of him. Jesse glanced up to hear it better, and when he did he caught sight of something he hadn't yet noticed, which went to show just how horrified he'd been when they'd gotten ambushed back there and poor Debbie was eaten alive.

Jesse aimed his light straight ahead.

Emma's skimpy jean shorts stared back at him.

That lowering feeling gripped his stomach, a sensation not unlike the onset of nausea.

Emma stopped moving and when Jesse halted behind her, his face was only inches from the soles of her sandals. An arm's length behind her smooth, round calves. Mere feet from her dusky, glimmering thighs. Jesse swallowed.

And stared at the underside of Emma's jean shorts.

She was half kneeling, half lying on the tunnel floor; the frayed denim spanning from her zipper to her rear end seemed to float like a navy blue island in a tan sea. On either side of the denim he could make out slender strips of underwear. Black ones that didn't entirely cover the flesh of her undercarriage.

His throat went bone-dry. The pale skin around the lacy underwear was smooth. He aimed the beam there and had time to wonder if Emma had the area waxed.

Not entirely, he saw. Within the diaphanous black netting, he glimpsed dark curls—

"*Wanna touch it?*" a voice behind him asked, and Jesse gasped in surprise.

Anger immediately flooded through him as he craned his neck and shined the helmet back at Ruth Cavanaugh.

"Excuse me?" he said.

"*Her pussy,*" Ruth said in a cackling crone's voice that scarcely resembled her normally diffident one. "I'm asking if you'd like to touch her *pussy.*"

"Why don't you—" Jesse gritted his teeth and threw a nervous glance at Emma. He fixed the light on Ruth's face. "Just shut up, all right?"

Ruth tilted her head in mockery. "Shut up, huh? Don't like me tattlin' on you? Afraid your pin-up girl's gonna know you jerk your little weed to her every—"

"*Hey.*"

"—night before you turn in?" Ruth's shrill voice swelled. "Pitiful little fantasies, Miss Emma sunbathin' on her belly and askin' you to rub some oil on her back."

"*Shut the hell up! What if she hears—*"

"Hears what? That you wanna peel back those black panties inch by inch and run your tongue up her buttcrack?"

Jesse kicked at her white moon of a face.

She recoiled, an infuriating brew of surprise and merriment in her eyes. "Now don't get your feelin's hurt. Ain't nuthin' wrong with giving your little carrot a tug now and then, 'specially when you ain't got a snowman's chance in hell of ever stickin' it inside the real thing!" Ruth cackled again, a throaty, wheezing sound that chilled his blood.

And now he noticed something peculiar. Ruth's hair, which before had been frizzy but cut fairly short, now seemed to cascade over her shoulders and continue down the middle of her back. Her face had also undergone some strange elongation, the chin more angular, tapering to a witch-like point. This, combined with the cracked voice, caused him to make an unconscious movement forward. He was practically lying on top of Emma's legs before he realized it. She shifted, and then her light was blaring at him.

"What's going on?" she asked.

He blinked, warded off the beam with a forearm. "I was just wondering why we stopped."

She seemed to relax slightly. "I don't know yet. Marc's saying something to Clevenger. Something about a cavern."

"Oh yeah?" he said, trying to look interested.

"You're sweating," she said.

He tried a laugh, but it came out an octave too high. "Aren't you?"

"I guess." Her eyes flicked down. "You're also on my legs."

"Oh, I'm—"

"I don't mind," she said. "It feels sort of nice."

Before he could respond, the others commenced crawling. Emma turned and followed them. He felt something tap the heel of one sneaker and directed the light at Ruth's ugly face.

"*Atta boy!*" she rasped. "*You might get to fuck something other than your hand yet!*"

Jesse turned away, disgusted. He was thankful for the darkness of the cave. It hid the plum-colored blush on his skin.

He crawled after Emma, but he hardly glanced at her crotch. Hardly at all.

Chapter Eight

Sam decided he'd just ask. He'd kept quiet about the monster that slaughtered Larry Robertson, assuming someone else would broach the subject. But Charly'd been too busy kissing him—not that he had any complaints on that account—to discuss nine-foot-tall creatures or what would happen if they encountered another one. Melanie was too busy taking up for Eric Florence to philosophize about the beast—girl had it bad for the coach, as hard as that was to believe. *Thinks she's in love with him*, Sam thought. And on top of that she had a mothering complex that made her bristle like a nursing porcupine every time Florence got mistreated, which admittedly had been often of late. Florence himself might've mentioned the white-skinned monster, but he seemed lost in his thoughts, which would've been fine by Sam if not for the odd expression Florence sometimes wore as he trudged along behind them. Like he was relishing some secret revenge fantasy in which Sam and Charly were the unfortunate stars. Sam glanced back and discovered Florence was wearing that grim smile now, likely imagining how it would feel to lock Sam's head in a table vise and crank. He suspected the gleaming-eyed, open-mouthed expression on Florence's face was very similar to the expression a suicide bomber wore right before he pulled the pin on the grenade inside his jockey shorts.

Sam said, "What do you all think that thing was?"

"Or more importantly," Charly said, "where did it come from?"

"That too."

Melanie's voice was sulky. "I can't believe you guys talked me into staying down here. We'd be back at the house by now, those FBI guys would be—"

"My dad had a saying," Sam interrupted. "Second-guessing is for fools."

Melanie crossed her arms. "Thanks a lot."

"That's why I'm here," Sam said agreeably. He stopped and regarded her in the gloom. "The main reason we kept going, if you'll recall, is the cry we heard. Had we gone back, we would've lost baby Jake's trail."

"You don't know that."

"I don't know anything, and neither do you. All I know is that we made the best choice we could with what we knew at the time."

"You don't know anything about leadership. We've got a finalist for the NCAA Coach of the Year, and you think you know more than he does."

"This isn't collegiate athletics," Charly said.

"No it isn't, it's your baby. And you trust this jerk to save him when he failed miserably in his only chance at being a father?"

"Ouch," Sam said.

"This isn't helping," Charly said, taking Sam's arm.

"And *you're* the one who put him in charge," Melanie spat. "Your *family's* at stake here, can't you see that? One of those things took Junior—"

"Jake," Charly corrected.

"—and you're ruining everything else. What'll the girls think when they find out you've been kissing this piece of crap?"

"Man," Sam said, chuckling, "she sure does get warmed up, doesn't she?"

"My *girls*," Charly said, her voice eerily serene, "are none of your business."

"Oh yeah?" Melanie said with a nasty little shimmy. "Maybe they *will* be my business before all this is over."

Charly slapped her.

It wasn't just the flat, meaty sound Charly's hand made when it cracked Melanie's cheek that made Sam and Florence both stare gape-mouthed in amazement, it was the force with which Charly delivered the blow. Melanie was fifteen years younger and a moment ago had seemed on the verge of making Charly cry. Now the younger woman was reeling toward the wall and holding her cheek like it was about to slide off her face.

"You can have Eric if you want him," Charly said. "I'm filing for divorce after we find my baby. And you'll never take my children from me." Turning to Florence, she said, "I want full custody."

Eric shrugged. "Whatever you say, Char."

Sam swept the beam closer to Florence's face, and what he saw there made his balls shrivel. The words had been spoken like a man with a superb marijuana buzz, the face both euphoric and slack. Yet there lurked something else in the man's features that made Sam uneasy. Florence's hair, unless it was some illusory trick, had thinned since earlier that day. His dark complexion seemed pasty now, his skin brushed with a queer translucence, only it wasn't just Florence's eyelids that showed blue runnels zigzagging beneath the epidermis, it was his whole face. Even more disturbingly—and this was enough to cause Sam to train his flashlight as far away from the coach as possible—the man's eyes had begun to look green. Not just the whites, but the whole damn *things*. Irises, pupils...very much like, Sam was loathe to admit, the monster with which he'd done battle back there. Was it possible, he wondered, for the thing's condition to communicate itself to one of them? And if it did, how did that bode for Sam, who might as well have taken a bath in the filthy creature's blood? The memory of the black liquid spewing over him like the world's least sanitary shower reminded him of his sodden clothes, the way his T-shirt clung wetly to his back. And the smell—ah, why the hell had he focused on that again?—made his gorge clench.

The odor of the creature's blood contained a sickening tinge of dog shit, but its dominant trait was something even less pleasant, something that took him back a dozen or so years to a hospital room at Shadeland Memorial. His mother had been prone to circulation problems, a product of her diabetes. Because of this, she'd had several blood clots in her legs and was on a destructive cycle of medications, most of which were meant to undo the side effects of the Coumadin she took to thin her blood. One nasty February had seen her admitted to the hospital with a deep vein thrombosis, a diagnosis that had chilled Sam even before he knew what the hell it was.

Evidently, the bored-looking doctor informed Sam and his father, Rita Bledsoe's femoral artery had been completely clogged for some time by a large clot. That she hadn't told anyone didn't surprise Sam; his mom would've been embarrassed to ask for a life preserver if she were drowning. Her diabetes and her silence had conspired to give the thrombosis free rein on her leg, and in the short interval between the faint tingling she detected and the soul-shattering pain that had sent her to the emergency room, her leg had begun to rot.

Internal necrosis, the doctor had told him and his dad.

Internal what? Sam had asked.

His dad put a hand on Sam's shoulder. *He's telling us your mother has gangrene.*

Gangrene, Sam repeated.

It was common in 'Nam, his dad said, and though his voice was even enough, Sam noticed how moist his eyes had gotten. *One of my buddies died from it after taking a bullet to the thigh.*

Which is our main problem, the doctor said, by way of steering them back to Rita Bledsoe. *The condition is quite advanced, and we're not sure if amputation is still an option.*

Wait a minute, Sam said.

I'm sorry, the doctor said, not sounding sorry at all. He stood, a short man with a wispy tumble of fine black hair. *We'll do what we can.*

Sam turned to his dad when the door closed. *What's he saying?*

His father looked at him square in the eyes, one large tear spilling down his grizzled cheek.

He's saying your momma's gonna die.

The next couple days, which proved to be all Rita had left because of the blood poisoning, had been a hazy, interminable hell. The stench hung over the room like a green miasma. Sam avoided looking at the leg whenever the nurses arrived to change the dressing, but one time he made the mistake of stealing a glance at it. This had been at the end, so he should have expected something bad, but the sight of his mom's rotting foot had still made him rise from his chair and exit the room with poorly concealed haste.

Now, looking at Eric Florence's altered skin, he remembered that awful rotting foot: the jaundiced toenails a yellowish brown, the little toe purpling like a ripened cherry. The next three toes, gone the same green as the helmet his dad brought back from the army. But worst of all was the big toe, the putrefying bag of tissue as black and bloated as an overripe banana.

And though Eric Florence's skin didn't resemble Rita Bledsoe's, the stench radiating from him did.

Can't you smell that? Sam wanted to ask Melanie Macomber. *Couldn't you taste that sour death smell when you kissed his cracked lips?*

He realized Eric Florence was watching him in the dark. Startled, Sam returned the man's gaze.

Florence opened his peeling, cracked lips and said, "She suffered a lot."

His throat as dry as parchment, Sam said, "I don't know who you're—"

"Mommy," Eric Florence said.

The hackles on the back of Sam's neck stood rigid. He grappled with the black tide of horror welling up in him, but the broadening grin—Jesus, the man's teeth had elongated and grown sharper, he was sure of it—threatened to undo him.

Take it easy, he tried to tell himself. *The man did some snooping around on you. He's already admitted as much, hasn't he? If he can go down to the lumber yard and find out about you cheating on your wife, who's to say he didn't learn how your mom died?*

That should have calmed him, but it didn't.

Why did he wait until the exact moment you were thinking of your mom's death to clobber you with it? How long has it been since you've thought of that putrescent big toe? A year? Longer?

And more importantly, how long ago did that creature infect the coach, if that indeed was what it had done?

Eric Florence was leering at him now, his curved teeth like a row of scythes eager for a bloody harvest.

"Sam?" a voice asked.

With a Herculean effort, he finally unlatched his gaze from the greenish orbs smoldering in the hollows of Eric Florence's eyes.

Sam frowned down at Charly.

"Are you okay?" she asked.

My God, he thought, *she didn't even hear her husband utter the word* Mommy.

Which meant Florence could not only read his thoughts, the man could communicate telepathically as well. And in thinking this, it was as though Sam had unwittingly tuned in to some far-off radio transmission, one that broadcasted carnage and sadism, a blood-soaked call-in show:

(enjoy guzzling your lifeblood)

"Sam?" Both Charly's hands on his arm.

(you and the infant, your essences commingling as they gush red over my lips)

"...scaring me, Sam. Please..."

(no escape, no hope for you)

He took Charly's hands, nodded with an expression he hoped was reassuring.

(your sepulcher)

"It's okay," he told her.

(this is your)

"I thought I heard something is all."

(sepulcher)

"Let's get going."

Charly continued watching him with the same alarmed expression. She shook her head. "If you need to rest for a few minutes—"

"Not a chance," he said between shallow breaths. "Your boy is close. We can't waste time sitting on our thumbs."

You're right, Sammy Boy, we shouldn't waste time, the buzzing voice murmured. *Within the hour I plan on eviscerating you and feasting on the child while his mewling bitch of a mother looks on.*

Sam swallowed but did not look back. And when Charly offered her hand, he gladly took it.

Chapter Nine

Jesse sensed the passage expanding around him and thought of how wrong he'd been about newborn babies. He used to think birth was rather a cruel thing: first, content and warm and safe and wet inside the mother's womb; the amniotic sack bursts and the child is pushed screaming into a cold, vast space of blinding lights and harsh voices. But now he viewed it all differently. The baby had been confined, grown too large for its surroundings, with no space even to flail its limbs. Then the beautiful release, the suffocating fluid vacuumed from its throat...

"*Oh thank God,*" he whispered, able to crawl on hands and knees again. Ahead someone was squatting and sweeping a flashlight through the blackness. It was Greeley, he now realized, and Clevenger was crouching alongside him.

Jesse chanced a look back at Ruth—the treacherous bitch—and marveled at the way her features had softened. She seemed to be staring through Jesse and beyond the figures ahead.

"You believe this?" Emma asked in a wondering voice.

Jesse frowned and stood abreast of her. Then he realized why everyone had fallen silent.

The flashlight beams carried by the others did slow, awestruck passes along the wall opposite.

It was at least fifty feet away.

He and Emma had hung back, but now they scuttled forward to see what Greeley and Clevenger were seeing. Both men, he noted with confusion, were now on their knees. They reminded him of a pair of crewmates on a storm-tossed ship, clutching the deck of their vessel and praying the surf wouldn't sweep them shrieking into a watery grave.

The walkway, it appeared, ended in a kind of curving promontory. Above them hung innumerable stalactites, many longer and thicker than full-grown men. Their glistening contours reminded him disquietingly of dangling shrouds.

Jesse directed his gaze downward and felt the strength go out of his legs.

The valley seemed endless.

He didn't want to venture too close to the edge—he'd always been a little afraid of heights—but his curiosity won out. He got down on all fours, pointed the mining helmet straight down.

Far, far below, perhaps ten stories, something shimmered. An underground river?

No, he realized with an inchoate sense of wrongness. The odor came next, and with it a desire to whirl and return to the tunnel, claustrophobia be damned. He scooted backward and yelped when he bumped someone's knees.

He spun and saw Colleen squinting down at him.

"You mind getting that light out of my face?"

"Sorry."

She nodded toward the others. "What's everyone so...holy *shit*," she said when she saw the dropoff.

A scratching sound behind him. Jesse whirled.

And let out a startled cry.

Demonic eyes stared at him from a bloody red face. Just when he was sure the Big Nasty had somehow tracked him here to finish the job, he discerned Frank Red Elk's longish black hair, usually glossy but now clotted with Debbie's blood.

"Want me to hold your hand?" Red Elk said.

Jesse let out a shuddering exhalation. "Shut up," he muttered.

Red Elk scrunched his nose. "The hell's that smell?"

"Guano," Greeley called back.

"That's bat shit, right?"

Greeley nodded.

Emma was casting restive glances around the yawning cavern. "So...where are they?"

"All over the place, would be my guess," Greeley said. "This is the perfect environment for bats."

Emma's face had gone slack with dread. "This isn't the perfect environment for anything."

Greeley started, an animation permeating his face that had been absent since the playground. "Actually, this is positive for us too."

"For a professor," Red Elk said, "you sure are a dumbass."

Greeley seemed not to hear him. "Don't you see? Bats are cave animals, but they do their feeding outside."

Clevenger nodded. "There's a way out of here."

Greeley flitted his flashlight beam over the walls. "Must be some...means...of egress..."

"*There*," Emma said.

They crowded around her—too hastily, Jesse thought. He could just imagine the whole group tumbling over into the abyss, shrieking and gibbering the whole way down. Cautiously, he joined them.

He leaned forward and gazed where the others were gazing.

To the left and perhaps eight feet below the promontory, there was another, narrower foothold which wound to the right before disappearing into what appeared to be a good-sized tunnel. Jesse studied the black opening with a mixture of hope and dread. It might lead them back to the surface, or at least to the main tunnel. But it was just as likely that a hellish tide of vampire bats would come shrieking out of the darkness for some wholesale bloodletting.

"I had no idea it would be this beautiful," someone behind them said.

They turned and found Ruth Cavanaugh gazing around the cavern with something akin to ecstasy. Jesse noted with unease that her face had continued its uncanny alteration. Longer, the chin was now a ghastly witch's caricature, the nose narrow and protuberant, almost— Jesse tried but could not escape the word—like a snout.

Emma said, "There might be a way out, Ruth. There's a tunnel—"

"No one will be leaving."

Colleen turned to Ruth, her eyes baleful. "What the hell's that supposed to mean?"

"I saw this place last night," Ruth said dreamily, "I saw it, but it was fragmented. Diffuse." Her voice went thick and unnaturally low. "My eyes weren't refined enough then...but now..." The rough, meaty sound of her voice, as though there were wet stones clogging the back of her throat, made Jesse's arm hairs stand up. Emma was very close to the little woman now, though Ruth Cavanaugh seemed to have grown taller. Last night she'd looked a few inches shorter than Emma. Now it seemed Ruth was a head taller. But that, Jesse thought as the acid of terror began to eat away at his composure, could have been because of the frizzy black hair, which was now a glorious mane that spread over her shoulders, all the way to her waist. Her ears also— *what the hell?*—had grown freakish and pointed, the ears of some fairy-tale elf. Only there was nothing friendly or playful in Ruth's bearing anymore. Nothing meek, either.

Emma shined her light in the little woman's eyes. "Ruth?"

"*So beautiful,*" Ruth said, her voice an alien buzz.

"*Ruth?*" Emma repeated, crowding into Jesse.

Ruth's lips spread in a grin that devoured the bottom half of her face, which was now a goblin's face, the stuff of a child's nightmare. Her eyes had taken on a swirling, pinkish hue, the crazed gleam penetrating Jesse's mind.

You thought you knew, the voice rumbled. *But you had no idea. Now watch. Watch what I can become...*

A sound like ripping paper came from behind Ruth. Emma sucked in frightened breath, her body rigid against Jesse's. The ripping sound echoed through the vast chamber, its quality both harsh and somehow pulpy. At first he was sure something had followed them through the tunnel, was coming out of the tunnel now to murder them where they couldn't escape.

But the sound wasn't coming from the tunnel. It was coming from Ruth's back.

Dark tendrils poked out of the sides of her green shirt, the fabric tearing in fitful tremors. He caught sight of her right armpit, now exposed.

The flesh there was as black as polished obsidian.

"Shoot her," Jesse said.

"That's madness," Clevenger said. He took a step toward Ruth, but she was swaying on her feet, listing drunkenly toward the drop-off.

"Jesse's right," Emma said, squeezing his arm. "We have to shoot her."

"*Ruth*," Clevenger implored.

She staggered toward Clevenger. He caught her, held her tremoring body, which now—Jesse fought to override his senses, but he knew his eyes weren't deceiving him—dwarfed the professor's. Ruth had grown as tall as Marc Greeley, who was all but melting into the cave wall to escape from the mutating woman.

"*You have to kill her!*" Greeley shouted.

"Kill her?" Clevenger said, his arm around her. "She's sick. My God, can't you *see* that?" His watery eyes darted pleadingly from person to person.

"We gotta shoot her, Professor," Red Elk said with finality. "Better step away."

Ruth was mumbling something into Clevenger's shoulder, but Jesse couldn't make it out because of all the black hair in the way.

"What?" Clevenger whispered to her. "What's that, Ruthie?"

"...*wanted you*," she muttered. "...*wanted...*"

"What, dear?" he prompted tenderly.

She drew back and Jesse bit his knuckle in fright at the buzzing voice.

"*Wanted you to like me,*" the thing that could not be Ruth said as its face swam into view. The face was a discolored triangular mask, the eyes blood red. Slowly, it rose to its full height, rising, rising, seven feet tall now. Eight. *Jesus Christ*, Jesse thought. *Jesus Christ.*

"What happened to you?" Clevenger whispered.

The red eyes beamed at them, the lurid expression simultaneously coy and obscene. Jesse realized with horror what the ripping sounds had been.

Giant, veined wings were expanding from the Ruth-thing's back.

"You're not..." Clevenger said, his voice scarcely audible above the squishy, popping noises emanating from the transmogrifying body. "You're not…"

"*Ruthie?*" the creature asked, the underjaw yawning wide in an unspeakable grin. Slaver drooled from the serrated teeth.

Colleen started forward and gripped Clevenger's arm.

"*BACK!*" the Ruth-thing rumbled.

Colleen jerked her hand away as if stung.

A gunshot exploded to Jesse's left. He whirled and saw Red Elk aiming the Ruger at the Ruth-thing's face. It was impossible to tell if he'd struck the creature or not because it was already a riot of folds and recesses, shifting darknesses and crimson splotches. The gun jumped again, but the creature barely reacted. Red Elk had to have hit it; Jesse had seen him shoot other targets at considerably farther range. Clevenger, who appeared as though he were in a trance, gawked at the ever-rising figure.

"Come on, Frank," Emma called. Jesse felt a tug at his arm and turned to see Colleen and Emma creeping toward the edge of the drop-off. They meant to leap down to the narrow ledge, he realized with sudden misgiving.

Red Elk nodded like he needed no more convincing. The pistol trained on the Ruth-thing's grisly face, he extended a hand toward Clevenger's shoulder. "Better come along, Professor. This isn't going to turn out well."

Clevenger peeled his eyes off the Ruth-thing. When he regarded first Red Elk, then the others, his lips quivered and his eyes were rimmed with tears.

"I can't," he said.

"*What do you mean, you can't?*" Red Elk growled. "Get your scrawny ass—"

Jesse's insides went cold.

Some thick, black, wormy-looking appendage—the Ruth-thing's tail?—had coiled around the Professor's right leg. It covered the upper half of the leg from bare, white knee to the upper thigh of his khaki shorts, and its sluglike tip was swishing threateningly over his crotch.

"Oh my God," Clevenger said in a trembling voice. "Please do something."

The creature lowered its head, then the wings snapped out like a pair of wind-caught sails. Before anyone could react, the Ruth-thing swept Clevenger over the drop-off, flapping its tenebrous wings, and hung suspended in the air before them. The wings beat in great whooshes, reminding Jesse of the illustrations of prehistoric birds he'd been fascinated by as a child. The appendage coiling around the professor did indeed appear to be a tail. Jesse watched in revulsion as the Ruth-thing's feet—three claws with a single heel talon—curled toward Clevenger's hovering frame.

"Come on," Emma said, her face steeled in grief. "We can't help him."

Jesse saw the grim truth in her face. But he wasn't keen on jumping down onto the narrow strip of rock below. What if they fell? What if the creature dropped the professor and swooped down—

His thoughts cut off when Clevenger began to scream.

Chapter Ten

Though the beast hovering in the air looked like some artist's sinister creation—a demon from a Bosch painting perhaps—the animal it most resembled was a bat.

The Ruth-thing began to rip Clevenger to pieces with its taloned feet.

The hovering creature's arms clutched the professor in an almost loving embrace while the feet did their gruesome work. Clevenger thrashed his head in agony as the digging talons dug gaping trenches in his sides. The blood began to spray in a messy cloud, and it was at that moment that Jesse heard the new sound, the cave seeming to spring to life around him, the very walls rustling.

Emma had been on the verge of leaping—Colleen had jumped and was safe on the lower ledge and screaming for them to follow her—when Emma too paused and looked around at the noises. Jesse chanced a look back at Red Elk, who'd aimed his beam at the ceiling and was staring open-mouthed at what he saw.

Jesse saw too.

They weren't stalactites.

They were winged creatures.

"Night Flyers," Emma whispered.

"Jump," Jesse said. "*Now.*"

She jumped to the lower ledge. He was about to follow when something whipped by his right side, nearly toppled him over the verge. A thump and grunting noise told him Greeley had made the leap too.

Jesse cast another look up and beheld the dangling creatures, their bodies much larger than the Ruth-thing's. They appeared to be well over ten feet long, their wingspan even greater than that. Their wings were unfurling now, the membranous rustling making Jesse's guts roil.

"Get moving," Red Elk commanded.

Jesse tore his eyes off the creatures and jumped. He made it easily, though his knees cracked painfully on the unyielding stone surface. He crouched on all fours and shot a look ahead. The walkway wound down for perhaps thirty feet before the tunnel swallowed it up. He didn't know if they'd be safe from the Night Flyers in there, but he knew if they didn't find shelter soon they were going to end up like Clevenger.

"Come on, Frank!" Colleen yelled.

Red Elk stood poised on the lip of the promontory, his feet braced far apart, the Ruger bobbing erratically as he took aim at the creature annihilating the professor in mid-air.

"Put your head down," Red Elk commanded, the Ruger coming to rest.

Jesse had been sure all awareness had left the professor, but now Clevenger surprised him by straining his head lower to give Red Elk a clean shot.

Red Elk fired, and the Night Flyer's gnashing teeth unfastened from the professor's shoulder. It snarled at Red Elk, the professor's blood dribbling from its fangs in soupy rills. Red Elk popped off another shot, this one nailing the Ruth-thing in the forehead. Jesse watched with new horror as its talons loosened their hold on Clevenger's bleeding body, the man slipping down its black frame toward a blacker abyss.

"Um..." Red Elk said.

"*Do something,*" Colleen shouted.

"Like what?" Red Elk asked. "I left my cape back at the house."

Clevenger's body slipped farther, only one talon snagged in his cotton shirt.

"*Frank,*" Emma said in a scared voice.

"I know," Red Elk said impatiently. He made a helpless gesture at the Ruth-thing. "Uh, bring him over here and I won't shoot you anymore."

The winged creature pumped its wings in foggy, drunken whooshes.

"Shit, man," Red Elk said, "just don't...drop—"

Clevenger fell.

"Noooo!" Emma screamed.

Jesse's throat boiled, the rest of his body numb.

The professor's body plummeted in nightmarish slow motion, the torso dipping lower and the legs describing an almost graceful somersault. Dimly, Jesse was reminded of water ballet.

Then a dark shape spiraled down from the ceiling. Jesse held his breath in awe. The professor's body disappeared into the gloom, and a split-second later, the twisting black projectile followed. There was a pregnant moment in which no one spoke or even breathed. Then a screech ripped the silence of the valley and the enormous, bat-like creature arose from the depths, clutching the professor's body like it was some overgrown rabbit. It swept past Red Elk and veered toward Jesse in a jarring loop. So swift was its passage and so powerful were the beats of its wings that Jesse and the girls were slammed against the wall. One wing tip cracked Greeley a glancing blow on the shoulder, spinning him off his safe haven and sending him tumbling to the thin ribbon of rock on which they stood. Greeley rolled, his momentum and the grade of the walkway working in ghastly collusion. He tried to stop his progress, but it was too late. He went over the edge, and was just able to avert the fatal drop by catching the rock lip with his fingers. Jesse knew he couldn't remain dangling there for long, had actually taken a step in that direction to give him aid, when the rustling noises morphed into a fiend's chorus of blood-freezing shrieks. The Night Flyers were falling toward them, their red eyes agleam with insatiable need.

Red Elk was the first to be lifted. The beast that seized him and hoisted him screaming into the air was obscenely large, fifteen feet or more across with a body like a black pterodactyl. In a moment the air swarmed with the swooping beasts, their trenchant squalls vibrating his eardrums like lunatic teakettles.

Something rammed him and Colleen. Jesse struck the wall hard, rebounded and landed with his head dangling over the walkway's rim. He twisted his head back and discovered the revolver lying next to him. Unthinkingly, he crammed it into the knapsack.

Merciless talons clamped over his shoulders and jerked him effortlessly into the air. He hung facedown as the thing soared over the fathomless canyon. To his left he distinguished a pair of flailing bodies borne screaming into the darkness.

Colleen and Emma.

The former dangled by one leg, the Night Flyer clutching her sneakered foot the way one would a briefcase. But the sight of Emma being swallowed by the inky darkness was somehow worse. The bat creature cradled her like a lover, and for a fleeting moment, Jesse was reminded of Fay Wray and King Kong. The last thing he saw was her fists pummeling the Night Flyer's hideous face, in her pluckiness perhaps forgetting that if the thing dropped her she'd fall screaming to her death.

It was the sound of her shrieks that smashed through Jesse's trance. He swiveled his head as far as physics would allow and in the lucent gleam of the mining helmet—thank God for the chinstrap; he couldn't imagine losing his only source of light—he beheld the iridescent underbelly of the Night Flyer, the vulnerable-looking, ribbed flesh.

Both his Night Flyer and Frank's were arcing back toward the place where they'd initially been ensnared, and from there it would be the same monolithic darkness into which he'd seen the others disappear.

For no reason at all he recalled one of his first assignments at the newspaper.

He'd been sent with a disgruntled grad student to the local YWCA to do a story on a self-defense course being given by the state police. None of it had been very interesting until a woman had asked, "What if a guy pulls a gun on you and tells you to get into his car?"

The state cop said, "You don't get in."

The woman smiled as though he'd gone crazy. "But what if he shoots you?"

The cop didn't smile. "If you get into the car, you're dead anyway. Maybe worse. If he shoots you in some parking lot, at least you die right away. If he gets you to an out-of-the-way spot—say a cornfield or maybe his basement—he'll rape you and torture you. Then he'll kill you."

On the heels of this memory, which careened through Jesse's mind at warp speed, he thought of the whole ceiling becoming a sea of black wings. Even now he could hear the throng of Night Flyers filling the valley with their screeches and slowly throbbing wings. If he let himself be taken to a place where all of them congregated, the possibilities were endless and unutterable.

Jesse glanced again at the ribbed, iridescent underbelly. Then he reached into his knapsack and fished out the cleaver.

His eyes happened on Frank Red Elk and the creature clutching him. The pair flew parallel to Jesse and his airborne host, with Frank and his creature about ten feet above and to Jesse's right. Frank had evidently come to the same decision Jesse had, for he was twisting in the creature's taloned grasp, the Ruger sweeping toward the thing's fleshy torso. Without hesitation, Red Elk squeezed the trigger, and the Night Flyer let loose with a howl so strident it made Jesse cover his ears. The thing spiraled up and over Jesse and his captor. The creature lunged down as if to chomp the man's face off, but Red Elk was too quick. He whipped his head to the side, thrust the Ruger into its large, pink earhole, and popped it again. The Night Flyer's red eyes became glowing moons; its klaxon bray penetrated Jesse's head, made it vibrate like a malfunctioning power tool.

It finally dropped Red Elk. For a moment, the dark man was breast stroking in the air toward the Night Flyer that carried Jesse. Then the creature jolted, and Jesse realized Frank hadn't fallen after all, had landed on the thing's back, on which he now sat astraddle. Immediately, the Night Flyer pitched sideways and veered toward the canyon wall. Though Jesse's view was obscured by the creature's body, he heard all too well Red Elk's *oomph* of surprise as he was driven into the wall and scraped savagely along its coarse surface.

In the uneven glow of his mining helmet light, he watched Red Elk place the Ruger's barrel against the Night Flyer's temple. There was a concussion and a spray of wetness. Then he and Red Elk were tumbling into the darkness.

Part Four
The Arena

Chapter One

Jesse awakens in his grandpa's living room. He knows this isn't possible, but the ratty green carpet, the recliners worn shiny with use, even the huge console television are items he recalls from his childhood. It occurs to him he might be dead, that he's in some unremarkable purgatory—this isn't glorious enough to be heaven and it's way too mundane for hell—but he also suspects he might be in a coma. He has a vague recollection of the Night Flyers, of their earsplitting screeches and the dizzying sight of Emma being borne away over the endless drop. He wonders if the others have been eaten the way Clevenger was. The thought troubles him, and he brushes it away.

The living room is just as he remembers it, only there is no sign of recent habitation; this too troubles him. The television is not only dark, but its enormous, olive screen is dusty from disuse. There is no glass of 7-Up fizzing next to his grandpa's favorite recliner. No morning paper either.

Yet the house is not devoid of life. He is as certain of this as he is that something terrible is about to occur. He pivots his head with a slow creak of tendons and peers fretfully down the hallway. It's not much of a hallway, only two rooms on either side and a bathroom straight ahead, yet now that short hallway seems interminable. He does not want to walk the fifteen paces to his grandpa's room, but he finds himself doing just that, his nerveless feet treading the tattered green carpet, and then he is outside the door.

Jesse imagines the room within: redolent of talcum powder and Old Spice aftershave and arranged with militaristic order. Grandpa was in the service—Air Force mechanic—and his time there instilled in him the habit of making his bed each morning, of folding his underwear neatly within his bureau drawer even though no one—not even his wife—would ever know he folded them.

A brutal railroad man begins swinging a sledgehammer within Jesse's chest cavity, the iron head striking just under his right pectoral muscle, the ache spreading down to his solar plexus, his belly, and Jesse leans forward breathlessly on the wooden door.

The door opens, and his discomfort and fear curdle into revulsion. The familiar smells of powder and aftershave have been routed by old feces and the halitosis of one who is being eaten from the inside out.

The croaking voice from the bed makes him jump.

"Ten years too late."

Jesse shakes his head, mouths the words *Tried to come, Grandpa,* but he can't make a sound.

"Tried to come, my ass," his grandpa says, and despite his anxiety and breathlessness, Jesse is compelled to study the wasted figure on the bed to confirm it is indeed his grandfather. In life the man had seldom sworn, and never in such a curt, sarcastic voice.

"You either go somewhere or you don't," the corpselike face growls. "You want to see a person, you see him. Nothing stops you if you care about someone."

Jesse can't respond. What's there to say?

The face, he notes with quiet dismay, is sunken and creased, the folds like some old, musty tarp heaped in a corner and colorless with age. The whiskers are black and sparse, with salty tufts sprouting from the jawline, where the nurse's razor has missed. His grandfather was a thin man most of his life, but the figure on the bed is an animate skeleton, the splotchy skin bagging down around the elbows as though a molting process has begun.

"You're a superficial little bastard, you know that?"

Jesse looks up, stunned, and sees his grandpa watching him. As if to confirm the caustic declaration, Jesse finds himself looking not at his grandpa's irises but rather at the red troughs of sagging eyelid that form their southern borders.

"That's right," his grandpa says, "focus on the ravaged body."

Jesse shakes his head.

"The one time I needed you."

"No."

"Rebounded how many missed shots for you? Ten thousand?"

Jesse closes his eyes, the hot tears squeezing through.

"How many times I pick you up from little league practice?"

"Every afternoon," Jesse whispers.

"I ever miss a game of yours?"

"Not one."

"Didn't I read you books?"

"You know you did."

"*Frog and Toad* and Dr. Seuss and those goddamn Clifford books."

Jesse hangs his head.

"We looked at the sports page together," his grandpa goes on, "talked about who was hitting and who wasn't."

"Every day," Jesse agrees, "all summer long."

A palsied finger shoots out, jabs him in the arm. Jesse sucks in a startled breath.

His grandpa's crooked teeth are gritted in rage. "And don't you give me any of that modern crap about brainwashing you with sports and letting a kid find himself. You loved that stuff as much as I did, and you know it."

"I did, Grandpa."

"And when you got into taking pictures, who bought you a brand-new Polaroid?"

"You did."

"And film. Christ, you went through it like it was free, but did I complain?"

"You never complained, Grandpa."

The corpselike body astonishes him by sitting erect, the yellowed nest of pillows around him retaining his shape.

"Then where were you, Jess? Why'd you abandon me?"

Jesse is holding back the tears now, humming in misery.

"You're not gonna run away this time," his grandpa growls.

The door behind him slams shut.

Jesse murmurs, "I failed you, I'm sorry."

He moans at the flare of hostility in the man's rheumy eyes.

"You failed, huh? I'm sorry, Grandpa, and all is forgiven? *Well, to hell with that.*"

His grandpa thrusts the covers down, revealing impossibly skinny legs, bare and hairless below the hemline of the stained hospital gown. The legs swing toward Jesse. The feet are swollen and plagued by open sores.

"Please let me go," Jesse whispers.

"Ohhhh," his grandpa says, bloodshot eyes stretching wide, "'let me go', the boy says. Well I'd say you *did* go, didn't you? Went everywhere but the hospital."

"Grandpa—"

"Went to your made-up girlfriend's house for dinner, took her to the drive-in."

"Grandpa, please."

"Named her Juliet. Kind of an idiot you think I am anyway? *Juliet?* Why didn't you name her Ophelia or Miranda or Lady Fucking Macbeth instead?"

Jesse tries to grope for the door, but his hands hang limply at his sides.

"That was the biggest insult," his grandpa says. "The condescension. Why didn't you just tell the truth, 'I'm scared of coming over there and I'm a lazy, selfish prick'. It woulda hurt, but at least I wouldn't think you thought I was an idiot."

"I didn't think—"

The curtain-rod arms shoot out. "*The hell you didn't!*"

The praying mantis body rises toward him.

"And the worst part," his grandpa croaks, the exposed lower teeth so crowded Jesse can see several places where one tooth overlaps another, "the worst part, my unfaithful, lying grandson, is how I only asked for one thing from you your entire goddamned life. Just one thing."

Now the livid face hovers inches from Jesse's, the death smell rotting out of the wet mouth.

"You remember what I asked, boy?"

Jesse squeezes his eyes shut, shakes his head weakly. Of course he remembers. One day late in his senior year of high school he'd been worrying about how he'd pay for college, his mother having saved next to nothing, and Jesse himself with only a hundred or so in his account. His grandpa matter-of-factly fished an envelope from the table next to his recliner and handed it to Jesse. When he opened it he discovered it was a college fund with more than enough to carry Jesse through his undergrad years and maybe a little further. He took in his grandpa's quiet smile, too moved to speak, and his grandpa had said, "Just be there for me when I need you."

Jesse sobs, makes high, keening sounds, but he can't sink into his grandfather's arms because the man he loved is gone and has been replaced by this vengeful doppelganger.

"'Just be there for me'," his grandpa repeats now. "Was that too much to ask?"

"No."

"*Yes!* Oh yes it *was*, my boy. All I wanted from you was a little time, some diverting conversation. We cancer patients tend to value that, you know. It makes the end more bearable."

A rustling sound fills the small room, and at this Jesse opens his eyes and sees his grandpa has opened his gown to reveal a horror of a body. The skin of the chest is peeling in charred curls, revealing portions of the ribcage and the pink-black lungs within. The belly too is being eaten away by maggots and slugs, the purple organs within a squirming refuse heap of decay.

Jesse gags, claps a hand over his mouth.

"Sure, puke your guts out," the thing that could not be his grandpa says. "It's what I did. And I did it all alone, didn't I? Your mom came around sometimes, but we were never as close as you and I were. Or at least as close as I *thought* you and I were. But you—" jabbing a finger into Jesse's sweat-soaked shirt, "—*you* proved me *wrong*, didn't you? It was like you wanted to punish me for making that one request of you."

The dying face shoves into his, rancid spit flying from the wasted lips. "*Well, you punished me good, didn't you? I saw you every week of your life until I went downhill, and then you didn't show up for six stinking months! Didn't even come to the hospital when I was so drugged up I couldn't move. Your mother begged you and begged you, but you used every excuse imaginable to make sure I didn't sully you with my death.*"

And now the face is altering. Even through Jesse's tears he can see the rheumy eyes turning green and changing shape, the nubby brown teeth elongating and tapering at the tips.

The thing that had been his grandpa but is now one of the Children seizes Jesse by the wrists and thrusts his hands into the writhing cesspool of its belly, the maggots squirming hotly against his fingers, the pulpy intestines perforating around his nails, seeping their shitty discharge over his knuckles. The now-pale face looms before Jesse's. It opens its flyblown maw and clamps down on Jesse's cheek and crunches through cartilage and gristle. Jesse wails into the scalding wet stench as the creature's black tongue snakes out...

"*...sorry,*" he mumbled, "*...sorry I failed you...*"

Something hard struck his cheek, and at first he thought it was the creature chewing his flesh. In terror, Jesse opened his eyes and immediately closed them, the light slanting down at him too fierce.

The palm tapped his cheek again, with even less finesse than before.

"...you with me, kiddo?" the voice said.

Jesse nodded, his skull suddenly awash in pain.

"You better get your ass in gear," the voice said. "I don't think we have much time before they find a way through."

Jesse brought up a hand to block the light. "Could you..." he said. "Can't you point that thing somewhere else?"

The light immediately went away. He remembered the cache of supplies under the house, the explosion. Remembered the ambush in the cave, Debbie's scissoring legs drizzling blood. Recalled the endless passage through the tunnel, Emma's black lace panties. Thought of Ruth becoming a hideous bat creature, the thing digging Clevenger to ribbons. Saw with sinking dread the Night Flyers swooping down and snatching Emma and the others.

Looked up into Frank Red Elk's impassive face.

"Sounds like you got some issues to work out," Red Elk said.

Jesse groaned. He endeavored to take in the immediate area, but the vicious pulse in his skull overwhelmed him.

"My dad got cancer too," Red Elk said. "Only his was from smoking four packs of Lucky Strikes every day."

"Grandpa didn't smoke," Jesse said.

"Still died, didn't he?"

Jesse returned Red Elk's pitiless gaze a moment longer. Then he made it up on an elbow, looked around. "Where are we?"

"Where you think? We're underground."

"Yeah, but...where'd the Night Flyers go?"

Red Elk shook his head. "Those things were attacking us, and I thought we were finally gonna get our tickets punched. I shot the one carrying me and ended up riding with you and your creature a few seconds.

"We got lucky. I got that cocksucker in the head. It let us go right before it slammed headfirst into the entrance of this tunnel. You and I tumbled inside, and the rocks over it gave way. That Night Flyer got buried under the debris, and the only thing we got was a knock in the head for you and a messed-up back for me."

Red Elk tapped the mining helmet on Jesse's head. "Good thing you were wearing that. I think you landed right on your head."

Jesse sat up. "They took the others?"

"Others are probably better off. We might die in here."

"They took Emma."

"All of 'em," Red Elk said. "Carried 'em the same direction they took the professor."

Jesse thought of the Night Flyers winging down into the stygian valley. It made him want to cry.

As if reading his mind, Red Elk said, "You and the girl were gettin' on well, weren't you?"

Jesse glanced at him to see if he was being mocked. But for once Red Elk seemed serious.

Red Elk studied his face a long moment, turned and aimed his light down the tunnel. "We go that way, we'll follow the same general path those Flyers took when they kidnapped the girls. But there's a problem."

"Looks okay to me," Jesse said.

"From here," Red Elk agreed. "Until you round that bend up there and the tunnel narrows to the width of a bratwurst."

"What about..." Jesse started to ask, but when he turned and his mining helmet lit up what was behind him, he understood how truly screwed they were.

The tunnel was choked with rocks.

Red Elk said equably, "Reckon we'll have to blow up the place, see if this old thing still works."

Jesse watched him slide the ancient stick of dynamite out of the red gym bag with quiet alarm.

"Question is," Red Elk said, "which side do we blow?"

Jesse eyed the pile of crushed rocks with mounting dread. "It's got to be here, doesn't it? I mean, it leads back to where we were attacked, but at least it leads somewhere."

"That's one argument."

Jesse became aware of the grit in his mouth, the taste of it chalky and highly unpleasant. "What's the other argument?" he asked.

"We could jam this," Red Elk held up the faded red stick, "in the bratwurst hole."

"You said yourself, that tunnel is impassable."

"As it is," Red Elk said. "But I shined my light into it and was pretty sure it opened up about six feet in."

"And then?" Jesse said. "What if it narrows again after that? What if the tunnel just ends?"

"I don't think so. You've been out a good twenty minutes. I spent the majority of that time at the hole listening."

"So?"

Red Elk's face grew doubtful. "It sounds crazy, but I swear I heard a baby crying."

Chapter Two

He feels big. Not just big, but *big*, a sensation not only of physical strength, but of actual size as well. He's not holding the flashlight, but even as he stares down at his hands he can detect a difference in their size. The growth of his knuckles, the length of his fingers, hell, even the expanse of his palms is *substantial*. At first he was pissed as hell about Sam Bledsoe putting them all on a flashlight battery ration. Who the hell did he think he was, the goddamn chancellor of the cave? In fact, for a good while he'd been pissed about *everything*. From Charly's grinning treachery to Bledsoe's general assholery, it had pretty much been a carnival ride through his worst nightmares since heading belowground.

But none of that stuff seems to matter. He's *big* now, bigger than he's ever been, and he's surcharged with an energy that makes his teeth vibrate. His dick has been hard for a good twenty minutes, and it's not just Mel's proximity that's causing his dog to howl. Sure, she's driven him crazy since the first time she showed up in his office wanting a grad assistant's position... Eric smiles at the memory of how coolly he put her through the motions of interviewing:

I see, I see. So how long have you been interested in coaching at the collegiate level?

Mel answering while he leans over the desk to get a good look at those endless brown legs and a hint of aquamarine panties peeking at him from under the hood of skirt.

Eric pretending to be impressed with her answer and telling her what a sacred responsibility it is to be entrusted with the futures of thirteen female athletes.

Mel's eyes, deadly serious, lock on his in that solemn way. He pretends to write something on his blotter so he can risk another glance at that maddening V of underwear. He hunches closer to his desk, scribbling nonsense—maybe she'll just think he's nearsighted— and actually begins to sweat from the strain of peering up that sober black skirt. He spies her panties again, and they're darker than he'd originally thought, closer to green than blue, some color his wife would call Sea Foam or Essence of Birch Leaf.

When he looks up from his graffiti-scrawled blotter, she's staring right at him. And not just at him, but *into* him. She knows what he's been up to, or at least she thinks she does, and he tries not to blush, but he knows from the hot feel of his cheeks that his face is redder than a beet.

But amazingly, her expression is not one of disappointment or outrage, but of naïve excitement. The face of a young woman who's heard about such clandestine things but has been so isolated from those who might do them to her that standing on the brink of this world is exhilaration enough to make her chest heave.

And it *is* heaving, he realizes with amazement. He watches her perfect, softball-sized breasts bulging above the sensible white business casual shirt, and he looks up to find he's been caught yet again, and even more tellingly, her glazed, horny, sexually repressed expression has intensified. *Jesus,* he thinks. *If this goes on any longer she's either going to hurdle the desk and mount me or bolt screaming from the room.*

But she does neither. She only asks, *What will my duties be, Mr. Florence?*

Flo, he tells her through the thickness in his throat and resists naming a dozen naughty duties he'd just love to bestow upon her, the first of which being to lift that skirt and let him—

"You okay, Flo?" a voice asks, startling the hell out of him. He glances up through the sludgy gloom and realizes it's Mel herself soliciting his well-being. He stares hard at her and at once can see what she's thinking: *...doesn't look well, but my goodness, who can blame him? The way his stupid wife is treating him, any man would be sick to death...*

And holy crap, he thinks, it's just like tuning into a radio station, and not one of those gauzy AM stations that sound like a man trapped in a well shouting up through a severe rainstorm, but an honest-to-goodness, big city FM rock station, playing all your favorite hits. The Steve Miller Band, AC/DC, The Rolling Stones, and Melanie Macomber's Innermost Thoughts and Desires. What a trip! He considers setting aside the next half hour to do nothing but listen in on his companions—well, Melanie mostly, with a little of that newly minted slut Charly thrown in to keep him edgy. Bledsoe's mind he has no interest in. He knows well enough what's in there anyway: *Fuck Charly, fuck Charly, fuck Charly.* And oh yes...something else. Something about a dying mother and a foot rotting off. Eric hadn't needed to do a thing, merely gazed at the wife-stealing cocksucker, and there it was, like his own personal drive-in movie theater, except there was no tinny speaker-on-the-window sound; it was all hi-def. Man, he could even *smell* that putrefying big toe, the fulsome stench of it boiling in the closed air of the hospital room like a Glade Plug-In from hell. He could almost gag remembering the smell, and how vivid was that? It had been a long-ago memory in someone else's mind, yet it still resonated in Eric's thoughts as though he himself had been sitting in Sam's bedside chair.

"Flo?" a voice urges. "You okay, Flo?"

He tunes in and hears, *You poor baby, someone who appreciates you is what you deserve. If Charly weren't here I'd caress you and make you feel all better, all better ...*

And though Eric's erection rages at this, her words are eerily close to those purple nightmare words from his childhood...

She's your new babysitter, his mom tells him

Eric nods. He's nine, what the hell does he know?

Patricia, this is my son. He's a trifle small for his age, but he played up a level in AAU this spring.

Patricia looks at him, her frowsy clothes and her shoebox of a face and her tight brown curls and most of all those recessed beady eyes that remind him of a bespectacled weasel.

She takes a step forward and two warring scents close over him like a noose: baby powder and ketchup.

Patricia, his mom says, *is second in her class at Shadeland High and is planning on becoming a surgeon.*

Pediatrician, Patricia corrects, smiling all the time.

Won't it be fun to have a regular sitter, honey? his mom coos. *Patricia will be here every day.*

Eric glances from the fleshy, shoebox-faced weasel to his mom and back to the weasel again. He doesn't know a thing about class rank or pediatricians—hell, he doesn't seem to recall his own name at the moment. The stink of ketchup with its airy, talc-scented counterpoint render him unable to breathe, much less form a coherent response.

Say something, his mom demands, her face tightening.

Eric feels small, like he always does, and he stares into those recessed eyes and wonders if they have a color.

Eric! his mom snaps.

He forces his mouth to open, makes his tongue move.

Hi, he says.

Hello, Pumpkin, Patricia says.

And the most hellish experience of Eric's life begins.

"Coach Florence?" Mel asks, seriously worried now. "Are you feeling faint?" She whirls and shouts over her shoulder to the others. "Hold on, dang it! There's something wrong with Flo!" Turns back to him and searches his face. "Tell me where it hurts, Flo. Tell Mel where it hurts."

And man, does he like this, the way she's talking and looking at him now, and it's as if a nimbus cloud has been bleached white by some divine meteorological providence, and the memory of Patricia and her man-hands and ketchup breath are gone, long gone, and so is her frowsy hair and her boxy face, and replacing them he sees nothing but Mel, sweet, delicious Mel, and she cannot see inside him, of course she can't, he is as closed to her as he's always been, perhaps more

(*because she wasn't touched*)

and she thinks he's merely caught a bug or something

(*the nail didn't harrow her flesh*)

or is distraught over his son's disappearance

(*but yours, it did, it slashed you deep, all the way to your core*)

and he'll let her go on thinking it, if it gets him closer to possessing her.

(*malignant to begin with, but repressed, God, so repressed*)

He puts a hand over hers, cups it to his face.

(*but no longer, he won't hold it in any longer, by God*)

"You feel so warm," Mel says, her breath sweet and near in the darkness. "It's like your skin's on fire."

(*now it's time to become*)

"Mel," he says softly. "I've never been better."

217

Chapter Three

Jesse listened. The voice was distant. There was a raw edge to it that suggested the baby had been screaming unheeded for many hours.

Jesse asked, "How can you be sure it's human? It could be one of the Children's children. Though I don't want to imagine it, I'm sure the Night Flyers have sex..."

"One got taken last night," Red Elk said.

Jesse gazed at the man's expressionless face. "What do you mean, one—"

"Debbie told me when she..." A bitterness rippled across the man's face a moment, then he staunched it as quickly as it had appeared. "Debbie saw it on TV last night after she got done dancing."

"Wait a minute. Debbie was a *stripper*?"

"That surprise you?"

Jesse thought of her firm, naked body tremoring from Red Elk's thrusts. "I guess not."

"The baby belonged to the ladies' basketball coach up at the college."

"I didn't hear about it."

"That's because you were too busy watching Emma's tight little can."

"I notice her tight little can wasn't lost on you either."

"Oh I noticed, all right. Wouldn't deny it, either. Girl has the kind of butt I'd like to eat off of. Spread a little whipped cream on those cheeks, stick a cherry in her crack—"

"I got it," Jesse said.

Red Elk began rummaging through the gym bag.

"Can I ask you a question, Frank?" he asked.

Red Elk grunted, fished out a graying stick of beef jerky.

"Have you always been this interested in sex?"

"It doesn't interest you?"

Jesse stuck his hands in his pockets, shrugged. "Sure it does, but it's like you don't think about anything else."

"You never find your hand when you're fantasizing about Emma?"

"Come on, we're not—"

"You never wondered how it'd feel to have her gobble that little knob of yours?"

"*Hey*," Jesse said. "Jeez, she might be dead for all we know."

"She ain't dead," Red Elk said, coming up with the silver lighter.

Jesse opened his mouth to answer but decided to keep quiet. Better to believe Red Elk's assertion. Better to ignore the sinking feeling in the pit of his belly...

Without looking at him, Red Elk said, "You see me ride that Night Flyer?"

"Sure did. Reminded me of some movie where a kid gets to ride a dragon."

"I was thinking that too," Red Elk said, "but in pictures the kids don't get as banged up as I did."

Jesse studied his unseamed face. "You look fine to me."

Red Elk gave him a wry look, reached back, and drew up his black Horror Drive-In T-shirt. Jesse fought off an urge to retch.

When the Night Flyer had dragged Red Elk along the cave wall, it had gotten its money's worth. In addition to the innumerable lacerations and welts festooning the man's back, there was a ragged trench that spanned from one shoulder to the other, ugly along its entire length, and in one gruesome patch flaying open the meat of his back to reveal a glistening glimpse of his scapula.

Half turning, Red Elk asked, "How's it look?"

Jesse swallowed. "I'm not hungry anymore, if that tells you anything."

"Figured," Red Elk said and mercifully let the shirt fall. "Just as well. The Twinkies and granola bars were in the other bag."

Jesse groaned, realizing the water was too.

"Well," Red Elk said, stretching his arms. "Might as well get on with it."

Jesse eyed the red tube of dynamite with alarm. "You're going to do it now?"

"What, you wanna snuggle first?" Red Elk said.

Jesse threw a desperate glance back up the corridor to where the rockslide was. "Are you sure we shouldn't...you know, try to move some of that away beforehand?"

"Don't see the point," Red Elk said. "That way isn't getting any more blocked. If this doesn't work, we can always try to unpile it later. For now, we may as well see if this does us any good."

Crap, Jesse thought. His stomach clenched into a tight ball.

Red Elk took the dynamite fuse and straightened it with a thumb and forefinger. To Jesse, he looked like some mischievous dad getting ready to set off an illegal firework for his kids.

"Speaking of the pile," Red Elk said, throwing a nod behind Jesse, "you better take refuge over there while this thing does its job."

Jesse backpedaled. "How far will the blast reach?"

"Don't know," Red Elk said amiably. "Never messed with dynamite before."

"If it kills us, we won't be able to help the girls."

"That what you reckon we're gonna do?"

"It is, isn't it? I mean, we can't let them die."

Red Elk pursed his lips and examined the fuse, which now poked straight up like a birthday candle. "I expect you're right. We better go after them."

"Then why'd you ask?"

A shrug. "Maybe I wanted to see if you were like Greeley."

"You couldn't tell the difference already? Thanks a hell of a lot, Frank."

"I could tell," Red Elk said. "But when you're going to war, you like to know what your friends are made of." He gestured toward the narrowed hole. "Whatever we find down there, it's gonna be hairy. There might be a hell of a lot more of those Night Flyers where they took the girls, and I expect we'll have to deal with more of those white bastards too."

Jesse felt a chill course down his spine. "How are we going to save them with all those things around?"

"I don't know," Red Elk said, considering. "Surprise, I guess."

"We're going to surprise them."

"Sure."

"The exploding dynamite ought to help."

Red Elk grinned crookedly. "I expect so."

Jesse blew out tremulous breath. "Okay. Let's blow up the cave."

This time the detonation wasn't as dramatic as it had been at the house. One moment Red Elk's elongated shadow was crouching on the moist cave wall, the next the man himself was barreling around the corner with a demented smile on his face.

"Cover up!" he shouted.

Jesse had a moment to wonder what the hell he was supposed to cover up with, but by that time the gravelly roar was blotting out all thought. Jesse flung himself on the rock pile and clasped his hands in his hair the way he'd been taught during elementary school tornado drills. Somewhere in the middle of all the rending and popping, Red Elk had joined him, had even girdled his shoulders with one meaty arm. The gesture would have been touching if Jesse weren't so terrified of having the cave fall on them. And for a long and torturous moment he was sure it would. The creaking groan bellowed louder, like some foghorn sounding from the bowels of the earth, and when Jesse cast a feverish glance up at the ceiling he saw that the rock face was chipping, large sheaves of the brown stuff crumbling off like plaster. A fissure scurried along the ceiling from the direction of the explosion, and as Jesse watched, a fascinated dread sweeping through him, the fissure broadened, became finger width, then he was screaming at Red Elk to run, they had to *run,* dammit, the whole mess was coming down on them. He yanked Red Elk away from the falling section of the ceiling. Powder sifted over them as they rushed toward the site of the explosion. There came a colossal groan followed by a crashing thud as the corridor behind them caved in. Jesse had a moment of confusion when they reached the place where the narrow area surely began. Yet the corridor no longer narrowed here—became, if anything, a good deal wider—and despite his coughing and the eye-watering dust choking the air, his helmet light indicated the blast had worked, they'd opened things up after all.

He was dragging Red Elk ahead when he glimpsed something that froze his blood.

A figure approaching.

The gritty murk here was worse than any they'd yet encountered, but despite the swirling caul of a billion dust motes, Jesse could see well enough to know they were in trouble.

He fumbled for the cleaver, realized he'd lost it when the Night Flyer had dropped him. And the revolver? Either Red Elk had it, or it was lost. The emaciated figure drew nearer. They'd stumbled upon more of the Children, but this time there was no hope for them. They didn't know how many they were up against. This could be one of the monsters, or it could be the whole damned hive.

Another shape was clarifying in the dust.

He coughed hard, his eyes watering badly now. But Red Elk strode past him with the Ruger extended like some zombified waiter hell-bent on distributing his tray of hors d'oeuvres. The figure immediately ahead of Red Elk froze, threw its arms up and the sound it made gave Jesse an odd feeling.

Then he realized why.

He'd begun to open his mouth to stop Red Elk before he did something catastrophic, but the Ruger expelled its flat, cracking noise, and the figure grunted. Then there was a flailing commotion ahead, the sounds of struggle.

He heard a woman shout, "*Sam!*"

His paralysis shattering, Jesse lurched forward.

Chapter Four

In the brown haze he made out a blonde woman, her face sweaty and fierce. She was cradling a man somewhere in his forties; it was difficult to tell in the swirl of dust motes and light. Red Elk was standing over them, the Ruger hanging limply, almost apologetically, at his side. A pretty brunette with freckles crouched beside the blonde girl and the unconscious guy. Another face loomed out of the shadows toward Jesse, and though the tall man's complexion was an unsettling white, something about it reminded him of Ruth Cavanaugh.

"Who are you guys?" the tall man said, but there was something not quite right about his voice. He wasn't incensed by the sudden shooting of one of his companions—if anything, the set of his mouth suggested it was all sort of a rush.

Jesse made himself answer, "We're trying to find our friends."

"Bet they took them too," the tall man said in his strange, exhilarated way.

Yes, Jesse thought, it was the eyes that were spooking him, the glassy, staring eyes. If one peered deep enough, one might see terrible things in those eyes, one might see

(*abandoned him, your grandpa*)

secrets laid bare, his worst mistakes replayed and exploited

(*all he wanted was your time*)

Jesse tried but could not detach his eyes from the unblinking doll's eyes of the pale man, the green eyes

(*coward*)

"Jesse," someone said.

Jesse turned his head, appalled at the hypnotic turmoil he'd just endured. Red Elk's huge hand was squeezing his bicep, shaking him hard enough to clip his teeth together and command his full attention.

"What?" Jesse asked.

"Help them with the man I just shot."

Still uneasy, Jesse obeyed.

As he knelt close to the blonde woman—the *gorgeous* blonde woman, he now realized, despite the sweat matting her hair and the grime on her cheeks—he saw her stare fiercely up at Red Elk.

"And where the hell will you be?" she demanded. "Finding a doctor for Sam, I hope."

"Sam?" Red Elk asked. "That isn't Sam Bledsoe?"

"If he's your friend," the blonde woman said and visored her eyes, "you've got a horrible way of showing it."

"We're not friends," Red Elk said.

The blonde glanced at Jesse. "Help me get him over to the wall."

Jesse got hold of the man's side while the blonde got under him and backpedaled. The freckled girl helped a little, but it was the blonde who did the lion's share of the work. *Strong lady*, Jesse thought. He made a mental note not to piss her off the way Frank had.

Charly mopped sweat off Sam's brow. He seemed to be breathing steadily, and the big, black-haired man who'd shot him had succeeded in staunching the flow of blood out of his left side. She wished she could say Sam had only been grazed, but the holes—one just over his hip, the exit wound even with it in the small of his back—were leaking too freely for her liking.

A shadow crept over Sam's face, and she shot a glance up at whoever it was, ready to tell him to get the hell out of her light.

The man who'd shot him.

Charly spoke through tight lips. "Would you move?"

"His color's a little off," the man remarked, as if commenting on the weather.

"That tends to accompany blood loss."

Red Elk's dark eyes appraised her.

"What do you want?" she asked.

"Lauren Hays."

Charly stared at him.

"She was in *Temptations* and *Womb Raider*," Red Elk explained.

"*Womb Raider?*"

The one named Jesse came forward, his hands shoved in his pockets and the face below his curly hair a mask of embarrassment. "I don't think she—what's your name, ma'am?"

"Charly."

"I don't think Charly wants to talk about movies right now. She's—
"

"You don't have the same dark complexion," Red Elk continued as though Jesse hadn't spoken, "and your face is nicer, like that other actress..." He glanced at Jesse. "You know the one I mean—she's in mainstream stuff. Like that cool horror flick about the dude who gets infected with something from space, and his whole body starts to get huge and freakish while they play that Air Supply song—"

"*Slither*, Elizabeth Banks. Why don't we make sure the guy here...what's his name?"

"Sam," Charly said.

"Sam. Why don't we make sure Sam's all right, then we can figure out—"

"Lauren Hays is shorter, too, and she ain't a blonde," Red Elk said. "So maybe it's not such a great comparison. Susan Featherly, maybe. The breasts—"

"*Frank,*" Jessie nearly shouted.

Sam opened his eyes, rolled them at Red Elk. "Oh Christ."

Red Elk nodded. "How you been, Sam?"

Charly looked from one to the other. "Wait a minute, how do you two—"

"He's the one my ex-wife cheated with," Sam said without heat.

They all looked at Red Elk, who could not suppress a self-satisfied smile.

Sam winced, teeth bared. He picked up the Maglite and aimed it at the wound in his side.

"What the hell is that?" he asked.

Jesse said, "A plastic Wonder bread bag."

Sam cocked an eyebrow at him. "Come again?"

"Your side was leaking like a sumbitch," Red Elk explained. "We had to cram something in the holes to stopper it."

Eyeing the bag, Sam said, "Hope you didn't have to toss out a fresh loaf."

"Oh, it didn't have bread in it," Jesse said. "Just batteries."

"Batteries," Sam repeated.

"For the flashlights."

Sam glanced at Red Elk. "At least tell me the bag was clean."

Red Elk shrugged. "I couldn't guarantee it."

"That's reassuring," Sam said. He closed his eyes again, appeared to rest.

Melanie uttered a high-pitched moan.

"What's up your butt?" Red Elk asked.

"Have any of you considered that the gunshot and that...nuclear *bomb* these two idiots set off might have gotten the attention of the white monsters?"

Jesse and Red Elk eyed each other in surprise.

"She's got a point," Red Elk allowed.

"Let's go back the way we came," Melanie said. "Now Flo and Sam are both hurt. I'm worried Flo's got some kind of infection from that creature."

Red Elk smiled softly. "Ah, I get it."

"You get what?" Melanie said.

"The old switcheroo."

"Excuse me?"

"You wanna scrog your boss here, who by the way doesn't look very spry," Red Elk said. "And he's dyin' to lay the pipe to you."

"Hey!"

"And the blonde here has moved on to Sammy Bledsoe."

"My name's Charly," she said.

"And if he's got half a brain," Red Elk went on, "he'll drop everything and make a play for you."

Unaccountably, Charly felt some of her dislike of the man diminish.

"First of all," Melanie said, "I don't want to *scrog* anybody. I don't even know what that means."

"It means fuck," Jesse told her.

"*Thanks,*" she spat. She turned to Red Elk. "Secondly, your attitude toward women is shameful. You shoot one of our party, act like it's no big deal, then you start comparing Charly here to a porn star—"

"Soft porn," Jesse corrected.

"What's the difference?"

"Well," Red Elk said expansively, "the production values are completely different, not to mention the lack of penetration—"

"Enough!" Melanie yelled. "Good God, what the hell did we run into? A smart-alecky dork and a sex-crazed Indian? We were better off on our own."

Red Elk was eyeing Melanie with a speculative gleam. Charly smiled even before Red Elk spoke.

"What do you—" Melanie started before breaking off and shaking her head with emphatic disgust. "Oh don't you even start—"

"Daneen Boone."

She tossed her arms in the air. "Just perfect."

"It took me a while because your hair is darker."

She rolled her eyes. "Thanks a million. Can we—"

"Your tits are smaller too."

Her mouth fell open.

"Oh don't get me wrong," Red Elk hastened, "I think you're mighty cute. Those freckles like to drive a man crazy."

"Eric," she said, turning, "could you please do something about this jerk?"

Charly craned her neck around to see what Eric's response would be, but he was mostly obscured by shadows.

"*Eric?*" Melanie demanded. "This person is sexually harassing me!"

"This ain't harassment," Red Elk said. "I'd have to take out my schlong and waggle it at you for it to be harassment."

"Schlong?"

"Dick," Jesse said.

"*I know what it means!*"

A weary groan drew their attention. Charly looked down at the face in her lap.

Sam's eyes were open again.

"Do you think you can move?" Charly asked.

He shook his head, wincing. "No, but I'm afraid if we don't get going soon, Frank and Melanie are gonna kill each other. Help me up."

Charly got behind Sam, and Jesse jogged over to help. Together they stood him on his feet, and though he swayed a moment and looked as though he might pass out, his eyes soon cleared.

Jesse said to Melanie, "Earlier, you said 'white monsters'."

She gave him a petulant scowl. "So? They remind you of porn stars too?"

Jesse glanced at Red Elk. "They haven't seen the Night Flyers yet."

Charly felt a chill course down her spine. "Night Flyers?"

"Whoa," Sam said, and Charly got her arms around him in time to prevent him from collapsing.

"You need to rest," she told him.

"I do," he agreed. "But first we need to get downwind of this dust factory. I can't take a breath without it tasting like someone's pounding erasers." He nodded at Jesse. "Plus, it sounds to me like you've got something to tell us."

Jesse opened his mouth.

"Not yet," Sam said, holding up a hand. "Not till we find a better place to hole up."

"We can't hole up for long," Jesse said. "The girls need us."

"Well my baby needs *me*," Charly said louder than she'd intended. "But we can't do this without Sam."

Sam took Charly's arm from around his back—kindly but firmly—and set off in a straight line.

"Sam?" she said. When he turned, she motioned to her left. "We were heading that way."

Without argument he changed course and was soon lost in the shadows. Jessie trailed Sam, Red Elk behind him. Melanie hung back to wait for Eric.

Charly had started to catch up with the others when she happened, for no reason at all, to glance backward.

What emerged from the murk didn't look much like her husband.

The figure was both skinnier and more muscular than Eric, with a complexion that reminded her of some sun-bleached reptile. Even more upsettingly, he was three or four inches taller than he was supposed to be. That was impossible, she knew—a growth spurt at age forty. But a cursory check of the cave floor, which was level where Eric and Melanie now stood side-by-side, their arms linked like Dorothy and the Scarecrow, confirmed Charly's suspicion. Against all logic and possibility, Eric was growing taller.

His greenish eyes pierced the swirling dust and knifed into her brain. *I'm going to dine on your viscera,* a voice proclaimed. *You're never going to see your baby again.*

The taste of copper corroding her throat, Charly hurried forward. She reached Red Elk's side in a few short moments, but not before one final thought catapulted toward her from Eric's diseased mind.

The Old One will want Junior for himself, and I'll not interfere with His plans. But you, Loving Wife, are going to experience what true pain is.

Charly shut her eyes against the voice.

Exquisite pain, my dear.

She finally reached Sam.

"You okay?" he asked.

Exquisite.

"Not yet," she said. "Not until I get Jake back."

Chapter Five

As they walked, Jesse and Red Elk tried to explain the Night Flyers to Charly and the rest. Charly gave them a brief account of how her party came to be in the caves, as well as a description—though it obviously cost her an effort—of how her baby was abducted.

Red Elk was double checking to make sure the guns weren't safetied when a noise made them all turn. Jesse was the closest, so it was his helmet light that picked out the pair on the ground first. Melanie was on her knees curled over Eric Florence, and though Jesse couldn't see the man's face, he could see well enough the way his feet drummed on the damp rock floor, the hands balled into white-knuckled fists.

A lingering glance at those freakishly long fingers with the pallid, membranous skin made Jesse suddenly very grateful he couldn't see Florence's face.

Melanie squinted up into the blaring beams of light, her pretty face messy with tears.

"What's wrong with him?" Sam asked in a tight voice.

"Like you give a damn," she spat, her words half-slurred with distress.

"No time for that stuff," Red Elk said, stepping closer. "He's either well or he isn't."

Jesse's money was on "he isn't."

"Or what?" Melanie asked, her pretty lips thinning. "What'll you do if he isn't okay? Shoot him the way you did Sam?"

Red Elk brandished the Ruger. "He won't walk away like Sam did."

"You'll have to kill me too, then," she said.

"She wants to stay, that's her business," Charly said. "We're getting Jake."

"It's not that simple," Red Elk said. "We had one turn Night Flyer on us earlier, and it cost us dearly. It's safer to shoot him now, save ourselves the trouble."

Melanie wrapped her arms around Eric Florence, met Red Elk's gaze with fierce defiance. "You're not gonna shoot anybody. And I'm staying right here until he's better."

"Take him," Charly answered and surprised them all by walking away.

Sam and Red Elk discussed something quietly. As Bledsoe jerked a thumb toward the others, he cringed and bent double.

Maybe the sandwich bag's not doing the trick, Jesse thought and felt a moment's hopelessness. He realized with a species of shame how much he'd relied on the absent members of their party for courage. Clevenger, despite being the oldest by a good margin, had acquitted himself admirably. Emma had been tough too, but not as tough as Colleen. It was she, Jesse now realized with dawning amazement, who had proven the backbone of their little party. Without Colleen, he would have died a hideous death back on that playground. Without her, they wouldn't have rescued Emma. And they almost certainly would not have gotten from the RV park to Red Elk's house without her stalwart presence. Even in the tunnel she'd been a warrior, blasting those grinning monsters like some video game heroine.

And now she was gone.

Last night he'd considered her an occasionally funny but just as often irritating accessory to the girl he had a crush on. Now he missed her almost as much as Emma.

Almost.

Now here they were, he thought, casting a dreary glance around the cave: a pipsqueak newspaper photographer, a housewife half out of her mind with maternal terror, a contractor who might be worth something if he hadn't been shot, and a Native American soft-porn aficionado on whom they were all counting to lead a suicidal rescue mission.

Jesse had an image of a snowball in hell.

Red Elk shook his head, spat. "I don't like leaving them here, but I guess we go on."

"You lead," Sam said.

Red Elk appraised Sam a moment. "We interested in settling old scores, Sammy?"

"We might be. But that's not why I want you to lead."

"Enlighten me."

"No one's shot you in the side, for one thing."

"There's that."

"Secondly, you're better with a gun than any of us."

"How you know that?"

"You got me, didn't you?"

"Just luck."

"Some luck," Sam said. "I need to give a third reason?"

"What, my Indian blood makes my eyes keener or something?"

"Only thing you're keen on is tits and ass."

Red Elk gave the slightest of grins, then handed Jesse a pocketknife. "This is better than nothing."

Jesse took it, but he had his doubts. He tried to swallow but couldn't. God, he'd never been thirstier in his life.

Red Elk held out the revolver to Sam. "You carry this. Two shots left."

Sam accepted it without comment.

"What do I do?" Charly asked. "Shake my pom-poms?"

Red Elk's eyes lowered. "They're nice pom-poms."

"That's all you'll ever see of them," Charly said.

"Never know. Sam's women have a way of crossing enemy lines."

"That what you figure I am?" Charly asked. "Sam's woman?"

"Aren't you?"

"If he'll have me," she said.

She didn't look at Sam, but Jesse did. He was sweating like hell, and his face had gone a sallow, olive hue. But the emotion in his eyes at Charly's words was unmistakable. Charly hooked an arm around Sam's waist.

Red Elk watched the pair, his dark face expressionless. "Well that was touching."

The others started forward, but Jesse hung back, examining the pocketknife and telling himself he wasn't stalling.

"Something on your mind?" Sam asked.

Before he knew what would come out of his mouth, he heard himself saying, "Emma and I saw something earlier. The rain was heavy, but it looked a lot bigger than the other Children."

Red Elk heaved a deep sigh. "I hope you're wrong."

"What was it?" Charly asked, eyes suddenly very large.

Red Elk shook his head, his expression dour and perhaps a little fearful. "They say that all the things that live down here were created by the same infernal being." He laughed mirthlessly, studied the ceiling of the cavern. "It's all turned out to be real so far, but for our sake I hope you just saw some sort of mirage."

Charly shook her head. "You're not telling us what—"

"The Old One," Red Elk said flatly. "Many tribes called it the Wendigo, though I've heard other names too, like Witiko and Kokodjo. Around here they always just called it the Old One."

Sam was eyeing Jesse. "You sure you two saw something?"

Jesse caught an afterimage of the stilt-like legs, the impossibly tall figure stooping toward something on the ground.

"I'm sure of it," Jesse said.

They regarded him in silence for a long moment.

Then Sam said, "It doesn't change anything."

Wordlessly, they started down the rugged decline. Jesse cast one final glance at Melanie and Florence, and what he saw made his steps quicken. Eyes closed with worry, she was still cradling the coach's sweat-soaked head like some wartime nurse comforting a dying soldier. Florence's body was unmoving like a dying soldier, too, but that's where all resemblance ceased.

For on the coach's face was the most hideous grin Jesse had ever seen.

Chapter Six

Eric waited until the voices had disappeared entirely. Then he waited another five minutes. He wouldn't have been capable of that before the change; he'd never been a patient man.

But now he was...different.

His sense of smell was immeasurably keener. He could still scent the dank cave walls, but now the odor was three-dimensional, contained dozens of other elements as well. The smell of the rainfall that had so altered the landscape these past several weeks was pungent down here. He could detect the crisp, natural minerals in the rainwater. He could also taste the chemicals, the taint of man.

This displeased him in a fundamental way.

Beneath the scents of the downpour he tasted the alkaline in the soil, the fetor of rotting vegetation. Somewhere, he noted with displeasure, a fox or even a wild cat had gotten swept away in one of the storms and had ended up starving to death down here in the caves. He smelled the animal's maggot-infested flesh, as well as the numberless microscopic creatures breaking down its body. Stronger than this, thankfully, was the fragrance of the Den. He'd never seen it with his current body, yet some race memory allowed him a glimpse of it.

It was glorious.

The others would soon be upon it, and when they did arrive there, many new aromas would permeate the Den.

The smell of the Indian's marrow being licked out of his cracked femurs. The astringent tang of that little newsboy's piss as it dribbled down his legs. The full, radiant fragrance of Sam Bledsoe's blood as a hundred creatures lapped at his writhing body.

The scent of Charly's breasts as his brethren chewed her soft, white flesh to hamburger.

Eric opened his eyes.

Melanie was still weeping, bless her delectable body.

He could take her right now, but the longer he waited the more he could relax and abandon himself completely. Soon he'd have some *serious* fun, and man, his body ached thinking about it. He'd actually taken a peek inside his shorts to confirm what he suspected was happening, and when he discovered how long his cock had already grown—he'd added two inches, perhaps more—he felt like a kid staring at a gleaming new bike. And like a new bicycle, he'd mount Melanie, oh would he mount her. He could already feel her luscious body beneath him, moaning, undulating, likely crying a little.

Or a lot.

Then the real fun would begin.

Eric grew erect thinking about it.

He could feel the tight muscles in his arms, man, like high-tension power lines. The strength was indescribable. He felt big, so damned *big*, and another scent came to him now, the scent of Melanie's deodorant. It would have some stupid name, Morning Mist or Fresh Mountain or something, but what it smelled like was Patricia the Babysitter.

Yet he was astonished how little her memory was affecting him now. In years past he couldn't stomach the odor of ketchup—a couple times he'd blown up at the kids for slathering their goddamn fries in it—without feeling small, without feeling reduced. The first time she'd sat for him she insisted on being in the bathroom while he took a piss, and though he pleaded with her to leave—he was for chrissakes old enough to hold his own peter and flush the toilet—she simply sat on the edge of the sink until the scalding tingle in his bladder won out. He'd hated her a little that day, had considered the whole thing abnormal and more than a little unsettling. But what chilled him worst of all was how she bent low so they were eye-to-eye and told him he better not tell his mommy about how she watched him tinkle. She actually used that word, *tinkle*, and that had been the beginning of the reducing. Big boys did not tinkle, they took a piss, or a leak, or if they really wanted to impress their friends, they drained the radiator, they had to see a man about a horse, or his personal favorite, they bled the weasel.

That night he dreamed of bleeding a weasel. Not his own two-inch weasel, of course, but the six-foot-tall weasel with tight brown curls and ketchup breath that made him want to puke.

She returned the next day, and it was as if nothing had happened in that upstairs bathroom. She didn't seem the slightest bit concerned about Eric informing on her, and that too represented a further reduction, that she was so confident in the terror she'd imposed on him that she hadn't made him repeat his pledge.

When his mom went out, the tall, blocky weasel girl turned to him, and with that wheedling, sinister smile, she said, "Take off your shorts."

Eric recalled how scared he was and how badly he wanted to escape through the back door. But worst of all, he remembered how excited he was too, how deliriously naughty the prospect of taking off his shorts was to his nine-year-old self.

When they were balled on the floor, he faced her in his Jockey shorts.

Patricia waited.

He gave a little start when he realized what she wanted. "The underwear too?" he asked, and it came out way too agreeably, way too eagerly, and when had he become such a servile little mouse?

He tried to reclaim a shred of his pride. "I don't want to."

Patricia's smile never wavered. She merely raised her eyebrows a fraction of an inch and waited. The living room was awash with buttery morning sunlight, and in the glow he could make out the miniscule beads of perspiration forming on her upper lip. Soon he realized just how much she sweated, which was why she coated herself in that patina of talcum powder, and by the time she was done doing things to him that day, the sweat had eroded the powder into white runnels that caked every one of her many crevices.

And the things he she did to him, the things she made him do to her...they had changed him. Prior to Patricia, he'd been mildly interested in sex, and of course he'd been interested in the female body, but despite her stertorous ketchup breathing and her sow-like appearance, she'd transformed him into a sex fiend, one who wanted more than the mere act—one who needed to mess around with power as well. To avoid that reduced feeling as an adult he most often insisted on being in control. Being *emphatically* in control. He found most women dug that, liked their men and their sex strong. But on a couple occasions—once with a college girlfriend who'd laughed at him and whom he'd punched in the belly and threatened to kill if she told a soul what had happened; the other time with Charly—he'd suggested that maybe, you know, they could do things to him that were a little out of the ordinary. In the college girlfriends' dorm room, both of them quite drunk, he'd insinuated that rather than walking down to the restroom she might relieve herself on him instead. She blinked at him a moment and then burst into laughter. That ended badly, almost life-in-prison badly, so he kept his secret desires hidden until he and Charly had been married a couple years. One night he'd asked her if she would humiliate him, spit in his face and call him cruel names and slap his genitals with a damp towel. Her face clouding, she'd blundered her way through it until she achieved the effect he was after, and though the release had been sweet, her silence afterward forbade any further requests on his part.

Yet again, he felt reduced.

Patricia was still with him after all these years.

It had gotten so bad that during his worst times coaching—at the tail-end of a six-win season and a potential suspension for inappropriate contact with a player—he'd become enshrouded in a smothering cloud of ketchup and talc that dogged him wherever he went. It was like Patricia had transmogrified into a ghost and was preying on him at his darkest moments, enveloping him in her stink and whispering those long-ago words that made him want to cry, scream, ejaculate and shit himself all at the same time: *Is Wittle Ewic's wittle peeny lonely? Let Patwicia make it better. Now roll over and tell me how this feels and if you're good I'll let you lick me in the wet place.*

Small, small, it made him feel so sickeningly small. But now...

Now everything had changed.

Because now he was large. Now he was *invincible*. His puling, execrable weakness had been expunged by the creature's touch, and he was thrumming with his desire to experience the world anew.

And now he can smell myriad odors baking out of Melanie. The salt of her tears. The febrile moisture of her skin. He can smell her crotch, and it almost overwhelms him: the clammy undercurrent of exertion commingling with the maddening juice of her arousal.

The scent galvanizes him. He looks into her eyes and sees a new fear there, not of losing him, not the fear of a concerned lover, but of a person who suddenly realizes she might be in danger. It is the exact expression the sunfish had exhibited that day back in junior high. He'd swiped that greenish, iridescent fish with the big net, slapped it down on the dock, and watched it flop around for a good minute or so, always of course making sure the little cocksucker didn't find its way back to the lake.

When he was sure the sunfish wasn't going to flop off the dock, he hustled to the house and found one of his dad's hypodermic insulin needles.

He told himself in the intervening years that he'd done what he did next without premeditation, that it was a harmless act of preadolescent cruelty. But that was bullshit, and deep down he'd known it all along. That gimlet eye of the sunfish had fixed on him before, and its name had been Patricia. That eye had reduced him and reduced him, and he refused to let it happen again. Emasculating him. Deriding him. And he was *big* as he dipped the syringe into the foul brown lake water. He was bigger as he flattened the fish with a trembling hand. He was huge as he brought the needle slowly down toward that gaping, lidless eye, grew even larger when he recognized real fear in the creature's silent stare. He became positively *colossal* the moment the needle tip pierced the cornea of the gasping fish, and when he depressed the plunger and the eye began to swell like some overfilled balloon, he felt an atavistic lust superheating his penis. He ejaculated at the exact moment the sunfish's eye burst, and then he sat back on the dock, his energy spent. He watched with a loopy kind of apathy as the one-eyed creature struggled in anguish, and when the fish actually got lucky and flopped into the water again, he was amazed to find he really didn't care.

Until the nightmares began.

He'd dreamt of that little sunfish ever since. It had been especially awful when he still lived with his parents on the lake. He imagined that sunfish—which had been nine inches long at most—swelling to a barracuda and eventually to great white shark proportions. He'd lie in bed shivering, certain the one-eyed beast awaited him in the waters, was out there trawling in the moonlight, ever watchful, ever filled with wrath.

Melanie has lost that fearful look, is talking to him now. He endeavors to reply, but his tongue is a sluggish wad of meat, his lips rubbery and gummed together.

"Can you hear me?" he hears her ask.

Oh, I can hear you, he thinks. *Now that we're off that godless dock and in this beautiful dark place, yes, Melanie, I can hear you just fine.*

"The others went on," she explains.

I know, he tells her.

She wipes her nose, sniffles. "I can't believe your wife…" She trails off, her eyes filling.

He sends her the thought: *It's okay, I've got you.*

She is looking down at him now, abruptly attentive.

You're better than Charly anyway, he goes on. *I want to make you feel as good as you've made me feel.*

"Are you…" she asks, an incredulous smile dawning. She's shocked, a little scared, but mostly she's amazed.

And turned on?

Yes, he realizes, she's definitely turned on. He can smell it on her.

Yes, he sends to her, *I'm talking to you in your mind.*

"You can—" she begins, but he puts a finger to her lips, reminding her she no longer needs to speak.

But she speaks anyway. "What am I thinking now?" she asks, and in her mind he sees them last night in her car, sees himself from her vantage-point, feels his own sweaty hands plunging inside the rear of her basketball shorts, and then the memory is fading, and he knows why. Because soon after that she shut him down, told him not yet, she wanted to wait.

Do you still need an engagement ring? he asks her now.

A troubled look. Then she peers at him with such coyness and such lust that it's all he can do not to throw her down and take her by force.

But the longer they wait, the sweeter it will be. The others are almost certainly out of earshot, and perhaps they are dead. He doesn't want that. He wants to kill them. To eat them. To screw Charly one last time with his huge new cock and laugh at her while he does it. Then he'll strip her flesh, he'll do it slowly. Keep her alive as long as he—

"Eric?" Melanie asks, her eyes huge.

What? he replies.

"Your face," she says and actually gestures toward her own face, as though he doesn't know what a goddamn face is, and since she obviously can't get the hang of this telepathy thing he talks to her in his own voice, and that's a mistake.

Because when he says, "*Stop looking at me,*" it's in a different voice, and the sound of it surprises even him, its deep, cicada-like drone at once demonic and insectile. The voice he imagines Satan having.

Melanie scuttles away from him, her mouth a gaping black O, and *fuck*, she lets his head smack on the rock floor, and for the barest fraction of an instant Eric feels human pain.

Then what remains of humanity is suffocated. He scrambles onto all fours and glares at Melanie in the meager glow of the flashlight. She screams, and a perfunctory glance down at himself reveals why. His limbs are tight and knobby, his penis a jutting pylon. The cumbersome coaching attire he still wears has already grown taut in most places, and he helps it now, peeling it effortlessly off his body like old skin. Out of simple curiosity he fingers his teeth, and the flesh pads come away bloody. The blood is black, of course, which he should have expected, but it still astounds him. He realizes she's been retreating and he's been following, and they are well clear of the light now, her human eyes useless. But his glorious new eyes reveal all: her gorgeous legs streaked with urine, the crotch he will soon violate, the succulent fat of her supple breasts, and then...

Her huge, blind eyes...like the blind, popped eye of the sunfish. It has followed him down here, after all these years it has wriggled into the waterless cave to indict him for his atrocity.

Eric begins to pant, the sound a feral growl in the blackness of the cave. *Oh no*, he tells the sunfish, tells Patricia, tells Melanie, *I will not be frightened by you, I will not be reduced!*

Eric springs.

In a whir of limbs he is on her screaming, maddeningly sweet body, and her thrashing only makes it better. The sharpened key that Bledsoe gave her pierces the flesh of Eric's shoulder, but he hardly feels it. He spins her, wrapping his elongated black tongue around her neck and gives her a squeeze that cuts off her scream, and then he tears off her shorts and plunges his phallus into her anus. She utters a silent shriek, and he hears her think that this is the worst thing that can happen to her, the most painful thing, and he tells her, *This is only the opening ceremony, Sweetie, this is only the beginning.*

How does it feel to be reduced? he demands as he punctures the pulpy lining of her rectum. *How does true love feel?*

Melanie batters at his tongue and he relaxes it slightly to allow her to breathe. As he listens to her gasp, his bony hips thrusting and tearing, he tells her, *You must stick around for the duration, my love. You mustn't die too quickly.*

Slowly, exulting in Melanie's unfettered screams, he begins to eat her right ear.

Chapter Seven

What Jesse expected to see when they reached the upcurving slant of the tunnel and the vast cavern beyond it was some kind of hive. They'd heard the weird chatter of the Children for the past couple minutes and the bloodcurdling screeches of the Night Flyers for twice that long. He hadn't said anything to the others, and they hadn't spoken it aloud either. None of them had to. They understood they were about to run into both species, and maybe this was why Jesse had expected some kind of elaborate hive.

What he found instead reminded him of a domed amphitheatre.

Entirely comprised of stone, the lofty walls were steeped in shadow. What he glimpsed there were carvings. The lower carvings, he realized, were of Children and the upper images of the Night Flyers, all the figures etched in the walls and created to scale.

Light came from a circle of fires roughly fifty feet in diameter near the center of the amphitheatre. They'd come upon the arena, he now saw, from one of more than a dozen openings in the rock walls, which reminded him crazily of box seats at an opera. All they needed were those fancy binoculars and a bunch of women singing Italian, and the effect would be complete.

To the far left of the domed cavern he spotted an immense vertical tunnel and immediately wondered where it led. When he continued his scan of the capacious room—hell, it was nearly the size of a college basketball arena—he discovered scores of the white monsters.

All around the arena, there were pockets of Children dining on what Jesse assumed were the gory remains of campers they'd captured aboveground. But many of the beasts had apparently become interested in the fresh catch of humans the Night Flyers had ensnared. There were at least three dozen Children skulking forward to have a look.

A score of Night Flyers had formed a ring within the seething circle of fire, and inside their snarling ranks crouched four more Night Flyers.

Each one with a captive.

Clevenger was long dead. The Ruth-creature had upended the professor's severed head and was gobbling the goodies within. Jesse watched, grotesquely fascinated, as her face darted up from her meal, her maw smeared with gore, to snarl at a pale Child who was tall enough to peer over the panoply of guards. The Night Flyers forming the protective circle, Jesse now realized, weren't noble sentries standing a post to ensure their buddies enjoyed an uninterrupted repast. Nearly every one of the bastards was chewing gobbets of flesh or innards from the professor's eviscerated body.

Colleen thrashed in a Night Flyer's arms. As it clutched her in a bear hug, the creature did not evince a desire to use Colleen sexually. What Jesse thought he read in the thing's face, though it was difficult to tell due to the distance, the tenebrous lighting, and the darkness of the creature's skin, was a cruel antagonism akin to a schoolyard bully. Only rather than consummating its teasing with a nasty rubbing of Colleen's face in the dirt, this creature was on the verge of devouring her.

The terror on Colleen's face would have been understandable if it were begotten solely out of fear for her own safety, but when Jesse followed her wide-eyed gaze and glimpsed what lay just ahead of her, he realized there was another reason why her terror was so extreme.

The Night Flyer sitting astride Marc Greeley's stomach had begun to carve up his handsome face.

All Jesse's jealousy, all his petty resentment of the man for his having messed around with Emma vanished the moment he beheld the deep incision along Greeley's hairline.

The Night Flyer was slowly scalping him.

Now and then one of the sentry Night Flyers would creep over to Greeley's wailing body and scoop out a bit of his flesh. The sooty gouges and trenches cut in his body made the once-handsome man look like he'd been besieged by giant leeches.

Jesse swallowed, strove to look away but couldn't. Even worse, he couldn't shut his ears against Greeley's tortured wails. Jesse felt a powerful surge of hatred for the Night Flyers. This slow murder of Marc Greeley was somehow worst of all, worse even than what had happened to Tiara Girl, who'd already been dead when Jesse happened upon the Big Nasty's defilement of her body.

Then Jesse heard a whimper that surcharged his body with adrenaline.

Emma.

He crawled to the far corner of the promontory and spotted her.

And the Night Flyer holding her captive.

She was pinned by the throat. The Night Flyer holding her down kept sniffing her, not in the salacious, would-be rapist manner of the Big Nasty, but the way a dog will inspect a bug he has trapped and will soon bite in half.

So maybe lust, Jesse reflected, was more indigenous to the Children. Lending credence to this theory was the proliferation of long, waxen creatures massed near that area of the circle.

They want Emma more than the other hostages, he thought sickly.

Movement to his immediate left snapped off his thoughts. Sam was wrestling Charly away from the edge. One of Sam's hands was clamped over her mouth, the other arm cinched tight around her torso. If he didn't know better, he'd have thought Sam was making off with her. Something, Jesse realized, had caused her to cry out, and though he knew what it was, could hear it even now, he hadn't yet spotted it.

He scanned the crowd of murderous monsters below until Red Elk literally grabbed his chin and pointed it straight down.

One of the children clutched Charly's baby.

Taller and stronger than most of the other Children—the thing looked twelve feet tall, at least; its muscles swam like eddying water with each of its panther-like movements—the creature grasped the poor child by one chubby leg and was holding Jake aloft like an unscrupulous barker enticing patrons with some prize, a teddy bear maybe, at the county fair.

The Night Flyers, who were staring with rapt attention at the squalling infant, had all but forgotten about the four victims trapped within their circle.

The huge, pale creature strode forward, his own kind parting before him in two neat rows. The Children were avidly watching the child, but something—fear of the creature clutching the baby?—precluded them from acting on their desire. When the creature and its quarry reached the edge of the fire-lit circle, Charly pumped an elbow into Sam's chest, loosening his grip, and for an awful second Jesse was sure her screams would be heard.

When the sentinel Night Flyers reached up for little Jake Florence, the creature carrying him yanked him back and out of reach. With a single nod, the creature seemed to indicate the humans in the circle.

Jesus Christ, Jesse thought. *They're bartering.*

The creature brought the baby close to its mouth and clipped its teeth together an inch from one tiny hand. The Night Flyers screeched in protest, and Jesse looked away in helpless dread.

There was a flurry of movement within the circle, and Jesse looked up in time to see the Night Flyer that had been slowly feasting on Marc Greeley scuttle forward to the edge of the circle of guards. It extended Greeley's blood-splattered body, the man's sneakered feet kicking weakly.

Several Children leaped forward to claim Greeley, but the Night Flyer hauled him back into the circle, dark teeth snapping menacingly. The ranks of sentries closed, and the two races of creatures stood growling at one another with palpable loathing. The Night Flyer holding

241

Greeley flapped its great wings until it hovered in the air above the circle. Again it extended Greeley's body in trade, and again the Children lunged for it. When the alabaster bodies surged into the winged black ones, the sentinels attacked. Jesse watched in nerveless horror as the Night Flyers leaned back and braced themselves on their arms and sent their appallingly lethal hind legs into action. Within seconds, a half dozen Children reeled back from the circle, their fronts shredded like paper.

One of the bleeding Children, Jesse discovered without a great deal of surprise, looked a lot like the college kid Austin, the spiky blond hair mostly fallen out and replaced by a leprous-looking white pate.

Again the Night Flyer holding Greeley let the man dangle over the reaching arms of the Children, but again it drew back, this time floated a good thirty feet above the pale creatures. The Children who hadn't been injured in the initial skirmish growled their fury at the hovering Night Flyer, but still the winged creatures remained intent on the baby. This time the Child holding the baby actually lowered Jake's upside-down body and opened its mouth as if to devour the head in one ferocious bite.

Behind him Jesse heard Charly and Sam wrestling again and knew the wounded man couldn't prevent her from breaking loose much longer. Charly was a smart lady, but that intelligence was no match for her maternal love. She was ready to dive into the crowd of monsters for a chance to touch her baby again.

It was at that moment that one of the Night Flyers darted at baby Jake.

Chapter Eight

Sam spotted the creature before it lunged. Granted, it was difficult to see much of anything with the bad lighting and especially with Charly bucking against him, but he'd noticed the oversized Night Flyer early on because of two things. One, it was gigantic and mean-looking, even meaner than the others, and that was saying a hell of a lot. Secondly, it had been chewing on what appeared to be one of the professor's white butt cheeks.

That wasn't the kind of thing a person could ignore.

When the Child holding Jake refused to relinquish him, Sam had seen the alteration in the big Night Flyer's posture. Until that point it had been borderline uninterested, merely doing its job while enjoying a fine cut of severed ass. But the kidnapper's second refusal—and Sam strongly suspected it was the same creature that had abducted the baby to begin with—had flipped some switch within the large Night Flyer. It dropped the meager remains of the butt cheek, its eyes going wide and murderous, and fluttered its wings like a hawk about to dive-bomb an unsuspecting field mouse.

Sam didn't see it launch itself at the kidnapping creature too clearly because when it happened, Charly went apeshit. But what he did see was the kidnapper spin away to protect its prize as the Night Flyer drove in with its razor talons splayed. The kidnapper arched its back as the talons striped its exposed flesh in deep vertical slits. And though some primitive facet of Sam's psyche was gratified to see the vicious fucker in pain, he knew Jake was now in even graver peril than he'd been. The kidnapper shot an elbow back at the whirring hind claws of the Night Flyer, but it was obviously a lost cause. In addition to the black ichor showering the already-black Night Flyer, Sam saw the kidnapper's exposed entrails, its dark brown lungs, its darker intestines.

The rest of the Children had watched, frozen in shock, as the attack took place, but now they surged forward as one body to destroy the offending Night Flyer.

All of this happened in the space of fifteen seconds.

The dying and perhaps already dead kidnapper pitched forward, baby Jake still clutched in its pestilent white fingers. Before the kidnapper's face smacked the cave floor, Charly let loose with an inhuman wail, and this time Sam did nothing to muzzle it. Instead he did the only thing he could think to do.

He leaped forward and slid down into the pit.

Frank Red Elk had just turned to Jesse, the words, "*We gotta get down there,*" falling from his lips, when Jesse saw Sam Bledsoe rocket past them and go skittering down the endless decline. Even as Sam began his descent, the scene below devolved into a hellish maelstrom of Night Flyers and Children. As the kidnapping Child fell, the baby in its hand lowered to the cave floor too. When the hand met the ground, Jake flopped over in a short tumble that could have been far worse but was still difficult to behold.

He couldn't imagine how awful it was for Charly.

But the child appeared unharmed, and soon baby Jake's heartbreaking, hoarse cries could be heard beneath the chaotic din.

Tearing his gaze away from the screaming child to see what had become of Emma and the others, Jesse was reminded of footage he'd seen of sharks attacking chunks of bloody bait, only in this case there was no bait, only sharks attacking on both sides.

The carnage was unspeakable.

Jesse couldn't imagine moving into such a churning sea of mayhem, but when Red Elk grabbed his arm and dragged him over the lip of their box seat, he didn't protest. At the same moment, another figure skidded down the steep slide to his left, and when he glanced that way and glimpsed Charly's grim face, he experienced an evanescent glimmer of hope.

Then he faced the pit and his hope was incinerated.

Several Night Flyers had taken wing and were swooping about the arena in screeching loops, reminding him very much of all the dragon movies he'd seen. Only these weren't benevolent, tractable creatures who breathed pretty fire and permitted their owners to strap on leather harnesses. These were homicidal beasts bent on destruction, their furnace-red eyes aglow and their stygian wings beating a dreadful cadence. From above he saw scores of Night Flyers arrowing down toward the melee and chided himself for not noticing them before. *Of course,* he thought. *They planned this. They probably welcomed this war, and had ensured themselves a tactical advantage. Why else drag their victims into the arena in the first place?*

With real awe Jesse glimpsed one large Night Flyer snatch a pale creature up in a mad lover's embrace and proceed to puncture the creature's midsection with its lethal hind claws. Before Jesse could look away, the black legs thrust down hard, and the Child's dusky entrails plopped out like a farmer's slop bucket at feeding time. The guts poured over a grappling pair of creatures, who didn't seem to notice.

Under his roughly sliding body, Jesse felt the scabrous rock wall grinding through his cargo shorts. He'd started out using his palms for brakes, but after losing much of the skin there, he relied on his sneaker heels to slow him. Beside him Frank Red Elk bounced over a rise, his face jerking forward and his arms pinwheeling in instant terror. He tumbled awkwardly, somersaulting twice before getting his big body under control. Just as Red Elk ceased his tumbling, a Night Flyer, evidently ready to take a break from the fighting, whooshed over him, its talons grasping the air Frank had just vacated. It let loose with an enraged shriek and whorled back down into the chaos.

Jesse saw immediately that the Children were faring much better on the ground. They swarmed over the Night Flyer sentinels, and here the bloodshed was worse. Two dozen of the Children hurled themselves onto the scythe-like hind talons with suicidal abandon. One pale creature was slashed from throat to belly. Another Child got it in the mouth, the force of the Night Flyer's pumping leg unhinging the mandible with a meaty click that turned Jesse's stomach.

The Children battled their way through the pistoning talons, and once they reached the torsos and faces of the Night Flyers, the tide of battle began to shift. One Child, its guts spilling over its crotch in a glistening mass of coils, broke through the whirring, motor-like legs of its winged adversary and clamped down on the Night Flyer's face with its dripping teeth. The hind talons flared out like dual exclamation marks and then started to convulse as the Child chewed through its face and bored its relentless way into the brain. Another pair of Children had gotten hold of a Night Flyer's legs, but rather than wishboning their quarry, they lifted the screeching Night Flyer into the air and in one astonishing movement whipsawed their victim downward. The Night Flyer rammed the cave floor with such concussive force that its brains blew out the back of its head.

With a quick glance Jesse saw that Sam had nearly reached the ground.

About five more seconds and he would too.

Charly sees it all happen in slow motion. She's heard about traumatic events unspooling in this muffled, protracted manner, but not even when that pale creature kidnapped her baby had she truly understood what it meant.

Until now.

She'd wanted to kill Sam—honestly would have killed him—had she been given the means a few moments earlier. She *had* to get down there to Jake. Those nightmarish moments during which Sam had refused to relinquish his viselike grip on her body had been the longest of her life. But then Sam was barreling by her, leaping, and then she was watching with something like love as he skidded down the rock wall. It had only taken her a second or two to follow his lead, but while those seconds played out it seemed to her that she was stuck in neutral, the hard rock beneath her feet abruptly congealing and sucking her down. The most torturous moment of all was little Jake's vertiginous drop. The creature, she discovered as she began her own descent, had not loosed Jake from its vile grip. Even from this maddening distance Charly could see the ugly brown stains on Jake's light blue pajamas. The onesie had little sharks on it, which she liked because she imagined them guarding her baby at night, when she'd awake at two a.m. and worry about sickness, about SIDS, about lightning striking the nursery or a sudden tornado. She'd worried about everything, and now she is sure she won't be able to save baby Jake.

But Sam is almost there, Sam is extending his legs to meet the ground. Charly shoots an anguished look at her baby and moans at the mass of brawling bodies stomping and thrashing all around him. Jake's a good ten feet inside the churning area of bloody combat, and she knows he will be trampled, and she's the one who deserves to die for letting this happen. Oh God, why didn't she lock the nursery window, why didn't she keep Jake in bed with her?

She is nearing the bottom. She'll be there in a moment, but Sam is already up and dashing straight for Jake. One of the black creatures spots Sam and swoops down at him, hind talons extended. Sam pauses, feet apart, and aims the revolver at it. He squeezes off one shot, two, and the Night Flyer is screeching, tumbling, blood spouting from its face. Sam tosses the revolver aside, but he's only twenty yards away from Jake now. Fifteen. He is moving like a running back, head down, strong arms pumping, and she loves him then. He is closer, closer, and Charly reaches the ground in time to see Sam disappear into the writhing, snarling creatures, and her feet hit the ground perfectly. She pops up like a gymnast and immediately sights Sam, whose body she can make out because it's much shorter than the others, childlike amidst the towering Night Flyers and the stiltwalking Children. She sees Sam stop, whirl, an agonized, questioning look on his face. She realizes he cannot find Jake. Sam is searching, scanning the ground, and then his eyes open wide. Charly is almost to Sam now, and Sam is crouching next to a lifeless white body.

When she sees Sam rise with something in his arms, she is sure she's hallucinating.

It can't be, she thinks. *Please God, let it be true.*

Sam looks up at her, his eyes brimming with tears, and she knows it's real. Something inside her explodes, and she's sobbing and moving toward him on legs that have no feeling. Sam starts forward too, his body hunched over her baby—who is moving, still alive, oh Jesus—and she knows he will protect little Jake. And they are only a few yards apart when the cave fills with the most horrifying noise she has ever heard, a deep, rending roar like the earth is exploding, and she and Sam and the creatures all turn and stare at the immense, vertical tunnel that leads into this airplane hangar of a cavern.

Charly's heart stops when she sees what is making the noise.

Chapter Nine

Jesse landed in a tangle and felt a fiery pain in his groin. He'd either pulled it badly or given himself a hernia, but that didn't matter at the moment. He spotted Frank Red Elk, his normally hooded gaze stretched wide in feverish urgency. Red Elk was shouting something, and after a moment Jesse got the sense of it: *"This way, dammit, this way!"*

Jesse gestured toward Charly, but Red Elk shook him hard enough to make his neck ache.

"This way," Red Elk commanded, hauling Jesse to his feet. "Let those two take care of the baby. We don't get the girls now, they're as good as dead."

Jesse followed Red Elk toward the hellish battleground. There were bodies everywhere, the guts and limbs of three different species strewn about like litter. Night Flyers feasted on Children; Children disemboweled Night Flyers. One Child, having bested a downed Flyer, scooped out its red eyes and popped them into his mouth like oysters on the half-shell.

Intrepidly, Red Elk waded forward into the massed bodies, looking every bit like some film protagonist. His gun was drawn, his head lowered slightly as if against a stiff wind. Jesse followed in his wake and prayed the creatures wouldn't attack. His whole body thrummed with terror, his hands quivering little birds that threatened to drop the pocketknife at any moment, but one thought recurred, bolstering him just enough to keep him from swooning:

If they could just wrest the girls free and get out of here before the carnage subsided, they might just stand a chance.

They were almost to the fires. Jesse discovered with real surprise that Colleen was alive. The creature still encircled her with its small, insectile arms, but its attention was now diverted to the surging tide of Children. Jesse was heartened to detect just a glimmer of fear in its satanic red eyes. Not fear for its own life, but fear of having its prize taken away. Its great black wings fluttered, preparatory to escaping perhaps, but something—Duty? Outrage? A desire to spill the Children's lifeblood?—kept it grounded.

"I'll get Colleen!" Red Elk shouted back. "You find your girl!"

Without another word, Red Elk charged toward the creature and Colleen. Then the mass of bodies shifted and swallowed Red Elk up. Jesse hustled by the battling creatures. So far they hadn't marked his passing, and for maybe the first time in his twenty-eight years Jesse was thankful for his diminutive stature. Perhaps sensing he'd never grow beyond his current five feet, eight inches, his parents had bombarded him with children's books about how wonderful it was to be small, characters like Piglet and Percy the Tank Engine experiencing the same tired epiphany after completing some task that could only be accomplished by someone little. Even at the age of five, Jesse thought the stories were bullshit. Who cared if Piglet could crawl under a bush or Percy could fit through a narrow tunnel? If they were bigger in the first place they wouldn't have been given such shitty jobs.

But now, as he slipped through a throng of hissing Night Flyers and came within two feet of a snarling Child, Jesse thanked God he was such a little man.

He cast about looking for Emma. The fires spat out sufficient light, though their lurid glow danced and undulated with the fighting. Jesse stepped past one of the fires and squinted into the maelstrom of bodies. A sudden dread that Emma had already been borne away for a private dinner fell upon him with dreadful certitude. The shifting bodies all looked the same, the earsplitting shrieks and the withering stench of the creatures blending in a hellish uniformity.

Something seized his ankle.

Jesse bellowed in horror and twisted away, but the monster held on. He was going to fall, and once he was down the things would close over him like a horde of marauding ants. Only, he thought as his back slammed the cave floor, *he* was the ant, not them. And being small hadn't helped a goddamn bit.

Whimpering, Jesse kicked out with his free leg, heard a grunt of pain and felt the grip on his ankle loosen. A voice made him freeze.

"Don't leave me!" was all the voice screamed, but it was enough to get Jesse's attention. He rolled over, peered through the orange firelight, and beheld Marc Greeley facing him on his belly.

Or at least, what was left of Marc Greeley.

Jesse experienced a moment of clarity. In zombie movies people were always being ripped apart and munched gradually, far too gradually to sustain Jesse's suspension of disbelief. The human body, he'd always reasoned, could not survive when its guts were being strung all over the place like police tape.

The sight of Marc Greeley disabused him of this belief.

Where before the Night Flyers had limited their damage to those leech-like commas of scooped flesh, they had since graduated to some serious desecration of Greeley's dying body.

The man's lips were gone, resulting in a grisly, sardonicus grin. Equally horrifying was the excising of the man's eyelids. Greeley's brown eyes now bulged from their messy crimson sockets like some horny cartoon wolf's. The scalping had been consummated. One Night Flyer's head was buried in Greeley's groin.

"*Please,*" Greeley moaned, shaking Jesse's ankle like a weary puppy.

Jesse tried but could not tear his eyes off the glistening black bat's head tremoring as it chomped through Greeley's sexual organs.

"*Please kill me,*" Greeley wailed.

Jesse covered his mouth, coughing with revulsion. He knew he'd lose his nerve if he thought about it. He sat on his knees over Greeley's ruined body.

With a moan, Jesse plunged the knife into Greeley's neck, just under the ear. Then, with the man's huge eyes goggling at him, he yanked the knife hard, unzipping the man's throat.

For a moment Greeley's Adam's apple bobbed, a gurgling cough chuffing from his grinning mouth. Then the eyes took on a bleary glaze. Sobbing, Jesse clambered away.

The Night Flyer rose from Greeley's mid-section and stood on its muscular hind legs.

It tensed to spring. Jesse brought up the knife, but it shook in his hand and felt absurdly small, like entering a swordfight with a plastic spork. He fancied he could see a diabolical grin darken the already black face.

Then the most frightening sound Jesse had ever heard thundered through the arena.

Sam thought, *This isn't happening.*

His dad answered, *You keep telling yourself that, Sammy. Right up until that thing kills you.*

The thing his dad was referring to had to be forty feet tall. More, probably. It was like the Children, only on a larger and far more sinister scale. The legs rose as high as two-story houses, though the way the monster moved made judging difficult. It strode upright a few paces then lowered to all fours and ambled forward like a panther for several more. The arms were slender but terribly muscled, the thing's physiology endowing it with a strength no other living creature could boast. The waist and torso were shockingly thin, which no doubt allowed it to navigate tight spaces. The fingers reminded him of crane claws, the long-toed feet of white pergolas. The entire monster filled him with a childlike dread that threatened to undo what remained of his composure.

But it was the face that made Sam want to scream.

Superficially, it was constructed similarly to the rest of the pale monsters. Green eyes—these the size of manhole covers—a vaguely vulpine facial structure. The ears had the same pointed tips. The mouth was crammed with teeth like those swords samurais used to carry...katanas, he thought they were called. One bite from that mouth would puree a man.

The Old One, Red Elk had called it.

It drifted through the cavern like a terrible white god, its lambent green eyes seeing everything at once, penetrating every creature's defenses and exposing each one's secret heart. Sam knew this because of the knowledge in its ageless eyes and the ghastly, rasping voice rumbling in his mind. He shook his head against the onslaught. It wasn't until he'd started to cover one ear with a quaking hand that he remembered he held the child, that he'd retrieved baby Jake, was maybe the child's only chance at survival.

No survival, the voice buzzed, like a cloud of raging hornets. *No survival for you or the child.*

The Old One was a hundred yards away, watching them. Then it halved the distance in three seconds.

Sam clutched Jake, who was baying feebly, and willed his body to cross to where Charly stood. She too had been arrested by the entrance of the monster, but when she heard her baby, her trance broke and she lunged toward Sam. As he handed Jake to her, Charly began to sob. Despite the tears and the snot, she was the prettiest he'd ever seen her at that moment. He longed to enfold her and her child in a steely embrace and spirit them away to some safe corner of the world where monsters were only in fairy tales, and green-eyed devils could not read his mind. But the buzzing voice shattered the tranquil moment and paralyzed his body with its malevolent promise.

YOU'LL FAIL HER, SAMUEL, the ageless voice assured him. *YOU'LL FAIL HER LIKE YOU FAILED YOUR WIFE AND KIDS. YOU'RE AS GANGRENOUS AS YOUR DEAD MOTHER'S TOES, SAMUEL BLEDSOE. YOU DESERVE AMPUTATION.*

Sam glanced back at Charly, and when he saw her eyes flutter wide, then flit to something behind him and above him, he knew it was the end.

Sam Bledsoe turned and stared up at the monster who had lived for a thousand years.

Part Five
The Old One

Chapter One

Jesse scrambled away from the approaching figure and gibbered breathless obscenities. He backed right into a Night Flyer, whose beady, vermilion eyes didn't blink, but instead continued gazing up in awe at the monster Red Elk had called the Old One. Turning his gaze back to the Old One, Jesse recalled the other name, the one that described the creature who made men cannibals.

The Wendigo.

He could feel the horrible intelligence crawling around his mind like some bloated and persistent sewer rat, uncovering his insecurities and his frailties and reveling in them.

Time to jump ship, eh, Jessie? it wheedled in its guttural, droning voice. *You get a little uncomfortable or a little inconvenienced, and you split town?*

No, Jesse thought, scuttling away from the approaching monster. He thrashed his head from side to side to shake free of the voice, but it only deepened, lost its specious jocularity.

YOU'RE NOT GOING ANYWHERE, ARE YOU? YOU ALREADY KNOW THE ENDING TO THIS STORY, AND IT DOESN'T END WELL FOR YOU, DOES IT, JESSE?

Jesse collapsed on the cave floor, barely noticing the black pool of liquid in which he lay.

He became aware that his sobs and the baby's cries were the only sounds in the cavern, a preternatural stillness having taken hold.

He ventured a look around him and saw that every face in the arena was upturned to the Old One. The Children had left off their campaign to gain possession of Emma, whom Jesse still had not located. The Night Flyers, too, were transfixed by the impossibly tall monster, who had risen to its full height and was surveying the scene.

The Old One's huge, green eyes took in everything and everyone. Its impassive gaze swept the dead creatures and the live ones, the people held captive by the creatures and those who had not yet been taken. For the briefest of moments its ancient pupils lit on Jesse. The effect was singularly disturbing.

The Old One closed its eyes.

And a deep humming sound began to fill the cave. The noise was unlike anything Jesse'd heard before. It was like a dissonant musical note transformed into a tactile sensation. Jesse's ears, teeth and body vibrated with the sound of it, the unearthly bass thrum. He thought at first it was coming from the Old One, and so it was—the creature's colorless lips were pressed together in a parody of musical ecstasy. But it also came from the Children and the Night Flyers, the races who'd moments earlier been adversaries but were now closing their eyes in rapturous communion. The Old One spread its interminable arms and the hum intensified, teeth-rattlingly loud and crackling with a baleful electricity.

Jesse heard a woman's voice behind him. He whirled and saw who was making the noise, and moreover, why she was making it.

Unlike the others, the Big Nasty was not transfixed by the sight of the Old One singing its unholy dirge.

The Big Nasty was too busy trying to rape Emma.

Charly tore her eyes off the towering creature and put her lips to Jake's ear. He was moaning weakly, his little arms paddling slowly against her chest as though he were under water. His legs moved hardly at all, and despite the horror all around her, she yanked up her shirt, pushed down one cup of her bra, and guided a nipple into Jake's mouth. But the poor little guy didn't react, just drew in a thin breath and sighed it out. Charly's shock and terror and worry burned away in a gust of mind-searing rage. *God damn them*, she thought. *Damn all of them. They won't beat us. By God they won't. I'll kill every one of them before they get my baby again. I'll—*

Her thoughts broke off as Jake latched onto her nipple. Weakly, he began to suck. Her breasts had been engorged for hours and hours, and she'd been leaking milk into her bra. The flow of it was too much for Jake, who immediately began to retch and gag. Charly unlatched him with a hiss, gritting her teeth in self-reproach. Her nipple continued to spray, so she held Jake to her shoulder while he caught his breath.

"He gonna be okay?" a voice asked.

Charly turned and saw Red Elk gazing at her baby.

She nodded. Then Charly saw the girl behind Red Elk, leaning wearily against his broad back.

"Think you can walk out of here?" Charly asked Colleen.

Colleen's eyes flitted lower. She asked, "Can he?"

Sam knelt beside Charly, both his hands braced on the cave floor. He was breathing heavily, his eyes pinched shut.

"Sam?" she asked. Against her, Jake writhed more strongly than he had before, his sick-looking face rooting against the flesh of her shoulder.

"Gotta go," Sam said, his voice a pained rasp. He grabbed her arm, began leading her back the way they'd come.

Red Elk turned to Colleen. "You go with 'em."

"Frank," Colleen said, "I'm not going to—"

"It's not a suggestion," Red Elk said, pushing her on.

"What the hell is this," Colleen asked, "Masculine Stupidity Day? I'm not just leaving you—"

"If I don't do this, we don't have a chance."

"Do what?"

"Look, goddammit!" Red Elk shouted and swept an arm toward the Old One. Colleen looked. So did Charly.

She realized what the song was all about. The Old One's long arms reached down, the broomstick fingers brushing the prone bodies of the fallen Children and Night Flyers.

When the fingers touched them, the dead bodies began to stir.

The sight of the monster's grinning face, a rictus of depthless cruelty, infuriated Jesse in a way he'd never thought possible. The Big Nasty sat astradle Emma's flailing body, flicking its serpent-like tongue at her, muttering garbled taunts. All around the pair the black and white creatures stood immobile in unbroken reverence, yet the Big Nasty carried on with his vile torment, unconcerned with the resurrections occurring around him.

Already, half a dozen of the corpses had begun to twitch and breathe again, the terrible song coupled with the Old One's healing touch somehow revivifying the damaged flesh and ravaged organs. Ranged around Emma and the Big Nasty, like a newly made Golgotha, there were severed limbs, decapitated heads. Jesse couldn't imagine how those pieces could be fitted back together, how the eviscerated bodies could be made whole again. But he didn't have time to muse on that now. Emma's shirt had been torn open, revealing the white bra beneath. The bright spire of fury within Jesse glowed hotter.

Jesse got to them just as the Big Nasty reached down and ripped away Emma's bra. The sight of Emma's bare breasts incited Jesse into unthinking action. He reared back and kicked at the Big Nasty's face, but quicker than Jesse would have thought possible, the creature's hand shot out, caught his sneaker and twisted. Jesse hit the ground with a rib-crunching *whump*. He lay next to Emma, each of them with a horrid, clawed hand clamped around their throats. Emma swung her head toward Jesse, and their eyes met. Hers were full of angry tears, but there was a gratitude there too.

Jesse thrust his face away, got both his hands on the wrist that pinned him down, but the Big Nasty's corded muscles only squeezed tighter. Jesse writhed beneath the viselike grip and something brushed his hair, something moving and sharp.

A Night Flyer talon. It belonged to a severed black foot that had moments before been lying motionless but was now starting to twitch, the blasphemous hum reanimating it.

"*No*," Emma moaned.

Jesse swiveled his head and saw the Big Nasty fumbling with Emma's jean shorts, its obscene phallus already tumid and thrusting at her crotch.

Jesse groped for the twitching Night Flyer foot. He grasped it and felt its scaly flesh squirm against his fingers. Jesse shifted the twitching foot to his other hand and batted it at the Big Nasty's face.

The blow was a weak one—Jesse's angle was bad—but it did the trick. One of the razor-sharp talons gouged a meaty divot out of the Big Nasty's cheek. It made a hissing sound, sat up and slapped a hand over the wound, and as it did it released Jesse, seemed to forget him for just a moment.

It was all the time he needed to push to his knees, raise the Night Flyer's foot—which was now twisting crazily in his grip—and strike down at the Big Nasty's stupefied face. There was a pulpy squirting sound as two of the talons punctured the Big Nasty's eyeballs, the barbed tips of the claws harrowing the soft ocular tissue and spilling milky fluid down the monster's cheeks. It squealed, a high-pitched siren that pierced the dreadful hum echoing through the cave. The squeal pushed Jesse's rage further, yet even as he rose, intent on finishing the job on the Big Nasty, the sound also kindled an atavistic fear in him very much akin to the one he'd felt at the beginning of the nightmare, when he'd first spied the creatures at the playground. The Big Nasty, he realized as the creature held its ruined eyeballs and wailed, had been one of those original monsters, the ones who'd ignored Jesse and preyed upon the younger people below. Why had they done that? he now wondered. Why had they not killed him first? Because they knew he was no threat to them, that men like Goliath and Musclehead possessed more valor?

I'll show you a threat, he thought as he raised a sneaker. *I'll show you a fucking threat!* his mind screamed as he shot the bottom of his foot at the creature's open mouth. The heel of Jesse's sneaker crunched through two of the Big Nasty's bottom teeth. The blind creature tilted awkwardly and came down on its side, and Jesse moved with it, bringing his foot up again and stomping on the side of the beast's head. He raised his foot and stomped again, harder. Again. *You ugly*—again—*vicious*—again—*motherfucker!* The creature's face was unrecognizable, but he stomped again, again. *Die, you*—

"Jesse!" someone was screaming. "Jesse, please. We have to go!"

Her words finally did it, finally broke through the crimson veil that had fallen over him. He blinked at her, disoriented, then he let her lead him back through the tall figures that stood still as statues. But there was a difference now, one that iced his blood and snuffed the sense of triumph that had seconds before coursed through him.

The creatures' eyes were open.

The creatures' eyes were on Jesse.

"*Run,*" Emma said, taking him by the hand.

He sprinted with her, and as he ran, the venomous eyes watched him, the Night Flyers and Children alike, the red and green glowing eyes now following him with a grim focus that scared him worse than anything had yet. He ran faster, faster; he was towing Emma forward now. Ahead he distinguished Frank Red Elk shoving Colleen toward the slope, the slide down which they'd skidded earlier. Sam and Charly had already begun to scale the slide, and he could tell by the way Charly was struggling that she was too busy trying to cradle her child to climb effectively. She would make it a few feet, then she'd lose her balance and land on her side, her screaming baby clutched against her.

Jesse and Emma dashed ahead. They were almost upon Red Elk and Colleen when the humming sound altered, a shrill, ululating cry slicing through it. Jesse threw a glance over his shoulder and saw one of the Children toss its head back and cry out with savage intensity. Several others joined in the high-pitched battle cry. The Old One, its huge luminous eyes open now, strode toward the opposite side of the cavern, its endless white arms extended.

As Jesse and Emma reached Red Elk and Colleen, Jesse realized he'd been in error earlier regarding the carvings in the walls. The figures weren't carvings at all. They were Children and Night Flyers, dormant but apparently waiting for the Old One to bring them back to life. And as the Old One's broomstick fingers caressed them, their period of waiting ended.

And they too stared down at Jesse and the others.

Sam grimaced and fought against the jackhammer throb in his skull. He got a hand on Charly's rear end, tried pushing her up the slope, but it was no use. She was doing a good job of protecting her baby, but at this rate they'd make it to the top of the hill some time next week, and Sam very much doubted they'd have that much time. Even now he could sense the monsters behind them marshaling their forces, and he could sure as hell hear them screaming their hideous war cry. Christ, like a bunch of insane kids playing cowboys and Indians.

(*NEVER MAKE IT, SAM, NEVER MAKE IT OUT*)

He scrunched his eyes and shook his head vigorously, as if he could dislodge the voice that reverberated in his brain.

(*I WILL DEVOUR THE WOMAN AND YOU AND THE CHILD*)

The voice clanged in his skull like a devil's migraine, and he gnashed his teeth, thrashed his head against it.

"Your side?" Charly was asking. "Is it bleeding again?"

"It's not my side," he grunted, and gazed up into her face. What he found there made him grin despite the death knell echoing in his head. Pure, sweet concern, the kind only a truly generous human being can feel for another.

Sam reached out. "Give me Jake."

Charly clutched her baby tighter.

He said, "I can carry him and crawl better than you."

Charly shook her head. "You've been shot, you can't—"

"The bleeding's stopped—"

"You're in pain though, I can see it."

Sam waved it off. "It's not the wounds that hurt, it's the voice."

Charly stared at him uncomprehendingly.

Sam aimed a thumb over his shoulder. "That big bastard keeps talking to me."

Charly was shaking her head, but dammit, they didn't have *time.* "Give me Jake," Sam repeated. "You lead us out of here. You can do that, right?"

Charly squeezed Jake tighter, her face uncertain.

"You can do it," Sam said. "You're the one found the way down here."

"That was luck."

"No it wasn't. You can do it again."

"Sam, I have to hold him."

He fixed her with his hardest stare. "I won't let them get Jake. With you leading, it'll be faster." He nodded toward the moveless creatures. "In a moment they're gonna stop whatever they're doing and come after us. You wanna be here when they do?"

That did it. Charly handed Sam her baby.

"Now get going," Sam said, ushering her up the slide.

Charly started to go, moving swiftly, far faster than he was able to manage with the baby. The ache in his side devolved into anguish. He'd lied to her about how much it hurt before, and now the pain was a conflagration.

Charly had only progressed twenty feet or so up the slope when she stopped.

"Charly, you've gotta—"

But he broke off as he saw her staring fixedly at something behind them.

Sam turned and saw.

The carvings in the walls were coming to life.

And as he watched in horror, the first of them leaped out of its resting place and made straight for them.

Chapter Two

It was pure instinct that started Jesse running. Emma followed his lead. And that was good, Jesse thought, because the creatures were coming fast now. The Children he'd mistaken for statues earlier were leaping out of their carved arches, too many of them to count. The monsters who'd helped bring about their awakening were still fixed in their spots, their green and red eyes closed and their throats emitting that awful hum. But their faces were no longer serene, and their muscles no longer hung slack. They practically vibrated with energy now, their fists clenched and their quadriceps flexing eagerly.

Jesse tripped, reeled sideways a moment, then regained his balance. A backward glance revealed the severed head he'd tripped over—a white-haired old man Jesse was certain had been taken from the campground.

He heard Emma moan and assumed it was out of dread, but when she tarried on the edge of the slope instead of scaling it he was forced to follow her gaze to see what the hell was important enough to delay them.

Oh no, Jesse thought. *Don't do it, Frank.*

Red Elk had apparently persuaded Colleen to save herself. She was shambling toward Jesse and Emma, though her eyes remained on Red Elk. Running that way, gazing over her shoulder, she wasn't making good time, and what was more, she appeared much the worse for wear than Emma did. If she didn't find another gear soon, they'd be on her within seconds. The newly animated Children were swarming through their closed-eyed brethren, and they didn't look at all lethargic. The way they bounded over the hard cave floor suggested they'd been storing up their energy for just this moment, and they weren't about to let a good meal escape.

Only one thing stood in their way.

Frank Red Elk.

Jesse recalled the story of Red Elk's great-grandfather's murder, the steel he'd heard in Red Elk's voice at the time...

Jesse swallowed. Tugged on Emma's hand. She moved with him. They started the climb, and Jesse let go of her so they could move faster. Colleen still hadn't reached them, but Jesse was too frightened to wait any longer.

Meanwhile, Red Elk stood stock still, the Ruger at his side.

The creatures were twenty feet away from him.

Jesse could not look away as the first one loped right at Red Elk, its eyes such a brilliant green that they seemed to glow. It moved on all fours with a terrible grace, its face stretched in a malefic grin.

Jesse was sure it would fall on Red Elk before the man could defend himself, but Red Elk was faster than Jesse would've imagined, even after all they'd been through. One instant the Ruger was hanging at his side. The next it was blasting a hole in the Child's forehead. It skidded clumsily and came to rest at the big man's feet. Two more creatures were coming fast, and though Jesse knew Red Elk couldn't hold the Children off for long, he knew if they didn't use this time, none of them would get out of the arena alive. Apparently Emma had the same notion because she began scuttling upward a moment before Jesse did. He pulled even with her, and together they scrambled up the verge. It was steeper than Jesse remembered, and several times he nearly pitched backward. Once he even windmilled his arms, at a ninety-degree angle with the floor for an endless, stomach-clenching moment. But Emma shot out a hand, snagged the front of his T-shirt and was able to jerk him back. Then they were crawling side by side again.

Three quick reports boomed below.

Jesse turned. Red Elk had aimed true again, both of the creatures convulsing at his feet. But there were a dozen more of them, recently revived and craving meat, bounding toward him. One of the pair Red Elk had just gunned down was already rising again, the wound having only delayed it momentarily. Jesse thought Red Elk would flee for sure this time, but again he held his ground, waiting until the last moment to blast away at the Children.

Buying us time, Jesse thought and cast a glance up the slope. They were halfway to the top, he realized, and what was more, Charly and Sam were almost there. Sam was moving slowly, but Jesse could see his burden was safe, the little baby feet tremoring against Sam's body as they moved higher, higher.

A cry from below scattered Jesse's good thoughts. It had come from Colleen, who hadn't made it far, too busy watching Red Elk to concentrate on climbing. Jesse glanced that way and watched it all happen in slow motion: the dozen or so creatures reaching Red Elk almost simultaneously; Red Elk lulling them into complacency by waiting until the last moment to start shooting; the barrel of the Ruger prescribing its lightning arc and spitting its ear-shattering thunder at the faces of two creatures, three; a fourth leaping at Red Elk and then spinning bonelessly to the cave floor. Jesse watched nervelessly as two of the creatures Red Elk had shot began to stir. They pushed to their knees, their slender fingers scrabbling toward the man who'd shot them.

Red Elk shot a fifth in the throat, a gout of black fluid sloshing over its white chest, but this creature kept coming, snarling as it choked on its own blood. Red Elk fired again at point blank range, and his aim was true, but the creature's momentum knocked him back, sprawled him on the ground in an awkward heap. Another beast leapt over its fallen brother, squealing with bloodlust, but Red Elk shot it between the legs, and the squeal became a plangent screech of pain. Red Elk shoved to an elbow, fired at another, which slapped at its shoulder and came down on Red Elk. Jesse watched numbly as Red Elk batted at the creature with the Ruger, but two more monsters lunged for him then, and the gun dropped uselessly to the cave floor, Red Elk's severed hand still gripping it. Red Elk flailed at the creatures with his remaining hand, but the other Children arrived then and immediately fell on the big man, their Caliban faces darting at his convulsing body, chunks of flesh crammed in their maws. It was over then, but a half dozen more arrived at the feast and set to work on Frank Red Elk, whose lifeless body was already a viscous ruin of blood and entrails.

Colleen screamed at the creatures, who took no notice of her. But they would any moment, Jesse knew, and then she'd be eaten too.

He shot a look at Emma, who'd made it higher.

Thinking of his grandpa, who died abandoned and alone, Jesse clambered down the verge toward Colleen. She turned when he seized her arm, and when their eyes met there was no recognition in her wet eyes.

"It's over," she said tonelessly. "They got Frank."

"*Get moving,*" Jesse said and yanked her forward hard enough to dislocate her shoulder. He didn't care; he wasn't going to let another of their party end up torn apart. Some of his resolve seemed to communicate itself to her because she began moving faster then. Not as briskly as she had hours earlier, but fast enough to put some space between them and the creatures. And that was a very good thing, Jesse thought.

Because the trance had broken below.

And the entire mass of beasts had begun to surge toward the hill.

As he had experienced earlier on the playground, Jesse moved with the torpid sluggishness of nightmare. He forced his legs to push harder, his hands to drag his body up the hill faster, but he kept having to reach down and haul Colleen upward. She was weeping freely now, her face dazed and spiritless.

He peered past her down the hill.

The creatures had begun to climb.

Jesse reached down, clutched a shoulder of Colleen's shirt and willed his legs to drive them both higher. If Charly or Sam remembered the way out of this hell, they might just have a chance. He recalled how the cave branched in several places near the arena, so maybe they'd finally catch a break, maybe the beasts would follow the wrong trail.

He'd begun to let himself hope for escape when his fevered gaze happened on the Children.

Jesse's blood froze.

They were clambering forward like gravity had no effect on them, their long talons piercing the hillside like steel pitons and propelling them upward. The creatures had halved the distance and would reach Jesse and Colleen in seconds. He watched the Night Flyers rise and hover, though they did not yet attack. The Night Flyers in the walls hadn't been reanimated. Maybe, Jesse thought, the Old One favored the Children since they were made in his image.

Below them, the Children surged closer.

Whimpering, Jesse looked up and glimpsed Emma's leg disappearing over the edge. He almost hoped she would keep going, would escape with Charly and Sam. But the next instant her face was peering down at him over the edge of the plateau.

Colleen pitched forward onto the hillside and slid down a couple feet.

Jesse yanked hard on her shirt. "Come *on*, dammit, we're almost there."

She started climbing again, but her face was a quivering picture of vanquishment. Jesse kept them going but when he glanced down he realized they weren't going to make it. The beasts were only twenty yards away, and they were coming fast.

Desperately, he looked up and saw he was only five yards from where Emma awaited. She extended an arm, leaning over the edge. Jesse dug in with the toes of his sneakers, pistoned his legs harder. Colleen was still an encumbrance, but at least she was moving now, moaning and moving at the same time. Jesse got them right under Emma, groped toward her hand, but Colleen fell. She wailed, dragging him backward. He opened his mouth to scream at her, but then he understood why she was still sliding away from him, why he too was skidding down the hill.

The beasts had reached them, had swarmed over Colleen and were clawing at Jesse's grasping hand. One dark talon harrowed his wrist. With a whimper he let loose of Colleen and watched the beasts teem over her, enveloping her in a maelstrom of digging claws and snapping teeth. One creature leaped for him. Jesse brought a sneaker up and kicked it in the face. It landed on the shifting pile of creatures, but another immediately took its place. Terror propelled Jesse up the hill, and then Emma's fingers were hooking him under the armpits, aiding his progress. She dragged him up, up, his shoes bicycling against the scabrous rock floor. A creature lunged for him, and by sheer luck Jesse's heel caught its underjaw and sent it backflipping down the slope, knocking three other beasts off balance, the ripple effect sending a goodly mass of the monsters tumbling downward.

Jesse scrambled onto the plateau. He thought he'd made it when a white blur burst over the edge and pounced on his legs. Emma's fist blasted over Jesse's shoulder and hammered the creature in the nose. The Child's head snapped back, and when it swung forward with the reverberation, Emma socked it again, the nose crunching this time under her bony knuckles. Jesse drew his knees up and smashed his shoes into the creature's chest. The blow knocked it backward just as another hideous face appeared, and when the creatures collided they both jarred and disappeared shrieking over the edge of the drop-off.

Without pausing, Jesse climbed to his feet beside Emma, and together they sprinted into the darkness. They swerved left with the curve and had gone twenty yards or so before they heard the Night Flyers swooping toward them.

Chapter Three

Together they shambled into the murk.

"There's Sam and Charly!" Emma shouted.

Jesse wrenched his attention toward where she pointed and saw two figures disappear around a corner. When he turned to face Emma and the mining helmet lit her up, he felt his stomach knot again.

"What's..." he began to say, but stopped when he heard it too—the sound their frenzied footfalls had concealed. A growing roar. Coming from behind them.

Coming from the arena.

Emma gazed at him in terror.

Unconsciously, he turned toward the drop-off, scarcely visible now, just a dim, flickering cone of light licking the far edge of the corridor. Then the flickering became frenetic, the massing shadows making the firelight dance.

They were coming. All of them. The awakened Children, the others who'd helped resuscitate them, the Night Flyers, even the Old One.

Every one of the beasts was bent on destroying them.

He turned away, moaning as he and Emma fled the onslaught. The corridor was fifteen feet high, but Jesse knew how it narrowed, how it closed to only a three-by-three shaft before opening up to where they'd gathered themselves earlier, after Red Elk shot Sam Bledsoe.

Jesse and Emma pelted down the corridor.

Emma was pulling ahead of him, but that was fine because the passage was narrowing. It was still plenty tall to stand upright, but it was no more than four feet wide now, so that he and Emma moved single file. He gave her a yard or so to make sure he didn't trip her—if he did they were dead—but he couldn't allow any more space than that.

The shadows were closing in.

Ahead, he could see a ghost of yellowish light. Sam and Charly? Man, he hoped so. Jesse knew he and Emma would have to duck soon. The ceiling got really low before the cavern ahead, and if Emma smashed head first into it, she'd be knocked senseless.

And yes, he saw by the glow of the mining helmet, the ceiling was only six feet high now; in moments they would have to run in a crouch. At least that would stop the Night Flyers.

He threw another glance back, and his breath clotted in his throat.

A Night Flyer was swooping toward them, its great black wings tilted sideways, its razor-sharp teeth hinged wide.

"*Down!*" Emma screamed. Before Jesse could complete his turn to see what the hell she was talking about, he was tripping over her, somersaulting, the Night Flyer smashing into him, the bones of its enormous wings snapping like wind-torn masts. He heard a wet click as its teeth sought his throat. A shape vaulted both Jesse and the Night Flyer, and it wasn't until it caught him by the collar of the shirt that Jesse realized it was Emma, Emma who'd seen the monster descending on them, Emma who'd saved them both by making sure they'd dropped at the right moment. She was hunched over, Jesse following her lead like a soldier fleeing enemy fire. The Night Flyer filled the corridor behind them in a broken tangle, its enraged maw snarling at them right up until the mass of creatures pushed over it, a nightmare glacier of white and black limbs and venomous faces, equal parts hunger and agony now because they were being wedged tighter and tighter by the crowd surging behind it.

The ceiling scraped Jesse's helmet, and for a moment the mining light blinked. He hunched down, cringing, and the light glowed full strength. He had no idea how much longer it would last, but if it did go out, they were done. This subterranean region was a labyrinthine madhouse of tunnels and traps. In the dark they were worse than dead; they would be sport for the monsters.

Emma was hustling forward as quickly as she could, bent over as she was, and for once the sight of her bared back, the exposed cleft of her upper buttocks, did nothing for Jesse's imagination.

He figured maybe he was maturing.

When they emerged into the small cavern, Jesse spotted Sam right away, handing Charly's baby up to her. They were just able to make the handoff, then Sam was ushering Emma forward, telling her to get her ass in gear. Jesse jogged after her, his body numb from the waves of terror that kept sweeping through it. Even now he could hear the bones breaking back there, the bursting of skin and organs, like a Bosch painting endowed with a soundtrack. He couldn't imagine how horrible the bottleneck of monstrous bodies had become in the three-by-three tunnel. The cavern seemed to creak like an old ship's hull in a vortex.

He was so fixated on the unearthly cacophony rumbling through the tunnel that he didn't at first notice what lay a few feet to their right. Jesse craned his head that way, and the yellowish mining light splashed over what had once been Melanie Macomber.

"Don't look at her," Sam said.

But it was too late for that.

Jesse was aware that Sam was helping Emma up into the opening, but he could not look away from Melanie's remains. It looked to Jesse like she had been bludgeoned to death with a meat mallet. Unbidden, his gaze lowered to the girl's crotch, which glistened with blood and viscera.

"Told you not to look," Sam said.

Jesse glanced up as Emma made it the rest of the way into the opening. Jesse moved forward to follow her, but Sam barred his way.

"I go first," Sam said.

Jesse gaped at him, uncomprehending.

Sam stared at him with unconcealed impatience. "Unless you're strong enough to haul me up there, I've gotta go first. With this side I can't climb too well, but if I step on your back, I can just make it."

"What about me?" Jesse asked. He hoped it was his imagination, but the sounds echoing from the corridor behind him seemed to be altering. Almost as if the bottleneck were breaking up.

"We'll figure it out," Sam said quickly. "Now kneel down, dammit. I don't want to be standing here talking when those bastards come through."

Jesse did as he was told, but a black dread had descended over him. He would die in here. After all these near misses, this would be the site of his death. Even now he could hear the sounds from the clogged tunnel morphing into a series of chunking beats, as if the stampede had been reversed and the victims of the deadly tide were being peeled off the pile and flung backward like sodden sand bags.

Jesse swallowed.

He placed his hands on his knees. Sam's shoe pressed into the small of his back. Jesse's body threatened to crumple under the load.

Jesse gritted his teeth, willed his arms and legs not to buckle. Bledsoe didn't look very big, but now Jesse understood just how much power Sam possessed. The guy was built like a powder keg, and if he didn't climb off soon, they were both going to collapse.

"*Hold still, dammit,*" Sam grunted.

Behind them the chunking sounds had grown more rapid. Jesse imagined a group of Children back there steam shoveling the mashed corpses out of the way, an assembly line of the beasts passing the dead and wounded back toward the arena. That's were the Old One likely was, in full resuscitation mode. *My God. Did they really have a prayer? What hope was there when your enemy never died, only returned with renewed vigor?*

Bledsoe's feet left Jesse's back.

Jesse blew out a relieved breath.

"Come on!" a voice from above hissed.

He strained his neck up and saw Emma peering down at him. The salty sweat dripped from his curly hair into his eyes, so that he had to rub them until he could see again.

"Okay," he said. "Coming."

But Emma wasn't listening.

She was eyeing the tunnel behind him.

Jesse turned that way and realized with foreboding how loud the sounds were now, the ghastly excavation of the occluded passage.

They would be upon them in moments.

"Grab on," someone called.

Jesse tore his eyes off the opening and saw Emma being lowered, arms first, down to him. It wasn't that far really, only nine or ten feet from the floor to the opening above, yet it seemed an impossible expanse. He could almost reach Emma's hands now, but once he did there was no guarantee Sam and Charly could drag both of them up.

He stood on tiptoes, his fingertips brushing Emma's.

"A little farther," she called back to the others.

Her hands lurched closer, and Jesse strained to grasp them. Their fingers twined, but they couldn't grip, their skin too slick from the strain.

"Lower," Emma grunted.

"*Can't go any lower,*" Sam answered. Jesse could hear the thinness in his voice. The man was tough, but the combination of dangling Emma down the verge and his earlier injury was close to breaking him.

But Emma's hands did jerk closer. It was only another inch or so, but it was enough for them to forge a stronger hold.

"Got him!" Emma called.

Jesse felt himself lifted off the ground.

The noises behind them swelled, the bottleneck nearly cleared. He was halfway to the opening. He threw a feverish glance at the tunnel, the mining light exposing a tapestry of swirling shadows.

Jesse heard a dull pop in Emma's wrist, but she didn't cry out, didn't loosen her hold on him. They rose higher, higher.

Then, impossibly, they were up.

Charly scooped up her child, whom she'd laid on the ground. Rubbing her wrist, Emma followed. Sam set off too. Jesse hustled after them until he was abreast of Sam, the tunnel just wide enough for the both of them.

"How far is it?" Jesse asked him.

"Hard to tell," Sam said with little interest.

"How long have you guys been underground?"

"Hours," Sam answered, "but I don't think we traveled all that far."

On the last word, his face stretched in a pained grimace, as though he'd just been given a jolt of electroshock therapy.

"You okay?" Jesse asked, his voice growing hoarse from running.

"Fine," Sam said. But he didn't look it.

Jesse asked, "Would you have left us if we'd have gotten to the cavern any later?"

Sam looked at him. "You really want me to answer that?"

Jesse decided he didn't.

Baby Jake held tight to her chest, Charly handed Emma the Maglite.

As they moved forward, the tunnel opened up into a broad cavern. Because they'd come from the opposite way, Jesse hadn't noticed how many openings there were in the walls, how many potential turnings there were. He decided that was a good thing if it threw the monsters off their trail. If, however, they got lost down here...

"We take this one," Charly said, nodding to a tunnel ahead and to the right.

"Are you sure?" Emma asked.

"Trust her," Sam said, and that was it.

They angled right and started up a gradual rise. Accelerating, the survivors hurried up the hill.

Chapter Four

The next hour crawled by in an unceasing tempest of nerves and uncertainty. Charly's sense of direction was awe-inspiring. She never hesitated, calling out their movements far before they reached the junctions of tunnels.

Emma was grimly determined as well. Comparably, Jesse knew, she'd been through far more than he had, but you'd never know it to look at her. Beneath the coating of grime and sweat, Emma was prettier than ever. Her resoluteness, her focus, her pragmatic attitude—all these things made her seem like Charly's younger sister. With the two of them in the lead, Jesse felt confident they would survive.

Sam Bledsoe, however, worried him a great deal.

Most of the time Jesse's helmet light was focused on the girl's backs. But whenever Jesse turned to check on Sam, the man's wan face seemed conflicted or downright tortured, as if he was being eaten alive from within.

By tacit understanding, Charly and Sam were the only two who handled the child, which was fine by Jesse. Holding babies always made Jesse feel inept. He was mortally afraid of dropping one.

Jesse continued on in a state of bleak distress. The tunnels had bizarre acoustics. At one moment the growls and footfalls of the monsters sounded right behind them. At others a preternatural quiet seemed to spread, the only noises their own breathing and the occasional whimper of the baby.

As they moved, numerous scents assailed Jesse. Earlier, the rank odors of the Children—fecal matter and rotten meat—predominated. Several times the ammoniac scent of the Night Flyers made his nostrils tingle. Yet increasingly it was the delirious smell of water that made its way toward them. Though he'd scarcely said a word since they'd escaped the arena, Sam did mention an underground river, saying when they reached it they'd be close to the surface. Then his face clouded and he said no more, no matter how hard Jesse pressed him on the matter.

After a time the tunnel became so narrow that it was impossible to run or even jog any longer, and they settled for progressing through the labyrinth at a steady walk. The corridor they were traveling narrowed so much that at times they had to move sideways.

"How far?" Emma asked, giving voice to the question perpetually on Jesse's mind.

When Sam didn't respond, only continued sidestepping along behind Jesse, Charly said, "We're over halfway there..."

"But what?" Emma asked.

Sighing, Charly said, "There're some problems up ahead."

"What problems?"

Charly didn't answer, continued to sidle along. A minute or two later, the tunnel opened up, and Charly raised her shirt to nurse the baby. Jesse turned away and regarded the wall.

"You said there were other problems," Emma prompted.

Charly glanced at Sam. "There's the river to cross."

"We're not crossing it," Sam said through clenched teeth.

Charly unlatched Jake, frowned at Sam. "But if we don't cross—"

"We're following it out," Sam said without looking up. "It's gotta come from somewhere, right?"

Emma seemed about to ask another question, but something made her freeze, open-lipped and staring.

A fluttering noise, somewhere ahead of them.

Like vast wings beating the air.

"Turn off your lights," Sam said.

Emma twisted off the Maglite. Jesse reached up and clicked off the mining helmet.

The sounds drew closer, slithery and batlike.

In the darkness, Jesse did his best not to make noise, but every time he exhaled, his dry throat rasped like cornhusks in a breeze. A hand slid into his, squeezed. He squeezed Emma's hand back but felt no better.

The Night Flyer—if that's what it was—seemed to pause up ahead. Jesse had no idea how far away it was, but it sounded way too close. He was painfully aware of being unarmed.

The noise slithered again, moving away from them this time. A sharp pain started in Jesse's chest, but he didn't dare exhale.

When the slithering noises ceased entirely, he blew out a shuddering breath.

"Let's get moving," Sam said.

So when are you going to tell her? Dad's voice asked.

I'm not, Sam answered him.

You're chickening out?

Wouldn't you?

Probably, his dad allowed, *but that doesn't mean it's right.*

None of this is right, Dad. Those things aren't right.

Can't argue with you there.

Baby Jake crooked in one arm, Sam lugged his aching body over the rim of the slide. The clamor was like a wrecking ball in his skull. He could feel his sanity splintering, the pain it brought on worse than any migraine he'd ever had.

SOON, SAMUEL. SOON. I WILL FINISH YOU SOON.

Sam handed Charly her baby. Jesse's mining helmet rose jerkily over the rim of the slide and splashed its amber glow over Charly as she bared a breast and guided it into Jake's rooting mouth. Sam hardly noticed. He longed to curl up like a pill bug and wail, to dash his brains out on this grimy cave floor. But the others needed help up, and if they were going to get out of here, Sam couldn't succumb to hopelessness now.

YES YOU CAN. YOU CAN AND YOU WILL. I WILL TASTE YOUR FLESH, I WILL HAVE YOUR WOMAN, I WILL DRINK OF THE CHILD'S BLOOD.

Sam jerked Jesse roughly over and then hoisted Emma up to safety. Charly was already done feeding Jake and was waiting impatiently for them to move on, and though Sam knew she was right to be in a hurry, he didn't know how much more of this his mind could take.

But he too rose and dusted himself off. Without the extra twenty pounds or whatever it was Jake weighed, Sam felt a good deal lighter. It didn't compensate for the maniacal clanging in his skull, but it helped a little.

He thought of asking Emma for the buck knife back, but she didn't offer, and he didn't have the energy to bother her. Getting Charly's baby up that last hill might just have been his last hurrah. But at least he'd done that.

They reached the river, the place where he'd first seen a white beast. Sam held Jake while Charly joined the others in kneeling before the water and drinking from cupped hands. Charly finished after only a few moments—he was sure she wanted more water but was just being considerate of Sam's thirst—and relieved him of baby Jake. Sam lay down on his belly and plunged his face in the water. He swallowed huge gulps of the turbid stuff, unmindful of how sick he might become or how foul the water tasted. Suddenly sick to his stomach, he brought his face out of the water and hung there panting.

Though tiny droplets still sprayed his face, the thunder of the water had diminished, which told him plainly that the deluge aboveground was over. For all he knew, it might have ended just after he and Charly had ventured inside the cave.

God, that felt like an age ago. Could it really have been only a matter of hours? If his internal clock was right—and Sam found it almost always was, give or take a few minutes—it was now approaching eleven o'clock. That could help them, he thought. The darker it was outside, the better. Though the creatures could see better in the dark than humans could, their night vision didn't seem to be faultless. Take the creature that had passed close by them earlier...

Sam realized everyone was staring at him.

"Lost in my thoughts," he said and mustered what he knew was a sorry excuse for a grin.

Charly's expression was concerned. "I asked if you thought we'd be able to make it out that way." She nodded upstream.

Sam started moving. "The water isn't as turbulent as it was. It's still high—even if the rain stopped completely, it'll take time for it all to drain down here—but I'm thinking we'll be able to..." He let the thought hang as he approached the arch through which the river entered the vast cavern.

"Gimme the Maglite a minute," he said to Emma. He trained it on the water where it met the cave wall on their side of the river. "Yep," he said, studying the ledge of sand and rock. "It's not ideal, but if we're careful, we should be able to get out that way."

"How far is it?" Emma asked.

"No idea," Sam said. "We didn't take this route in."

"Where did you enter?"

Sam gestured vaguely across the river, in the direction of the hole from which they'd dropped before battling the first creature they'd encountered, the one who'd devoured a good portion of poor Larry Robertson. Thinking of the sheriff's mutilated body, Sam could not suppress a shiver.

"Better get started," Sam said and promptly slipped, one work boot skimming the surface of the water. Sam settled back against the wall. He cast a brief glance down at the ledge. It was less than a foot wide in some places. The toes of his boots would poke out over the churning river.

"You sure about this?" Charly asked him.

"I'm not sure about anything."

She scrutinized him in the dimness.

"Gimme Jake," he said.

But she didn't.

"Come on," he said. "Those things aren't going to quit hunting us. All we know, they could be closing in right now."

"Sam..."

"Give him to me," Sam said more roughly than he'd intended.

"I've got him," Charly said.

Sam watched her for a long moment, saw she wasn't going to relent. Reluctantly, he began to sidle along the slick ledge.

And one by one, the others followed.

Chapter Five

The tunnel ate its way into the darkness far longer than he'd anticipated, so that Sam began to wonder whether they'd made a mistake. True, they'd been presented with no other viable options, but the situation was becoming bleak enough for Sam to second-guess himself. Maybe there had been another way out, one they'd missed.

And if unicorns were real, his dad spoke up, *you could ride one out of here.*

Go to hell, Dad.

You'd've never said that to me when I was alive.

Well, you aren't.

You were never a quitter, son.

Who's quitting?

Sounds like you are.

A wave of dizziness swept over him. He bit the inside of his mouth to fend off unconsciousness. The ashen stars in his mind bloomed, spread. The glow from the Maglite he aimed at the ledge wavered.

Charly said, "Are you—"

"I'm fine," he said.

I'm not quitting, either, he thought and continued on.

After a few more steps the ledge widened slightly. Another minute, and they had a three-foot walkway to travel on.

IT WON'T MATTER, the Old One told him. *I'LL HAVE YOU IN THE END.*

Not quitting, Sam told himself. *Getting them out of this cave. Getting them away from here.*

THERE'S NO ESCAPE, SAMUEL. YOU KNOW THAT.

"Name's not Samuel," he muttered. "Not even my teachers called me that."

FAILED YOUR FAMILY. YOU'LL FAIL THESE PEOPLE TOO.

"Sam?" Charly asked. "Who are you talking to?"

Getting you out of here, Sam thought.

"How much farther?" Jesse called from behind.

Sam scowled, was about to tell the kid he had no idea how much farther, what did he look like, a human GPS?

But the words died in his throat.

Ahead, he could see the river. Not just the infrequent glimmers cast by the Maglite and the mining helmet, but the kind of glow made by the moon, by the honest-to-goodness stars. He realized there was a mild stirring of breeze on the flesh of his cheeks. My God, had they found their way out?

Without ruminating more on it, Sam began a hurried shuffle forward. The surface of the ledge was slick and treacherous, but the shimmering water was so close, so deliriously close, and if he weren't so deathly afraid of being swept back downstream toward the Children and the Night Flyers, he'd kneel down and toss more scoopfuls of the black water into his mouth, he'd revel in the brackish taste of the stuff because they were almost out, dammit, they were almost safe!

"Ohmygod," Charly breathed, and though he knew it was unwise, he turned back to see her face. It was the most beautiful thing he'd ever seen, the most extraordinary thing. It was the apotheosis of all things good, of all things not lost, and for the first time in hours he allowed himself to wonder how their life might be if they survived all of this, how their life might be together.

The baby uttered a sudden and ecstatic cry, and for the first time since they'd rescued the child in the arena, Sam gazed down into the child's face. It had never occurred to him till now to examine the child, to study the curious little eyes, the tiny pink nose, and the mouth, God, Charly's mouth, the same shape and the same perfect lips.

Sam saw they were nearing a bend in the river, a place where the silvery moonlight spilled its brilliance onto the chugging water. The ledge there narrowed, but it didn't matter; they were nearly out.

A hand fell on his back, Charly's hand. She was moaning expectantly, sounding even more excited than he was. Jesse started to laugh and Emma joined him, and Sam had a sudden, ghastly thought, that all this was a final joke being played on them, that the moment they rounded the corner and beheld the world again, the mouth of whatever cave they'd reached would be circled with leering faces, the Children and Night Flyers mocking them one last time before ripping them apart.

Sam listened for the confirming voice of the Old One, but the blaring presence in his brain was silent for the moment. Sam reached the bend in the tunnel, pressed his back against it, began to navigate the diminished ledge. And as he did he saw it—the low-hanging ceiling ahead, the opening overhung with weeds but unmistakably a gateway to the outer world, the one he'd been sure he'd never see again.

"There it is!" Jesse cried out.

Sam winced, almost reminded the kid to keep his celebrations to himself so they didn't alert the creatures to their whereabouts, but Charly beat him to the punch, telling Jesse firmly but kindly that they weren't safe yet, they had to be careful until they were far away from this godforsaken land.

They sidled forward, the illuminated waters bubbling with grasses and sticks. The exit was only forty feet away now, no more than that.

Sam wondered how far away from the original cave entrance they would come out. He estimated that they'd moved in roughly the same direction as the original cave entrance, but what did he know? His head was full of dead fathers and godlike monsters—how could he be trusted to know anything?

The Old One hasn't spoken to you for several minutes now, he thought.

Biding its time.

No!

They were twenty feet away.

Ready to snatch you up and make good on its promise.

Closer, the outline of the cave exit was resplendent with pallid light.

Ready to eat you alive...waiting

Ten feet. Charly's hand on his back, patting him in excitement.

...waiting...just outside the cave—

Sam lunged through the opening, the down-hanging weeds dragging wet streaks through his hair.

Into the moonlight.

He reached back, helped Charly and Jake into the limpid brilliance. She threw herself against him, kissed him on the mouth, then Jake several times, then him again, the three of them gripped tightly in a laughing cluster. They barely noticed Jesse and Emma stumble out after them. When Sam finally looked up, tears streaming down his face, he saw Jesse kissing Emma, the two looking like something from a movie, and he supposed they deserved to look that way. Then he reminded himself to enjoy this moment, to by God kiss his own girl, which he did. Then he kissed Jake too, and the boy smiled. Sam laughed and was still laughing when he discovered something that made his spirits rise higher, which he hadn't thought possible.

The entrance to the cave they'd found earlier that day lay less than a football field away, its frowning black mouth like a scar on the pearlescent nightworld.

They didn't need any prompting to get them going. Sam moved ahead of Charly. Hand in hand, Jesse and Emma came after.

The ground underfoot squelched with each step. These lowlands were flooded—in many places the sable waters glittered like dark gems—but it appeared there was enough decent ground on which to tread. As they moved, Sam cast frequent glances at the cave entrance ahead. He'd not be taken by surprise.

A nagging worry that this was all a snare tickled at the nape of his neck, but that was giving the beasts too much credit. Or rather overestimating what the creatures thought of Sam and the rest. The beasts would consider their quarry too helpless to find a way out of the underground labyrinth and would therefore focus their hunt on the network of tunnels. Maybe after several hours the creatures would allow for the possibility that their prey had escaped, but by then Sam and his group would be long gone. Sam patted the pocket of his jeans to make sure his truck key was still there and was spared the ultimate cruel joke of finding it missing.

They were almost upon the original cave entrance now. Without thinking about it, Sam positioned himself between that black scar and the others. They moved slowly past it, Sam's eyes never leaving the dark semi-circle.

They skirted the cave entrance without issue.

Less than a minute later they reached the base of the hill.

This time Charly let Jesse have a turn carrying the baby. The two ladies moved on either side of Jesse to make sure he and his precious cargo didn't slip on the sodden ground. Sam hung back for several moments surveying the hill rising before them. It would only take them a few minutes, even with the slick scum of dead leaves and mud impeding them. But it wasn't time that was bothering Sam.

It was being exposed.

Funny, he mused, how much he'd hated being underground earlier, scurrying around the dank catacombs like some sightless mole. Nevertheless, there was a part of him now that longed for the obscuring darkness. Out here he felt like he'd been thrust onstage just before some unrehearsed show. Who knew where the creatures were? They could still be underground, but what if they were up here already, lying in wait on the hillside or up at Charly's house, ready to—

An icy tingling started at his shoulders.

Like he was being watched.

Sam whipped his head around and stared at the cave entrance.

Empty.

But still, he stared at it a full ten seconds longer, somehow convinced an ancient, leering face would materialize in the shadows.

Nothing was there.

He swallowed.

Turning back to the hill, he saw the others had made good progress, were already a good thirty feet up.

Sam followed them, moving as quietly as he could.

He took care to step on patches of ground that were free of debris. He didn't want to crack a twig or trip over a downed branch. Sure, the

Children and Night Flyers would be able to spot them if they passed close enough, but it still seemed wise to do all they could to avoid detection.

His mind drifted to the Night Flyers. He hadn't paid them enough mind, hadn't thought about how their ability to fly could change things. What if they'd been sent out on patrol, winging their way through the moonlit night to reconnoiter the area? He tried to estimate their numbers, but the sheer size of the underground world defeated him. Who knew how expansive that labyrinth was, how many other arenas just as large or even larger were hidden down there?

Sam looked up and was stunned to find they were nearing the top of the climb. *This is where they'll attack us*, Sam thought. *Just before we make it to the truck. They'll hit us with everything they've got— Children, Night Flyers, the Old One.*

Especially the Old One.

Sam shook the thought away, a superstitious dread of attracting the monster's attention making him grasp for other thoughts, other images: pink elephants, burning buildings, little kids playing in an opened fire plug.

Charly nude on a bed of rose petals.

Sam smiled. That one did it.

When the picture of Charly's gorgeous body dissipated from his imagination, he saw that the others had waited for him. Charly clutched her baby again. Each set of eyes lay fixed on Sam, clearly hoping for guidance.

If you all are counting on me to lead you, he thought ruefully, *we're all screwed.*

He joined them about twenty feet from the top and did his best not to sound out of breath. He said, "We'll take my truck. That all right with everybody?"

Emma shrugged. "My car's back at Red Elk's house.

"Can we all fit?" Charly asked.

He nodded. "It's a crew cab. These two'll be snug back there, but I doubt they'll mind too much."

At that Jesse smiled shyly at Emma.

"You have the keys?" Charly asked.

Sam nodded. "Might as well head up now. We don't want those things getting wise to us."

They started up the hill, but Sam said, "Hold on a second."

They stopped and waited, their eyes wide and anxious.

He said, "Just in case there's trouble up there, you need to know something."

"Robertson's hunting rifle?" Charly said.

Sam nodded. "It might not be loaded, so be sure to check. And there's a crowbar under my seat. It's for fixing a spare, but the spare has a hole in it."

"Mr. Prepared."

He chuckled. The others did too.

Then their smiles faded.

Sam peered up the hill with narrowed eyes.

There were voices up there, screaming.

Charly said, "Oh no."

Sam looked at her, his heart hammering in his chest.

"That's Kate's voice," she said. "My daughters are up there."

Chapter Six

They took off up the hill, moving as fast as they could against the steep angle and the sloppy terrain.

Sam kept his voice as low as he could. "You said they were at your mother-in-law's."

"They were," Charly said, her voice edging toward panic. "They were supposed to spend the night there."

"You suppose she..." he began, then broke off lamely. Wasn't it obvious? Florence's parents had brought them back. The girls probably missed their mom, and who could blame them? Their baby brother had been abducted.

Sam got an arm around Charly and helped her reach the crest of the incline. Then they were in the vacant lot to the left of Charly's, gazing diagonally at her house. Sam could see nothing wrong with it from the outside, but the shrieking from within told a very different story. Little girls' voices and a grown woman's, each of them a shrill of terror.

Sam said, "Get Jake to the truck."

Charly was shaking her head. "Can't...got to get my girls..."

"We will," Sam said. "But first you and Jake are gonna get safe. Emma too." He looked at Jesse. "We go to the house."

Jesse nodded.

But Charly was moving forward.

Sam took her by the shoulders, stared hard into her eyes. "You don't wanna let your baby get taken again, so you have to stay with him. You can't bring him in the house because there might be some of those things—"

Charly cried out, took a step that way.

"And that's why," Sam hurried on, "this is the only way."

He nodded at Emma. "Give me the buck knife, and get them to the truck." He held out the George Strait keychain and put it in Emma's palm. Nodding, she took Charly by the arm and led her through the tall grass, moving toward the road where Sam's blue Chevy sat parked.

Charly obeyed, but her eyes kept flitting to the house.

Sam and Jesse jogged toward the back deck. The screams were still blaring into the night, which he took for a good sign. Before he and Jesse slipped behind the garage, he caught one last glimpse of Charly, who was almost to the truck.

Then the image of her was gone. Sam tried to banish the certainty that he'd never be with her again, but it crystallized in his mind like an immutable fact.

He and Jesse stepped onto the deck and moved to the sliding glass door.

Jesse didn't see it until they stepped inside, and he supposed that was for the best. Had he known what awaited him in Charly's house, he might not have followed Sam.

The furniture had been tumbled against the walls as though some surly giant had decided to redecorate. And, Jesse realized as he took in the macabre scene, that was exactly what seemed to have happened.

Charly's daughters were both huddled behind an overturned sofa, their eyes huge and starey. They were screaming themselves raw, which Jesse felt like doing too if only he could find his voice. What they were screaming at was a giant white creature, one of the Children, but larger than all save the Old One. It was mostly naked, but there were still scraps of clothes hanging off its hips.

Eric Florence had transformed.

At the Eric-thing's feet were the remains of a man.

At least, Jesse *thought* it had been a man. The corpse was so mutilated it was difficult to discern its former shape.

Charly's daughters continued to scream, but it was Florence's mother that shrieked the loudest. The Eric-thing held her aloft, its hands squeezing her by the hips. Her white sneakers kicked the air ten feet off the ground. The woman had short black hair, looked like she was in her sixties. Even in the wan light of the family room, Sam could see how deeply tanned she was.

Sam was saying, "Put her down, Eric."

The beast glanced at Sam without comprehension.

At the sound of Sam's voice, the girls behind the sofa looked up, a flicker of surprise on their little faces, followed by recognition.

Sam was staring at the beast, but at waist level he was gesturing for the girls to come out. They stopped screaming, but they didn't budge from their hiding place.

"You're not going to hurt anybody..." Sam soothed. Then his eyes flickered down at the mangled body of what once might have been Eric Florence's father. "You're not gonna hurt anybody else," he amended.

The Eric-thing continued watching Sam.

Sam said, "A few hours ago you were one of us. Am I right, Eric?"

Eric's mother was sobbing quietly now, her mascara-smeared eyes on Sam.

"You're gonna put your mother down," Sam said to Eric. "Then we're gonna get you some help."

Sam shot a look at Jesse, jerked his head savagely at the girls.

Jesse realized he'd been gaping at the tableau like an idiot. With a start, he hurried over and bent down to the kids. One looked six or seven, the other a few years younger.

"Your mommy's outside," Jesse said, trying to keep the edge off his tone. "She's waiting for you."

That broke through the membrane of terror holding them inert. They accepted Jesse's hands, and he'd started to lead them around the upended couch, when a gasp sounded from across the room.

Where Charly stood transfixed, baby Jake in her arms.

Sam reached into his pocket, grasped the handle of the buck knife. He caught a distant screech and wondered whether it was some harmless night bird or something far deadlier, something with black wings as wide as this room.

Peripherally, he could see that Jesse had the girls just about herded outside, and that was good. When he stabbed the Eric-thing, he didn't want the girls anywhere near. He wanted Charly and Jake far away from the Eric-thing too, but damn her, she was stepping closer, talking to it now.

Charly said, her voice barely more than a whisper, "Please put her down, Eric. You've already killed your dad."

The Eric-thing opened its mouth in a lurid grin. Jesus, the teeth in there like mottled spears. Its head swiveled slowly toward Charly's mother-in-law, whose kicking grew more frantic. Eric's mother began to scream.

"*Please,*" Charly said in alarm. "*Please, don't.*"

Sam slid out the knife.

Behind him, Jesse and the girls glided through the open door and into the night.

Its huge hands wrapped around the woman's waist, the creature drew her mid-section and the womb in which it had once lived closer to its open maw. Eric's mother batted at the Eric-thing's face, her stumpy legs scissoring in the air.

"*Don't do it!*" Charly shouted.

Sam strode toward them.

The Eric-thing's bear-trap jaws clamped down on his mother's blue-jeaned crotch.

The woman threw her head back and wailed.

Blood washed over the creature's flexing jaws, and beyond the struggling pair Sam glimpsed Charly rushing over and slapping at the

Eric-thing's shoulder.

With all the strength he could muster, Sam pumped the buck knife into its ribs.

The Eric-thing tossed his shrieking mother across the room, her neck snapping as she struck the wall. Then it seized Sam by the throat and lifted him into the air.

When the Eric-thing hauled Sam toward its mouth, Charly was certain it was all over. If Sam got killed, it was only a matter of time before she died too. And of course if she died, Jake was lost as well. She was thinking of her son transforming into one of *them* when Sam kicked the handle of the knife and the Eric-thing erupted in fury and pain. Sam dropped to the floor in a boneless heap, and the Eric-thing doubled over. And though it cost her a supreme effort, she placed baby Jake on the carpet and reached into her pocket. Jake began to fuss.

Her eyes never leaving the bent-over Eric-thing, she whispered to Jake, "Mommy's here, honey. Mommy's not leaving."

Charly stood, Sam's pocketknife in her hand, and stepped toward the Eric-thing. The kick had been a good one, Sam's boot driving the handle so far in it was flush with the Eric-thing's skin. She stepped closer, her fingers swinging the knife on its hinge so the business end pointed out.

The Eric-thing was still doubled over, its head maybe four feet off the ground. It had gotten its fingers around the antler handle of Robertson's knife and was succeeding in sliding it out of its entrails. There was very little time, maybe no time at all before the knife would be free and Sam would be dead. She saw Sam, God bless him, getting unsteadily to his feet, and she knew he would fight as long as he could draw breath, knew he wouldn't abandon her.

The Eric-thing's eyes latched on Charly's.

Charly pumped the knife.

Then the Eric-thing was squalling, its long fingers batting at the pocketknife Charly had jammed in its left eye.

It staggered backward, black liquid dribbling over its knuckles. Charly advanced on it, got hold of the buck knife waggling in its ribs. She ripped it out, and the Eric-thing folded forward with shock and pain. Before it could attack her she grasped the antler handle with both hands and, like a volleyball digger, thrust the big buck knife at the Eric-thing's remaining eye.

It sheared through the cornea and unleashed a torrent of viscid black syrup over her fists. The Eric-thing jerked back, and she was actually lifted off her feet before the sharp edge of the buck knife unseated from the creature's skull. The Eric-thing stumbled and sprawled on its side. The sounds issuing from it were indescribable, the kicking of its legs oddly reminiscent of a toddler throwing a tantrum. Perhaps it was this thought that caused Charly to hurry forward and kneel beside her husband. He had always been very much like a toddler, she now realized, but not a loveable one, not like a real child. Only the unreasoning anger, only the unmitigated spoiledness of the raging child existed in Eric, none of the sweetness, none of the love. She remembered the knife in her hand, remembered the monster he had been even before the change, the pathetic creature who'd made a mockery of their marriage, who'd emotionally scarred their daughters, who'd planned on twisting their son into a hideous facsimile of himself. These thoughts in mind, Charly raised the buck knife, point down, and slammed it with every ounce of force she could summon into the Eric-thing's heart.

A powerful whooshing sound emanated from its mouth; its cadaverous hands shot straight into the air, like a caricature of a sleepwalker. The hands hung that way a moment, the sightless head straining up from the floor. Then the Eric-thing collapsed and lay without moving.

She sensed someone beside her and turned to see Sam holding Jake against his shoulder. The Eric-thing was motionless now, but Charly heard a low thrum that chilled her blood.

She looked at Sam in the near blackness and saw the fear in his eyes.

Then they stood and hurried through the kitchen. Without stopping, Charly grabbed a carving knife and followed Sam through the side door.

Chapter Seven

After retrieving Sheriff Robertson's rifle, which Sam loaded with bullets from the glove box, they got in Sam's truck. Her daughters flanking her in the back seat, Charly clasped Jake to her and nodded at Emma to drive. Charly desperately wanted to give her baby a diaper change, but there wasn't time. Afraid one of her kids would get hurt with it, she handed Jesse the carving knife. Jesse took it gratefully and placed it on the seat beside him.

Emma threw the Chevy into gear, Jesse sitting shotgun beside her. Through the back window Sam offered them a tired grin, perhaps hoping the madness was over. But as they motored through the driveway and onto the lane, Charly realized it wasn't.

For out of the hole Sam's men had excavated in the next lot over, a head as long as a house door and a body three stories tall was rising.

The Old One had found them.

At first Charly thought they'd outrun the monster. The Chevy blew by the Old One as it stood erect, its expressionless face tracking them as they passed. Then, with awe-inspiring swiftness, it stepped across the yard and began to stride after them, its incredible legs swallowing thirty feet or more with every step.

Still, they had a lead, and Emma was pushing the pickup ever faster, motoring toward forty now, the big dually's frame vibrating with the acceleration. Charly glanced in the rearview mirror and sucked in breath. The Old One had somehow closed the distance, was still closing in, and then it vaulted into the air, disappeared above the roof, and reappeared ahead of them, landing with an agility Charly wouldn't have thought possible.

The monster blocked the road.

Before the truck crashed into it—and in that moment Charly wondered if they should chance it, just ram the unmerciful giant and take their chances that the truck would still drive after the impact—Emma stood on the brakes. The Chevy skidded sideways then shuddered to a halt only ten yards away. She reversed the truck, its headlights bathing the monster's legs in a grim amber glow. Charly leaned forward until she could see the Old One's face, that hideous, unblinking mask that had lived for hundreds, maybe thousands of years. That had claimed an untold number of victims.

Sam was hopping out of the truck bed.

"*No, Sam!*" she cried through the open passenger's window.

Charly jerked forward, but Jake's weight and her daughters' arms kept her moored in the backseat. Sam stood beside the truck, his gaze crawling over the dark, sleek surface of the rifle.

"You can't," she said, though her voice broke.

Sam said under his breath and without looking up, "Take a sharp left and head out through the field. Cut across it a few hundred yards or so, then make for the road."

"We gotta move," Jesse said, and when Charly turned she saw them coming from behind, all of them, scores of Children eating the distance between them in loping strides.

"Jesse's right," Sam said. "The moment I start shooting, you take off."

Emma searched Sam's face, an agonized expression on her own. Then she nodded sadly.

"You can't—" Charly began.

"No other choice," Sam said. "Tell my kids I'm sorry for what I did to them."

"*Sam...*" she said, willing him to look up.

But he didn't.

"One more thing I want you to know," Sam said, his voice raw. "I've been coming out here the last few weeks, just walking around. It sounds sad, I know. But the reason was, I wanted to see you. You're a great girl, Charly. The best I've known."

Charly reached out for him.

He levered the rifle.

Looked up at her.

His wet eyes blazed. In that moment he looked very afraid. And very determined.

"Keep these kids safe," he said.

Then he started away.

"*Sam!*" she yelled.

But he was striding toward the Old One.

Any advice for me, Dad? Sam asked.

Nothing you don't know, came the answer.

The Old One watched him as he approached.

This is suicide, isn't it?

Of course it is.

But it's a good death.

In his head, his dad laughed softly. *I don't know that I'd call it that.*

Sam swallowed. *You know what I mean.*

I know what you mean, his dad said tenderly. *And I'm proud of you, boy.*

Though he knew it was silly, Sam felt a lump in his throat. He was halfway between the Old One and the pickup now, the beast towering over him and watching him without emotion.

Would've been nice to settle down with Charly, though, he thought.

You got that right.

Give those kids a real father, treat Charly the way she deserves.

You'd have done a great job this time, his dad told him. *Both as a daddy and a husband.*

I would have, Sam thought and raised the rifle. The Marlin 336 felt ridiculous in his hands. What could it do to such a monster?

The Old One didn't move. Distantly, Sam heard the Chevy idling behind him.

Should've told Charly not to look, he thought.

Can't worry about that now, his dad said.

Sam heard other sounds behind him, the rabid snarls of the Children.

Suddenly shaking, Sam put his eye to the scope, drew a bead on the Old One's left eye. Sam blinked away sweat, the barrel lowering.

I'm scared, Dad.

I know you are, and I don't blame you. But it's gotta be done.

Sam swallowed hard, but it stuck in his throat.

Now scoot your feet further apart, his dad went on. *A little wider than your shoulders, like I taught you.*

Sam moved his feet wider.

Keep your knees a little bent so they don't lock on you, throw off your aim.

Sam bent his knees a little, heard the Children striding closer. Heard one of Charly's daughters scream.

Put the crosshairs on its heart, Sammy. You might hit one eye, but you won't get the second. But if you get the heart, bring the big bastard down, who knows what'll happen?

Sam lowered the rifle until the crosshairs lay on the skinny beast's heart. If it had one.

Sam's whole body trembled.

Wish me luck, Dad.

You don't need luck, Sammy. You just need to focus. After the first shot's off, you've gotta lever that rifle fast. Use the scope as much as you can. I'm sure Robertson kept the Marlin calibrated.

It's dark, though, Sam thought. *It's mostly just shadows.*

You can see just fine in this moonlight, his dad soothed. *Just focus.*

Okay, Sam thought. He placed his finger on the trigger.

And Dad? he thought.

Yeah, Sammy?

He imagined his dad's whiskery face watching him, the eyes steady and kind.

"Thanks," Sam whispered.

See you in a little while, his dad said, the same kind expression in his eyes.

Sam pulled the trigger.

The Old One jerked sideways, a cloud of black droplets spuming from its chest.

Behind Sam, the Chevy roared to life.

Good, Sam thought and levered the rifle. The spent cartridge flicked to his right and twirled on the pavement.

Sam sighted the Old One, which had stumbled back, and fired again. A black hole opened up in the middle of its chest, a foot or so below the first wound. The Old One rocked again, but then it seemed to steady. It bellowed in rage, a mind-shattering sound.

Sam levered the rifle.

He fired again, the spent cartridge clittering on the pavement. This shot wasn't as good, the bullet grazing the beast's skinny ribs but doing no real damage. Behind him, Sam heard the thunder of a hundred pairs of white feet, the outraged screams of the Old One's followers. He also heard the Chevy bouncing off into the grass, and that was good.

He levered the Marlin and swung the crosshairs up to the Old One's face. It crouched and snarled at him, the sound so loud and deep Sam could feel it in his bones. It loomed closer, only twenty yards away now.

Sam tracked its left eye, centered the scope on the black pupil inside the lambent green oval.

Fired.

The Old One bellowed, straightening, its great arms upflung in agony and outrage.

Sam raised the Marlin until the crosshairs fixed on the soft flesh of its underjaw. He squeezed the trigger.

The Old One's throat opened up, the black fluid gushing from its wound. The horde of Children behind him shrieked and growled, their bloodlust and wrath unspeakable.

They were almost upon him.

The Old One's bleeding face lowered until the one remaining eye fixed on him.

One more bullet, Sam thought.

Could use it on yourself, a voice somewhere in his mind whispered.

"Hell no," Sam said and sighted the Old One's right eye.

He squeezed the trigger, but as he did the Old One got a hand up. The bullet vaporized the tip of its middle finger, then it juddered again as the shot slammed home. But Sam could see right away the wound open up in the Old One's cheek, the right eye still intact. It glared at him with fathomless loathing, snatched him off the ground like a toy someone had left lying around. The army of Children behind him brayed a hell's chorus of delight, their god having defeated this brazen mortal.

Sam threw a quick glance to his left and saw what he'd hoped for, the pickup truck surging across the field, the deep mud thus far not bogging it down.

Make it across, he thought.

He turned back to the Old One.

Dying was inevitable now, but if he could do one last thing, maybe the truck could get away. Or at least his death would be quicker.

Sam rose, rose, the filthy fingers clamped around his body below the armpits. It was a miscalculation by the Old One, Sam knew, to allow Sam's arms to hang free. He still had the rifle, and though the cartridges had all been spent, the weapon was solid steel. And reasonably sharp.

The Old One reached toward him with one taloned finger, and in that instant Sam understood what the thing had planned for him, and this was worse than death, worse than anything. It was damnation.

The ragged fingernail loomed closer to his forehead, the Old One intending to mark him, to make of him what it had of Eric Florence, and Sam would never allow that. The remaining eye was a good six feet away, but the nail had nearly reached the flesh of Sam's face. He couldn't delay any longer.

With an inarticulate cry, Sam reared back and thrust the rifle forward, released it like a javelin, and watched in savage triumph as it embedded in the Old One's remaining eye.

The beast squalled, its long arms whipping Sam around like a maraca. It squeezed him, squeezed him, all its awful strength seemingly pouring into those fingers, and Sam felt his torso giving way in one colossal deathblast of pain. His ribs crunched, the lungs within gored by jagged bones. Blood jetted out of Sam's mouth, but he felt a weary satisfaction, the pain diminishing rapidly as a comforting lethargy spread through him.

With his darkening vision, Sam watched the Old One jerk its head at him, its wounded eyes staring at him in hateful disbelief. It hadn't meant to kill him this quickly, he knew, and though he hadn't blinded it all the way, at least he'd hurt it badly and bought himself a better death.

Maybe Charly will get away yet, Sam thought, smiling.

He was still smiling as the Old One's tombstone teeth closed over his throat.

Chapter Eight

"Drive faster," Jesse whispered. His throat was burning with acid, his guts churning and queasy.

He couldn't believe Sam was dead.

Jesse turned back to the gruesome site of Sam's demise and beheld the Old One pivoting toward them. The Chevy was bouncing roughly over the bean field, but at least they were still moving. What with the rains and the mud, they were lucky they hadn't gotten stuck.

If Emma keeps us going, Jesse thought, *we should be all right.*

The Old One started to follow them.

Nothing should move like that, Jesse thought. Though its legs knifed through the air like giant pendulums, and the arms splayed forward to grasp the earth and propel the wraithlike body forward, that face, that evil, omnipotent face hardly moved at all.

"Get to the road," Jesse said, his voice overcome by the squeal of the shocks, the groan of the Chevy's axles. A breath-stealing pain rumbled up his spine. Jesse winced and impulsively fingered his front teeth. Searing pain in his fingertips. He lowered them from his mouth and discovered he'd slit the pads of his fingers, his teeth unaccountably sharp.

Uh-uh, Jesse thought, swallowing. *Don't even think about that.* He gripped the door to steady himself against the rocking of the truck, but even more so to combat the stretched, weightless feeling that was taking hold of him, the buzzing in his mind.

No!

"Please get to the road," Jesse said in a failing voice.

Emma only shook her head, her lips tight.

"Listen to Jesse!" Charly demanded. "Drive toward—"

"Sam said a few hundred yards!" Emma shouted back.

Charly leaned forward. "He said that so we'd get around the monster. Now that we are, we've gotta get the truck on pavement. That thing's going to catch us."

But Emma kept mudding through the bean field, the big dually lurching and bouncing like an airplane besieged by turbulence. Jesse looked back, saw that the Old One was coming fast, its strides swallowing the distance effortlessly. Meanwhile, the Chevy trundled along at an uneasy thirty-five, its headlights bouncing wildly.

"You want me to drive?" he asked.

"No," Emma responded.

"Why not?"

"Because I'm a better driver."

"You've never even been in my—"

"I've seen you leaving work," she said, a small, radiant smile permeating her face despite the mortal danger closing in on them. "You drive like a grandma."

"I don't—" he began.

"*It's right behind us,*" Charly said, her voice tight with terror.

Jesse whirled in time to see the Old One's galloping body storming nearer, the broomstick fingers groping for their tailgate.

"It's going to—" Jesse started to say.

Emma whipped the wheel to the right.

Jesse slid against her, but almost immediately the Chevy got traction and surged toward the road. A white shape tumbled by, the long fingers actually thunking against the rocker panel of the dually. Jesse glanced up and watched the Old One skid, catch itself before it went over, then scramble toward them.

It was a race to the road.

The Chevy bounced insanely now, Emma giving it everything. The bean field's ruts jounced the frame terribly, the puddled soil sucking the tires with unperishing hunger.

They didn't have far to go, only thirty yards more, but the Old One was closing on them again, its speed appalling. Jesse wondered fleetingly if reaching the road would do any good. If the monster moved that swiftly over messy terrain, how much faster would it lope on asphalt?

"It's gonna get us!" Charly's younger daughter called.

The older daughter, the one right behind Jesse, gasped and recoiled from the window. Following her gaze, Jesse realized why. The Children were teeming over the bean field, now moving at a diagonal to make up for the Chevy's head start. And though the creatures did not advance as rapidly as the Old One did, they were still making good enough time to become a concern.

The country road was racing toward them. The asphalt strip seemed perilously thin. If they didn't slow now, they'd skid right over into the cornfield opposite, and then there'd be no escaping the Old One, who'd snatch them up one by one like a bird plucking worms from the ground.

"*Emma,*" Charly moaned.

"Almost there," Emma shot back.

Jesse spun and saw the Old One's knobby knees pistoning nearer, the groping hands now directly over the bed of the Chevy.

Emma cut the wheel left. They skidded sideways, their back end whipsawing through the muck. Jesse was thrown against the passenger's door and had a moment to wonder why he hadn't put his seatbelt on. Then the Chevy jounced over the lip of the road and began to tilt.

"*Come on,*" Emma pleaded through clenched teeth. She spun the wheel back, fought the skid, and for one horrible moment Jesse was sure they'd overturn.

Then the truck's tires gripped the road and they shot forward.

Jesse smiled in amazement. Emma grinned back at him, her expression equal parts joy and disbelief. He was about to compliment her on her driving when Charly screamed, "*Look out!*"

Moving so fast Jesse scarcely saw it, an enormous white hand loomed in the driver's side window and exploded through it, glass shrapnel pelting their faces and chests. The jagged yellow fingernails passed within an inch of Emma's face and clawed over the seatback. Before Jesse realized what was happening, Charly's oldest daughter was rising toward the gaping window, one of the Old One's dirty nails snagged in her purple shirt.

"*NO!*" Charly shrieked. She wrapped her arms around daughter's waist, but the Old One's fingers plunged deeper into the cab and seized the screaming little girl by the torso. Charly squeezed her daughter tight, but the Old One began dragging both daughter and mother out the driver's side window.

Jesse pawed the seat for the carving knife, but it wasn't there. Where the hell had it—

"Take the wheel!" Emma shouted.

Jesse glanced at her confusedly, but Emma was already twisting in her seat, on her knees facing the Old One's hand, which had already dragged Charly's oldest daughter half out of the cab. Charly hung on desperately, but she too was sliding headfirst through the window.

Jesse grasped the wheel just before they veered off the road. Left foot on the accelerator, he guided the pickup away from the muddy shoulder. Something silver flashed in his periphery. He turned just in time to see Emma slash the Old One's index finger with the carving knife. From outside the cab there came an unearthly roar, a sound somehow high-pitched and deep at the same time. Emma immediately hacked at the Old One again, this time gouging an ugly trench down the monster's middle finger, the flesh over its knuckles splitting. Its grip on the little girl loosened enough for Charly to haul her back inside the cab.

Jesse jerked the wheel to the right, hoping to remove them entirely from the Old One's reach, but one of the jagged fingernails sank into the beige ceiling, spilling fragments of white foam from the lacerated fabric.

Emma grasped the carving knife with both hands, drew the handle even with the side of her head, then slammed it with all her might into the Old One's middle finger just below the nail. Severed, the top of the Old One's finger thumped onto the seat between Emma and Jesse, but Jesse scarcely noticed.

Because the quality of the Old One's bellowing had altered, and somewhere deep in the recesses of his mind Jesse understood the power of the creature's rage. Though the noxious black fluid was spurting from the stump of its severed finger, it was not blinded by its pain or its fury. Jesse had no idea how he knew this, but he knew that if Emma didn't get down now...

It happened in an instant. Jesse had scooted across the seat to hold the wheel with his right hand and pull Emma away with his left when the Old One's dripping fingers jerked at Emma's face. Jesse grasped the side of her shirt, but before he could tug her out of the Old One's deadly range, the powerful fingers crashed into Emma's face, propelling her backward into the steering wheel. Her head snapped back with a dull crunch, the back of her skull smacking the windshield with brutal force. As she rebounded off the steering wheel, the Old One's hand turned sideways and with astonishing speed lashed out at Emma's face. Blood sprayed everywhere, and then Emma was slumped in Jesse's lap, her broken body twitching senselessly. Jesse screamed and without thinking relinquished his hold on the wheel. The Chevy arrowed toward the cornfield, decelerating. The Old One's fingers no longer scrabbled inside the cab, but that didn't matter. If Jesse didn't get them going again, they would be dead within seconds.

With Emma's limp body lolling in his lap, her face a bloody ruin, Jesse leaned over, gripped the wheel and tried to steer it back onto the road. He struggled to get his foot on the accelerator, but the console and Emma's body were both in the way.

"Jesse!" Charly pleaded.

"*Trying*," he grunted.

Thunder filled the cab as the roof crumpled.

Since seeing Sam murdered by the Old One, Charly had vacillated between a state of sorrow and horrified confusion; the only thing keeping her sane was her determination to shield her children from the monsters.

But when the Old One damn near wrested Kate from her grasp, Charly's trance broke. She took baby Jake from Olivia's arms.

"Get down," she said to Olivia and shoved her roughly between her seat and the front seatback. Moon-eyed, Olivia did as she was told. Charly commanded Kate to join her sister on the floor as well. Charly handed the baby to Kate. Maybe, Charly reasoned, looking after Jake would take Kate's mind off of how she'd nearly been snatched from the truck by the Old One.

"Stay down," she told her girls and climbed into the passenger's seat. Jesse was settling in behind the wheel, moving them from the grassy shoulder back to the road. The Chevy leapt forward as he depressed the accelerator, but the Old One's fist bashed down again, this time right over Jesse's head.

"*Jesus!*" he shrieked, the torn metal slicing into the back of his head, the windshield spiderwebbing so badly the road before them became a ghostly mosaic.

Charly sucked in air and looked out the rear window. The Old One had dropped back a little, the Chevy topping fifty now, but its fists were raised for another attack. Jesse goosed the accelerator, and the Chevy's rear bumper evaded the plummeting fists by a matter of inches.

"Faster," Charly told him.

"I know," he said, pushing the Chevy up to sixty, then moving briskly toward seventy. The asphalt road wasn't in perfect condition, but it was smooth enough. Charly glanced back and discovered the Old One still in pursuit.

Go faster, she almost said, but she didn't have to. Jesse had the Chevy up to nearly eighty now, and they were leaving the monster behind. Jesse sat hunched over the wheel, the torn metal shards poking down around him like gleaming stalactites.

Charly remembered the cave. Remembered Sam...

Something in her periphery caused her to turn.

"Can't take it too fast," Jesse said in a low voice. "The road's still wet."

Charly didn't answer. Couldn't answer. She watched the sky above the road with horror.

"What's wrong?" Jesse asked.

But then he saw it too. He eyed the side mirror in dread.

The Night Flyers were drawing nearer.

Chapter Nine

Charly strained with the effort of dragging Emma's body toward the door.

"What are you doing?" Jesse asked her.

"What's it look like?"

"You can't."

"She's dead, Jesse."

"But you can't just..." He swallowed. "What if she's still alive?"

"Look at her."

Jesse kept his eyes fixed on the road ahead.

Charly hated herself, but said it anyway. "Look at her, Jesse."

Reluctantly, he did. His eyes only remained on Emma's lifeless face for a moment, but that was more than enough to see what Charly already had: the cheek torn clear off, exposing the jaw like a medical anatomy book; a bloody trough ripped through Emma's temple, the gouge deep enough to expose a pale swath of skull; worst of all the dangling eye, the socket black in the darkness of the cab.

Something peculiar flitted across Jesse's face. Something not sorrowful and certainly not indignant. It was almost like desire, but that was absurd. With a psychic shiver, Charly pushed the thought away.

Charly positioned Emma's dead body against the door.

"Stay down back there," she told her girls. Then, in a lower voice, she said, "I'll wait till those things get right up on us. Then I'll shove her out to distract them. Hopefully they'll take the bait."

Jesse's voice was thick. "I don't think that's necessary. Look how far back they are."

"Put as much distance between us as you can."

"That's what I'm doing."

"The road turns gravel in another mile."

Jesse stared at her. "You're kidding me."

"Wish I was."

The Chevy moved up to a rattling ninety.

"Are we safe, Mommy?" Olivia asked.

"No," Charly said. "Stay down and cover your head."

"How far until town?" Jesse asked.

"Haven't you been out here before?"

"We came another way. Emma..." he said, but broke off. He cleared his throat. "Emma said it was faster."

"To the campground, it is," Charly said. "But this is the quickest way from our house."

"So how long?"

"Ten more minutes."

Jesse was quiet a moment before he asked, "Are we doing the right thing?"

"What, trying not to die?"

"Leading them toward town."

Charly didn't respond.

"If they follow us..." Jesse said. "Think of all the people they'll—"

"I'm thinking of my kids," she said, an edge to her voice. "They're the only people I'm concerned with."

Ahead, the gravel loomed like a gray specter.

You'll want to slow down, Charly was about to say, but Jesse beat her to it. The Chevy decelerated to a shade over sixty. It was still a dangerous speed on wet gravel, Charly knew, but what choice did they have? If Jesse lowered their speed too much the Night Flyers—and the Old One—would overtake them, and dying in a high-speed truck accident was infinitely preferable to being eaten alive by monsters.

"How long is it gravel?"

"Three miles?" Charly guessed.

"Damn."

The tires barreled over the last section of asphalt and crunched over gravel. Jesse grimaced with the effort of keeping her straight, but the Chevy still began to slue wildly.

"Better slow down," she told him.

Jesse brought it down to fifty-five, but the Chevy still yawed erratically.

A silvery snatch of moonlight skittered across Jesse's face. Charly didn't like what she glimpsed there. Wan, sallow, and an ill-defined impression that his face had elongated. Had to be her imagination, she knew. Jesse was fine. Was doing all he could do get them out of here. But still... The disquiet lingered like the taste of bile after a violent bout of vomiting.

Jake began to cry. Charly could hear Kate back there, bouncing him in her lap and trying to quiet him. *Good girl*, Charly thought.

She glanced through the back window.

No sign of the Night Flyers.

"Think we're okay?" Jesse asked.

"Drive."

"I am driving."

"Then drive without talking."

"Are you always this mean?"

Charly smiled at him, and he brightened a little.

She turned to gaze out the back window.

Her smile evaporated.

The Night Flyers had reappeared. Not only that, but they were angling off the road as though to cut across the cornfield. Charly remembered, her stomach plummeting, that the road ahead did indeed veer right.

They're heading us off, she thought.

They'd ticked off about a mile of gravel, Charly estimated. But there were hills and curves ahead, the gravel loose and hazardous.

Charly thought for a moment, thought hard. Then she came to a decision. "When we get to the blacktop again," she said.

Jesse glanced at her. "Yeah?"

"There's a gravel road about a half mile up. Through the woods."

The pickup shimmied a little. Jesse gritted his teeth. "You want to drive on more gravel?"

"The road it leads to is County Road 1200."

"So?"

"1200 leads to Highway 65."

"You wanna take the highway?"

"The longer we're on this road, the more they're gonna gain. The faster we can get to 65, the better we can outrun them. Plus it's less populated than town, at least at this time of night."

"Then let's take the gravel road," Jesse said. "I don't see the problem."

"The gravel road goes back toward the campground."

Jesse's mouth hung open. "Charly..."

"You said yourself you don't want to lead those things toward town."

"Anonymity is looking really attractive right now. We could park at a gas station, hide inside a bathroom."

"They'll find us."

"Not necessarily, they could—"

"*Can't you hear them?*"

Jesse stared at her a moment longer, then fixed his eyes on the road. It was all the answer she needed.

It was a sensation unlike any other, like tuning into radio stations from countries that spoke other languages. They hit her in bursts, sometimes faintly. She knew these voices came from the Night Flyers. First the voices were garbled in that alien tongue—clicks and weird choking sounds. Then it was like her mind adjusted to the language barrier and the English translation kicked in.

Get youuuu...going to get youuuu...

But the voice that came through the clearest was the voice she hadn't heard until Sam's death. She was able to mark it so clearly because it had begun at the exact moment that the Old One had turned to watch the truck after biting off Sam's head. As if the monster was implanting a trace in her mind, one it could follow no matter how far she roamed.

Since then she'd come to understand all too well the pained expression on Sam's face earlier, during the passage through the tunnels. For whatever reason, the Old One had marked him and had tortured him up until the confrontation on the lane. And when Sam's body had been flung into the crowd and butchered by the Children, the Old One had fixated on her.

She cringed as another thought missile ripped through her brain.

YOUR BABY IS GOING TO BE ONE OF US, CHARLY. AFTER WE EAT YOU AND YOUR DAUGHTERS, YOUR BABY BOY WILL BECOME ONE OF US.

No, she thought weakly.

JUNIOR WILL BE ONE OF US.

That did it. She tightened the muscles of her legs and squeezed her fists until they ached. She would not allow the Old One to touch any of her children. She wouldn't allow it to take her baby. Not again.

The cornfields disappeared ahead, the forest taking hold. She thumbed down her window, squinted through the night to locate the mass of slowly flapping wings. She leaned out into the chilly air to better see, the wind blasting the side of her head, her blonde hair streaking against the side of the Chevy. She thought she could make out...

Yes. The prehistoric-looking beasts were nearly to the forest. The Chevy would beat them there, but not by much. Plus, the road trended right, toward the creatures, before it serpentined left. Then there was a long descent, a series of ravines and rises. Then they'd hit blacktop again. Moments after that, they'd turn onto the gravel lane that'd lead to 1200. A minute or two after that, they'd be on 65.

A total of five minutes, she estimated. No more than that. If they could survive the next five minutes, they'd make it out of this nightmare.

Jesse was eyeing the impending forest warily.

"The road is pretty straight until the trees," Charly said. "Things get kind of wild after that, like an amusement park ride. Kate and Olivia always want to go this way because it's so up and down."

They were almost to the woods.

Jesse swallowed. "This is it, isn't it?"

"This is it," Charly agreed.

"We make it through here and the other gravel road, we'll be safe, won't we?"

"We'll be safe," Charly said, and was amazed to find she believed it. *Five more minutes*, she thought. *Five more minutes.*

Chapter Ten

The forest swallowed them up.

The headlights illuminated the gravel lane, which might as well have been a tunnel. The overhanging boughs of the great oaks and sycamores formed what amounted to an unbroken canopy of branches and leaves.

Charly thought of the bend looming ahead, the place where the Night Flyers might attack them. "Step on it, Jesse."

"If we wreck, we're done," he said.

"If they catch us, it's not gonna be pretty either. Did you see how many there were?"

"I saw."

It was tough to tell with the darkness and the shifting mass of wings, but to Charly it looked as though there were easily fifty of the flying beasts.

Another thought from the Old One blasted through her mind, but she was able to focus on the road despite the glancing pain the telepathy brought on. Jesse was accelerating. If they could make it through the stretch where the trees were sparse...

The thought struck Charly like a club blow.

It was almost as if the Night Flyers had led them to this spot.

Impossible, she thought. *They weren't even awake until the last couple days or so—how could they know the terrain aboveground that well?*

Yes. She realized that she believed this, that the monsters that had authored this blood-soaked horror show had only recently awakened. How else to explain the sudden attacks? There had likely been some catalyst, but that hardly mattered now. Whether it was the Indian Trails subdivision or the construction of the campground or something else entirely, what mattered was the plight they were in.

Jesse hugged the inside of the curve, doing a nice job of it, holding the pickup steady as it scuffled through the loose rock and puddled potholes. The gravel under their tires crunched and pinged against the rocker panels as though they were being strafed with machine-gun fire.

"You see anything?" Jesse asked. He was leaning over the wheel, his eyes darting from the pitted road to the open patch of sky. Their brightened headlamps showed everything ahead of them, yet the sky remained a mystery. If the Night Flyers attacked, it would come without warning.

The road straightened out and Jesse depressed the accelerator. They reached the open stretch.

And the Night Flyers fell on them.

Two struck the Chevy like torpedoes, one smashing into the front corner of the bumper and crunching like a broken kite under the wheel, the other crashing into Charly's window, spraying glass over her body. Its mangled face shot up, snarling, and Charly drove the heels of her shoes into the creature's face. Its head snapped backward, and Charly kicked again, this time propelling the Night Flyer clear out of the opening. She saw it tumbling end over end, squalling in fury, but in the same moment a new beast swooped down and fastened onto the roof. It swung its head low and stared at them upside down through the starred windshield. Jesse pumped the brakes and it tumbled off, its vicious talons ripping grooves through the metal until it disappeared, screeching over the hood. The crunching sound came again. The Chevy jounced, fishtailed, then caught and motored toward the enclosing forest. A Night Flyer ventured to beat them there and impaled itself on an oak branch, the wood punching through its belly and holding it like a baited hook twenty feet off the ground.

The road jagged a sharp left, but before the open splotch of sky disappeared, Charly watched several winged forms swoop into the tunnel of trees.

"Mommy?" Olivia called from the backseat.

Charly eyed the side mirror with dread. "Not now, honey."

"I think Jake filled his pants."

"I think I did too," Jesse said.

Charly spotted them against the tapestry of arched boughs, their tenebrous wings whipping them closer and closer, their crimson eyes like tiny, bobbing reflectors.

The Chevy trundled up a rise, then its front end dipped as it shot over a sudden declivity, the tires actually leaving the road for one stomach-fluttering moment. The pickup crunched down roughly, the top of Charly's head bouncing off the ceiling. Jesse braked to avoid a spinout, but that allowed a Night Flyer to lunge forward and clatter down into the bed. Without bothering to right itself, the winged beast dove through the open back window. Its upper body half in, half out of the cab, the Night Flyer snapped at them with teeth as sharp as rapiers, missing Charly's face by inches.

Retracting its head, it discovered Charly's children.

Its face transformed from unthinking ferocity to a sadistic species of cunning, the jaws unhinging in a hissing drip of saliva. Kate howled in terror, Olivia too horrified to do anything but gape. The creature's muscled shoulders tensed as it prepared to dart at them.

With a strangled cry, Charly leapt over the seatback and clawed at its eyes. The nail of her index finger scooped out a glob of red tissue. The Night Flyer screeched in rage. She backhanded it, but the demonic face scarcely jolted at all.

Its untouched eye remained fastened on Charly.

The Night Flyer plunged toward her.

Charly collapsed on the floor, covering her children. The back of her hand brushed something on the Chevy's carpet, and she recalled Sam's words:

There's a crowbar under my seat.

Charly shot a hand under the vinyl seatback and groped for it. Her fingers spidered over a pencil, what felt like a crumpled fast food container, then she touched something cool and hard. She got her fingers around it, slid it out, but when she turned to smash the creature's hideous face with it, she was aghast to find it climbing into the cab.

Its face and shoulders had wriggled inside, but its wings impeded it. Charly glanced down at the crowbar, saw its chiseled end, and flipped it around.

The Night Flyer had nearly gotten far enough inside to have its way with them. It was already close enough to snatch the children from the floor, to decapitate Charly or Jesse with one lethal swipe of its claws. Charly gripped the crowbar, got on her knees. A couple feet above her, the Night Flyer's head scraped the mangled ceiling. The straining creature's neck was exposed.

Charly drove the chisel into its throat.

The Night Flyer squealed and began thrashing in agony. The black lifeblood sluiced down over Charly's hands. She yanked the sharp end of the crowbar out with a meaty *zlip* and thrust it up again, this time just under the chin.

The creature gave off fighting and thrashed to escape through the back window. Charly longed to bludgeon its hideous face until it was a pulpy stew, but the crying of her daughters drew her attention to the shadowed floor.

Olivia was lathered with the foul black fluid, her face pinched by soundless tears. Baby Jake was pushing against Kate, whimpering. Kate only stared at her mom through eyes that were doing their best to stay brave.

The Night Flyer finally backed its way out of the window and fluttered away, but there was another winged creature touching down on the bouncing pickup gate and a couple more closing in. Jesse had just about gotten them out of the forest, which meant the first stretch of gravel would end soon. But that didn't matter if the Night Flyers were riding along in the bed with them. What if one of them got smart enough to puncture the tires?

The thought doused Charly with icy terror. She clambered through the back window. The Night Flyer that had landed moments earlier was stepping forward with spider-like delicacy, its wings furled behind it. The other Night Flyers were keeping pace with the shivering Chevy, their infernal red eyes concentrating on landing on its side panels.

The Night Flyer crouched nearer, its face level with Charly now, grinning in anticipation.

Charly cocked the crowbar like a big-league hitter and cut loose with everything she had.

The crowbar smashed the Night Flyer's underjaw, knocking it clear to the side of its face, the thin flesh that bound its jaws together tearing like paper.

The creature's expression switched to wide-eyed bewilderment. Charly lifted the crowbar above her head and chopped down at its face. The turned corner of the bar crushed the bridge of its nose as easily as a boot heel crushes an egg. This time it staggered back, and Charly went with it, swinging again. She knocked it off-balance and sent it tumbling off the open tailgate in a stunned flurry of black wings.

Immediately another Night Flyer took its place, this one landing on the rocker panel to Charly's right. The way the creature's hind leg talons punctured the hard steel wasn't lost on Charly. If it kicked at her...

Charly swung the crowbar, but as she did the Chevy jounced over a pothole, throwing her off-kilter. The crowbar glanced harmlessly off the creature's shoulder, and what was worse, the beast was lowering into the bed, moving with infinite patience, apparently intent on not making the same mistakes its comrades had made.

She swept the crowbar back up at the Night Flyer in a desperate backhand, but it feinted the blow, the swing carrying Charly forward into its willowy black arms. The great wings enfolded her. The demonic face loomed closer.

The Chevy braked, and they both slammed into the back of the cab. The impact hurt Charly—her shoulder felt like it had been dislocated—but the Night Flyer got the worst of it, its left wing snapping under its weight.

The creature shrieked in demented fury. Charly reeled away, landed against the opposite rocker panel. The Night Flyer stepped sideways toward the back of the bed so it could examine its crumpled wing. Charly lunged forward, planted her hands on the thing's rear end and shoved. The long, swooshing tail slapped the skin of her leg as the creature stumbled toward the bouncing back gate. The Night Flyer ran out of room, stepped into open space, its other wing crushed beneath it as it pounded the gravel road and rolled forward in a ruined ball.

More Night Flyers winged down at the bed of the Chevy, their extended talons grasping for purchase. She knew she couldn't hold them off any longer, knew she must get back inside. Head down, Charly waded toward the open back window, plopped into the back seat. Climbing over the seatback, she reminded her daughters to stay down, but she knew she needn't have. They were as close to the floor as they could possibly get, Kate lying on her side with baby Jake curled up in front of her.

Jesse was swerving back and forth across the road to deter the screeching Night Flyers, driving skillfully enough that Emma would have been proud. But he couldn't hold them off much longer. Behind them, the corridor of trees was choked with the winged monsters, all of them hungering for human flesh.

Especially the flesh of children.

Charly glanced down at Emma's body, which had lolled to the floor. With a disconsolate moan, Charly slid forward, straddled the corpse and dragged it toward the door.

This time Jesse didn't protest.

Charly got the door open, the weeds along the road thwacking against the metal. Jesse angled toward the left side of the lane so Charly's door would be centered. She lifted Emma's body toward the gap. Charly held the door ajar, while with her free hand she seized the waistband of Emma's shorts and dragged her farther into the opening. The dead girl's hands bounced off the lane, her bloody hair hanging down over her face. Charly felt a wave of guilt for desecrating Emma's body. Grimacing, she grasped one of Emma's smooth calves and lifted. Gravity and speed did the rest, Emma slithering out the open door, then rolling over several times in their dusty wake.

The Night Flyers darted toward the body.

Charly suppressed a cry of relief. Nearly all the creatures had been diverted by the corpse, were now ranged around it scratching and snarling to get at the fresh meat.

The gravel ended, and smooth black asphalt took its place. Like a bucking stallion unleashed from its pen, the Chevy bolted forward, rapidly putting distance between them and the remaining Night Flyers. The forest gave way to cornfields.

Jesse's pale face was runnelled with dirt and sweat. He looked like he might throw up. But he was doing a fine job of moving them away from the creatures.

Charly said, "We can keep going toward town if you want. Just get us away from them."

"I thought you wanted to take 65."

Charly regarded him, a chill coursing down her arms. His voice had been raspy, lifeless.

He's been through a lot, she reminded herself. *And just like you, he's parched. When's the last time he had a drink of water?*

Still, she couldn't shake the worm of worry wriggling through her.

"The turn-off is up here," she said. "It's up to you."

Without further comment, he slowed the dually and veered left onto the gravel road. Charly glanced back. As she'd expected, the Night Flyers immediately set off over the cornfield in an attempt to cut them off. But this stretch of gravel was much shorter than the last one. They'd gain County Road 1200 before the Night Flyers could catch them. She'd begun to believe they'd make it to the highway without any more problems when she turned back to the road and saw the Old One waiting for them ahead.

Chapter Eleven

"Run him over," Charly said.

The Old One stood a football field away, its lean, alabaster body limned by the black sky beyond. The telephone-pole legs were poised just far enough apart that the Chevy could neither split them nor sneak around either side of them without mowing down cornstalks. The drop-off into the field was only a foot or so, but what ground she could see among the stalks glittered with undrained rainfall. If they did chance it and set off through the fields, they'd likely get bogged down, this field in worse shape than the one through which they'd traveled earlier.

"Hit him," Charly said, gripping the crowbar tighter. "It's the only way through."

Jesse said nothing, but despite the treacherous gravel, the Chevy was accelerating, making its unswerving way toward the creature's ghostly shins. Charly glanced down behind the seat, saw that Olivia had taken a turn holding Jake.

Nearly there. As before, the Old One's pitiless face watched them; it seemed neither enraged nor ravenous for their flesh. Was it patience she saw in its unblinking eyes? Or doubt that they'd go through with it?

They rocketed toward the Old One's legs. The ghastly, staring face tracked them, its skin taking on a pearlescent sheen in the moonlight. *Go*, Charly thought. *Go faster and rip the monster's legs off.* She knew the beast was strong, appallingly strong, but there was no way it could withstand three-and-a-half tons of hurtling steel.

They drew closer, closer, the Chevy up to eighty now. Jesse hunched over the wheel, his face grim and cold. Whatever happened, she knew he wouldn't relent, knew the collision was inevitable.

"Hang on girls!" she called over her shoulder. "Hold Jake tight!"

Only a few seconds left. Charly squeezed the crowbar.

The Old One stared at them, the huge green eyes unblinking.

Three seconds, she thought. *Two...*

The Old One stepped aside.

The Chevy swept by in a chalky cloud.

"*What?*" Charly said. She spun in her seat and peered into the darkness and saw the jade effulgence of the Old One's eyes painted red in the Chevy's taillights. On the Old One's staring face she thought she glimpsed a triumphant jack-o-lantern grin. She turned to Jesse...

...and saw the same ghastly grin on his face. He leered at her, his face stretched and white, his teeth splotched with brown, the tips hooked and sharp. He leaned toward her, sighing rancid breath, one hand on the wheel but not even minding the road.

With a sob, Charly jammed the chisel into his left eye.

There came a wet, ripping noise, and he shrieked and the truck veered toward the shoulder. Charly jabbed him again, caught only his collarbone this time. The pickup coasted toward the cornfield, and the Jesse-thing slapped a hand over her forearm and drew her closer. Dimly, Charly heard her daughters screaming.

Leering at her with its one good eye, the Jesse-thing slithered its attenuated tongue toward her, the pink darkening to black. Charly swung the crowbar at the Jesse-thing's head, but he caught it, squeezed her wrist until something within popped. Charly moaned, felt the Jesse-thing fondle one of her breasts through her tank top. The Chevy bounced over the grassy shoulder and into the cornfield, the stalks thunking like helpless pedestrians.

The pickup ground to a halt in the flooded field.

She pushed against the Jesse-thing's chest, but its strength was too great, and God, those glowing green eyes now beamed at her, laughing, the tongue drawing a sticky line along her jaw, the stench—

There was a flurry of movement to her left. The Jesse-thing jerked away and covered its face, and when Charly glanced that way she saw, illuminated by the greenish-blue light of the dashboard, her oldest daughter shaking the Jesse-thing by its curly brown hair. Kate's face was wet with tears, her nose bubbling snot, but she was wrenching the Jesse-thing's head back and forth and shouting incoherent threats at him. Charly realized her own wrist was free. She drew the crowbar back and swung with everything she had at the Jesse-thing's temple. There was a cracking sound as it smashed through the skull. The Jesse-thing cried out, shoved away from Kate and flailed its hand at the crowbar, but Charly jabbed the hard chisel into its face again, this time shattering its front teeth. Its hands clapped over its spewing mouth, and Charly aimed another blow at its remaining eye. She cried out as the blow struck home, blinding the Jesse-thing. It howled, thrusting its head back into the open window, but Charly was on her knees after it, straddling it, swinging the turned end of the crowbar like an axe and striking the monster squarely in the forehead. The iron bar staved in the Jesse-thing's skull, but she raised it and struck, harder this time, snapping the fingers it had thrown up for protection and bashing its skull. She brought the crowbar down again and again, screaming now, all the pent-up fear and rage gushing out at the Jesse-thing, and she no longer cared that this monster had been an ally only moments before, no longer cared about the pain she was inflicting. She smashed down, down, the black blood spraying the interior of the Chevy, the frothing ruin of a face no longer reacting to the blows. The arms had fallen to its sides, its body convulsing in a twitching dance, and Charly smashed and smashed, heedless of her daughters' screaming, Olivia saying something about the monster, and Charly thought, *Yes, I'm killing the monster,* until Kate's frantic cries broke through the haze of fury.

In the silence that followed, Charly heard the Old One's approaching footfalls, turned and saw the Chevy's engine light blaring an angry red. Sitting on the Jesse-thing's twitching legs, Charly keyed the engine, but it was stalled, and through the shattered windows she heard the monster's feet splashing into the pooled cornfield. She moved the gearshift to *Park*, thinking that would help, but it didn't. Charly twisted the key again, but the engine only sputtered and stalled, the livid red light telling her it was over, over, she and her children were going to be eaten right here in the cornfield. All but Jake, who would be taken away, who would be...

NO! her mind screamed.

Charly turned the key. The engine coughed to life.

"*Oh God,*" Charly whimpered. She threw the truck into gear and jammed her foot on the accelerator. The Chevy's tires vomited muddy gouts of water, but the back end only slid sideways, and she knew the Old One was nearly upon them now. Sweat dripped from her greasy hair into her eyes. She thought she smelled the creature coming, the very air tainted by its noxious odor.

Charly let off the gas, let the Chevy settle back, then she depressed the accelerator again. The four-wheel drive fared better this time, the tires slipping some but grabbing enough of the underlying soil to rumble forward. The cornstalks started to thunk down again. She heard a strident scream and realized it was in her mind, the Old One's surprised voice. In the overhead mirror she saw it coming, hurrying forward now, hands outstretched in eagerness, but the Chevy was gaining traction, mowing down the cornstalks and veering back toward the road. Ahead and to her left the cornstalks thinned, the road fast approaching. She urged the Chevy faster, but the splashing footfalls were very near the truck bed now. The Chevy left the field. Charly heard the screech of a Night Flyer in the distance, but that no longer mattered; only the Old One was near enough to stop them.

"*Hang on,*" she said to her girls.

Teeth gritted, Charly jerked the wheel. The Chevy hopped over the edge of the gravel road. She depressed the pedal as hard as she could without spinning them out. A white shape hurtled at her in the overhead mirror as the Old One swiped at the bed of the truck, but it was a desperate swipe, the Chevy almost to County Road 1200. If she could make one more turn...

Charly stomped the brakes, cut the wheel. The tires screeched as the Chevy swept around the corner. A ditch on the other side of County Road 1200 loomed closer, a drop-off of nearly six feet. She was sure she'd taken the corner too hard, had consigned them to that ditch. Grimacing, Charly gripped the wheel.

The pickup caught the road. In the overhead mirror the Old One swiped a hand at them, grazed the open tailgate, shuddering the truck but not enough to knock the Chevy off its forward trajectory.

On blacktop again Charly floored it, the big truck moaning with pleasure as it picked up speed. She watched the Old One set off after them again, but she could see she'd beaten it this time. The winged shapes in the moonlit sky looked even farther away. Soon, the Old One was a small white spire on the dark horizon. She allowed herself to breathe.

Then Charly remembered the creature she was sitting on.

The monster that had once been Jesse.

She didn't want to stop, but she'd seen enough horror movies to know there was always one more scare, one more boo moment when the bad guy leapt at the heroine. It seemed to her that an increasing number of movies ended badly, the woman dying in the end.

Charly slowed the truck. She reached out, pushed open her door. The Jesse-thing had been scrunched against it, its face dripping reddish-black blood onto the beige door fabric, and when the door swung open the head and torso simply slumped backward and hung upside down in the doorway. Charly lifted her rear end, and without her weight, the Jesse-thing slithered slowly over the seat. She got a hand under one of its ankles, shoved, and the whole lifeless body somersaulted onto the road. Charly stepped on the pedal before bothering to close the door, so anxious was she to get away from the Jesse-thing. The door slammed on its own. Watching in the side mirror, she half expected the body she'd just dumped to scramble to its feet and charge after her. But the Jesse-thing lay huddled in the road as the Chevy moved steadily away.

Chapter Twelve

They'd been motoring down Highway 65 for several minutes before Charly finally allowed herself to breathe deeply. She tilted the overhead mirror and peered at her children. Olivia watched her with tired eyes. Charly ached to turn around and stroke her hair.

Kate asked, "When can we stop, Mommy? I'm really thirsty."

Charly ignored the sandpapery feel of her throat and looked at her older daughter. Despite her thirst, Charly smiled at the way Jake was slumped against Kate's belly, his chin tilted down as he slept.

"Not for a while, honey," Charly said.

"Are we safe?"

Charly eyed the road meditatively. She wanted to tell the truth.

So she said, "I think so."

She and Kate gazed at each other for a long time, the sound of Jake's breathing audible under the rough hum of the engine.

Charly said, "You want to keep holding him?"

"Uh-huh."

"It's not uncomfortable?"

"I like it," Kate said.

Charly pressed her lips together and faced the road so Kate wouldn't see her tears.

"Any sign of them?" Kate asked.

Charly scanned the dark skies. "Not so far."

"Are we going to Indianapolis?"

"I think we have enough gas."

"How far is it?"

"We should make it."

Kate nodded. Olivia said nothing.

A few minutes later, Kate said, "Can we pull over yet? I have to go to the bathroom."

"Not yet, honey."

A silence fell over them. Charly kept the Chevy moving at a steady seventy-five. She didn't want to get pulled over.

Olivia kept watching her with that same speculative look.

To break the silence, Charly said, "The truck sounds like it's gonna make it."

Kate said, "I thought the wheels were gonna fall off back there."

"Me too," Charly said.

She looked up at Kate in the overhead mirror, discovered that her eyes were happy.

But Olivia wouldn't speak.

Terrified of the answer she'd get, Charly asked, "Can you talk to Mommy?"

Olivia frowned, the crease in her forehead giving her a careworn expression that hurt Charly's heart. There were drying splotches of the Night Flyers' blood on her cheeks, and though the thought of any part of those things touching her children made her queasy, she didn't think she could pull over to clean them off. Not yet.

"What is it?" Charly asked.

"That man," Olivia said.

"Which one?"

"You know."

Charly forced herself to say, "Jesse?"

Olivia nodded.

Charly swallowed the thickness in her throat. "What about him, honey?"

"He changed into one of them, didn't he?"

Charly said slowly, "He was changing. You saw the cuts on him?"

Olivia nodded.

Charly said, "I think he got...infected."

Olivia said, "You have cuts too."

Charly opened her mouth, closed it. She had no idea at all what to say, had not even considered the possibility that what had befallen Eric and Jesse could happen to her.

"Mommy?"

Charly looked at her daughter.

For the first time, Olivia's lips began to tremble. "I don't want you to change."

"I'm not going to, honey. I promise."

Olivia said nothing.

"Do you believe me?" Charly asked.

After a time, the child nodded.

Kate asked, "Was there a bigger bat?"

Charly frowned at her in the mirror. "What do you mean?"

Kate shrugged. "The white ones...the ones Daddy and Jesse became. There was a bigger white one. A taller one. Like their leader."

"Yeah?" Charly said slowly.

"What if the black ones—the ones with wings—have a leader too?"

Charly's stomach did a somersault. *I hope to God they don't have a leader*, she thought. She said nothing out loud.

Kate said, "It's sad."

"What's sad, honey?"

"I liked him."

"Liked who? Jesse?"

"Well, him too. Until...you know." Kate frowned. "I meant the other one."

"You mean Sam," Charly said.

Kate nodded. "Sam. I thought he was nice."

Charly's eyes filled then, and she focused on the road to try to take her mind off of Sam.

But she couldn't do it.

Jake went on sleeping. Kate and Olivia leaned against their seats and said nothing.

Charly drove south.

After

It was a week after Charly and her children had escaped.

The creatures had gone below.

Though aboveground there were police, government officials, grieving family members and all manner of media swarming the state park like carrion flies, deep within the earth the Children and the Old One lay in a state of hibernation.

But their sleep was uneasy.

Unlike past feedings, this one had not occurred without struggle. The species on which they fed was still weak and easily killed, but its machines had improved, and many Children had been injured. A few had been so badly hurt that the Old One had been unable to revive them. Even the Old One, for the first time in his long existence, had experienced physical pain.

The Old One's eyes rolled behind the great white blinds of his lids. He and his Children would not rest for long this time. The Old One's hunger was too great.

And his anger was even more powerful.

The Old One remembered Sam, the one who had stood his ground, firing pieces of steel into his flesh. He remembered the man's hubris and the mocking smile he wore even as the Old One ended his pathetic existence.

The Old One's finger had regenerated, but the wound still throbbed.

He could not understand the young woman's brazen attack on him. Yes, he had killed her, but now he wished he could kill her a thousand times more. Like the man earlier, the young woman they called Emma had died too quickly. She deserved to be made a plaything of his Children, to die the slow death they were accustomed to granting.

Most of all, the Old One thought of the woman with the yellow hair, the woman who had escaped him and taken her three mewling whelps with her. The Old One had transformed her mate into a useful servant and had done the same to her final companion, the young man with the curly hair. The one that had been called Eric and the one that had once gone by Jesse were his now, and he would use them well. He had acquired over a dozen new Children, but he had lost five of his own. Five too many.

The Old One ground his teeth in his sleep and concentrated. He would find a way to bring the yellow-haired woman back. With any luck, he could give her the death she deserved.

In a different area of the subterranean labyrinth that honeycombed the earth under the Peaceful Valley Nature Preserve, the Night Flyers clung unthinkingly to the ceilings of a dozen large caverns. In number they were roughly equal to the Children, though very few Night Flyers had been awakened by the humans who had so foolishly ventured into their territory. The sleep of the Night Flyers who had done battle was anything but restful, for their desire for flesh and marrow had gone almost entirely unappeased. Worse, they had been routed by their pale rivals because the majority of their winged race had been unaware of the battle and the subsequent pursuit of the humans.

But soon all the Night Flyers would be aware of what had transpired. They would know of it because their dark mother had dreamed of it. In her seemingly endless fever dream, she had witnessed the skirmish in the arena and the escape of the humans that had inexplicably eluded her glorious offspring. This troubled her, but what troubled her most was the fact that there had been human children in the strange blue conveyance, the machine that had coughed and rumbled and ultimately outrun her offspring. Somehow, the succulent young meat had eluded her winged minions, had eluded *her.*

The thought made her massive, furled wings rustle against the cavern floor. She could not depend from the ceiling like her offspring, of course, not when she weighed nearly two tons. Now those two tons of stygian malevolence trembled with wrath and yearning.

Nearly a mile under the Peaceful Valley Nature Preserve, in one of the largest and deepest undiscovered cave systems on the planet, the great mother dreamed of her revenge.

Her slumber would soon come to an end.

And when it did, the bloodshed that occurred a week ago when the humans had attempted to declare the valley their own would prove less significant than a single drop of rain.

The great mother sighed in her sleep and imagined the storm that would soon rage. A tempest of carnage and wailing. A blood feast that would prove forever which species was truly dominant.

A demonstration of why humans were right to fear the night and to shudder at the darkness.

A mile under the earth, the great mother dreamed.

And prepared her revenge.

About the Author

Jonathan Janz grew up between a dark forest and a graveyard, and in a way, that explains everything. Brian Keene named his debut novel, *The Sorrows,* "the best horror novel of 2012". The Library Journal deemed his follow-up, *House of Skin,* "reminiscent of Shirley Jackson's *The Haunting of Hill House* and Peter Straub's *Ghost Story*". Samhain Horror also published his third novel, *The Darkest Lullaby,* in April. *Savage Species* is his fourth full-length work. Look for his fifth novel, a vampire western called *Dust Devils,* in early 2014. He has also written three novellas (*The Clearing of Travis Coble, Old Order,* and *Witching Hour Theatre*) and several short stories. His primary interests are his wonderful wife and his three amazing children, and though he realizes that every author's wife and children are wonderful and amazing, in this case the cliché happens to be true. You can learn more about Jonathan at www.jonathanjanz.com. You can also find him on Facebook, via @jonathanjanz on Twitter, or on his Goodreads and Amazon author pages.

Beware when the vampires come to town.

Dust Devils
© *2014 Jonathan Janz*

When traveling actors recruited his wife for a plum role, Cody Wilson had no idea they would murder her. Twelve-year-old Willet Black was just as devastated the night the fiends slaughtered everyone he loved. Now Cody and Willet are bent on revenge, but neither of them suspects what they're really up against.

For the actors are vampires. Their thirst for human blood is insatiable. Even if word of their atrocities were to spread, it would take an army to oppose them. But it is 1885 in the wilds of New Mexico, and there is no help for Cody and Willet. The two must battle the vampires—alone—or die trying.

Available now in ebook and print from Samhain Publishing.

Enjoy the following excerpt for Dust Devils...

Cody peered over the rim of the cliff and felt his throat tighten. *Jesus Christ*, he thought. *Jesus Christ Almighty.*

There, cupped in the rocky basin far below, were the devils. Stripped of their acting garb, the five powerful men capered about the fire like cackling demons. Blood slicked their chests, their rugged chins glinting like sloppy jewels. Over the fire revolved the corpse of an old man, spitted from anus to mouth on a cottonwood pike. Price, their leader, was thrashing something on the basin floor, pounding it as though in the thrall of some childish tantrum. And though Cody's mind revolted at the very thought, he realized the object Price wielded was a human leg. As the scene wavered out of focus, the fire heat shimmering the naked men, Cody saw the pale ragged bone stub jutting out of the severed leg. It was all he could do to keep his gorge down.

He was so transfixed by the grotesqueness of the scene that he hardly noticed the boy on the ledge below him. Small, frail-looking, aglow with moonlight, the boy resembled some creature of the desert, a lizard or a scorpion washed pale by the sun. The boy crawled forward, toward the lip of the outcropping, and Cody realized how skinny the kid was. A slender cage of ribs stood out under a shirt that might once have been white. The wool pants didn't come close to touching the ratty shoes. Cody figured the pants for hand-me-downs.

Below, one of the men—Horton, Cody now saw, the youngest of the devils—kept time on a metal wash drum, dust puffing from his strong hands as he slapped out his arrhythmic tattoo. It was a damn good thing the men below were occupied, for the boy on the ledge was sitting straight up and peering openly at them now, making no attempt at all to conceal himself.

Cody thought, *What're you doing, kid? Get down before they see you.*

But the kid didn't, only continued taking in the scene, his legs dangling over the ledge as if he were watching a carnival sideshow. Jesus, if the boy didn't watch out, he'd lose his balance and plummet straight down at them, and if the impact didn't kill him—which was nearly a sure thing; the drop was a hundred feet easy—the devils sure as hell would. They'd enjoy it, too. Cody had seen them slaughter ones almost as young.

The distance between Cody and the boy was only fifteen feet or so, yet it was a sheer drop down bald sandstone. He could no more make it to the boy unobserved and unhurt than he could bring Angela back from the dead.

The thought of his wife blurred his vision, made his nose run. He ran a savage wrist along his upper lip and choked back the tears. No, by God. Now wasn't the time for that. He'd come all this way to study them, to learn their tendencies. Not to shed more tears over the woman who'd betrayed him.

The little boy below—the stupid son of a bitch—had rolled over onto his stomach, head toward Cody now, clearly intending to slide down the verge on his belly. *And then what?* Cody's mind demanded. *Become their next meal? Serve yourself up on a platter?* If they spotted the kid, they might well spot Cody too, and he knew that once they saw you there was no escaping.

Not knowing why he was doing it but knowing he had to do it just the same, Cody mimicked the boy's movements, lay flat on the stone ledge and lowered himself down, hoping to God the drop wasn't as sheer as it looked, hoping he'd slide down and land gracefully instead of freefalling toward a broken leg or much, much worse.

As Cody's hips grated over the scabrous edge, he did his best to cling to the rock wall, but the perpendicular drop eluded his reaching legs. *Damn it all*, he thought. *Here I go.*

It's all about the story...

Romance

HORROR

www.samhainpublishing.com

CPSIA information can be obtained at www.ICGtesting.com
Printed in the USA
LVOW08s1115300716

498409LV00006B/575/P